Blood Secret

Books by Sharon Page

"Wicked for Christmas" in
SILENT NIGHT, SINFUL NIGHT

BLOOD WICKED

BLOOD DEEP

BLOOD RED

BLOOD ROSE

BLACK SILK

HOT SILK

SIN

"Midnight Man" in WILD NIGHTS

Blood Secret

SHARON PAGE

APHRODISIA

KENSINGTON PUBLISHING CORP.

www.kensingtonbooks.com

APHRODISIA BOOKS are published by

Kensington Publishing Corp.
119 West 40th Street
New York, NY 10018

All Kensington titles, imprints, and distributed lines are available at special quantity discounts for bulk purchases for sales promotion, premiums, fund-raising, and educational, or institutional use.

Special book excerpts or customized printings can also be created to fit specific needs. For details, write or phone the office of the Kensington Special Sales Manager: Kensington Publishing Corp., 119 West 40th Street, New York, NY 10018. Attn. Special Sales Department. Phone: 1-800-221-2647.

Aphrodisia and the A logo Reg. U.S. Pat. & TM Off.

ISBN-13: 978-0-7582-5095-7
ISBN-10: 0-7582-5095-9

First Kensington Trade Paperback Printing: April 2012

10 9 8 7 6 5 4 3 2 1

Printed in the United States of America

1

The Proposition

The Home of the Duke of Greystone
London, March 1818

The Duke of Greystone gave her an appraising smile, the devil personified, then he tipped his tumbler and drained his drink. Lady Lucy Drake held her breath for the time it took His Grace to set down the glass.

What was he going to say?

Surely, it would be yes. The duke was a notorious rake and libertine. He was called a thorough and absolute rogue. How could he possibly turn down the chance to debauch a maiden?

But instead of giving her an answer, the duke slowly, gracefully rose from his wing chair. Groaning, he gave a sinuous stretch, one that made his muscles flex and ripple beneath his coat. Then he turned his back to her and took his glass to the decanter. He did not look at her. He filled the tumbler half full with a dark liquid—perhaps port—and threw that back in one swallow. Then he filled it again.

While she waited.

While her heart thundered.

Lucy tapped her foot in fury. For heaven's sake, she was offering him the only thing she had left of value: her innocence. She was going to surrender her very future. If he said *yes,* she would be ruined and considered a scandalous wanton. She would be destined to remain unmarried forever. She would never have a husband. Or children. She would never, ever have love. If Father had been alive, he would have suffered despair and a broken heart over what she was about to do.

Yet the blasted Duke of Greystone did not even have the decency to give her an *answer.*

She cleared her throat.

He sipped his liquor—she could smell a strong metallic aroma—and walked to one of the windows. Sumptuous curtains of sapphire blue framed the floor-to-ceiling windows. This room, his drawing room, was massive and luxuriously decadent. Watered blue silk covered the walls, elegant Grecian chaises were placed here and there, and gilt glimmered everywhere.

The duke continued to drink. His long, graceful gloved fingers were wrapped around the cut-glass tumbler. Her nose detected a blend of delectable scents on him. Sandalwood, citrusy bergamot, the crisp bite of shaving powder. He was partly *en dishabille:* coatless, with his collar open, his cravat dangling over shirt and waistcoat. His unfashionably long, golden hair brushed his shoulders. He was wearing black leather gloves, trousers, and polished black boots as reflective as a mirror. He was utterly gorgeous and he looked thoroughly . . . bad.

Obviously, he knew it. He wore arrogance the way some gentlemen wore cologne: liberally applied and rather overwhelming. Lucy rolled her eyes. If her siblings' lives did not depend on the success of this plan, she would turn and stalk out of the duke's residence right now. This man might be astoundingly handsome, rich as Croesus, and reputed to be wickedly intelligent, but in her opinion he was an utter boor.

She was inured to a handsome face: a chiseled jaw, the light shadow of a beard, a strong aristocratic nose, and long lashes did nothing for her. True, her breathing was faster, her palms damp in her gloves, and she could feel perspiration beneath her hair. . . .

But that was because she knew the weight of her responsibility. It was nothing to do with the careless way he lounged, and how muscular his legs looked in his trousers.

Boor. Most definitely.

After all, he must know how nerve-racking it was to make this proposition. Finally, after several more infuriating minutes of foot tapping, Lucy cleared her throat again. She added a gentle reminder, forcing her voice to softly prod, "Your Grace?"

He drew a cheroot out of a pocket in his waistcoat and paced to his well-polished walnut desk, where he struck a match and lit his cheroot. A shake of his hand extinguished the flame and he puffed circles of rich-scented smoke into the air.

This was outside of enough. "Your Grace," she snapped. "Are you considering my proposal or have you drifted off into a drunken stupor?"

She could see his profile—admittedly remarkable. His cheekbones were sculpted ridges, his forehead broad and noble. He possessed a perfect, straight nose. The lashes framing his unusual silver-green eyes made her want to grind her molars in envy.

Remember, Lucy, you know better than to let a gentleman's appearance turn you into a giddy, careless girl. She knew the most gorgeous man could prove to be the most dangerous. A man could look like an angel, but be willing to kill you. Even after he'd said he loved you.

Her courage quavered.

From where she stood, she saw His Grace's lips twitch. Then lift in a smile.

He turned, crossing his arms over his broad chest. White teeth dazzled her. As well as rugged lines framing his mouth and the wink of dimples.

His golden brows lifted superciliously. "This, my dear, is your idea of a seduction? Snapping at me for my answer? You are asking me how much I'm willing to pay to debauch you. You should feel flattered that I am taking some time about this. It is a matter that requires a great deal of consideration."

"Flattered?" Lucy gaped at him. "Are you saying I am *not* worth my brother's vowels?" She had expected she would be fighting now for the courage to do what she had proposed: go to bed with him so he would forgive her brother's massive gaming debt.

His gaze raked over her, blatantly assessing. His smile vanished and she almost expected him to stride to her and run his hand over her legs, the way gentlemen did with horses they planned to purchase. "Lady Lucy, your brother's debts are a small price for your virginity. I wonder that you would sell yourself so cheap."

She flamed in humiliation. It was a wonder the scorching blush on her cheeks didn't set her hair on fire. "You have left me no choice, Your Grace. It might not be very much money to you, but it means devastation for my family."

"You don't like me, do you, Lady Lucy? Some men would find that appealing in a bed partner. Some men enjoy rogering an angry woman. I don't. I like my ladies to admire me."

Oh dear God. This was what he needed to agree? Well, she would have to fake it. She gave a simpering smile. "Of course I admire you."

"Good God, is that hideous look on your face supposed to be a smile? I preferred your expression of extreme distaste." He stubbed out the cheroot into a crystal dish. Three long strides brought him right in front of her. She expected he would stop a respectful distance away. But he didn't. He moved so close, she had to retreat. For his every step forward, she took one back. Until something firm and velvety pressed against her back. A chair.

She could retreat no further. Smiling, the duke took one more step so his broad chest brushed her breasts. Her stays lifted them and the low scoop of her tight bodice let them almost spill over. She had hoped to look enticing. But now having her bare flesh brush against his satin waistcoat had her trembling with nerves.

She had to look up to meet his eyes. Foolishly, she tried to hold her breath—if she drew a deep one, it would push her breasts against his chest.

The duke literally had a wicked glint in his eye. His large green eyes sparkled at her as though reflecting the light. It fascinated her so, she suddenly realized she was gawking at his handsome face.

"If I'm going to ravish you, Lady Lucy," he rumbled, in a lazy, drawling baritone, "I intend to take my time. It won't take me one night to properly debauch you. I'd need at least a week."

"What are you talking about? How could it require a week?"

"Give me seven days as my lover and I will show you."

Seven *days*? She'd thought she would have this business done within just a few *hours*. "I cannot do that! How could I return here night after night? Someone might see me. Someone might suspect . . . my reputation would be *ruined*."

He stepped back, as though giving her space to breathe. Greystone ran his hand over his jaw, his expression thoughtful. "Given you proposed to trade your quim for your brother's vowels, I assumed you had already accepted ruination, love."

Quim. The word left her lips flapping in mute shock.

"You do understand what you are offering me, don't you?" he asked.

"Yes." Somehow, she found her voice. "But I thought it would happen tonight. I thought it would be one night. Then I could sneak home and no one would have to know."

"I will accept your proposition, Lady Lucy, but not on those terms."

Panic turned her voice to a high-pitched squeak. "What do you mean?"

"There are my conditions, my dear. I will tear up your brother's vowels, forgive his debt to me of thirty thousand pounds—"

"*Thirty* thousand," she cried. "He told me it was five!"

An expression of sympathy tugged at the duke's handsome mouth. "It was thirty. And I will forgive every penny of it if you spend a fortnight with me, here, in my house, as my partner in carnal pleasure."

Lucy had never fainted. Not once. Not even the time when her life had been in danger. But the room seemed to take flight around her now. Her brother owed this peer an absolute fortune. She took deep breaths. She put her hand behind her and gripped the chair to steady her. Her hand curled hard enough that her fingers punctured the velvet. Unfortunately, there were times she could not quite control her unusual, remarkable strength. She must restrain it now. She could not let the duke know she was not a normal lady, at all. That she, like the rest of her family, could change her shape and transform into a dragon.

She fought to regain control while one thought whirled in her head. The duke was willing to forgo thirty thousand pounds to take her to bed.

It was a fortune. And he was willing to trade it for sex with her. Sex for a—

A fortnight. Had he truly said a *fortnight?* "I—I think two weeks is a bit unnecessary, Your Grace."

Slowly, he stripped off his right glove without a word. She was so struck with shock, she couldn't help but gape at the slide of black leather over his hand. He revealed tanned skin and long, elegant fingers.

"Nonsense," he said, as he removed his left glove. He laid

both of them on the arm of a chair. "I don't doubt, at the end of two weeks, my concern will be convincing you to leave." He gave a careless gentlemanly shrug. "If you want to save your family, you will contact whoever is now the head of your household. You will inform them you will be away for a fortnight. Have them send any clothing or . . . feminine things that you will require."

"You want me to stay here? For two weeks? You mean night and day? Constantly? Every minute?"

With one deft motion, he pulled off his cravat. This he also dropped on the arm of the chair. "Exactly. For what I intend to do to you, I need time, my dear. Besides, I can hardly send you home with rope burns on your wrists, can I?"

The velvet in the chair back beneath her fingers tore with a soft *rrrip*, the frame gave an ominous *crack*. She released the chair. "You have no need to tie me up," she declared. "I am going into this willingly. You don't need to restrain me and have your wicked way with me."

He laughed. The impossible, annoying man *laughed* at her.

"This is impossible," she cried. "I cannot stay with you for a fortnight. I cannot . . . live with you. Here."

He undid his waistcoat and removed it. He stood in his shirtsleeves, and she couldn't stop staring at his broad shoulders, the bulge of muscles at his arms, his broad chest.

She shook her head, trying to put sense back in it. "What are you doing?" she gasped. "Why are you taking off your clothes?"

He shrugged and tugged the hem of his shirt out of his trousers. "You are offering sex in return for a debt. Sex is best enjoyed when both partners—or all participants—are naked."

With his fingers on the tails of his shirt, Sinjin Montjoy, the Duke of Greystone, could not quite believe what had just happened.

He had been trying to get the information he needed from this woman's brother, the young Earl of Wrenshire, but with no success. The earl was only twenty-four, but his mind was too strong for Sinjin to penetrate with his vampiric mind-reading skills. And the earl was too damnably loyal to his damned dragon family to give Sinjin what he needed to know.

He had been at his wits' end, unsure what to do next to the young earl to make him talk. And now one of the sisters had come to his house and served herself to him on a silver platter.

This was perfect.

He had tried to look into her thoughts, but she was also a preternatural being—an immortal. He could not see inside her mind. To gain information from her, he would have to do it the old-fashioned way. Seduce her, win her trust, make her fall in love with him, then coax her to tell him what her family had done with his nephew.

Damn them for making a child a pawn in this battle. But what else could be expected of dragons?

Poor Lady Lucy stood, her mouth slack with appalled shock, as he pulled his shirt over his head. He saw her eyes go wide and her gaze race over every inch of his naked chest. She had pretty eyes—deep, indigo blue, fringed with dark lashes. Her hair was raven black and fell in lovely curls around her face. As much as he hated dragons, it would be no hardship to seduce her.

"You must reconsider, Your Grace. I will do anything you wish . . . but I cannot stay with you."

Laughing, he settled into a chair, and with quick tugs, pulled off his boots. "It is not worth thirty thousand pounds to you to invent a fabrication? Lady Lucy, you came here intending to relinquish your innocence. Yet you are unwilling to tell a lie and say you are visiting a friend."

She gave him a fierce scowl. Given her beauty, her scrunched-up forehead and screwed-up mouth even looked fetching. Those blue eyes were annoyingly naïve and innocent. She appeared young—perhaps two-and-twenty. The poor thing certainly had a fool for a brother—

He broke off that train of thought. Lady Lucy Drake was a dragon and he could not let himself feel sympathy for her. Innocent she might be now, but she would ultimately prove to be like every other member of the Drago species: ruthless, destructive, and predatory. Dragons looked on humans as prey. Dragons killed families. And the monsters stole innocent young boys to hold as hostages—as they had done with his nephew. If he felt his resolve softening, if he felt her large blue eyes begin to tug at his empathy, he only had to remember that her family had stolen his young nephew and were keeping the boy as a hostage.

With his hands on the waistband of his trousers, Sinjin paused. "It is a bargain, Lady Lucy? If you aren't interested, I may as well preserve my modesty."

She sputtered. Her cheeks flushed a vivid red. Hades, this innocent could prove to be explosive in bed. The thought intrigued him. As flinty and cold as his heart was toward dragons, there was no reason he couldn't indulge in some pleasure before he had to do what duty demanded of him. But he had to be careful—he could not let her discover what he really was.

A vampire. He was one of the most powerful dragon slayers; he had been given the gift of immortality. It made him indestructible. And to get what he wanted—his nephew—he couldn't let her find out he killed her kind.

"Lady Lucy?" he prompted.

She breathed a heavy sigh. "All right. I will do it."

"Good then." He left his trousers fastened. "I will have a footman show you to the appropriate bedchamber. A maid will help you undress. I'll be along in a few minutes."

* * *

It was going to happen.

Lucy wrapped her arms around her chest and paced along the beautifully woven Turkish carpets strewn on the floor of the bedchamber. An elderly footman had led her to this room. It was a guest bedroom, apparently, not the duke's room. In the center stood an enormous oval bed, with a canopy that soared to the heavens. A fire blazed, warding off the cold dampness of a March evening. Fog wreathed the house—she could see it from the windows. It blanketed Upper Brook Street, and rolled down Park Lane.

On the mantel, a clock ticked. She had been here for only five minutes, waiting for the maid, but it felt like one hundred years. She let her gaze go to the licking flames of the fire.

And her lips twisted in a grimace.

What would she do if it happened again?

She had never done more than kiss a man. The first time she had, she'd felt the change sweep over her as she responded to the kiss. She'd gone hot. Her blood had turned to fire. Her body had felt sort of molten, the way it did before she shifted shape. She'd broken free of the kiss, and had astonished the gentleman who was kissing her—a mortal—by running away.

She couldn't run away now.

But if she started to change shape, she would have to. She couldn't let the Duke of Greystone learn she was *unusual,* that she was one of the Drago clan, who could transform from a human into a dragon.

Fear made her shoulders tremble. If a kiss could trigger her shape-shifting ability, what would lovemaking do?

But this wasn't lovemaking, was it? She didn't want to do it. This had nothing to do with *love.* This was something she had to endure to save her family.

The kiss had been something she had wanted. She had been in love with the gentleman—the younger son of the Earl of

Montley. It had been years and years ago, when she had been just sixteen. Desire, love, emotion—somehow they had scuttled her control, and the experience of losing control over her shape-shifting had taught her she could never marry a mortal.

She didn't even like the Duke of Greystone. There would be no risk of feeling heat and excitement with him. So no risk of having her body shift shape involuntarily.

A knock came at the door, but it opened before she could say a word in answer. Dressed in a simple gray gown, wearing a white mobcap, a young maid came in. A very buxom maid. It shouldn't surprise her, Lucy thought coolly. No doubt a libertine duke hired his female servants based on their appeal in his bed.

"C-c-can I help you w—with your dress, m-m-miss?"

Lucy couldn't prevent the small jerk of shock as the maid forced her sentence out. The girl stuttered. Was it nerves? "Thank you. I hope I haven't frightened you."

"N-no." The girl hastened over, and Lucy found herself in capable hands. She was down to her shift in no time at all.

She could see her reflection in a large cheval mirror. Her blush deepened with every passing moment. The maid worked efficiently, without speaking, but Lucy knew what the girl must think. That she was a lightskirt. A wanton.

"This is not what it appears—" She stopped. What else could she say it was? She couldn't say she had to take off her dress because she'd been caught in the rain, for heaven's sake.

"It—It's not m-m-my business, miss."

Lucy saw the maid's face. She wasn't stuttering with nerves. She had seen the girl's small frown of frustration as she got stuck on one of the words.

"Y-you'll like H-His G-g-grace," the maid whispered. The girl smiled tentatively.

"Like him?" She thought him wretched. Then her blush rushed like wildfire, like dragon's fire, over her face. "Has he . . .

been intimate with you?" Had the maid meant she would like him . . . in bed?

"N-no, miss. 'E d—don't allow that. With me s-stutt—" The girl sighed.

With an ache of sympathy, Lucy supplied, "Your stutter. Yes, I understand."

"C-c-couldn't keep a place. Th-thought me d-d-daft. Not His Grace. Not him!" The girl spoke vehemently at the end, so filled with force, her stutter left her.

It surprised Lucy. Apparently, the arrogant rogue had done something kind for this young woman.

"Y-your shift, m-miss."

The maid took it by its lace-trimmed hem and slithered it up, over her head. As the muslin flew past her hips, Lucy felt a breeze through her nether curls and between her thighs. As it brushed past her breasts, it made them bounce and they jiggled, heavy and naked, as her shift was pulled off completely.

Instinctively she put a hand to cover the juncture of her thighs and used her other arm to shield her breasts. The maid gave a shy giggle and turned away. She scooped up Lucy's clothes and laid them over a chair, keeping her back to Lucy. Then the girl hastened out, closing the door behind her.

Lucy let out her breath with a whoosh. Even alone, she covered her body with her hands. She had never stood anywhere utterly naked. Not even in her bedroom. The mirror threw her image at her. Her hair loose and falling to her hips, her curvy nude hips. Her breasts squashed by the pressure of her forearm into round and jiggly spheres. Her full thighs, her calves, her bare feet. She looked like some sort of wild creature. In her mind, she looked more like a wild thing now than she did when she changed to dragon form. She turned away, flushing more vigorously.

You have to let the duke, this man, this stranger, see you like this.

Goodness, she couldn't even look at her body in the mirror, much less show it to that . . . to him.

She hurried to her clothes. Her hands were on her shift before she got control of her thundering heart and spoke sense to herself. "You cannot run, Lucy. If you go, your family will be ruined. If you go, you know Helena will marry the Odious Earl to save the family."

The Odious Earl. She shuddered. He was a dragon-shifter, a distant relative in the Drago family tree, but he was also a fifty-year-old, grossly fat earl. And he wanted to marry Helena. The Odious Earl was certain he was going to be given Helena, because he knew how desperate they were due to her brother's debts.

Lucy had almost wed a horrible, terrible man. After the Earl of Montley, she had determined she would only marry another dragon. And she had been fooled by a handsome face. For her fiancé had been the worst beast imaginable.

She couldn't let Helena be forced into a horrible marriage. Her sister was nineteen. Lovely and innocent. Helena deserved to marry for love. The earl was a lecherous old debaucher. If Lucy erased a thirty-thousand-pound debt with a fortnight of sex, the Odious Earl could be booted out of the house on his backside.

She heard a soft sound. A footstep? Was the door going to open and the duke walk in, wearing just his trousers?

She stared at the doorknob so hard, she was surprised she did not set it on fire with the ferocity of her glare. A soft, sliding sound came behind her and a man's voice said, "You have a delicious derriere."

She almost jumped out of her skin. Jerking around, Lucy realized her breasts had moved a few moments before her arm caught up to cover them. No doubt he had seen her curves, even her dark brown nipples, which looked so scandalously . . . hypnotic when they were unclothed. Even she could barely tear her gaze from her bare nipples when she caught a glimpse of them.

But the Duke of Greystone was watching her face. He calmly sauntered through the secret opening, one that had been covered by a sliding wall panel. He strolled into the bedroom the way some men strolled through the park on a pleasant afternoon.

Except he was completely naked. And he was obviously, rigidly, shockingly aroused.

2

Stripped Bare

Lucy spread her fingers to cover her private place again and clamped her arm over her breasts. She desperately tried to look everywhere but at this naked man who stood before her. But her eyes betrayed her, and her gaze slid to him. She caught glimpses of broad, straight shoulders. Glimpses of his pectorals, with the dark circles of his nipples, and the long, hard muscles of his thighs.

And once or twice her gaze strayed back to that part that revealed how much he anticipated having her.

"Lady Lucy," the duke said coolly. "You offered me the free use of your lovely body. Please move your hands. I wish to enjoy the view."

"I—" She couldn't. She simply could not stand in front of him so boldly. Already she was blushing like fire because he could see so much of her, just as she could see every inch of him. If she wanted. If she *looked*.

He could see her generous thighs, her hips, and her stomach. He had already seen her naked *bottom*, even if it was only for moments. She felt so . . . embarrassed, ashamed, humiliated. Her body was too lush, too curvaceous. Her body had always been a curse. When she'd been just thirteen, she had begun to shift into dragon shape. That had been bad enough, for it had taken her years to learn how to control it, to learn how to live with the pain of the shift. Then her body changed from slender and boyish to this rounded, embarrassingly wanton-looking shape.

Lucy glanced at the duke through her lashes, but he had turned his back to her. He strode to a cupboard. At least he wasn't ogling her, but she was surprised he wasn't. As he opened the door, he said, "Lady Lucy, just because you are paying with your innocence, does not mean the surrender has to be unpleasant."

Unpleasant? It was mortifying. She'd had no idea she would feel this awkward and embarrassed. She'd thought she could do this, but all she wanted to do was run for the door. She kept her gaze fixed on her arm, ensuring it shielded her breasts. And ensuring she did not look at his muscled back. Or his naked buttocks. "Could we not just . . . just go to the bed and put out the lights?" she asked desperately. "I did not think you would want to stand in front of each other without any clothes."

A flash of red flew at her and she jerked back. A robe, she realized, as it billowed and floated to the floor. His Grace kept his back to her as she pulled it on. She firmly fastened the belt and knotted it.

She had to get this over with. Keeping her eyes downcast, she moved to the bed. She would lift the covers and get in. Surely, he would then join her. She was shaking at the thought of what would happen once he got into bed with her. His naked body would rest over hers. She would open her legs. And he would go inside her. She knew that much of this business. She would close her eyes and not think of what was happening to her. She'd overheard the maids in her home whisper about sex. They said for some men, the act did not last long. Only minutes. Hopefully the duke would be such a man.

Before she reached the bed, he turned. Lucy sensed it out of the corner of her eye and she looked at him. She saw the firm, taut plane of his stomach, the bulge of his chest muscles, the taut indents of his haunches. His hair was gold and spilled to his shoulders, the way men had worn their hair decades before. Her gaze went down, where it should not go, and fixed on the wobble of his erection as he moved toward her.

Really the dark would have been much better. She could have faced this if they were beneath covers in a shadowy room. Tears burned at the corners of her eyes—tears of frustration over her predicament, of anger over her brother's stupidity.

The duke prowled across the bedroom and this time she couldn't look away.

His erection was so . . . astonishing. It was long, thick, topped with a acorn-shaped head. It was flushed as much as she was sure her cheeks were. Pronounced veins twined along it. Golden hair curled above it and his large testicles dangled below. It was a primitive-looking thing. It looked so . . . odd on the smooth, sculpted planes of his body. Yet it was intriguing, and a strange ache shot from her belly to the place between her legs. She clutched the belt of the robe.

Fear. Anger. Nerves. And illicit, forbidden, wrong physical desire. How could she feel so many different things at once?

Lucy had been supposed to marry four years ago, just after she had turned eighteen. Her father had brought him to the house as a suitor from the Drako family. Allan Ferrars. He had been handsome, charming. Dragons had to marry dragons, her father had said.

But Mr. Ferrars had hidden his true person behind a gentleman's gloss. He was rough. Cruel. She had caught him attacking one of the maids. She had rescued the girl by shifting to dragon-shape. Forgetting Mr. Ferrars could change, too. He had thrown her across the room, had swiped her stomach with his brutal claws. As she'd struggled to her feet to attack him in return, she had realized Allan Ferrars didn't love her at all. Then Jack had caught them. . . . Jack, her brother, had shifted shape and had fought Mr. Ferrars. They had been forced to destroy Ferrars to survive. . . .

She mustn't think about that. Not now. But she would never forget that moment when she'd realized she could have married such a man. She could have blindly gone to her wedding night without any idea she had wed a vicious brute.

It had scared her. It had made her vow never to marry. And here, now, she felt the old fears surging up. She was going to be intimate with this man, this stranger, and she was . . . terrified to know what it would be like.

"Look up for a moment, my dear." The duke's baritone voice was gentle in the quiet room.

She jerked her gaze up, her cheeks burning as hot as dragon fire, but her blood felt ice-cold.

He smiled, and lines bracketed his full, firm lips. He was a handsome man. Mr. Ferrars had been terribly good-looking too. That was what she had learned. Beautiful men believed they could get away with anything.

"I know you are nervous, my dear," he said softly. "I promise I will be very gentle. I will make this good for you."

How could it be, when she'd been forced to do this by the actions of the brother she had always adored, by his debts? And by the arrogance of the duke? She stalked to the head of the bed and pulled back the covers. "I just want to get on with it."

"All right, then, we shall."

She didn't look at him. She clambered onto the bed and slid beneath the sheets still wearing the robe. Her toes touched something hot—a bed warmer—and she squeaked.

A low, seductive laugh made her scowl. Her fiancé had possessed the same sort of deep, sensual laugh. It used to make her heart beat fast. It had made her blood hot and her skin feel too tight. Now, hearing it on the duke, it screamed a warning in her head.

How had she thought she could do this?

She *must* do it. Lucy nudged the warming pan aside with her toe and slid further under the covers in this strange, unfamiliar bed.

But she had changed. She used to tremble with girlish desire at a deep, masculine laugh. She used to look at a handsome man and feel desire. She had dreamed of kisses. Of more . . . of pleasure and sex and intimacy.

Allan Ferrars had changed her. He had ruined everything for her. She didn't feel those things anymore. She was only two and twenty, but after his attack upon her, she'd felt so much older. So wary. So cynical. She had been afraid of love after that, afraid of any stirring of desire. Certainly, her heart would never be touched—unless by a man she knew she could trust completely.

Sinking her teeth firmly into her lower lip, Lucy looked up at the duke, who stood at the foot of the bed. She could not trust this man at all—he had carelessly, cruelly ruined her brother, and by extension that meant he had ruined her family. Her heart hammered like the thunder of dragons running. "Stop laughing and come and ravish me. I cannot stay out all night. I simply cannot."

The duke sighed. So loudly she could hear it. "My dear Lady Lucy, I do not approach sex as you seem to think I do. I'm not just going to get on top of you and plow you while you grit your teeth and shut your eyes. You will enjoy this or I will not consider it payment for your brother's debts."

Sinjin folded his arms over his chest. Lady Lucy Drake, who lay beneath his sheets, grimaced as though she was about to take foul-tasting medicine.

He scratched his jaw, his fingertips grazing over his smooth skin. After he had become a vampire, unlike others, he had never grown stubble again.

Lady Lucy had come to him. She had offered her body. Why did he feel as though he was the villain, about to ravish a terrified and unwilling victim?

Worse, his mind was urging him to do it. He drank blood, but while he was the type of vampire that fed on blood, consuming the fluid didn't satisfy him unless he could also drink in the powerful emotions of his prey. It was his victim's desire, or fear, anger, horror—along with coppery-tasting blood—that satisfied his undead body.

Emotions rolled off Lady Lucy like fog pouring down London's twining streets. She would be a feast for a vampire like him. And she was a dragon. He should feel no pity for her. Had dragons felt anything for him when they had murdered his family? Had those dragons showed a scrap of pity when they had killed his younger brother and sisters?

Anger. In him, it drove his sexual desire instead of quelling it. It washed away pity and sympathy. It hardened his heart. It brought ice flooding through him. Ice gave him the hardness to slay dragons.

He was going to pleasure Lady Lucy Drake. He was going to use her to find his nephew. Then he was going to do to her what he did to every dragon. He would summon the ice to toughen his heart, he would take out his sword, and he would rid the world of one more deadly beast.

But he said gently to her, "You're afraid." Which was obvious—she had her robe wrapped around her up to the base of her throat, the covers pulled up to her chin. He sat on the edge of the bed.

She tipped up her chin. "I don't understand why you don't just get in here with me. Why are you drawing this out?"

Sinjin cupped her cheek. The feel of her dewy skin against

his palm—it made his jaw ache with hunger, with desire, with need. She went tense beneath his touch.

"Drawing it out is supposed to be part of the fun," he informed her, watching the way her eyes widened in obvious dismay. Softly, he let his thumb brush her lips. Velvet and plump, just as he liked them. "It is called foreplay, my dear. Most women enjoy it."

"We made . . . a bargain. I will do what you want. I promise you that."

He could terrify her and feed off that emotion. He could do what she so obviously wanted—fuck her without conversation or care, thus evoking her anger and hatred. The power of her hatred would sustain him for a week.

But there was another way he could satisfy himself, he realized. Make Lady Lucy enjoy her seduction. He imagined she would feel so many emotions, he would feel like a drunkard unleashed in a brewery.

She was lovely. Her skin was alabaster and the scarlet robe was an erotic splash of color against it. Her lips were a deep wine red. Her hair, still pinned in place, was ebony, and promised to feel like silk. She had fetching dark nipples, the kind whose bounce could hypnotize a man. And she had the covers drawn almost up to her throat.

"As for going home . . ." He lifted her hand to his lips. "I think not, my dear. Not tonight."

He whisked the bedcovers down and had the belt of her robe undone before her hands could move. One of the advantages of vampiric speed was how quickly he could disrobe a maiden.

Ironically she would be the first maiden in his bed—he normally seduced experienced women. Ironic because the dragon slayer was supposed to save the maiden. And he was bound—bound by duty and by the vow he had made on the day his family had died—to slay Lady Lucy.

He left her robe on but open, then drew the covers over her again. Stretching out beside her on the bed, he propped his head with his hand. He lay on top of the covers, while she was securely ensconced beneath.

Pink flooded her cheeks. Her chest rose and fell swiftly beneath the blanket. But her dark brows had knitted together in a deep frown, and fire snapped in her eyes. "That was . . . unconscionable. You did that without even asking! And how did you do it so—so quickly?" She scuttled away a few inches beneath the covers and looked as indignant as a fishwife.

"You did encourage me to get on with it quickly. Now, would you prefer me to take my time, my dear?"

"I would prefer—" She closed her eyes and her teeth ripped at her lip. "I don't know what would be best. In my head, I know it would be best to just do it now. But then my courage fails me. . . ."

"Shhh." Sinjin bent over and lifted her fingers to his lips to kiss them. It was the first touch of his mouth to her skin. It was just a light caress of his lower lip across her knuckles, but it hit him with surprising force. It was like tasting fire. His head swam with lust and desire. The taste of her skin, the scent of her blood—it was remarkable. It was all that was sweet and delectable about pretty young ladies. But there was spiciness too. Her blood smelled of heat and cinnamon and cloves and jasmine. That had to be the dragon blood in her.

Wide, nervous blue eyes gazed at him as he gently pressed a kiss to each knuckle. "There's nothing to fear, you know, Lady Lucy," he lied smoothly.

Her brow rose. "I'm giving up everything. That does tend to make a woman fearful."

"No one has to know what has happened between us. Most English gentlemen are not very clever. I'm sure you could still convince one you are a virgin on your wedding night." For the first time in his life, he felt a flicker of conscience. She was not going to have a wedding night, was she? Not after he did his duty and destroyed her.

She shook her head. "I will never marry."

He jerked guiltily. But he had to play his part. Seducer, not dragon slayer. "You are a beautiful woman. Irresistible to most gentlemen, I should think."

"N-no."

He flicked out his tongue and touched the very tip of her index finger. She squeaked softly, like a startled mouse. "I think you liked that. Let me show you other places that will like to be kissed."

"My lips?" She drew back. "Could we not do this without kisses?"

Sinjin blinked. Strange. Most women wanted the kisses. Most women hungered for kisses. They seemed to believe kisses were the proof of a man's regard. "As you wish. No kisses on your lips. But you cannot deny me the pleasure of putting my mouth everywhere else."

"Everywhere?" she gasped.

Lucy blinked. He could not mean *everywhere,* could he? Where else could a man kiss a woman but on her hand and her lips?

The duke bent to her and pressed his lips to her neck. The oddest jolt of fire leapt from there. It rushed through her veins like flames licking at the sky.

His long hair also tickled as he stroked his mouth along her throat and reached the rim of her ear. He brushed back her hair. Surprisingly, his breath was cool. Almost icy. She'd heard her maids speak of men blowing their breath by their ears—something that hadn't sounded at all enticing—but the maids had described warm breath. The duke's breath was cold.

Still, the brush of it did feel surprisingly . . . good.

He nibbled her ear, making shivers tumble down her spine.

"Where do you like to touch yourself that pleases you, Lady Lucy?"

"W-what on earth do you mean?"

"What parts are sensitive to your touch? Have you touched here?" He stroked the exposed skin at her collarbones. Goodness, how could it feel so hot—like a candle's flame flickering close to her skin? But fear crawled back inside and nestled around her heart. This was wrong. Forbidden. She was supposed to do it, but not like it. She might be committing the sin of sex without marriage, but it was for necessity. Forgivable—as long as she didn't behave like a wanton and actually like the sin.

But try as she might, she could not deny his caress made her ache inside. The sort of ache she'd known before Mr. Ferrars had attacked her and had frightened her so badly.

"Well, of course I have touched there," Lucy said simply, embarrassed. "I would scratch it when I have an itch."

The duke laughed. A low, rolling laugh that rumbled like thunder. "Have you ever scratched here?"

Sinjin tugged the sheets from her hands and slid them down enough to expose the swell of her breasts. His body tightened with arousal at the sight of the full, generous curves. His erection bucked against his stomach.

Tracing her full breasts with his lips, he heard Lady Lucy whimper. From fear? Or desire? He couldn't be sure. She was tense beneath him. He waited for signs of resistance. But she stayed still. So he lowered the sheets lower, until it slipped below her nipples. Marvelous dark brown nipples. Applying the lightest pressure, he drew the left one to a hard peak. It plumped up beautifully in his mouth.

Bringing out his vampiric skill, he flicked her tongue around her nipple. She let out a soft groan. And he recognized it as a sound of pleasure. "Yes, Lady Lucy, you like that." Pursing his mouth, he suckled. Beneath him, she squirmed. A smile played at his lips.

If things had been different . . .

Hell, she was one of the family who had stolen his nephew. She was one of the clan of beasts who had mercilessly killed his family. Things could never be different. Yet still, he had to pleasure her.

He gave a tug at her nipples. "No! Oh goodness, you can't do that!" But he didn't stop and her moans grew deep and throaty. He knew the dragon in her could take and enjoy a great deal of sensation. Her fists pressed against his shoulders as though she was trying to push him away. But she did it weakly, as though she was beginning to understand she didn't want him to cease—she wanted more instead.

He suckled. God, she was delicious. And she was moving beneath him. She arched to press her breast to his mouth.

She was so damn delicious. Enough to make him want to forget who she was . . .

No, he wouldn't. He couldn't let himself forget what dragons like her had cost him. He couldn't forget his mission—if he did, he could lose his nephew forever.

While he sucked each nipple in turn, he shoved down the sheets. Lady Lucy didn't protest. She was lost to the sensation now—he could feel the emotions roiling in her. No doubt she was fighting her response, but at the same time, the pleasure would be flooding through her. She would hate herself for feeling this for him, a man she didn't know, who held her in his power. Yet she would want more. Hunger for it. Do any wanton, naughty, sinful thing to get it.

He pushed the sheets to her thighs. She gasped in protest. He ignored it, and slid his hand along the smooth curve of her stomach. She had generous curves, Lady Lucy Drake. For a fleeting moment, he wondered what she looked like when she became a dragon. They were beautiful creatures—not the fearsome beasts of storybooks. Their scales glowed like pearl, their forms were graceful and strong, their eyes as brilliant as diamonds. It was almost possible to forget how vicious and deadly they were.

Crisp curls met his fingers. He stroked there, then lower, pushing his fingers between her nether lips, and he touched the hot, slick skin of her quim. His fingers coasted along her clit—she cried out at the contact.

"Good, is it?" He played with her until she quivered beneath him like a frothy dessert. Her eyes were shut tight. She was lusciously moist.

Her scent reached his nose. And hell, he was lost. Lost in wanting her. He rolled over her, coaxed her legs apart with his, and settled between, playing with her sweet cunny all the while.

Then he released her taut clit, grasped his cock, and he guided it to touch her. She moaned. Then gasped. Her hands flew up to push on his chest.

"I—Oh! I'm not ready. Please. Can we wait? Just a bit longer?"

He circled the tip of his finger on her clit and watched her squirm. Watched her cheeks turn pink, and her breaths turn to gusty gasps. "I thought you were in a hurry to be ravished, so you could get home."

"I—I just need a moment. I thought I could. But I can't—"

His senses drank in pure fear. She was terrified. Actually frightened out of her wits. "Why are you so afraid of me?" he murmured. "I've done nothing to hurt you."

"It—It's not you. I was . . . my fiancé . . . I can't stop thinking about what it was like, when he attacked me. When I realized he was willing to *kill* me, that he was not going to hold back because he had asked me to marry him." She shook with fear. Her dark blue eyes grew wide with remembered horror.

"I don't understand, love. Your fiancé tried to kill you?"

"Oh goodness. It—I shouldn't have said anything. It doesn't matter."

She was wounded, this dragon. He needed to seduce her to pry the information from her, but obviously he could not seduce her until her fear abated. "Shh," Sinjin soothed. "It does matter. I don't want you to be so afraid." He lay beside her and drew the sheets up over them both, covering them in warmth.

"I can't—"

"I'm just going to hold you, my dear. While you tell me what happened to you."

3

Dragon

At first Sinjin thought Lady Lucy would keep her secrets to herself. As he cradled her to his chest and brushed soft kisses to her head, inhaling the rosy scent that clung to her silken hair, she whispered, "I should not have said anything. I—I've ruined everything."

"You haven't. Come, you can trust me. We're lying here naked together. What did your fiancé do to you? Should I find the gentleman, and duel him at Chalk Farm for you?"

"N-no. He died."

"At the hands of a member of your family?" Since he was her intended husband, this man must have been a dragon. Why would he attack? Strangely, for all he hated dragons, Sinjin felt his fists clench at the thought of one hurting Lady Lucy. There was something vulnerable about her—something he had never sensed in a dragon before.

"I caught him, you see." She burrowed closer to him. In answer, he cuddled her tighter. Her full breasts were a soft cushion against him, her generous hips pressed to his. What a magnificently lush and beautiful woman she was.

"Caught him? What do—" Then he could guess. What would break a woman's heart? "You caught him with another woman?"

"Y-yes," she admitted shakily. "But it wasn't . . . he was forcing himself on her. She was a maid and she wasn't willing. She was so terrified. And I—I was so *angry*. He was a brute, and I'd thought . . . I was so stupid. I had thought he was wonderful, charming, a true gentleman."

"What did you do? Try to stop him from raping this maid?"

Against his chest, she nodded her head.

Hell. "And he lashed out at you in return?"

"Yes. He threw me across the room. He slash—he hit me. I thought he was going to kill me. It didn't seem to matter that I was engaged to marry him. He was enraged. He was wild. Like a madman. If my brother hadn't come . . . I couldn't fight him, you see. I wasn't strong enough."

"You are a very brave woman. No wonder you are so afraid to come to my bed." Sinjin tipped up her chin, and met her gaze. Hades, just touching her delicate chin made his cold blood heat and sizzle. "You have nothing to fear. I would never hurt you. And I see why you would come to your brother's defense so admirably." Though the woman was a silly little fool for offering something she was too afraid to give.

Large, fetching indigo eyes gazed up at him. "I suppose it would not convince you to forgive his vowels without . . . without payment?"

"Now that I have you naked in my bed, pressing so delightfully against my naked body? My dear Lady Lucy, I hardly think so."

With those words, Greystone rolled over her. Lucy struggled, but the duke had parted her legs with his, and he had her wrists pinned to the bed. She was his captive. And she didn't like it.

"Trust me," he murmured. "Your fiancé was a monster, my dear. You cannot judge all men by his vicious behavior. Even the scoundrels."

With soft, relaxed lips, he kissed her. An openmouthed, hungry, shocking kiss. His tongue slid into her mouth, forcing her lips to part. Twining with her tongue. Exploring her mouth. She'd never had a kiss like this. It was so wet. So . . . undeniably hot. Steam seemed to rise from her body, perspiration dampened the valley between her breasts. He lowered his body against hers. She felt him, the rock-hard length of him, the lean muscles, and the length of his erection pushing against her belly. Lucy panicked.

No . . .

The duke bent to her nipple, his long golden hair spilling over her bare chest. She gouged her fingers into his arms, determined to push him away, even though she had promised him this. Even though she knew she had no choice. But he suckled her hard, dark nipple so tenderly. Heavens, it did feel good. It stole her strength. Her fingers softened against his hard muscles. His sucking made her body feel floating, lazy . . . good. It made her feel as though melted chocolate ran through her veins.

She was so mixed up. Greystone was a rogue. He had ruined her brother. He was a *villain*. But he was kind to his maid, unlike Mr. Ferrars who had thought a servant was there for his taking, willing or not.

She had been so wrong about Mr. Ferrars. She had thought he was wonderful and perfect.

The duke's large, long-fingered hand skimmed over her stomach. Then he stroked between her thighs again, touching her most private place, and she moaned, *"Yes."* She had no idea she would feel the roughness of his fingers—that her skin would be so sensitive. She loved the scratch of them over her delicate flesh. Her skin there was so soft and his hands were so sensually rough.

Dimly, she wondered how his hands could be so rough when he was a duke.

Oh goodness, he had flicked that most sensitive place—the little bump that lay between her nether lips, and she almost rolled her eyes back into her head at the pleasure. Her hips arched up. As if he could read her thoughts, he stroked her a little harder, as if he had known the rocking of her hips was a wordless signal that meant: *I'm begging you for more.*

How had the duke done this? How had he made her want, when she'd thought she would never feel desire ever again? How could she want *him,* when she knew nothing about him, other than he wanted to ruin her brother? But she sensed he had been serious of his offer to kill Allan Ferrars at Chalk Farm. She had believed him when he had gazed deeply into her eyes and called her *brave.*

It was only one word, yet it had made her heart quiver more than any of Mr. Ferrars's many compliments.

Oh goodness, Greystone was kneading her breasts now, his touch firm. She felt as though she was in the middle of a fireworks display, with things exploding around her everywhere.

Then he slid his finger inside her. Between her nether lips, parting them gently. Goodness, he was *inside* her. She was doing the most intimate thing possible. With a man she did not like, did not know, and should not want.

"Open your eyes."

As if he commanded her, she did it and the first things she saw were thick, velvet-soft black lashes and gorgeous green eyes. Eyes that glittered at her in the firelight. "Is it good?" he asked. Greystone looked truly concerned.

Then his finger slid deep inside her, and she gasped at the sudden sensations—an intense quiver that rushed through her.

Lucy heard a shocking wet, sucking sound as his finger thrust in and out. It was the sound of her arousal.

"Good?" he coaxed.

Biting her lower lip, she nodded. She didn't want to speak. This was wrong. Sinful. Naughty. But she wanted it, and the best way to deal with the war in her heart and her head was to do it quickly, not say a word, and never, ever think of it after it happened.

His hand moved and he stopped stroking the little nub that vibrated with such intense feeling. She gasped in frustration.

He wrapped his hand around the shaft of his erection—she could feel the brush of his fingers against her stomach as he took hold of himself. Then, with his hand tight around it, he stroked the head of his erection against her nether lips. They had stuck together, resisting him, but he gently eased them apart.

Her arms were splayed on the bed, pressing hard into the soft mattress. Her hands were clenched in tight fists. Her toes curled. But she bit her lip so she couldn't possibly let a "no" slip out from between them.

His hips arched forward in slow, easy strokes as he pushed his penis inside her. For the first time, she knew what it was like to have a man's thickness inside. He didn't go in far. Just enough that shock turned to need, and tension melted like ice beneath a flame. Just like his mouth on her nipples, this was good.

"You are a brave woman," Greystone said gently. "Very brave to face fears to save your brother." He rocked his hips as he spoke and the movement was as soft and relaxed as his words. It pushed him further inside her. Astonishing sensations . . . squishiness, warmth, wetness, pleasure . . . her fingers tightened on his arms. Her hips lifted.

His face came to life in great detail. Blond hair fell across his brow, glinting with strands of pale gold. His eyes truly sparkled. They were large, beautiful eyes, green and flecked with silvery-gray—so much, they shone. Astonishing, unusual eyes. Lines framed his mouth, lines of strain, which seemed to come out when he showed desire.

He drew back, withdrawing until she felt just the tip of his erection touching her and she moaned. Now, she just wanted him deep in her. "Perhaps I am brave and foolhardy?" Her voice was husky, hoarse, as though she hadn't spoken for years.

His lips curved. "Not foolhardy." He tipped his hips, going deeper inside her. Instinctively her arms slipped around his neck, her leg around his. She shouldn't behave so intimately—she didn't know him. He was a stranger to her. This was not about love. Yet she wanted it to be intimate. She wanted to feel close to him. To hold him. His body was so warm and strong in her grasp. She loved the weight of him against her. Her fingers touched hard muscle, velvet skin. Her leg lay against legs with muscles that felt as hard and solid as iron.

Deeper he went, and his penis stroked a place inside her that made explosions of light in front of her eyes. Then a twinge of pain rushed through her and she gasped in shock.

His fingers traced the curve of her cheek. "Shh," he whispered. "Easy. It will hurt, I'm afraid, when I go past your maidenhead. I wish it didn't, love. But after that it will be very, very good."

"No—"

He thrust. She squealed. She clenched. She tightened. She wanted to back away. But she couldn't vanish into the mattress. Nor could she push him off.

Greystone pressed against her, seating himself all the way inside, and he didn't move. He stayed motionless, and he rained kisses on her forehead, her cheeks, her lips. It was hard to feel pain with such glorious kisses stealing her breath. And little by little, the stinging sensation ebbed.

She whispered, "It's better. . . ." Then she saw his expression. He looked like a man in great pain. He looked raw, ravaged, tormented. His eyes were wild. His mouth was a slash, bracketed by harsh lines. He looked as though his control could snap in a heartbeat. "Are you . . . all right?" she asked.

"You are tight, sweet, and perfect, my dear. So no, I am no longer all right."

Lucy let her arms slip from his neck, but her legs were still wrapped around him, and his groin, hot and hard, was pressed tight against her. "What should I do?" she whispered.

"Have a screaming orgasm, Lady Lucy."

He circled his hips as he said it, stroking his long shaft within her. Her private place throbbed with need, her body ached with yearning. Amazing she could feel so much. She could feel the stroke of the head, the slide of his rod against in- credible, sensitive places. He planted one sweet, sensual kiss after another on her lips, which kept her gaze locked with his.

Lucy watched a smile touch Greystone's full, handsome mouth. Then groans deepened the lines framing his lips. His eyes glowed as if they were on fire, and his deep, throaty moans . . . she adored them.

Heavens, she was moving with him. Rising to meet his thrusts. Lifting to bang her pubis to his and take him deep in- side. Each slick stroke rubbed the taut head along the sensitive places inside her. And he angled his hips, so each collision of their hips left her little nub tingling.

She was weak with pleasure, yet driven to rock with him. She clung to him, arching her hips, panting. Her nipples had hardened, and each thrust brushed them against his chest. Her lips tingled from kisses, her nipples throbbed from swift brushes, her quim pulsed . . . and fire raged in her, hotter than any she'd ever breathed as a dragon.

Oh God. The flames burst in her, and she heard wild moan- ing, and she shouted, "Oh Your Grace! Your Grace!"

Her cries blended with a harsh masculine groan. She opened

her eyes to see his wide with astonishment. His hips banged hard against hers and he shuddered against her.

Oh. Oh, why hadn't she thought of this? This was what happened when men found release. She felt hot and wet inside, very wet, but too weak to move. Too weak from pleasure to say anything. She was clinging to him, and her body still rippled and throbbed around him.

His seed had gone inside her. She might . . . she might become pregnant. Why had she not thought of this? The ramifications of what she had done might haunt her forever—

"My dear Lady Lucy, I've never lost control so quickly before." He kissed her forehead. "I'd intended a much longer bout."

She was shaky, now, and her fingers gripped his strong biceps. She stared down, letting his chest fill her vision, for she couldn't face his eyes right now. Sweat glistened on his straight, wide shoulders and on his smooth chest. His skin was pale, and with his powerful, well-defined muscles, he looked as though he had been carved from marble.

Still staring below his face, she managed to ask, "Does that mean . . . are you pleased?" Pleased enough to rip up vowels? For what she had given up, what she had risked, surely she would achieve her goal.

"It is an auspicious beginning." He took a deep breath. "Our fortnight may exhaust me."

The duke was still speaking about her staying for fourteen days. Frustration and a sense of failure choked her.

"But first . . ." he murmured huskily.

He suddenly moved down her body, kissing a trail down her stomach. His lips brushed across her dark nether curls. Then his tongue delved in between her curls to touch her nether lips, to touch her most private place, wet and sticky with her juices and his.

She squirmed on the bed. He was a rake and he knew the most scandalous things. But his tongue . . . the plunges of his hot tongue were different from the thrusts of his shaft and teased her in a different way. She moaned helplessly. The tension built again, swirling inside her. . . .

She came again, her fingers stretching wide on the sheets, her legs weak. She sobbed with it. Then a fire seemed to explode inside her and wrap around her heart. Her skin tingled and felt as though it was moving. Changing.

Goodness, Lucy knew what was happening. She felt this way when she was going to shift into dragon form. When her bones moved and her muscles changed and her skin transformed to iridescent scales.

It couldn't happen now. The duke had no idea what she really was. No one in London did. Her family had kept their secret for generations.

But how did she stop the shift? When that kiss, that one she'd been given years ago, had made her shift, she had run away. She hadn't been able to stop the change. At least she had found refuge deep in the massive gardens of their hosts' estate. Her change had happened in a wooded area, where no one could see.

Heavens, what was she going to do here and now?

Hades, she was shifting. Sinjin knew it—he had seen people shift from their human shape to dragon form before. Her body was rippling beneath him and her skin felt hot enough to burst into flame.

"You must let me go," Lady Lucy cried softly. "I—I don't feel well. I need to—to use the necessary." She tried to push out from under him.

She was trying to hide what she was. She thought he didn't know she was a dragon.

It suited him to let her think she had succeeded. He swiftly moved off the bed, then whisked her to her feet. "Behind the screen," he said.

"Oh." Perspiration beaded on her forehead. She had gone white. "I need privacy, Your Grace."

"Of course." He bowed, despite being naked. "Summon the maid when you are ready to dress. This will be enough for tonight. After you are ready, you will return home in an unmarked carriage, then gather your things to return for two weeks."

"I—" Her muscles jerked. Sitting up, she hugged her bare chest tightly, as though she was trying to keep her body from flying apart. He read the strain in the face, in the way her muscles shuddered and jerked beneath her hands. Valiantly, she was trying to fight the shift, but it was obvious she couldn't.

Sinjin's nostrils flared as he scented the change in her smell. His entire body tensed, and his brain was hammering one message at him: *Do your duty and destroy her when she becomes a dragon. You cannot suffer a dragon to live.*

His hands clenched against his will, yearning to be wrapped around the hilt of a sword. He had vowed to slay dragons—it was not a vow he could walk away from. . . .

But he couldn't hurt Lady Lucy Drake tonight. He had to let her go and wait for her to come back. Once she returned, and had agreed to spend a fortnight under his control, then he would start questioning her about his nephew.

"I will give you some privacy," he said casually. He turned his back on her deliberately, for he saw how she was perspiring, and how her jaw was twitching and her muscles were popping under her smooth, satiny skin. He put his back to her as much for himself as for her.

He left and closed the secret door in the wall paneling. Using his preternatural hearing, he detected a smothered scream. It signaled that her body had changed—when the body transformed from mortal shape into the larger form of a dragon, it caused a great deal of physical pain.

Right now, he had a dragon in his house. By the code of his clan, he was obligated to slay her. But that would condemn his nephew to death.

Sinjin walked away feeling the crushing sensation at his throat. It felt as though his windpipe could collapse. It was the punishment for not doing his duty—but only a warning. It would ease.

What if Lady Lucy did not return to his house?

Sinjin stalked over to the dressing table in his bedchamber. A decanter stood on it, beside a large tumbler. Other men drank brandy—he had his servants bring him blood. He poured a glass and the aroma sent his fangs launching forward. He drained all the blood from the glass in an instant while he wondered what Lady Lucy would do.

She had made love with him when she was frightened of men and intimacy. She was a remarkably strong woman, and determined to protect her family. He knew what lengths a person would go to when their family was at risk.

Sinjin licked his lips, gathering up the last, tangy droplets of blood with his tongue. It was entertaining to think of the carnal games he would play with her. For he was certain Lady Lucy would come back.

Changing her shape was agonizing.

Lucy had sunk to the floor beside the bed and she clutched the bedpost as spasms of pain rocked her body. Why couldn't she stop it from happening?

Others could. Her father had been able to, and he had tried to teach her how to do it. Most of the time, she was able to keep her body from transforming, but there had been times, like this instant, where she lost control of her body.

She closed her eyes, bit her lips to contain any screams or sobs. And just tried to endure the hateful process.

She didn't want to be a dragon. She yearned to be normal. To be just a mortal. To have worries like the other human, ordinary young ladies she knew: such as snaring a husband, becoming mistress of a house, and being a grand hostess within the *ton*.

She had just given up her virginity and she could even end up pregnant.

All in all, her life was a disastrous mess.

Her arms and legs twitched and grew. Her skin rippled, changing by some mystical, awful process into scales. Heat swamped her, and Lucy fell dizzily back against the bed.

She couldn't stop it. She couldn't help but scream with the pain as her muscles popped, tore, heated, and re-formed.

Within minutes, she was no longer human, she was a dragon, and she was curled up on the floor beside the bed, with her tail tucked in around her. Firelight glinted off her scales. She took up the entire room.

If the duke were to come back, how would she explain this?

Lucy turned her sleek, dragon's head toward the secret panel in the wall and gazed at it with her large eyes. A small lick of flame came from her mouth.

She prayed the panel did not open.

4

Lies and Vows

"What are you doing, Lucy? Why are you packing?"

Lucy whirled to find Helena standing in the doorway of her bedroom. Her sister was tearing at a piece of embroidery, nervously shredding it. With her pale gold hair and enormous blue eyes, Helena was a beauty, and at nineteen, she was also old enough to understand what their brother's stupid gambling had done to the family. In fact, Helena understood all too well—Lucy knew her lovely sister was noble enough to agree to a wretched marriage to save them all.

Lucy let the blue silk gown in her arms fall into her open trunk. She was still shaking. It had been draining to face her fear and painful memories and go to bed with the duke. It had stunned her to actually like it. She'd been wild with terror when she'd started to shift into dragon form.

It had been a miracle she hadn't been caught. At least she had been alone in his bedroom when she had shifted shape, but as a dragon, her head had brushed the high ceiling and her tail had been curled and pressing against the wall. Then she'd managed to regain control of her body and change back. Trembling, exhausted, disheveled, and itchy with dried perspiration, she had summoned his maid, dressed, and come home.

In her carriage, she had concocted a story. Now she faced the elder of her two sisters and used it. "I have an invitation to a house party."

Helena frowned. "Lucy, it is the beginning to the Season. Who on earth would be having a house party? Everyone is in London."

"Not all the Drakes," she said, amazed at how smoothly she was able to lie. "Since we can't shop for our prospective husbands on the marriage mart, many of the dragon clans do not bother to attend Society events. There will be eligible men in this house party, Helena. Drago men. Men who are dragons, like we are. If I can snare one and marry well, then I can rescue us."

Helena crossed her arms, sighed heavily. Lucy flinched as her sister's perceptive gaze searched her face. She tried to give no hint that all this was a complete fabrication.

"Lucy," Helena said. "You said you would never think of marrying—"

"I am ready to marry now," Lucy broke in. "I've recovered from Allan Ferrars." She went to her wardrobe so Helena could not see her face. The more impassive and natural she tried to make her expression appear, the more Lucy was certain she wore an enormous sign on her head that read LIAR.

"Are you certain?" Helena came over to her, and touched her arm. Doubt furrowed her sister's smooth, pretty forehead. Helena knew her far too well.

Bother. Lucy had never lied to any member of her family before. . . .

Well, that was not true. Neither of her two sisters knew exactly what Ferrars had done or what she had seen when she had yanked open the bedroom door. They did not know he had battled with Jack and that their brother had been forced to kill him. Not telling them why had not been a direct falsehood. It had more been a lie by omission.

She didn't want Helena to know what she was doing. And anyway, she had no choice now: She had already done it. She had given up her virginity, and she certainly couldn't retrieve it. The problem—losing her virginity made her feel different. She felt more world-wise and experienced, older, and more . . . more aware of everything around her. The lavender sprinkled on her underclothes smelled more sweet and intense, like a field of wildflowers. She was aware of the touch of things—the caress of her muslin petticoats as they brushed her thighs. The tug of her garters on the sensitive skin of her legs. The way her bodice bound her breasts. And since she felt so . . . different, she was afraid someone who knew her well would guess what she had done.

"It's not just to save us," she said firmly. "I *want* to marry. I know Father would have wanted it, and I can't live with myself for disappointing him."

She hated herself in that moment. Using their father's wishes to convince her sister.

As she expected, Helena's eyes teared. But to Lucy's surprise, Helena vehemently shook her head. "Father would not have forced you to do something you didn't want. He truly thought Mr. Ferrars was a gentleman and a noble dragon. Father would not want you to marry if you didn't wish to."

"I know. I'm going to open my heart and fall in love, Helly. I promise. I know wonderful gentlemen will be at this party and one will sweep me off my feet." The lie was so very much the opposite of what was going to happen that her throat felt thick.

"How long will you be gone?"

"A fortnight."

Helena's eyes widened. "With Jack missing?"

"Creadmore will look after both you and Beatrix." Creadmore was loyal—he had been Father's butler for twenty years. He would ensure the family was safe. But Helena's ingenuous question reminded Lucy that she could not look for Jack for the two wretched weeks she had to spend with the duke. "I will write every day, Helena," she promised impulsively. "I'll send letters by footman or by the express." Which would save her from having to explain a London postmark.

She was weaving a tangled mess.

But in two weeks, the debt would be paid. They would be safe. Then she could find Jack, and she would give him a kick in the breeches for all the trouble he'd caused.

As for her ruination and possible pregnancy . . . she wouldn't think of that now. She would give Jack an extra kick in his behind if she was expecting a child.

At least, she was certain Jack was alive and safe. He always ran away when he got into trouble. It had driven Father mad. Now it was going to do the same to her.

Late in the night, but before dawn began to touch the sky, he walked to his sister's grave.

Sinjin flicked up the collar of his greatcoat and stalked through the cemetery, toward the massive crypt that held his sister's coffin. He carried a bouquet of roses.

He had lost all his family except Emma when he had been nine years of age. The dragon slayers had found him, had taken him in and raised him. With his father dead, he had become the Duke of Greystone. But the only title that had mattered to him had been that of dragon slayer. Wreaking vengeance on dragons had helped him survive the pain of losing his parents, his younger brother, and his other two sisters.

Emma had never been able to heal. She'd always been lost in a sort of make-believe world. She had believed she had fairies for friends, and she would not even speak to anyone but him.

Emma had been made into a vampire by the dragon slayers,

just as he had been. When she was as old as he was, when he had been turned, he had insisted she be given immortal life.

All members of the dragon slayers clan were given immortality. Their souls were taken and their bodies were made stronger by the transformation. As vampires, they were almost invincible. Emma should have lived for eternity. But Emma had fallen in love with a forbidden man—a dragon. She had run away with him. Other dragon slayers had hunted the man down and destroyed him. After she had lost her husband, Emma had gone mad. She had destroyed herself. She had walked out into the sunlight, had screamed with agony as the light burned her to ashes and dust.

With her death, he had lost everyone in his family—except Emma had a child. And when she had killed herself, she had left her son alone, without parents.

Sinjin pulled open the door to the crypt, ducked his head, and stepped into the dark. It was pitch dark, but as a vampire, he could see easily. Emma's cool marble sarcophagus stood in the middle. Her likeness was carved into the top. On it, with her marble eyes closed and her sculpted hands resting on her chest, he could imagine she was still alive and she looked this way, as though she was merely sleeping. But all that was inside the coffin was a small pile of dust.

His heart cold, he laid the roses on top of the marble hands. "I know James is safe, Emma," he said aloud, into the quiet of the tomb. "I will have him home soon. I promise."

And he would. James was the only family he had left.

He had to ensure he acquired Lady Lucy Drake's trust. After that, he could question her, and try to find clues to where James was being held by her family. If he could coax her to trust him, he would be able to slowly break through the defenses she carried as a shape-shifter and see into her thoughts.

But before dawn, he would try one more time with her brother, Jack.

One of his servants had brought him word this evening: they had discovered where her damned brother was hiding.

Maybe the Earl of Wrenshire would be more forthcoming with his information when he found out what his sister was willing to do to save him.

Her trunk was packed. Lucy swiftly tied her bonnet ribbons beneath her chin, her gloves tucked beneath her arm.

She was ready to go—to run for the carriage before she lost her nerve—when the front door opened, the scent of smoke whirled in, and one of her investigators bowed, gave her a crooked smile, and said softly, "I have findings to report, my lady."

She led him into the study, which would have been her brother's room if Jack had not disappeared, and sat at the desk. Arching her brow, she waited for her investigator to begin. He doffed his beaver hat and gave her another grin, looking relaxed and devilish. A former Bow Street Runner, Mr. Armstrong did not look like the sort of man who respected the law, but he reputedly took cases without payment or hope of reward when he felt justice should be served.

He had agreed to find her missing brother and accept his payment later. Lucy suspected it was because the handsome, dark-haired man admired Helena.

"I believe I've traced the last movements the earl made before he disappeared, my lady." Armstrong drew a notebook from a deep pocket and flicked the pages with his black-gloved hands. "At eight of the night, the earl left his club and proceeded to—" He stopped abruptly, then ran his fingers around his collar. "Beg your pardon, my lady, but the rest might not be suitable for a lady's ears."

Lucy sighed. "You cannot shock me, Mr. Armstrong. I assume it was either a seedy gaming establishment or a brothel."

"Indeed it was a combination of both, my lady. At midnight, he took his leave and visited several gaming halls."

She arched a brow. "Several? Could he not lose enough money at one?"

She didn't expect an answer but to her surprise he gave her one. "It appears he was not engaged in deep play but in the pursuit of a duke," he said.

"A duke? And this was on the night he disappeared?" Normally her brother stayed out all night, but returned in midmorning, where he would collapse in a drunken stupor on his bed. But on that particular day, he had not appeared. He had gone out the night before and he had not come back. "Which duke?" Though, really, what other duke would it be?

"The Duke of Greystone," Armstrong confirmed. "They encountered each other in a tavern near the London Docks. According to several witnesses, they left together."

"They did?" And the wretched duke had said nothing about it. Did he know what had happened to Jack?

"I take it, my lady, you wish to know what they spoke about? They were overheard."

"Yes, of course I do!"

"They spoke of the duke's nephew. The duke accused the earl's father of kidnapping his young nephew."

5

The Pleasure Room

The Duke of Greystone possessed an enormous house on Upper Brook Street—one crafted of severe gray stone and rows of sparkling windows. A footman in sapphire-blue and silver livery escorted her past the drawing room in which she had first encountered the duke.

Inside Lucy was ready to explode. And not with desire.

Had Greystone done something with her brother? Had his words frightened Jack so much they had forced him to run? Had the duke hurt her brother over this bizarre accusation?

How could her father have kidnapped the duke's nephew? It was impossible. Father never would have done such a thing. The accusation was utterly insane.

Was Greystone insane? He had not seemed so when she had . . . oh God, when she'd had intimate relations with him. He had been astonishingly kind to her. He had comforted her about Allan Ferrars, soothing her, telling her she was brave. Had he done all those things while knowing what had happened to her brother?

And she, the utter fool, had been seduced by his words and

by his wonderful touches and the thrusts that had made her whole body quiver with pleasure.

But then a memory struck her, one that made her halt on the stairs. She clutched the banister to keep her balance. Father had rescued children who were shape-shifting dragons. He had taken in many orphans or abandoned children, and had supported them, and helped them understand what they were. Just before he had died, Father had been distraught. There had been a child he had taken in . . . one he said he had tried to protect . . . but that he had failed to do so.

How could that have been the duke's nephew? Father only took in children who had no family or who had been cast off and rejected by their relatives.

"Where is the duke?" she demanded of the servant, when they reached the stairs that swept up to the next story of the house. "Where are you taking me?"

The footman bowed. "His Grace wished to meet you in the Pleasure Room."

"The *what* room?" She stared. The servant, an elderly man, with bushy gray eyebrows and crinkled blue eyes beneath his powdered wig, held his face without expression. He did not even blush.

"It is a special room used by His Grace," the man replied. He began to mount the stairs.

"Indeed." Lifting her hems, she followed, rolling her eyes. Only the Duke of Greystone, scoundrel and libertine that he was, could have a room of such a name. A normal gentleman would have a library, a study, and a bedchamber. He would not openly call a room the "Pleasure" Room.

She had been a *fool* to come here and offer herself to him. The duke must have been laughing at her all the while.

The footman stopped at the end of the hall, at double white paneled doors. "Do not announce me," she said. She intended to take His Grace by surprise. Lucy threw open both doors and stalked inside. She planned to face Greystone and crisply ask, "What happened to my brother? You were the last person to see him."

But she was taken by surprise.

There was one astonishing thing in this room she had seen before, but quite a few things she hadn't. Dark paneling covered the walls. Glowing light came from a huge fireplace and tapered candles set in tall, wrought-iron stands. A large cheval mirror stood near a bench, reflecting the flickering candle flames. Strange wooden objects littered the room—stands and benches with ropes tied to them. A swing with a small velvet seat hung from the ceiling in the middle of the room. And manacles also dangled from the ceiling. This room looked as though it had nothing to do with pleasure.

"Lady Lucy. How delightful. You are early."

The duke's voice flowed to her. He stood in front of the fireplace, illuminated by the glow. She had been trying to look everywhere at once, and not at him. As the day before, he was not wearing any clothes.

But this time, when she saw him, her traitorous brain thought of what his body had felt like under her fingertips. What it had felt like when his narrow hips had been between her legs and his chest had been a wicked pressure against her naked breasts—

Lucy crossed her arms over her chest, refusing to blush, to show any intimidation. "Your Grace, I have learned you spoke to my brother on the night he disappeared," she said sharply. "He left a seedy tavern in your company, and then he has not been seen again. And you accused my father of kidnapping your nephew. That's impossible!"

Greystone plucked something off the mantel. He strode to her, at ease in his nudity. He held out a glass to her—a delicate glass with amber liquid within. Sherry. After what she had just said, he was offering sherry.

"Your Grace, what happened to my brother?"

He set the glass on one of the strange benches. There were chains attached to the legs. "And how did you learn of this, Lady Lucy?"

"I hired a man to hunt for my brother. He has been missing for a week! He vanished after telling me about his debts to you. I feared—I feared he had done something foolish."

"Hurt himself?"

"No—run away. Left England."

"Yes, your brother is the sort of wastrel who would do that."

"You have no right to say such a thing," she flared. "What did you do to him? Did you injure him because he has not paid his debts?" Bothered, she looked down. He was now very erect, as though their *argument* aroused him.

She glared into his eyes. "What did you do to him?"

"I questioned him. Which is a better treatment than he deserves, since he would not tell me where my nephew is being held."

"That is madness. My family did not kidnap your nephew."

"They did. And you must be very well aware of the fact. So you tell me, Lady Lucy, where is the boy? Where is your family hiding my nephew, James?"

"How could you think my family did such a thing? I do not know anything about your nephew. I am sorry if he is missing. I know how terrifying that is, since I have no idea what happened to my *brother*. But my family had nothing to do with his disappearance."

"Not true. They did, and I suspect you know where he is. It is a known fact that your family is a closely knit clan."

The way he looked into her eyes . . . as though he knew . . . but he couldn't . . .

Unless her brother, Jack, had told him they were dragons.

No, Jack would never do that. They had all been taught they must never reveal the truth.

His Grace walked around her slowly. She stood her ground—until he came against her from behind. His erection poked her bottom through her skirts. She tried to step away, but his arms went around her waist. "You are being loyal to your family, and you are lying to me."

"I'm not!" Lucy half-turned to protest, and her lips almost touched his. Breathing hard, she turned away.

"You hired a man to search for your brother. What do you think I did to find my nephew? I have sent two dozen men in search of him. But the reason I know your father took him, Lady Lucy, is because your father told me."

"It's—it can't be possible. My father would never have done such a thing. Why would he?"

"I believe you know, Lady Lucy." He breathed the words against her ear with his cool breath.

"I don't!"

Sinjin tried to see into Lady Lucy's thoughts. He could not, but her emotions flooded to him. Anger. Confusion. Frustration. Fear. Worry.

Why the fear? Was she fearful because she might be caught in a lie? Or was she feeling great fear because she was afraid for her brother? He skimmed his hands up her stomach, to rest just below the generous curve of her breasts. She wore a fresh gown, a fetching one of ivory silk. She stiffened. Her heart thundered against his fingers. "Your father assured me James is safe. But he also assured me I would never see the boy again. Why, my dear, do you think I worked to ruin your brother?"

"I—"

"I did it to get my nephew back. All I want is the safe return of an innocent boy. He is only five years of age."

Against his body, she shuddered. "I cannot believe this. I

have no proof my father said any such thing to you. I have witnesses who saw you leave with my brother."

He traced the smooth curve of her jaw. Was her outrage just an act? Was it possible her father had ensured she did not know that he had stolen a child to use the poor lad as a hostage? "I know where he is. I will take you to him. But first, my dear, you will submit to my every command tonight."

"What—what do you mean?"

"I want to make love to you. You will do everything I ask, and then I will tell you where you can find your wastrel brother."

Lucy glanced around the room—at the swing, the manacles, and the benches with their chains. She did not care about their bargain now. And the last thing she wanted to do was something sexual. "No. I wish to go to my brother *now.*"

Wastrel or not, Jack deserved her protection. She had vowed to Father that she would look after Jack, who drank too much, gamed too much, and was always in trouble. But also, Jack had protected her once, when she'd needed him most. He had rescued her from Allan, and she owed him her very life for that.

A wicked grin curved the duke's lips. He winked at her, which infuriated her. Lightly, he said, "Your brother is perfectly safe. I doubt he would appreciate your interruption too soon."

She did not appreciate his teasing tone at this particular time. "Why? Where is he?" She crossed her arms over her chest and glared at the maddening man.

"No harm in giving you a little hint, I suppose. . . ." He shrugged. "My men have located him in a brothel—he's been holed up in there for days."

"A brothel?" Pure fury rushed through her. Lucy clenched her fists at her sides. "We thought he was dead and he is hiding in a *brothel?*"

"Indeed."

There was much about this she did not understand. "How, if you wanted to find your nephew, did you not know where my brother was? Are you telling me that after you left that tavern together, when he had not given you the information you wanted, you simply let him go?"

Suspiciously, she watched his eyes, to see if he gave himself away. It didn't make sense. But his eyes merely reflected the light in the room, and she could get no sense of his private thoughts.

The duke sighed. "I allowed your brother to go as I intended to follow him. However, I was overly arrogant, and your brother evaded me. For as long as you have been looking for him, I've been searching for him. I want him to tell me where my nephew is. Now, come, Lady Lucy, we made a bargain. Sexual pleasure first."

She should go and find Jack right now. So she could boot her brother in his derriere, the thoughtless wretch. But her body relaxed in the duke's embrace, against her will. She couldn't help it. She was so tired—tired of trying to save Jack from himself.

Greystone's arms tightened around her. She could not deny they were strong, and inside the circle of them, she felt secure.

"Even if we had not made a bargain," the duke murmured, "I would move heaven and earth to make love to you."

His lips touched her neck. The most remarkable tingle burst like a fireball at the point where he kissed her. It rushed down her spine. Then he ran his tongue along her neck.

Inside, she was molten, as hot as dragon fire.

"Your brother should have taken much better care of you." Kisses trailed down the nape of her neck. Lucy whimpered.

She should go to Jack . . . but the duke was right . . . Jack would be furious at her for hauling him from a house of ill repute. She gazed down at the duke's golden hair. "You do believe I know nothing about your nephew, don't you? I truly don't."

His tongue ran over the swell of her breasts. "Yes, I believe you." He looked up. "I would say I was wrong about your father, except he admitted it to me."

"But why would my father take an innocent boy—"

He had turned her as she protested, and he silenced her with one hot, openmouthed, hungry kiss.

The duke must believe she had nothing to do with the kidnapping of his nephew—how could he kiss her like this if he did? Lucy wanted to know exactly what had happened but she was on fire, and she couldn't stop kissing him.

She must know about his nephew's kidnapping. Even as he assured her he did believe her, Sinjin could not understand how Lady Lucy did not know what her family had done.

True, she had appeared to be genuinely shocked, but she'd managed to keep London Society from learning she was a dragon. She knew how to keep a secret.

She wouldn't tell him the truth. He had to get inside her mind and see for himself. To do that, he had to coax her to trust him.

Her skin sizzled with warmth beneath his hands. What he intended to do was give Lady Lucy Drake an introduction to exotic sex in a way she wouldn't forget.

He could tie her up and have his wicked way with her.

Or he could let her tie him up.

The duke stretched his long, nude body on one of the benches, and he grinned. Lucy was still completely dressed, and she had crossed her arms over her chest. He had simply left her, walked to the bench, and lay down.

His feet rested by the legs, where ropes dangled. He held more rope in his hands. With his arms above his head, he looked both vulnerable and more muscular. In this position, his chest and back looked even broader. Unlike her body, which was soft, her curves defined by areas where she was too plump, his skin clung to the shape of his remarkable muscles. Then he shifted, and she saw his erection where it was trapped between the bench and his abdomen—goodness, he was very aroused, his penis long and straight.

She approached him cautiously. With his cheek resting on the smooth leather of the bench, he grinned. "I want you to lie like this, my dear. I would like to massage you."

"I cannot lie anywhere like that. I am wearing my stays."

His relaxed laugh rolled over her. He sat up, swinging his long legs over the bench, and crooked his finger. She couldn't help but stare at his wobbling penis. The head of it glistened in a way that made her blush. Trails of a silvery fluid dribbled from a tiny opening in the acorn-shaped head.

Lifting her hem, she walked to him. Holding her hips, he made her turn, then he swiftly undid the fastenings of her dress. He moved with more expert speed than her maid, and had her undressed to her stays and shift in no time at all.

He drew down her garters and her filmy stockings. Then he pushed up the lace-trimmed hem of her shift and kissed her inner thighs.

"Goodness! That tickles," she gasped. She half-turned and saw his smile. Locks of his golden hair shielded his face, but there was no doubt he was grinning gently at her.

He couldn't blame her for his nephew's disappearance—how could he continue to smile at her if he did?

Unlacing her stays, he drew them down. Balancing her hands on his shoulders, she stepped out of her stockings, then her stays. And he whisked her shift off.

She swallowed hard as her breasts bounced and her naked body was displayed, mere inches from his face. She had been intimate with him but she still felt shy.

"You are very beautiful," he murmured. He leaned forward, flashing a much naughtier smile and he buried his face in the fullness of her breasts.

Beautiful was something Lucy did not feel. She felt awkwardly naked. She didn't know how to stand, where she should put her hands, or if she should touch him. She rested her knee on the bench while he played with her breasts, but she felt unbalanced and awkward and slid her foot back to the ground.

Suddenly, he settled his hands on her waist and lifted her off the ground. He traded places with her so quickly she barely had time to register what had happened. Then he was easing her down, turning her to lie on her stomach.

His hands coasted over her back, firmly but carefully stroking and rubbing her. He massaged her muscles.

Closing her eyes—it felt easier to experience this with eyes shut—she gave a murmur of pleasure.

His fingers kneaded their way down her back. Each stroke made her relax more.

Suddenly Greystone lifted her bottom. Something slightly scratchy brushed against her cheeks—it was the thick hair at his crotch. His penis stroked her private place, and she was so wet, the taut head immediately slid in. She turned her head and saw him. He was balanced on the bench on his knees, and her bottom was lifted up in the air.

He thrust into her, in long, slow strokes, his penis driving deep. His hips bumped against her bottom with each thrust. He spread her legs wide, holding her with his hands to open her for him. It was rather erotic. She clung to the bench and focused on the way her bottom jiggled when his pubis hit her. She felt the sway of her breasts. Her nipples were hard and long.

Heat washed over her. She was panting, working toward her pleasure, sucking in breaths.

"Let me play with you here, Lady Lucy."

His fingers came around her hip and plied between her nether lips. He stroked her clit, and she gasped in shock. The orgasm slammed into her almost instantly.

She shook with it. Her body was so hot . . . she was melting. . . .

Heavens, her muscles were jerking and jolting. She was changing.

She tried to pull away, but he held her to him. He had plunged deep and was gripping her, so she would ride through her climax on him.

She had to escape. But he was too strong and he would not let her go.

Panic made her desperate. "Please. You must let me go. I need to . . . I must go to the retiring room. Please!"

His hand stroked slowly down her back. "It is all right, my dear. I know what is happening to you. I know what you are."

She blinked. Dazed from lovemaking and panic, shaking from the strain of trying to resist the change, she wasn't certain she had heard correctly. "What do you mean?"

"You are a dragon. I know that. I know your family are dragons."

She tried again to scurry away from him, but he held her too tightly. How could he know? Jack must have told him. But she could not allow him to know. She had to make him believe it was not true. "I'm not a dragon. I am a female. I mean, I am human. A properly brought up lady. Whatever you were told about dragons, I can assure you it was not true. How could it be? That is the stuff of fairy tales—"

She broke off. How could he have believed it so easily? How could he say it so calmly now? Why would anyone accept such a mad and preposterous story?

Greystone tipped his hips back, letting his erection slide free. For a moment she had the hope she could flee, but he pulled her back, drawing her onto his lap. "That's what you are trying to force yourself to be. You are trying to fight your dragon nature."

She bolted up from his lap and landed on the floor. Her breasts jiggled but she didn't care that she was naked now. She wrapped her arms around herself. "It is not true. There is no such thing as people who turn into dragons. Of course it is impossible for a woman to be both a lady and a dragon."

"That is exactly what you believe, isn't it?"

How gently he spoke.

"But you are both, aren't you, Lady Lucy? You are both a responsible lady and a fiery dragon. And the reason I know what you are is because I am not merely a duke. I am a vampire."

A vampire—could it be possible? She reared back. She knew of vampires—they were undead creatures, not immortal shifters like dragons were. Vampires tended to keep together, just as dragons did, and witches did, and demons did. She had been told there were peers of the realm who were really vampires.

"It's all right, my dear. I won't hurt you. I don't intend to drink your blood."

"You don't?" She hugged herself. "Are you sure? Is this why you lured me here?" If he attacked her, she would have to shift shape and fight him as a dragon. A vampire would be far too strong for her otherwise—

Suddenly she realized she had controlled her shift into dragon form. It hadn't happened. When he had told her he was a vampire, she had forgotten what was happening to her body. And somehow that had helped her control the change.

He regarded her with amusement, which she found preposterous at this moment—when they were discussing drinking her blood.

"With you, love," he growled, "I would prefer to feed on sex."

She frowned. "That's not possible. Is it?"

He grinned. "For me, it is. And you, my beautiful Lady Lucy, promise to be a sumptuous feast." Then he sobered, his eyes serious but still mirror-like. She now knew why his eyes glittered so much—it was because he was one of the undead.

"You are stunningly beautiful, love," he said. "Don't try to hide what you are. Being a dragon gives you incredible power." His smile dazzled her again.

"But," she said, warily, "I am not certain if it gives me enough power to subdue a hungry vampire."

With eyes twinkling, he murmured, "What would make you feel safe with me?"

She swallowed hard. "I don't know."

"You could tie me up."

She jolted. "Tie you up?"

"Mmm. Bind my hands together or tie me to the bench. Would that make you feel comfortable? I give you my word that I won't hurt you, but I understand, love, why you might be scared."

Would it make her feel more at ease? She was not sure. But he appeared to be so excited by the idea. Flushing, she nodded.

"All right, my dear. Let me teach you how to tie me up."

She had no idea it would prove so arousing to tie the duke's wrists together.

Lucy squirmed on the bench, very wet, very aroused, and quite pleased with her handiwork. Looping the ropes around his wrists, she had tied his hands together in front of him, then, following his instructions, she had crisscrossed the ropes, wrapping layer after layer, until he was well and truly captured.

He teasingly batted his eyelashes at her. "I wish I could touch you—stroke your silken cheek, push back your unruly curls, stroke your lush, beautiful mouth—but unfortunately I'm a little tied up right now."

It made her smile. It banished nerves and doubt. She didn't care that he was a vampire. How could she, when he accepted she was a dragon?

He wiggled his bound hands and flashed a grin. "Come up here, my love, and sit on my face. Even though my hands are bound, I can use my tongue to pleasure you."

A hot flush touched her cheeks. But to her surprise, as she stepped over the bench, and carefully walked until her quim was over his face, he winked. "A few more inches. Then lower down so I may kiss you."

Strange how she listened to his commands. She couldn't quite figure out what the duke wanted, and it made her willing to play his game. Heavens, it made her hungry to play his game. Her breath came fast, her heart raced, her legs trembled.

She lowered and the duke licked a place behind her quim—a bridge of flesh that made her moan helplessly. His tongue darted to the entrance of her bottom and lightly stroked.

Stars exploded before her eyes.

He dropped back. "Do you know, my love, how sensitive your bottom is?" he asked hoarsely. "You have the most lush and beautiful arse I've ever seen. I would love to give you an orgasm by pleasuring it."

"Pleasuring my bottom? What do you mean?"

"Lie on your stomach, my dear, and I will show you."

Slowly she did, but she stiffened as he approached. Why would he not answer questions and demand she trust him?

Something warm and wet stroked over the curve of her bottom, gently following, tickling her skin. Gasping, she glanced back, over her shoulder. Through the screen of her hair, she saw he had bent to her rump. He had licked the cheek of her bottom. Now, puckering, he planted a kiss on the plumpness of her right cheek. It jiggled.

"You are beautiful, love. So generous." He rained kisses over her curves, kisses that tickled, that made her giggle. Then he caressed her with his tongue, roving the wet tip over sensitive flesh.

Apparently a woman's bottom could be pleasured.

Greystone lifted his head. "That was just the beginning, Lady Lucy. If you say yes, there is more pleasure to be had."

She swallowed hard once more. And whispered, "Yes."

"Good. What I intend to do involves some sexual toys."

6

Wanton

The duke was lying on his back on the leather bench, and he held a long ivory rod in his teeth. The "sexual toy" as he called it was preventing him from speaking now, but he had made his request very clear.

He had told her to slowly, gently, carefully take the rod up inside her rump. Gently, he had caressed her bottom with oils. His finger had slightly invaded her. The pressure had shocked her at first, making her toes curl and her fists clutch into tight balls. But he had coaxed her to let him continue, to relax and accept the slow thrusts of his finger.

She'd had no idea she was so sensitive there. It was even better than his kisses.

But this . . .

Sinking her teeth into her lower lip, she straddled his hips, her legs on either side of the bench. The first touch of the entrance of her bottom to the rod made her squeak. It did feel good. She lowered a little—

Then quickly stood upright. That particular invasion had hurt.

"Slowly," he said, around the toy held in his mouth.

She blushed. She could not quite believe he wanted her to put her bottom down on his face, but he had seemed to be very enthusiastic about the idea. Taking his advice, she tried again, bending her knees to go just a bit further, to take a tiny bit more inside.

This time it didn't shock her and make her tense. She rose and thrust down again. Panting, moaning, she worked on him. Slick from the oil, her bottom took the long rod in easily. She kept her eyes closed, though, embarrassed by what she was doing.

She moaned. Oh, it was good.

Then he shifted, releasing the rod with his mouth. It was up inside her, the end sticking out a few inches. And she was blushing fiercely.

"Take my cock inside your rump, too, Lucy," the duke said huskily.

She blinked. "Two things . . . inside me?"

"Yes, love. You're a dragon at heart. Fiery, feisty, and you can indulge in pleasures that most gently bred ladies cannot."

She should say no. But she was aroused. Wet and aching with need, and she wanted to be filled. To bursting—goodness, the idea was so exciting. But he was big, too, and she wasn't sure . . .

She ached so much, she was so tense and shaky with lust, she had to try. Her bottom felt aroused and ready, and she wanted to push her limits, her boundaries. Maybe it truly was the dragon inside her, wanting a pleasure that would make her burst into flames.

"God, angel, yes." He growled. "Take me inside you," he rasped. Then he gave a raw laugh. "Would you move the mirror, love? Turn it to reflect us, so we can both watch."

In front of the cheval mirror, she frowned. Her naked rear was positioned in front of the looking glass. The beautiful ivory rod stuck out between her cheeks. She held it, and slowly lowered on the duke—but she was too unsure to take two in the same place. She slid him into her quim instead.

But she could see what she looked like when she was riding him. It looked so erotic, her knees almost crumpled.

She pulled back, then thrust deeper. Her bottom tingled with pleasure, her quim ached, and she wanted more. Wanted it deeper. Moaning, she worked furiously, thrusting the rod and his erection in further and further and the duke groaned with every stroke.

She was very well stuffed—so much so, her feet tingled. The duke was right. She was a dragon and she liked this.

"God, they are both all the way inside you, love. Right to the hilt. You are the most amazing lover I've ever had."

He was watching them in the mirror, too. His eyes glittered at her—vampire eyes, but eyes that snapped with desire. She'd never had a man look at her like this. As though she was the most delectable woman in the world.

Outside, the lights of the street gleamed, and there came the cacophony of clattering wheels, trotting hooves, the shouts of coachmen. The street would be packed with carriages, with outriders with torches, all the bustle of a busy Mayfair street.

"Christ," he muttered. "You are so amazingly tight."

She breathed hard, trembling. "I am not hurting you, am I?"

"No, my dear. I'm indestructible."

His words set her on fire. Made her wild and bold. She felt as strong and wild as she did when she became a dragon.

A grin twitched his lips. "Ride me, my dear."

She did.

"God, I can't hold it back," Greystone growled. Then his hips arched up, driving his cock inside to the hilt. She squealed as the thick rod and his huge size filled her completely, pushed deep. Her fingers curled. It was so good. But she didn't climax.

The duke did. His head arched back, and he howled in pleasure. Then he slumped back on the bench. "Lady Lucy, come here. Turn. Kneel on my chest."

She hesitated, but he chuckled harshly. "I can support you, love."

As Lucy daintily got into place, he grasped her hips and drew her forward. The duke held the rod in her bottom and began moving it in long slow strokes. He took it all the way out, then pushed it forward so it made a luscious pop going inside. Then he flicked his tongue over her clit. He suckled her and thrust the rod in her bottom.

In seconds, an orgasm screamed through her. She cried out and he slid his fingers inside her pulsing cunny. She felt her walls squeeze him.

God, she'd never felt anything like this. She was writhing wildly, and screaming so terribly loud—

Then everything went black.

When Lucy dazedly opened her eyes, she was lying on the duke's chest, and his arms were wrapped around her. He must have eased the rod from her rump, for she didn't feel it. He kissed the top of her head and smoothed her hair. "There, love. Do you feel all right?"

"I feel wonderful," she breathed. She should get up. She must. But her feet were twitching a bit, her legs were weak, and she felt overwhelmed with sensation.

Oh goodness, what had she just done?

All sorts of astonishing, erotic, wonderful things.

The duke turned her into something quite different than the well-bred lady she was trying to be. He transformed her into a wanton creature.

She had tried so hard to keep the dragon inside her captured within her tightly laced corset. But for the first time, she wondered if she would be better to let it out a little more often. Not actually change shape, but become wilder and stronger, more sensual, more aggressive, the way she was when she was a dragon.

Sinjin smiled. Lady Lucy gazed at him sleepily. He cupped her cheek, and used the contact to try to look inside her thoughts. Had she been lying? Did she know where his nephew was? Did she know *what* his nephew was? To his astonishment, thoughts slammed into his mind. The messages were snippets of swift thoughts and he fought to grasp them.

Something quite different than the well-bred lady I am trying to be, she thought. *He transformed me into a wanton creature. . . .*

Let it out more often. . . .

Jack, what have you done this time . . . how could you hide while we were so worried about you . . . please, let me find you safe and sound. . . .

Will the duke really take me to Jack . . . I want to trust him . . . but am I a fool?

He knew that vampires could trade thoughts with other preternatural beings, but only when both parties were willing to send their thoughts.

"We will go and fetch your brother very soon." He said the words softly, the way a mesmerist tried to push his will into another's mind. And he sent more thoughts back to her. *Was there a boy your father spoke about? Did your father ever tell you about a boy named James?*

She would not know where these thoughts had come from and, if she knew anything about his nephew, it would trigger her thoughts in response.

They rushed to him. *What Father said . . . the day before he died . . . he had done something awful . . . he had tried to protect a child . . . and he'd failed . . . what if it truly was the duke's nephew? What if the child he was speaking of was not an orphan or abandoned?*

Sinjin's heart picked up speed and he waited.

Why would Father take his nephew . . . I don't understand. . . .

With a sharp pain in his head, Sinjin lost the connection with her thoughts. He lifted her hand and bestowed a soft kiss. Damn, but he should despise this woman—this dragon—who was one of the family who had taken James.

But she was so different from any other dragon he'd met. Human emotions were powerful in her. She was vulnerable. But also she deeply loved her brother. He'd tasted the emotion she'd felt when she'd thought about his nephew. It was empathy, worry, fear, pain. None of those emotions suggested she was guilty.

Her father and brother might be vicious enough to hold his nephew hostage as a pawn in the battle between dragons and dragon slayers, but Lady Lucy Drake seemed to be astonishingly softhearted. For a dragon.

Sinjin gently lifted her so she was sitting up. "First we will get you washed up, my dear. Then we will get your brother."

At which point she would know what he was—a dragon slayer. What was he going to do then? His duty was to destroy both her and her brother. Unless they could help him find his nephew, he was supposed to do it.

For the first time in his life, he felt something other than ice-cold at the thought of carrying out his duty, damn it. He saw Lady Lucy push back her tangled raven-black curls and he felt regret.

7

The Hunt

She had done the most intimate things with this man—she had let him make love to her in the most shocking and scandalous ways. That, she'd had the courage to do, but speaking to him as they sat across from each other in a carriage? Suddenly it was impossible. And being in such a confined space with the Duke of Greystone felt like the most awkward thing in the world.

Lucy folded her arms in front of her chest. Her neck ached from the ramrod stiffness of her spine, but the duke looked far more pained than she. He was slumped in the corner, his head thrown back, his eyes shut. Harsh lines ringed his mouth. He kept making grumpy, growling sounds, like an angered bear.

"What is wrong?" she ventured. "Is it worry about your nephew? I am—I am sure he must be all right." He must be— surely Father could not have done anything else. "I am sure Father would take the best care of him."

"Are you?"

How could he make love to her, coax her to do such naughty things, smile at her while he did, then speak with such ice?

She knew why—it was this horrible thing he believed her family had done.

"Yes," she answered swiftly. But her father's tears and his words—*I failed a child*—rang in her head. She didn't know the truth, but she feared the worst, and it made her sick with guilt and horror.

"What of my brother?" she asked, and the silence seemed to shatter like fragile ice on a pond. "Was he all right? Did your men tell you anything about how he is faring?"

Greystone stretched out his legs, and lifted a brow. "You are worried about that worthless scoundrel? Lady Lucy, you are foolishly and unnecessarily sentimental. Your brother is hiding in a brothel. I assure you he is fine. Very fine, though perhaps a bit tired."

Something about the way he spoke . . . "Did you see him? You said your men found him, but you speak as though you have seen him for yourself."

"Indeed. I visited him last night. I wanted him to tell me where my nephew is being held. He refused."

Lucy swallowed hard. "You don't seem like the sort of gentleman who takes a refusal in stride. What did you do?" Her voice rose as her panic did. "Did you hurt him? Torture him? Kill him?"

"My dear, I would not be taking you to the brothel if I had either hurt or destroyed him. What would be the point? Also, he can't help me if he is dead."

It was true. "So you simply left him in the brothel when he would not help you?"

"That was my intention for the time being, while I determined the best plan of attack to make him help me."

Oh dear God, she had been a fool. Greystone wanted to force her brother to speak . . . and he had *her* alone in a carriage. "Are you planning to use me as leverage?" Her voice broke. Lucy began to laugh—laughter that turned to choking sobs. She regained her breath. "It wouldn't work. And you can't threaten to ruin me, can you? We've already done that.

What are you going to do? Threaten to kill me. Perhaps he would let you—"

"No, he wouldn't. You told me he saved your life once before."

"I do not know anymore what he is capable of doing. He can hardly care about us all when he simply deserted us to live in a brothel."

The duke's brow rose. "He would hardly let you suffer."

"I don't know. . . . I do not know anymore. . . . He didn't care if our sister was forced to marry an older, disgusting earl. He knew how afraid and desperate we were." She took a shaky breath. Ice emanated from the duke's glower. Softly, she asked, "Is your nephew like me? Can he change into a dragon?"

"Yes."

Through narrowed eyes, he watched her. "So the truth now comes out. You do know your family took my nephew."

"I do not." But she sucked in a harsh breath. Could Father have believed the duke's nephew was in danger? Perhaps he could have taken the boy, if he believed he had to protect the child. When Father took in abandoned children, it was to protect them from parents who thought them monsters, from villagers who intended to kill them, from dragon slayers.

But to *kidnap* a duke's nephew . . .

"Did my father speak to you about your nephew's power? Did my father want to take your nephew to help him?"

"No, Lady Lucy."

She waited for more explanation but he gave her nothing. "I—I thought perhaps my father insisted that your nephew should be with others of his kind. So we could help him adapt to the human world."

"No, my dear. Such things were never discussed."

Was he lying? Her father would not take a child unless he had no other choice.

"But you knew about your nephew's ability to become a dragon?"

"Yes, I had witnessed it. It was unfortunate, but it could not be helped. And as a vampire, I knew exactly how to care for James. Your father did not take my nephew to protect him. It was entirely selfish motives that prompted your father to steal a frightened boy."

"I am sure that is not true."

"What you believe out of loyalty is of no consequence. Anyway, we have arrived. Shall we get out and find your brother?"

What she thought was of no *consequence*? "Why?" she demanded. "So you can threaten me in front of him?"

The duke sighed. "Of course not. So you can obtain the information from him. If you wish to leave here with your brother, that is what you must do."

So he would not let her take Jack with her, unless he got what he wanted.

Apparently sleeping with the man had not made him feel anything for her. He spoke as dispassionately as he would about lint on his coat. Lucy pursed her lips as the carriage door opened, then his footman helped her down the steps. To think she had liked this rogue's kisses.

She whirled on him as he stepped down from the carriage. She stood on the sidewalk—of a not-quite fashionable street on the fringe of Mayfair. "What do you mean—if I want to leave here? What are you going to do? Kill me? Force me into captivity in the brothel? Hurt my brother?"

She'd expected he would look hard and cruel. Instead, the duke looked old, worn down, filled with pain. "Lady Lucy, if I have to keep you captive until I get the truth out of one of you, I will."

He would not. She doubted he could keep her captive—in

dragon form she was incredibly strong. Very strong, if she were fighting for her life.

She would find out about his nephew. But why had her father taken the boy? Had it been to protect him from his hard, unfeeling vampire of an uncle?

Lucy stepped over the threshold of the brothel into a beautiful foyer. A fountain bubbled in the middle and skylights bathed the sparkling water with moonlight.

Gasping, she turned in a circle, drinking in the elegance of this house of ill repute.

Her brother spent most of his nights in brothels like this, but she had never been in one. She had always imagined a whorehouse would be a house decorated with garish scarlet, filled with screeching women and drunken men.

This house was a beautiful white-stucco home, one of a row of elegant townhouses. Tasteful décor leapt to the eye—expensive furnishings, beautiful respectable paintings of nymphs in light and airy dresses, paneled walls. Two footmen respectfully bowed, murmuring, "Good evening, Your Grace. Madam." They drew open two large black doors.

The duke grasped her arm and placed her hand on the crook of his arm. She tried to break free but he would not let her. She glared at him.

He leaned close and whispered, "Be careful, love. There are brothels that cater to vampires, demons, and shifters. This isn't one of them."

Her eyes must have gone huge—she felt the abrupt lift of her hairline as her brows arched high.

The duke drew out a small stack of notes—and pressed it to the hand of a youthful footman who waited respectfully by the brothel's front door. "I am looking for Lord Wrenshire. I believe he has reserved a private room for several days."

"His lordship specifically requested he not be disturbed."

She wanted to smack her brother. The duke calmly withdrew a few more notes from his pocket. "I assume he was not as generous with his tips for your services?"

"Indeed he was not. If you will follow me, Your Grace—" With that, the young lad turned and strode toward a curved stair. They took that one up, followed myriad corridors until they reached a door painted a powder blue. The servant rapped. And rapped again.

"He's probably asleep." Lucy knew Jack—it was far too early for him to be up. Irritation made her slam her palm hard on the door. "Jack, get up and open this door right *now*."

The servant looked as though his cravat was strangling him. "I beg your pardon, Miss, but the gentleman might not have come because he's not—not decent."

"My brother is *rarely* decent."

The lock clicked and to Lucy's shock, the door opened. The duke had his hand on the door handle. The door swung wide, revealing a room with a huge bed. And bodies in the bed. Arms stuck out from the sheets, and dangling feet. There must be four women in the bed.

Four women in the bed . . . with Jack.

The duke grasped her shoulders. "You should wait outside."

"You must be joking," she gasped. "After what you did. After what you *threatened* to do to me—including keeping me a prisoner in here? Finding this particular scene is nothing."

"My dear, I never threatened anything specific. Your vivid imagination ran away with you. I would never keep you a prisoner. Not a courageous lady like you. Your brother, however . . ." He let his voice trail away as he tried to direct her away from the bedroom door.

"You said you would quite happily keep me captive."

"My own private captive. And not here."

She pushed his hands away. Anyway, now the shock had

gone and she knew what she was seeing, she could tell her brother wasn't in the bed. "My brother isn't here, so it doesn't matter what you planned to do with him."

"So he isn't. But I should make sure." The duke moved quickly and effortlessly to the bed. One girl sleepily tried to sit up, gasping, "Oo—er, what time is it?"

The duke yanked the sheets back. Lucy saw four voluptuous females intertwined on the bed, heard the girls squeal and protest and try to grab the sheets. She saw the duke look under the bed before he relinquished the blankets and allowed the women to cover themselves.

She suspected he was trying to shock her. Or perhaps show her Jack's true nature, in the hopes she would betray her family by telling him where his nephew was. She would tell—if she knew. She squared her shoulders and stalked to the wardrobe. She opened it—it had much the same scandalous sexual play-things in it, like whips and ropes, as the duke kept in his wardrobe. Regardless, Jack wasn't hiding there.

She shut the doors. Greystone was looking behind the curtains and one of the prostitutes cried, "What are ye doing? Who are ye?"

"The Duke of Greystone," came the deep, rumbling reply. "And a lady. What happened to Lord Wrenshire?"

The girl pushed tangled blond curls back. " 'E's not 'ere? Well, 'e was last night. 'E was in bed with all of us."

Lucy stepped forward and faced the girl squarely. "I am his sister—"

The duke made a strangled sound, but she ignored him. She was too angry to care that these women now knew who she was. "I did not know he was here. I thought he was in trouble, lost somewhere in London. He has three sisters altogether and we have been all frantic with worry."

"Well, that's gents for you. Thoughtless." Another girl extracted herself from the tangle on the bed. She jumped off the mattress to the floor. She wore a shift that was so translucent her dark pink nipples showed through. Red waves hung to her waist.

"Do you know where Wrenshire went?" Greystone asked. "To another room perhaps?"

The redhead shrugged. "He might have. Or he might have gone. He said he couldn't stay much longer. That he could not stay in any one place for a long time anymore, in case he got caught."

"Caught? By who?" Lucy glared at the duke.

He shrugged, palms up, with a look of innocence on his face. "Not me."

She was not so sure, but she met the eyes of each girl. "Was my brother afraid of someone? Did he say who?" She knew they would not say if Jack was afraid of Greystone, but one of them might betray the truth with a nervous glance to the duke.

They all stared at each other. A brunette rubbed her chin. The redhead yawned and stretched and the other two, both blondes, shook their heads. "He didn't say," they all said, almost in unison.

Lucy could see the duke searching the room. There were no masculine clothes, though the scent of cigar smoke hung in the air. She went to the bedside tables and pulled open drawers. The four prostitutes peered at her, and she knew her neck was blushing scarlet, like her cheeks, but she kept searching. The drawers held nothing personal to her brother. There were velvet ropes, manacles, and ivory wands.

She went to the dresser table, reaching it at the same moment as Greystone. "I should look—I would know what belongs to him."

"Be my guest then, my dear." He stepped back, but as soon as she began to search the marble surface of the table, Greystone returned to stand behind her. Very close. His hands settled on the edge of the table, his chest brushing her back. Soft puffs of his breath coasted over her neck. And against her bottom—

She had riffled through a glass tray on the vanity twice and could not remember what she had seen in it. "Stop it," she said to the duke. "Move back. I cannot think with you looming over me."

"It bothers you?" His voice lowered to a soft caress beside her ear. "Even after what we've done?"

"Yes. Of course, apparently that did not matter to you. It did not stop you from threatening me," she answered, keeping her tones so quiet, the prostitutes would not hear. She focused on her search. Hairpins were scattered on the vanity. The small glass dish held a key—perhaps for the wardrobe? A pocket watch, but a cheap one, and it certainly did not belong to Jack. There were ropes laid on the vanity top—when men wanted to do naughty things, ropes seemed to figure quite prominently. She pushed the ropes aside with a furious sweep. "There's nothing here. Nothing to tell me Jack ever was here. Or where he would go."

"He's run farther than a brothel this time," Greystone murmured.

"Thank you. How helpful of you," she said through gritted teeth.

"It is possible he has gone to where my nephew is being held."

She let out a long breath. "I don't know where that is."

His hands abruptly lifted from the dresser and he stepped back. "All right. I believe you, my dear. So where do you suspect your brother would go?"

She thought. Screwing up her forehead, shutting her eyes. Where would Jack go? "Another brothel, possibly. Perhaps he ran away because it was time to pay his bill here," she added. She was not proud of the sarcasm in her voice, but she certainly couldn't quell it. "Perhaps he ran away to the continent—men do that to escape debts." Would Jack do it? Once she would never have thought Jack capable of deserting them all like that. When he was a boy, he spoke of sea travel and voyages around the world. He wanted to see Tibet, the Himalayas, which was the place that their dragon clan was supposed to have originally come from. But that had been when he was young and hungry for adventure. She didn't think such things would interest him now. Now he just wanted liquor, women, and gaming.

She pulled open the first of the drawers below the marble vanity top. It gave a squeak of protest. It was empty . . . no, it wasn't. There was a glint of silver in the back. She reached in and drew out a coin. A shilling, she assumed, until she looked more closely. The coin was not one she recognized. It was stamped with the picture of a rearing dragon. A sword pierced the dragon's chest. "What is this?"

Greystone's large hand, clad in a brown leather glove, covered her palm. He plucked up the coin. His blond brows drew together sharply. Then a grin touched his mouth. "I do not know, but I suspect it belonged to your brother."

She moved to snatch it back from him, but it had disappeared from his fingers. He must have slipped it into a pocket. "I want that back—"

But he crouched, and drew open the last two drawers. "Empty. Come, there's nothing to help us here. Let's speak to the madam."

"She wishes to serve us tea?" Lucy asked the question aloud, not expecting an answer. She paced in front of a window in a parlor that had a view of the street, of people strolling and fashionable carriages rumbling past.

But the duke decided to answer. His sensual drawl fell into the quiet room. "Mrs. Siddons is quite the lady, my dear. And it gives you a chance to question her." He sat on a wing chair, looking large and muscular against the delicate pink silk cushions. He leaned back, his hand resting carelessly on the head of a walking stick.

"But she is a madam. Why would she offer tea?"

"She is a woman of business, and quite charming and polite."

"You know her!"

Greystone laughed. "That is a very vinegary face. I thought you already believed I was an unconscionable rake." Instantly he sobered. "I don't come here, Lady Lucy. And after our two sessions together, I suspect I would never find pleasure in such a place again. I doubt any of these women could compare to you."

Heat flared over her cheeks. "I suspect you don't really believe that—" She broke off, threw her hands up. "I do not understand you! You threaten me one minute and slather on flattery the next."

"Worrying about someone has that effect. Wouldn't you say so?"

She crossed her arms over her chest. "Worrying about my brother turned me into a madwoman. Until then I was very normal, very proper. Now I am not." She tightened her arms, pressing against her chest. "Of course I am not normal, am I? You know what I am."

"And you know what I am. Neither of us is normal or ordinary. I believe we understand each other."

She hesitated, then nodded. "I think we do. Do you think the madam will help us?"

"You will find out in a moment—I believe she is approaching."

Then she heard the footsteps and in a moment a footman opened the door. He entered carrying a tea tray and a voluptuous blonde followed him. Or rather, a prominent pair of breasts entered, and the lady followed those. Rubies glittered at her neck. The madam curtsied, wearing a pleasant and calming smile. "Your Grace. Lady Lucinda, may I wish you a good afternoon. I am told you are in search of your brother, the Earl of Wrenshire."

"Yes. I was told he was here."

The madam waved to a seat. "Please sit down, Lady Lucinda. Make yourself comfortable." She poised on a settee and waited for the footman to set the gleaming silver tray on a low table in front of her. "I am sorry, my dear. Your brother was here. One of my most treasured clients and a favorite amongst my girls—how could I deny him when he offered a fortune to stay in one of my rooms for as long as he desired?"

Calmly, the madam lifted the teapot and began to elegantly pour two cups for her guests.

Lucy watched, but it was as though the madam moved in slow motion and she was watching the woman through a pane of rain-streaked glass. Everything was blurry and odd, and her heart was thudding so fast she feared it might explode.

Damn, damn Jack! How could he! They had no money, Helena was contemplating a hellish marriage, she had given up her virginity. But Jack had paid a large amount of money that they did not have . . . to *hide*. In a brothel. All he had thought of was his own skin. When she found Jack . . .

What would she do? Jack would not change. Her heart felt so heavy, and she felt so frustrated, but she had come to accept that. Still, what in heavens was she to do with her brother?

The madam could give them no more help. She could not suggest where Jack might have gone, except perhaps to another brothel.

Then the duke casually mentioned that dozens of houses of ill repute operated in London. She had no intention of traveling from brothel to brothel to find her brother.

A quarter-hour later, she was on the street again. She looked up and down it, foolishly. Certainly she was not going to spot her brother running away. He was long gone. "What do you propose we do next, Greystone?"

The duke's hand rested on her small back, and she sharply took a step away from his touch. She would not forget that he had spoken of imprisoning her.

"Your brother might have gone to the place where my nephew is being kept."

She clenched her fists. "And you think I know where it is. You think I will reveal it, because I will go there to find Jack. I keep telling you I do not know where he is!"

But a thought suddenly shoved its way into her mind. If Father had truly taken the duke's nephew, he would not have kept it a secret from his most trusted servants. He would have required their help. Father would have told Creadmore. That was a way she could find out the truth, and also find where the boy was being kept, if her family did have him. "I—I might be able to find out, if it is true. We could go there and retrieve your nephew. And I could see if Jack is there."

"Retrieve my nephew?" he repeated slowly. His brow quirked.

She frowned, confused. "You wish to have him back, don't you?"

"Yes." He was staring at her with surprise in his silvery-green eyes. "But are you saying that you intend to just give him to me, Lady Lucy?"

"Of course. You are his family. You love him. If it is true that my father took him, I think I understand why he did it— he wanted to protect your nephew and help him live with his ability to shift shape. His intentions were good. But he should not have taken the boy away from you."

The duke stepped back. As though her words had shocked him. "Thank you, Lady Lucy. You are a unique and remarkable woman."

He lifted her hand to his lips. His mouth touched. Heat flared over her skin, even hotter than it did when she turned into a dragon. She gasped. Then Greystone straightened, swept her into his arms, tipped her so she was floating, held by his strong embrace.

His mouth pressed to hers, and that touch sent showers of sparks through her blood. He kissed her until her heartbeat roared in her ears. Until she was panting against his soft, beautiful mouth.

It was the softest, most enticing kiss she could imagine.

Greystone set her back on her feet. His eyes held hers. "Thank you. You do understand I would never willingly hurt you." But his mouth was grim as he said the words. Then he turned abruptly, away from her. "We should go."

8

Questions

Lucy did not know a man could kiss a woman so much. Or that a woman could truly be kissed breathless.

The duke had escorted her into his carriage. Then, instead of sitting across from her, he had braced his arms on either side of her head. As they'd lurched out into the street, he kissed her. An openmouthed kiss where his lips played over hers, hot, hard, and deliciously wet. His tongue tangled with hers. He kept kissing her, even though the carriage swayed as it made haste down the street, winding around other vehicles and carts. She could barely keep her balance, but he did, with his hands splayed on the velvet squabs behind her. He kept steady on his feet and drove her mouth mad with pleasure.

At first, she'd thought she should push him away, because he had irritated her. But then she thought of what he'd said. That he would never hurt her. He had taken her to her brother. He appeared to have accepted the truth: she did not know where his nephew was, but she was willing to help him.

Now he was kissing her senseless.

Greystone drew back so she could catch her breath, but she couldn't really, she was too dizzy from being kissed. Anyway, before she could take more than two deep breaths, his mouth slanted over hers again. Her lips felt puffy, full from pressing to his, but she loved the sensation.

She clutched the edge of the seat to stay steady, so her mouth would stay against his.

She had no idea a kiss could make her so . . . hot for more. For his mouth on her breasts, his hand between her legs . . . for his body lying between her thighs and his buttocks pumping as he buried deeply inside her.

The very thought made her privates ache, made a moan slip out as he broke their kiss.

"I know what you are thinking," he murmured.

"You could not—" she began, but he surged in again and took her mouth once more.

Strangely, even though she had no idea where Jack was, she couldn't help smiling softly against his hot, beautiful lips. She needed this. It kept her from worrying. And the duke looked so beautiful when he kissed her. His lashes lowered—it struck her as odd that such an experienced man would kiss with his eyes half-closed, as though he were shy. Her eyes were wide open, taking in every detail she could, though they were rather too close for her to see properly.

She could see the oddest things. Part of his right earlobe was missing. A deep scar—no, three scars—ran along his right cheek. His skin was pale, though that was not uncommon for some gentlemen, as men of the *ton* gambled and drank all night, then were too sick and sore-headed to face the light of day.

But he wasn't just a gentleman. He was a vampire.

Lucy knew nothing more about vampires than the tales that were told in villages—and there were two basic stories. Vampires were soulless beasts who mindlessly fed on blood. Or they were clever and beautiful and lured you into baring your neck.

When the duke kissed her, it made her want to bare anything for him.

But then, she'd already let him see, touch, make love to everything.

He stopped kissing her, rested his lips by her ear, and spoke. "Lovely one, I do not even need to read your thoughts to know. You are hot with desire. As much as you like to be kissed, you want more."

"What do you mean you do not need to read my thoughts?" Shock, then fear, tumbled through her. "You cannot do that, can you?"

He smiled. "Vampires can. But I cannot read yours, and I suspect that is because you are a dragon."

Never would Lucy have imagined a man would say that in a matter-of-fact tone. "But you don't really seem like a vampire."

"Because I haven't gone for your throat? No, my dear, I can control my craving for blood."

As though to prove it, he ran his tongue along her neck. It sent sparks of heat shooting through her. She quivered so hard with desire she feared she might dissolve.

"You are thinking about coaxing me to explore you with my mouth," he murmured. "Have my lips trail down your neck, down to the scoop of your neckline. You're thinking about letting me run my tongue over your breasts. See if I can coax them out of your bodice so I can suck your nipples."

She moaned against his mouth. The images he was painting in her mind set her on fire. How—how could he have guessed her thoughts with such uncanny accuracy? Could he actually read her mind despite what he'd said? Or had he read all of that in her kiss?

"You are thinking you want me to push up your skirts," he continued. His lips pressed softly against her neck. They parted and she felt the scrape of teeth. Instinctively, she tensed, and tried to draw back but the seat resisted. Even as fear coiled in her belly, her skin came alive at the very place his teeth brushed.

Pursing his lips lightly against her neck, he suckled. She squeaked. Goodness, that felt wonderful. Pleasure snaked down from her neck, warming her heart, heating her belly, making her throb between her legs. She was panting.

"You want me to undo the falls of my trousers and lie on top of you. You want my hard thrusts. You want me to drive deep into you."

She did, but it was as if he'd taken control of her. He could stoke desire in her with only a few sentences, with just a few naughty visions he conjured in her mind.

Lucy saw, with a jolt of awareness, that when he aroused her, he controlled her. She had always kept such rigid control of herself, but with Greystone, she surrendered control. Too much of it, she feared.

When she had made love with him, she had turned into a dragon.

Panic welled. She had to get out of this kiss before he stole all her control away. Never had she felt such a desperate need to escape.

But he kissed a sizzling path back to her lips. He whispered, "There's nothing wrong with wanting me. Desiring someone does not make you any less strong."

How could he have seen that? "It frightens me, that you seem to know everything I'm thinking."

"Apparently, I am beginning to understand you."

She pressed right into the seat's velvet and met his gaze. Surprise lit up his eyes and lifted his brows. He seemed more astounded by his pronouncement than she did.

The carriage stopped. She heard familiar sounds—the final creaks of the wheels, jingling traces, the shouts of her family's coachman, the crunch on gravel of her footmen's feet. Sounds she usually never noticed, but that tonight seemed to echo loudly in her head.

"What does that mean?" she asked him. "What do you mean?"

"My dear Lady Lucy, I don't know."

With a soft *clunk*, the steps from the carriage were lowered. The door was about to open and the duke moved across the carriage with the speed of a bolt of lightning. By the time the footman had turned the handle, Greystone was lounging casually on the other seat.

She was trembling. She didn't know why. She did know she didn't want to stop kissing him. Seeking equilibrium, to stop shaking, to regain control, she said, "I'll go in alone. I know Creadmore—my family's butler—would not reveal any secrets in front of a stranger. It is going to be difficult enough to get him to speak to me."

He smiled at her from across the carriage—a patient smile. Then he leaned across the carriage and pushed back a lock of her hair. She lifted a hand, asking as she did, "Is my hair a mess now?"

"A few pins have fallen out, I think."

"I'll say—I'll say it was while I was searching for Jack. Really, I could hardly be expected to look like the perfect lady while haring all over London in search of my brother."

He kissed her once more, this time on the bridge of her nose. "Your brother does not deserve you, my dear."

Lucy felt an odd tickle in her throat, and knew, from many tears shed after Father's death, what it meant. Hastily, she stood. He held her hand to help her, but she said, "I can manage."

She opened the door and hurried down the dropped steps by herself. How could kissing do this? She felt as though kissing him had unleashed some kind of magic, magic that let him look into her soul. Then Lucy lifted her hems, and she ran up to the front door of her house.

Sinjin was hungry. Kissing Lady Lucy had helped keep his need for blood at bay. To overwhelm his hunger, he would flood his body with sexual desire. It gave him the strength to control his instinctual yearning to go find some human prey and gorge on a slender, sweet-scented neck, and made it easier to slake his hunger with blood in a tumbler.

Hell. He did not want to do that. But now he was thinking about blood—the tang of it, the texture, the way it would fill him, satisfy his craving—and he was damned hungry.

He had been made into a vampire because his clan believed dragon slayers had to be immortal. He'd wanted to be a dragon slayer, but he hadn't wanted to become a monster who really did prey on innocent maidens and take their blood. He'd had no choice—he had been turned into a vampire. His clan did it secretly. No dragon knew they were actually immortal.

But he refused to kill any person just so he could be fed.

To distract himself from hunger, Sinjin leapt down from the carriage. Lucy was the daughter of an earl, so her family home was an elegant house on Mount Street. Many carriages clattered along the road, and lights blazed in all the homes, for it was the start of the Season. Balls, routs, musicals, and other entertainments were held each night.

He usually received invitations. He ignored them all. There was no point in being both a duke and a dragon slayer if he couldn't be known as eccentric, he thought ruefully. And if he went, he was not sure he could survive being surrounded by the smell of so much blood. Likely, he would feed on someone before the end of the night. If his hunger got too strong, he could end up drinking from some debutante on the ballroom floor.

Hell, the *ton* thought it had scandals. They had no idea what he could give them. Not just juicy stories, but abject terror.

This was humor that didn't make him smile. He was a duke who had to avoid mortals lest he kill them. He was a beast who had hungers he could barely satisfy. He was a dragon slayer who had committed his soul to protecting England from dragons. All in all, he was in a hell of a situation. He had to get James back, but James carried dragon blood in him, which meant the boy was in danger from other dragon slayers. It meant he had to ensure Lucy believed he would never hurt her.

He was finding it damned hard to imagine slaying Lucy.

Damned hard.

Sinjin paced up and down on the sidewalk. Stepping out of the carriage had been idiocy. The street was filled with people, and he could smell their blood. His fangs had pushed forth and now overlapped his lower lip. He kept his face hidden from the elegant members of the *ton* and entourages of servants passing by him.

He thought about Lady Lucy instead. Would she get the information he needed from her butler? What was his next step, if she—

Something moved in the air. Sinjin sensed the slight rumble of a preternatural being moving behind him. Cold rolled over him. He turned, leaning on his walking stick. With his vampiric vision he could see the "prince"—as the man was called by other dragon slayers. The prince was moving so quickly, he was invisible to the rest of the world. The dragon slayer's pale blond hair shone beneath a beaver hat, and his eyes were two silver circles of reflected moonlight.

Coming to a stop, the man became visible at once. A couple walking on the other side of the street stopped and stared in astonishment. But they quickly looked away and strolled on. No doubt they had assumed the prince had just stepped out of the shadows. No one would believe the impossible: that a man had been walking so fast he was invisible to their naked and inferior eyes. No one would believe vampires and dragons existed, and dragon slayers were not just men of myth.

"Greystone, what in hell are you doing?" the prince grumbled. "You are going to spare a dragon?"

He didn't answer. His answer was supposed to be *no*.

The prince's gleaming eyes narrowed. "You know the punishment."

Sinjin glowered. The prince was a powerful being. Reputedly he had fought battles on high snow-covered peaks of the Carpathian Mountains, five hundred years before. He had protected his small principality from the Turks, from other Europeans, from his neighbors. Reputedly the prince had made a pact with a strong evil being to acquire his power—some said Lucifer, some spoke of a powerful warlock, some claimed he sold his soul to an ancient vampire. He gained immortality, and the price was to become a dragon slayer for eternity.

But then, given that the prince had lost his family to dragons, just as Sinjin had, Sinjin imagined the prince had not considered it a "price" to become a slayer.

"I won't kill her," Sinjin growled, "until I have my nephew."

"Your nephew is a dragon, Greystone."

"And I had your word you would not touch him, as long as I removed the dragon clan of Drago for you. The father is dead. I will deal with the son and the other children. As I promised to do, in return for my nephew's safety."

The prince, who was thought in England to be a prince of a small principality near Transylvania, curled his lip. "I sense you do not want to hurt this female."

Sinjin flattened his lips and knew his eyes were cold and glittering, betraying no emotion. "I know what the females are capable of. I have seen female dragons fight and destroy mortals. I have no sentiment here."

The prince cocked his head, his silvery eyes filled with disbelief. "Do you not?"

"No."

The prince stepped closer. Sinjin flinched as his vampire sire's hand gently stroked along the line of his hip through his trousers.

"Remember what is at stake, Greystone," the prince hissed. "I should have ordered the slaying of your young nephew. If you disobey your orders to kill this clan—including Lady Lucy Drake—I will judge you unfit to care appropriately for a half-dragon like your nephew. The boy will have to be destroyed."

"Yes, you bastard." Sinjin wanted to rip the prince apart. But the old, powerful vampire would be too strong for him. He would be the one torn to pieces instead. "I understand exactly what you are saying. To protect my nephew, I will do what I vowed to do. And that includes slaying the entire Drake family."

The prince's hand slid down and cupped his buttocks. Sinjin gripped the bastard's wrist and yanked his palm away, but the prince grinned. "I worry about you. About your heart—"

"Don't," Sinjin snarled. "Have I not proved, time and again, that I am the most heartless killer you have?"

Lucy cornered Creadmore in the gallery. He carried a candle aloft, and with Father's hounds following him, sniffing at his heels, he was rattling the doors to ensure they were locked. Most peers did not bring their hunting dogs to their London homes, but Father had been unique. He liked to have his animals with him at all times. Since his death, the hounds were subdued and sorrowful. They slunk around the house with their tails drooped and heads hanging.

She knew how they felt. With Father dead, Jack had been able to run amok with his gaming, and now the weight of fear, of possible poverty, of horror of the kidnapping of Greystone's nephew was pushing down on her head.

Before she said a word, Creadmore stopped, turned, and swung the light in her direction. "Lady Lucy!" he exclaimed. "I did not expect you home yet. Certainly not in the middle of the night."

Bother. She had forgotten about her lie—that she was visiting a friend and would be away from the house for a fortnight. She decided to give some of the truth. It would make the further lying she would have to do sound more convincing.

"I lied about that," she said. "I was not with a friend. I was trying to find my brother—and I did, only to find he has gone somewhere else." Facing Creadmore squarely, she went on, "I learned my father took a child he believed to be a dragon. I think my brother might have gone to this child. I want to know where Father placed this boy. You must know this, Creadmore."

The butler lifted the candle and the glow blinded her. But only for a moment—after all, she could breathe fire, so she could look into flame. Her sight swiftly adjusted.

"You must tell me where this boy-dragon is, Creadmore," she insisted. "I know my father took the child without permission of his guardian."

"How do you know this, Lady Lucy?"

That she did not want to reveal. "You are not supposed to question me. I want an answer."

The butler sadly shook his head. "And I cannot give you one. The late earl swore me to secrecy." He turned away. The dogs whined, then followed him as he headed away down the gallery.

This was ridiculous. Fear made the hairs on her neck rise. Why was there such secrecy? Had Father done something wrong . . . ?

Impulsively, she ran after Creadmore and sprinted around him. She breathed heavily, as her chest tried to expand against her stays to draw in air. "I need to know. I want to know why my father essentially kidnapped a child. I must find out where that child is!"

The butler shook his head. "Your father would wish you to remain in ignorance."

"That is not your choice to make!" This had never happened before. Planting her fists on her hips, she warned, "I could dismiss you."

"I am afraid you cannot, my lady. Only your brother can do that."

She balked at having Creadmore point out how powerless she was, as a woman. "Then you should be afraid of me because I am a dragon."

"A gentle one." A kind smile touched the servant's lips. "You have never killed. I do not believe you would start with me. Honor your father's wishes. He did not want you to know."

A fierce sigh of frustration escaped her. "Father is gone. And he stole a *child!* Creadmore, I am determined to make it right. Tell me what has happened with this boy."

"Your father was ashamed of taking this child, it is true. He admitted as much to me. But I could see he was greatly worried and he told me he had no other choice. It was to protect our clan."

"From what?"

The butler slowly shook his head. "That he did not confide in me."

"And you simply accepted what he said—without rhyme or reason?" She flushed. Of course Creadmore would. He was a servant. He would not have questioned her father. Or would he? She knew her father allowed Creadmore latitude to speak and question that no other servant was given.

"Lady Lucy, the late earl was a kindly gentleman. He would never have taken a child away from its family without good reason. He did tell me he believed the child was in imminent danger from dragon slayers."

"Where did he hide the boy?"

"My lady, I gave my solemn word I would not say."

The Drago clan members had several homes. Her family alone had three. "Scotland," she said quickly. "Did Father take the boy to our home there?" She knew the butler could not openly tell her, but he might reveal the truth by betraying it.

He stood, looking impassive. He held the candle below his face, which gave an eerie glow to his sharp chin and pronounced cheekbones, and left his eyes as wells of shadow.

"Near Gretna—the estate near there?"

Nothing.

"The moors," she said. "Our home in Dartmoor."

Creadmore's face did not change but the candle wobbled slightly. Of course her father would take the child there. It was secluded. The house stood on a small piece of firm ground but was almost completely surrounded by the notorious peat bogs of the Dartmoor moors. Thus the house was quite safe. Dartmoor was a good place for shape-shifters to hide. It abounded with legends: ghosts who rode headless horses over the open moor, murdered brides who haunted churches, cursed white doves who were a premonition of death if they flew into your house, evil sprites who threw grown men into rivers. A wealth of myth made the people accept strange occurrences and merely take them in stride. In truth, the moors were filled with undead beings and shape-shifters that took refuge in a place that was mostly desolate and empty.

Though she was now certain her father had taken the child to their Dartmoor house—because of Creadmore's candle wobble—she did not want to make it obvious she had guessed. She frowned, hoping she did not look as if she was quivering in anticipation. "Father did not like the moors, though. He wouldn't have taken a child there. He would have taken a child to Hampshire—he loved the countryside there."

An almost imperceptible softening of the butler's expression revealed relief. He thought she had not noticed his slip. She rubbed her chin as though musing deeply.

"I cannot say," he responded quickly.

"I will have to go to each one and search. I will start with Hampshire."

"Do not search, Lady Lucy. The child is being kept in secrecy because of the threat of the dragon slayers."

"But my father made peace with the dragon slayers a year ago. He would not fear they would attack this boy—" She stopped. Father had made an agreement of peace with the dragon slayers a year ago. He had told her and her siblings about it, though he had warned them to still be watchful and careful. And a year ago, Father had taken the duke's nephew—

Did it mean the duke was involved with the dragon slayers? Could he be one?

No, that was impossible.

He would never have made a proposition to her and have taken her to bed. He would have . . . killed her. It was what he was supposed to do. . . .

But then, her family held his nephew.

No, Greystone could not be a dragon slayer. They were all mortal men. Father had told her that. And the duke had revealed he was a vampire.

But she stood in the gallery, with Creadmore watching her intently, as her mind tried to make sense of all these threads of thought. It couldn't be a coincidence that Father took the duke's nephew, and at the same time, he negotiated peace with the dragon slayers. . . .

But if Father had taken the boy to ensure there was peace with the slayers, that meant her father had been holding the boy as a . . . a hostage. It was like holding him for ransom. And it meant Father must have never intended to let the boy go home.

She couldn't believe that! Not even peace was worth doing such a thing to a child.

Now, she knew where the boy was. Lucy was certain he was at their house on the moors. To fetch him meant days of travel . . . with the duke. Who might be a dragon slayer. It sounded impossible. Slayers wanted to rid the world of demons and shifters. They would never have a vampire amongst them.

She didn't know what the truth was. But she had to find out.

And she had to survive days of travel with a gentleman who might want to kill her.

Town was not dark anymore—and most certainly not in Mayfair. Street flares burned every few yards to light the streets. A sea of carriages rolled down the street equipped with so many lights, they appeared to be streams of white ribbons, rumbling down the road. Houses glowed. Servants carried lamps and torches.

It was human nature, after all, to want to ward off the dark.

Sinjin had retreated to shadow—the small, protective stretch of it between streetlamps. He stepped out when he spotted Lady Lucy hurrying down to his carriage.

Her eyes were wide and he smelled fear and uncertainty rolling off her.

Hell, had she guessed what he was?

But she came to him and met his gaze. "I know where your nephew is—" She stopped and sucked in a deep breath. "I am sure of it. But it will be a long trip. It will take us days. I must pack a trunk."

"We will start tonight as soon as you are ready. Do you need anything from my house?"

She shook her head. "It might take me an hour or two to prepare my trunks."

He tried to search her thoughts, but nothing came to him. Did that mean she no longer trusted him? That she was suspicious of him? He lifted her hand to his lips and gave a gentle kiss to her fingers. "I will wait."

9

Carriage Pleasures

Only a very foolish woman would ask a man, when she was alone in a carriage with him and had no hope of summoning help in time, if he planned to kill her.

Lucy wanted to believe she was not a complete idiot. So she kept the question locked inside her.

The carriage was hot and confining. The lamps burned within. By the time she had packed a trunk for travel, and she'd done it as hastily as she could, the time had ticked toward two o'clock. Mount Street was still crowded with carriages, and it would be until just before dawn, when the *ton* finally left the balls, suppers, and routs, and returned home. But even amidst the crowd, she was alone with the duke in the carriage. If she screamed no one would hear her.

It would take days to reach Dartmoor.

If the duke was a dragon slayer, she was quite certain he would not kill her until he retrieved his nephew. Until then, she would be safe. It gave her time to find out the truth.

What would she do if Greystone was a slayer?

Slayers killed dragons—throughout history, dragon slayers had killed hundreds of her kind. Could she fight him? Should she even try fighting? Or should she try to escape, return to her home, and tell the other members of the Drago clan, so they could pursue him?

Enough members of her clan could kill him.

But she . . . could she do such a thing to a man who had kissed her over and over in his carriage?

If he planned to kill dragons, didn't she have to? Her first loyalty must be to her kind.

The duke sprawled in the seat beside her and she glanced at him out of the corner of her eye. She had taken off her bonnet, one she had brought for travel, since a woman could not give an effective sidelong glance with a bonnet narrowing her gaze. She could not watch him surreptitiously while wearing a hat.

He groaned and gave a long, catlike stretch. He looked like a tawny lion settling in the grass. He caught her gaze and smiled. "Lady Lucy, you are quiet and nervous. What exactly happened with your butler?"

She gave a startled jerk. She had been lost in thought. Lost in wondering if she should run for her life now, or wait for the lion to pounce. "Nothing." Which wasn't a complete lie. All she had done with Creadmore was guess the location of his nephew—nothing more. Now she wished she had told the butler what she was doing. At least someone would know where she was. "I am . . . simply anxious. I wish we could arrive there at once and find your nephew."

He idly tapped his hand on his thigh. With his head cocked, he surveyed her. "Again, I must thank you. But you are not sure he is there, are you? That's why you are nervous, isn't it?"

She had told Greystone only that she *believed* his son was at her family's home in Dartmoor. "Creadmore did not tell me directly. He refused to. I had to guess."

"How did you do that?"

How deep and alluring his voice was. How it tempted her to talk. "We have three houses. I spoke of each one to him and gauged his reaction. He fought the hardest to contain his reaction when I mentioned the Dartmoor house to him. After that, I went to my father's study. Father kept journals. He did not mention your nephew in them, but early last March, he wrote entries about the Dartmoor house. I didn't know he had visited there—he kept it a secret from all of us. The only reason I can think he did that is because he took your nephew there."

She fiddled with her cloak, drawing it closer around her, pretending her shiver came from cold and not fear. She was sitting in a small, heated carriage with a man who might be planning to kill her. Of course she was afraid.

Could she be wrong about the duke? How could he have made love to her if he was a dragon slayer?

He laid his arm along the back of the seat and she tensed, drawing away from him, huddling closer to the side of the carriage.

"Now you are scurrying away from me, like a rabbit, not a dragon. What is it, my dear?"

It was madness—she wanted to ask, bluntly, *Are you a dragon slayer?* But also she wanted him to *kiss* her. She wanted his arms around her. How could she want to touch someone whom she thought wanted to kill her? But for some crazy reason, she could not just stop her desires so easily.

That made her press further against the side of the carriage. Not to protect her from him—to protect her from herself. The moment she had seen Mr. Ferrars hurt another woman, her feelings for him had vanished. Her heart had gone ice-cold. She should feel the same about Greystone. If she didn't trust him, how could she *want* him?

But now, looking at the duke's mouth, cranked down in concern for her, she thought of kissing it, and then she felt an aching throb between her legs.

Bother it. She could not stand it. "Are you a dragon slayer?" The dangerous, forbidden, foolish words fell out. "Is that why you didn't even flinch when you say what I am? Is that why we've had peace with the slayers—ever since my father took your nephew?"

She had to know. Had to, because she wanted to have sex with him. She was willing to risk her own life to go to him, touch him, press her body to his, strip naked and have him.

He blinked. His brows disappeared beneath the gold locks of his hair. "A dragon slayer? A knight in shining armor, do you mean? A hero? I'm sorry, my love, but no woman who has known me has ever called me that. I'm a rogue."

"No." Her face was hot, her heart racing. "I mean a true dragon slayer. I mean someone who hunts down dragons—like me and my family—and kills them."

"I'm a vampire. I wouldn't hunt and kill any preternatural being."

That was what she had thought. But she wasn't sure she believed him.

She had thought she loved Allan, then learned he couldn't be trusted. She would not be foolish enough to trust a man who had openly told her he was a rogue.

He frowned, his eyes narrowed to slits that reflected the glow from the carriage lamp. "You are saying there are dragon slayers? Men who hunt . . . *you?*"

"Yes."

"Christ," he muttered, which seemed incongruous for a vampire.

Was his surprise, his shock, real? She gazed into his eyes, but they reflected the light of the carriage lamps and told her nothing.

The carriage was filled with silence. Her mind whirled. He truly had seemed surprised to learn there were slayers. But was it real? Was it? Was it?

Finally his words fell into the quiet, splashing like stones cast in a still pond. "I would kill any man who hurt you."

＊　＊　＊

Did she believe his act? She had stunned him so much with her blunt question it had been easy to appear surprised.

But what surprised Sinjin was the honesty in the last thing he'd growled. If another dragon slayer attacked Lady Lucy, there was no way he could stand by and watch her be hurt. If the prince were to touch her, he would tear the vampire apart. At least, he would try to and likely be destroyed in the attempt. But he would be willing to be torn limb from limb to protect her, if not for protecting James.

Yet he was damn well supposed to kill her. If he didn't, James would pay.

He had no choice.

He had to assure her he was not a dragon slayer. He had to gain her trust. But she was seated as far from him on the velvet seat as she possibly could. It wasn't time to move closer to her. He couldn't use touch yet. He had to seduce her into believing him with his words.

"I didn't know dragon slayers existed beyond the legends of Saint George," he said. "I know there are vampire slayers. There is a Royal Society for them. Secretive and not known to most mortals, but it exists."

"I know about the Royal Society for the Investigation of Mysterious Phenomena. They used to capture people of my clan to study their shape-shifting ability. Then the Royal Society members would give those dragons to the slayers to kill them."

She kept speaking quickly and nervously. Apparently her father had told her quite a lot about dragon slayers—she knew of the different clans of slayers, knew their history. But she must not know about the prince, Sinjin realized, and the fact that the dragon slayers who served him had been made into vampires.

He knew he was safe the minute she told him, "I thought at first you couldn't be a slayer, because you are a vampire."

"I know vampire slayers hate shape-shifters," he said quickly, "almost as much as they hate vampires. It would stand to reason that those who destroy dragons would hate vampires, and would not let them become dragon slayers."

She mulled that. He could not read her thoughts, but she wore the fierce stare she took on when thinking deeply. His lie appeared to convince her. She hugged herself still, but not as tightly. "It is strange, though," she murmured. "It was at the same time my father took your nephew that he negotiated a truce with the slayers. After that, they left us in peace."

"Thank heaven for it," he said huskily. "Or my nephew could have been killed."

She sank her teeth in her lip at that. He saw the pain in her eyes at the thought. Lady Lucy Drake had a very soft heart.

Now was the time to distract her with sex and seduction. And in truth, he needed it—to take the edge off his hunger for blood, give him strength to control his vampire nature.

As he had done on the very first night he had made love to Lady Lucy, Sinjin began to casually remove his clothing.

Lucy could not help but stare.

The duke pulled off his leather gloves, then with one tug of his strong hand he undid the elaborate knot of his cravat. He dropped the rectangle of white fabric, and opened his collar.

She swallowed hard. Her gaze riveted to the sight of his strong neck, the hollow of his throat. He had been made into a vampire. An undead creature had sunk fangs into his throat and had taken his blood and his soul.

It made her shiver to think of it.

She wanted to kiss his exposed neck. She wanted to do it and not fear she was being weak and stupid for wanting him. The way he had said he would kill anyone who hurt her . . . it had sounded like the truth.

Suddenly, she thought of his nephew. Was the child truly at their Dartmoor home? Was she right?

The duke pulled his shirt over his head. She lost her breath as his muscles flexed. But her thoughts were filling with worry. Was the child scared? Surely, he would be all right. Her father would never hurt a child, but he might be fearful, being parted from his family.

The duke reached for the fastenings of his trousers. She was panting with the anticipation of seeing him naked, yet she was all mixed up inside with the worry that his nephew wouldn't be there. And if the boy wasn't, then what—?

Trousers slid down lean hips. The duke wore nothing underneath. He was hard, his firm shaft pointing toward his navel, glistening with moisture already. He wrapped his hand around his shaft, and her heart raced and her cunny pulsed as he gave a long, slow stroke.

"H-How can you?" she asked shakily.

Greystone looked up in surprise.

Finally she said it. "How can you want to do erotic things when your nephew is missing? My brother is missing and even though I know he is all right—he is just being selfish and annoying—it makes it hard for me to give myself completely to pleasure."

He sighed. "I don't have a choice. Sex keeps me distracted. It keeps me from drinking blood."

"Oh." Then she realized. "Oh. You mean, if we do not have sex, you will attack someone."

He nodded. "It helps a great deal."

She frowned. "Is that really true?"

"It sounds like a lie intended to get me beneath your skirts, you mean? No, it is the truth, my dear."

Lucy swallowed hard. She had wanted him, now she had a reason to make love to him that had nothing to do with feminine foolishness. She was agreeing to sex to simply . . . protect innocent mortals from his hungers. "All right. Then what do you want to do?"

What didn't he want to do? Mainly he wanted to make their erotic games last. The longer they did, the more they sated his need for blood.

"Relax on the seat, my love, and spread your legs."

Sinjin lifted a small valise from the other seat and flipped it open. Inside were all the toys he had brought to use on their trip—he had also made a quick stop at his own house before they had left. Taking out a long, slim wand of smooth ivory, he put it to his lips and licked it to moisten it. Lady Lucy breathed in sharply and her eyes widened. Smiling, he laved his tongue up and down the length.

"Lift your skirts," he commanded.

She did as he bid, drawing up the silk mass of them. She was not wearing drawers and he coaxed her to lift her skirts until she could see the thatch of her dark nether curls. Well, she could barely see them, with the mass of her skirts bunched in front.

"Perfect." He licked the rod he held once more with the flat of his tongue, then bade her to relax against the velvet back of the seat and simply watch.

She did. His long fingers lightly stroked the curls between her legs, then he touched her nether lips and with small crooks of his finger he coaxed them to part. She was transfixed by the sight of his hands playing. Each jiggle of the coach made his steady hand caress her.

Slowly, he touched the tip of the rod to her passage. She parted her legs wider, moaning, and he took her encouragement and slid it deeply inside.

Gasping at being filled. Moaning. Blushing to have him

watching her. Overwhelmed with the eroticism of having her legs spread and her skirts lifted in the carriage to expose her. All these things washed over her.

Then the duke grasped her right leg and lifted it high, forcing her to sit further back. His hand slid beneath the cheeks of her bottom. His finger invaded her anus slightly. It was so good—to have the ivory rod in her quim and the tip of his finger teasing her bottom. She was swaying and not entirely because their carriage was.

He withdrew another toy from his small case and again attended to it by licking it. This one was smaller, with a carved flared end. Watching him suck at it made her pant, made her quim pulse and tug at the toy filling her. Winking at her, he took it from his mouth. Cupping her bottom, he parted her cheeks with one hand, then touched the rounded head to her snug entrance.

She moaned and arched toward his hand, delighting in the teasing, intense sensation.

The toy popped inside her. His eyes glowed like green-glass lanterns as he slid it into her bottom, pulling back, then thrusting again. Oh dear heaven, it was wonderful.

Slowly, he pushed it up inside her until the flare touched her cheeks and held it in place. She was sitting on the soft velvet seat, utterly crammed full. Heavens, each jiggle and jostle of the carriage thrust the toys inside her, teasing both her quim and her bottom. He took out another and after thoroughly licking it, he pressed it to her anus, beside the toy already filling her. She gasped. He worked slowly—they must have covered a mile of road while he nudged the ivory wand in her bottom beside the first.

She was on the brink of an orgasm, yet she wanted to draw it out. She tried not to move, for bouncing would make her climax in an instant. Then he grasped the two toys in her rump and the one in her cunny and thrust vigorously. Desperately she tried to hang on, tried not to surrender, but the orgasm struck her in a long, rolling, exquisite wave.

Her fingers clung to the seat and she was screaming in pleasure.

As the orgasm ebbed, she dazedly met Greystone's amused gaze. Slowly, gently, he drew the wands from her bottom and her quim.

She was splayed over the velvet seat on her tummy. She wore only her short stays so it was comfortable to lie this way. Her skirts frothed around her waist and her bottom was bared. She half-turned. Some of her hair had fallen from her pins and spilled down her back, and she watched as he clasped his hand around his shaft. He looked so intense. His long hair fell around his face. His lips were parted and his mouth was tense with desire.

"Where—" She broke off. She was not quite courageous enough to ask for what she wanted. It was too naughty. Too embarrassing. Even though she had just let him do it.

"Where do I plan to put it?"

Lucy nodded, blushing.

"Where do you want it?"

"I—" Again embarrassment won out over the desire to request what she wanted.

Greystone lightly stroked her nether lips, making her quiver. "There?"

"Ummm—"

"No, that's not what you want. You want me in your arse."

Her blush deepened. Even after everything they had done, her face was on fire and her throat was bone-dry as he spoke of it. "Yes," she managed.

"My pleasure, my dear Lady Lucy." He spoke hoarsely, too, as though lust and desire were having the same effect on him.

Over her shoulder, she watched as he guided his shaft between her cheeks. She gasped as she felt him stroke the head in the valley. She felt the slickness of his juices. And she could tell the head was taut but soft, and the thick shaft as rigid as ivory.

With his customary gentleness, he eased the head inside her. She closed her eyes, feeling everything. The exquisite pop as he pushed in. The glide of his thick shaft past her sensitive ring. The hot, full feeling of taking him inside.

He thrust into her, panting, moaning, and she rose up to meet him. They began slowly, then moved faster and faster. He was braced over her, holding the seat, and she was gripping it, too.

She pounded wildly back against him, taking him deep, and wanting it fast and hard. It was incredible. Her bottom was slick from his strokes, tingling and sensitive. She loved feeling his hips slam against her cheeks. Loved it. Needed it.

Her fingers played with her slippery clit. Until she was so close, she could not move her fingers anymore. She held them steady and rubbed against them.

"Ooooh," she cried, and her entire body tensed then seemed to turn to molten liquid. She was coming. Surrendering completely.

He gave a long, harsh moan, and his hips bucked against her.

"Yes," she cried. She loved having him come. Her bottom felt hot, full. His body pressed more heavily on her as he drank in ragged breaths, but he supported most of his weight. She liked having him lie on her, knowing he was weak with pleasure, too. But he withdrew from her rump and patted her rear lightly.

She saw him pluck a handkerchief from a pocket. With gentle swipes of the soft cloth, he cleaned her bottom with the square of ivory linen.

"When we reach the next inn, we will stop, engage a room to clean up. And you, my dear, will need to eat."

She sighed. Not quite words of love. But he was thinking of her. Taking care of her. He couldn't be a dragon slayer. She simply couldn't believe it.

10

Maiden Flight

"You are going to fall off the seat. Stop trying to stay awake with me at night, my dear. You need your rest."

The duke held out his arm. Sighing, Lucy fell into his embrace. She was exhausted. They had traveled day and night for three days. In daylight, they kept the shades pulled down on the carriage, and Greystone slept on the seat opposite her. At night, she had wanted to help him keep his feeding under control. So they had engaged in a lot of sex and had not shared very much conversation. They had mostly traded moans and groans while licking, sucking, and pounding. It was their own private sinful world, where they did all kinds of erotic things. It was a wild fantasy that Lucy could have never even dreamed of experiencing.

But after three days of many orgasms and almost no sleep, she was tired.

The duke kissed the top of her head. "Relax against me and go to sleep, love."

She intended only to rest, not sleep, for she knew he would want to make love again. But her lids were heavy, his strong body felt so wonderful against hers, and she couldn't fight the droop of her eyelids.

She trusted him. Enough to relax completely in his arms. Enough to snuggle, to shut her eyes, to promise she would stay awake so they could make love again . . .

Lucy woke with a start. Something soft and wet pressed against her cheek. Her mouth was slack and open. Her neck ached and she felt as though twisted in a large knot. An arm slid around her, and she was drawn against the duke's chest once more.

Blearily, she focused on his handsome face.

A soft smile curved his mouth. "You were asleep," he murmured. "And you were sleeping in the most uncomfortable position. But when I tried to move you and hold you in my arms again, you hit me away."

Oh dear. The soft, wet thing had been the back of the seat. She'd drooled on it in her sleep. She felt strange, and disoriented. It had to be because she was sleeping. Normally she didn't feel so dizzy and odd in a carriage, even one swaying on a rough road—

The carriage was not swaying. The wheels were not rumbling. There was no jostling.

"We've stopped? Why? Are we at an inn?"

"No. We've reached the moors. I thought you might want to stretch your wings."

"You mean my legs."

He flashed a grin. "No. Come outside, Lady Lucy." Greystone stood, though he was too tall to straighten in the carriage. He pushed open the door. She could see nothing but blackness beyond. It was quiet, except for a rush of wind.

The cool air wrapped around her. The duke held out her cloak. She took it; then he jumped down from the carriage. Pulling on the cloak, she followed. She stepped down onto soft grass. Stars twinkled above in a vast, purplish-black sky. The lamps of the carriage sent fingers of light into the darkness, a feeble glow that quickly disappeared. A full moon gleamed in the sky, white and blue, and small. She shivered. The moors were desolate and almost completely empty. Hills surrounded them. Moonlight fell on the ruins of an ancient village, with circles of granite blocks the only thing left behind of a settlement several thousands of years old.

The duke drew her close. Even though he was undead, his body was warm against hers. Her breath made a puff of white in the air. It was March, but cold here, where the wind blew without anything to stop it. The hills were covered in new grass and dollops of snow.

Greystone rubbed his hands over her through her cloak. "A little colder than I'd intended."

"Should we go back into the carriage?" But the overheated compartment had left her groggy. Lucy enjoyed her breaths of bracing air.

The duke regarded her. "How often do you shift, love?"

"I never shift," she said quickly. But then she hesitated. "No, that isn't true. I try to control it, to ensure it doesn't happen, but sometimes I can't stop it. That was what happened in your bedroom."

"But you must let yourself shift at times. You must do it deliberately."

Against his chest, she shook her head. "No. I would *never* willingly do it."

He tipped up her chin. His eyes were pale and green, reflecting the carriage light into the darkness. "Why not?"

"I am not supposed to be a beast. I am supposed to be a human being." She put her hand to her mouth. How could she have called herself a "beast," drawing his attention to what she truly was?

"You are human, but you are a unique human, love. Just as I am."

Why was he speaking of this? "You said you try to control your feeding because you do not want to feed on people. That is how I feel—I don't want to do the awful things that dragons are capable of doing. I am afraid, when I shift shape, that I will lose control. That I will attack and kill." She gazed around at the emptiness surrounding her. This was why shape-shifters liked the moors. There were almost no people around to bother them.

Slowly, she asked, "You do feed on mortals sometimes, don't you? From what you said, I thought you tried, at all times, to control your cravings."

"I try to avoid it as much as I can. But my bad side is something I cannot completely evade. I have to drink blood. But you can shift shape and not hurt humans."

She shook her head. "When I shift, I become something different. I don't have the same control. The same . . . conscience."

He had no idea what an unleashed dragon could do. If she let down her control—heavens, she could destroy a village. She could burn innocent people alive. She could bite people in half, tear them to pieces with her claws. She could do everything it was feared mythical dragons could do.

Greystone clasped her hand. "Come with me."

Lucy let him lead her, though she did not like to be taken somewhere without knowing where it would be. He walked off the road, while she tried to become accustomed to the dark.

"There are bogs everywhere," she warned.

"I know. I can smell them. And, since vampires have excellent vision, I can see them. There is a track here. I assume if we stay on it we will be safe."

"Where are we going?"

"Trust me."

The moors were open, with dark quiet hills sloping beneath a wide, endless velvet black sky. Above, the countless stars glittered and winked. Lucy was accustomed to Town, to Mayfair, to streets illuminated at night with artificial light. It was so vast and quiet it felt heavy.

Finally, he stopped on a hillside. The road and carriage were many yards away and almost impossible to see.

"There's no one around," Greystone said. "No one to see. Why not shift into your dragon form and fly? You would find it would ease the tension and pain inside you. Fighting your true nature is difficult, Lady Lucy. In the end, it will destroy you."

"That's not true. It can't be." She frowned. No one had ever said that to her before. "If that were true, my father would have told me. He always approved of me controlling my shape-shifting."

"Tonight, just let yourself go. Be who you are."

"Are you planning to do that?" she demanded, her heart thudding in her throat. "Are you planning to be a vampire tonight?"

"Do I intend to find an innocent maiden and drink her blood? No, my dear, you do not have to worry about that. You've pleasured me well."

Lucy did not particularly like having the intimate things they had done likened to a good supper. And . . . well, she was stalling for time.

"Go ahead," the duke coaxed, and he might as well have been pointing at the juiciest apple on the forbidden tree. "You can fly here. Let yourself go."

"I have to . . . get into the appropriate position," she lied primly. Lucy stalked a few yards from him. She stepped into spongy grass and hissed as the cool damp seeped into her boot.

She did not want to do this. Why on earth should she shift shape just to fly about in the dark? He was *wrong*. She did *not* need this—

"You don't have to be afraid. There is no one to see you."

"That doesn't matter." It was though he had poked and

poked her, and finally she had lashed out. But he hadn't really goaded her. She was doing it to herself. This was who she was. For once, why not revel in it?

But it was wrong to do it. She wasn't normal, and she had spent her whole life fighting to behave as though she was. She could not just let go now and fly around the moors as though she had been wrong all her life, and in a few mere days, he had come into her life and brought in things that were right.

Everything she had done with him was wrong, by the eyes of Society, the eyes of her world. Greystone was wrong about this, too. But correct about one thing. She was afraid.

Lucy had never willingly shifted before. Even in her adolescence, she had never done so. Father had taught her what she was when she was a child. He'd warned her she would begin to shift when she began to transform into a woman. She had not been afraid, really, the very first time it happened, since she knew what it was. But she had fought it even then.

She'd never thought it was dangerous to keep tight control over her body's need to change to dragon form; she'd thought it was for the best.

If resisting her shape-shifting would ultimately kill her, wouldn't Father have told her?

Lucy took a deep breath. It was true that it was a constant battle. It was like wearing a full corset, and lacing it as tightly as possible. She was trying to hold everything in, and half the time it did feel like she would burst.

She bit her lip, let it start, but then she stopped before she changed. Suddenly, she did not want to do this alone. "Can't you shift shape and fly? Vampires can turn into bats, can't they?"

"I can't," the duke said, and even though she was yards away, she heard him distinctly. "I'm a vampire who cannot do any of the fun things. But you do it—I want to watch you."

She could do this. How could she be so afraid of it? Perhaps he was correct. Perhaps it was her fear of what she really was that could hurt her.

The duke came over to her. Slowly, carefully, he took off her clothing. Her heartbeat raced as his hands moved over her. Soon she was naked on the hill.

Naked. Out in the open. Where anyone could see. Except they were alone here. The carriage was so far away, surely the servants couldn't see her. And the duke stood between her and the sight line of their vehicle. He would have to do so, otherwise the servants might see her transform.

She was going to do it. Her heart thundered, but she was going to try.

Lucy closed her eyes, and in the magical way she never understood, she began the change.

Heat began to gather around her heart. The warmth flowed through her blood, slowly leaching everywhere under her skin. Here was the point where she should start to fight. Gritting her teeth hard, she fought against herself. Instead of trying to will the change to stop, she stopped her body from battling. She let herself change.

It was a strange feeling, as though her body was being wobbled apart. It didn't feel bad, but it felt like she was losing control of her limbs. The wobbling made them longer, as though giants were stretching her. Her body grew—or rather, the ground got farther away. It happened so quickly, she only knew she had become a dragon by the way she tingled and the way the jutting granite rock and waving grass receded in a swift blur. She stretched. The sound that rumbled from her throat was a little-used roar.

Her arms were longer and tipped with claws that glowed blue-white in the moonlight. Scales glittered, catching the light, and they looked blue and green and silver all at the same time. Her legs were strong, muscled. Her body was slender and her face had changed completely. She now had a muzzle, a snaking tongue, and large, heavy-lidded eyes with long, curling eyelashes.

She had wings on her back—large wings that spanned ten feet across, and were made of gossamer-thin, shimmering panels of skin stretched on a bone-like structure. She gave her wings a flick, feeling the way they stirred the air. Her tail lifted behind her. It was a beautiful thing, long and sinuous, and the spine of it was marked with diamond-shaped scales that stood upright in a line. The end held a flat, silvery, arrow-shaped piece that glinted when she moved her tail.

Female dragons could use their tales to draw a mate. They used their tails for playful flirting the way human ladies plied their fans in the ballroom. Though Lucy couldn't—she'd never learned. She had never spent much time as a dragon.

But here, in the velvety dark and the amazing stillness of the moors, she felt like stretching out. She let her tail drift through the air, drawing patterns in the dark with the reflectivity of her scales.

Then, her dragon's heart beating swiftly, she looked to the duke.

He was watching her, a soft smile on his mouth. "You are beautiful," he said. "I would like to see you fly."

"All right," she whispered, but as a dragon, she could not speak in English. She used a language of whispers and snorts that was more musical that it sounded.

"And breathe fire."

She tipped up her muzzle and let out one small lick of flame. Breathing fire was dangerous, and it drained her of energy quickly. If a dragon breathed too much fire, the dragon could die—a dragon could deplete its life force without even realizing it was doing it.

Lucy gave her wings a flap. Never had she had so much open space in which to do it. She lifted them high, feeling the strain of new, different muscles. Then she pushed the wings down, so she rose gracefully from the ground. With beat after beat, she soared up into the cool, clear night sky. She cut cleanly through the velvety dark. Flying felt different. Flying over the moors felt utterly new.

She didn't feel guilty for letting herself become a dragon. Instead, her heart pattered in excitement. This was . . .

"It is fun," she cried out, though her sounds were soft growls, not words. Lucy twirled in the air, then swooped down and lifted to the sky. She flapped hard, pretended she was reaching for the stars, then she dove down, spinning like a barrel.

A new sound rumbled up. One she had never made as a dragon, and she had no idea what it would sound like.

It was laughter, and it tinkled like the light tap of a fork against glass.

Sinjin had never seen any creature look so happy and act so playfully. It was true that vampires were rarely playful in any place but bed. And he had never seen werewolves or shape-shifting dragons except in the midst of a fight, where they were struggling to survive, not having fun. In fact, he had never seen any shape-shifting creature when it wasn't trying to kill him.

He had never seen one while it was playing with its power like a happy child.

Lady Lucy as a dragon was very much like Lucy as a woman: strikingly beautiful. Her scales were dark green and they shimmered. When the moonlight played on them, the light rippled like silver waves on a dark blue-green sea.

He had always hated the sight of a dragon's muzzle and teeth. Anytime he saw a dragon's mouth, it was snapping at him, trying to rip him apart. But Lady Lucy's teeth were not large, and her mouth had a gentle curve that made it look as though she was smiling. Her tongue, which snaked out swiftly, was soft and pink. Her little line of flame had been a brilliant gold color.

And she had beautiful eyes. They were the same fascinating indigo as her human eyes.

She was whirling and twirling in the air, and making a soft, musical sound.

Her happiness made him smile. Yet he was supposed to look at her like this and hate her.

He had to.

For James's sake.

But she was playfully dancing in the air, obviously filled with delight. She would race up toward the twinkling stars, her tail streaming straight behind her, her wings sparkling with silver moonlight as they flapped. Then she plummeted toward the ground, so fast Sinjin didn't think she would be able to stop. His heart plunged into his gut with the fear she would hurt herself.

Instinctively, he ran forward to catch her, but she made a graceful arc with one beat of her wings. He laughed along with her tinkling sounds when she swooped up to the sky again. He watched in amazement as she played in the air the way he used to play in water when he'd been a boy. When he had been young and innocent, long before he'd learned about his duty as a dragon slayer. Before he'd lost his family and before he'd lost his heart.

How could he kill her? How?

How could he hurt a woman who amazed him at every turn? Who he was beginning to realize was the most remarkable woman he'd ever had in his bed.

He wished he could rescue James, then haul Lucy back to his bed and keep her there, and never let her go.

But he couldn't. His damned prince had made that perfectly clear.

* * *

She felt glorious, happy, powerful, alive.

Lucy landed on the soft grass of the hill, and she shifted back. She trembled and wriggled as her body shrank in size and her bones and muscles reshaped. In a heartbeat, she was in human shape again. She stood in the middle of the vast empty field, naked.

It was exhilarating. She had flown. Lucy felt as though she could have soared high enough to touch stars. Wildness—it was like it had taken root in her soul and was growing like a weed. She wanted to tend to this wildness, she wanted it to blossom.

She wanted to be wilder.

"You said you needed me to keep making love to you or you would lose control of your urge to feed."

The duke's gaze traveled over to her in a slow sweep from her head to her bare toes. He licked his lips. "Yes, I did."

She eyed her pile of clothing. The Lucy of a few days ago would have run to them to put them on. Instead, she twirled, enjoying the feel of bracing air on every inch of her skin.

"Then we should make love again. Now. Out here."

11

Thank You

The duke dropped to his knees on the trampled, damp grass, and he placed his hand on her hips, drawing her cunny to his mouth. He blew a soft breath over her curls, making Lucy quiver, then murmured, "Come here, love. I want to taste your sweet pussy."

Lucy blushed. Cupping her bottom, Greystone lifted her, and moved her so she straddled his face. He pulled her down so she was sitting on his mouth.

Then he did the most wicked, exciting things to her with his lips and his tongue, while his hands tugged her bottom's cheeks lightly apart. The sensation of having her anus gently pulled was arousing. The hot thrusts of his tongue into her, the intense, hungry way he devoured her made Lucy sway on her feet.

She clutched his head to stay steady. Her feet had sunk into the soft mud beneath the grass. He licked her clit with fast strokes. She'd intended to stay quiet—the moors might be almost empty of inhabitants here, but they were still *outside*. But when he did *that* to her—when his tongue flicked faster than a bow over a fiddle's string—she had to scream.

Above her, the heavens were vast and dark and dotted with jewel-like stars. Her cries of pleasure seemed to slice through the air, rising as high as she had done when she flew.

Her hands gripped his hair desperately. Having shifted shape seemed to leave her skin terribly sensitive. It wasn't just the brush of his breath, the wild flicking of his tongue that overwhelmed her. She felt *everything* so intensely. The whisper of cold air. The swirls of breezes. The clutch of his fingers in the cheeks of her bum. The tug at her puckered anus—

Oh. *Oooh.* "Your Grace! Your Grace! Oh, Your Grace!" Incoherent, mad screams tumbled from the lips. The orgasm streaked through her like a shooting star. She fell forward, he lifted, grabbed her, and fell to the damp earth, planting her on top of him. His thick, erect cock slid up inside her clutching, pulsing quim—her pussy, he'd called it. It ignited another, even stronger climax. She pressed her fists to his chest to brace herself.

Then he began driving up into her. While she was still coming. One climax flooded into the next and Lucy had orgasm after orgasm on top of him, while he thrust into her. Her fists flailed on him as her muscles went tight. Her head thrashed to and fro. Her screams could probably be heard all the way at Plymouth.

Laughing harshly, he surged up, his hips hard and insistent against hers. While she writhed on him, he bucked underneath her. Then he fell back, gasping down ragged breaths.

His arms settled around her and she collapsed on his chest.

Together they took in heaving breaths.

Then he laughed again. "While you were coming, you kept calling me 'Your Grace.' "

Dazedly, she lifted, propped her chin on his broad chest muscles. "You are a duke."

"Call me Sinjin, love. After this, nothing else will do." He gave her one last, long stroke down her back with his hands, then he lifted her. His cock flopped against his belly. He sat up, deposited her on his lap. "We should keep traveling, Lady Lucy."

"Just—just Lucy."

"Ah, there is nothing 'just Lucy' about you." He scooped her up by her bottom, then got to his feet and set her gently on hers. Amazing her, as he always did, with his strength.

Lucy suddenly felt the cold of the night air. She shivered.

Sinjin left her and went to the jumble of her clothes that lay on the grass, flattening it. He brought her shift, ghostly white in the moonlight and twirling like a phantom in the breeze. From behind her, he drew it over her head. She let the hem fall over her hips as he fetched her stays. She was pulling them on when he said, in his voice gruff and deep, "Lucy, love, we cannot drive up to the house and demand my nephew. Whoever is looking after him won't turn him over to me. I don't want to put you into trouble with your family, or your family's servants."

She frowned as he helped her put on her dress. Then he put her cloak on her shoulders. It was cold, from having been in the night air, but that wasn't what caused the chill around her heart. It was anger over what her family had done. And the realization that she was—for the first time—acting in complete defiance of her family.

"That's true," she said. "It would be best if I go to the house first. I can find James, and I can get him out of the house, without anyone knowing. . . ."

It meant betraying her family, her clan. But she heard Sinjin's harsh breaths behind her. When he spoke of his nephew, he breathed that way—as though he was trying to tamp down fear and panic.

She turned and laid her hand on his forearm. It was rock-hard with tension. "Don't worry, I will bring him home to you." Then softly, she asked, "What happened to your nephew's mother and father?"

He jerked his head up. She saw he had retrieved his hat, which had fallen when he'd dropped to his knees to lick her pussy. He jammed his hat upon his head. "Why do you ask? Why should anything have happened to them?" His voice was a raw rasp.

It was true. She didn't know anything had. She just sensed so much grief in Sinjin. "I assumed you are hunting for him because he is in your care."

"He is. You are correct about that. My sister died two years ago, when the boy was three."

"I am so sorry." She felt guilty—it was obviously hurting him to talk about it, but she could not stop her curiosity. "And the boy's father?"

"That was why my sister died. He went first. She didn't want to survive without him. And that's enough, Lucy. I have no intention of telling you more. I am the only family James has. That's all that matters."

She knew she deserved to be chastised, because it was not her business. But they had been intimate and she was going to take a huge risk for him. It hurt that he did not want to talk to her. That he wouldn't tell her more.

"All right." Then another thought struck her. "I am certain I can smuggle your nephew out of the house. Are you willing to trust me—to wait and be patient?"

He nodded. "Of course I trust you. I will do exactly as you ask."

But she wondered—would he do as she asked? Sinjin had never once been docile. She might trust him now and know he wouldn't hurt her, but she wasn't sure she could trust this particular promise. It would be easiest if he let her try to bring James out. She prayed he would understand that.

He clasped her hand, threading his fingers through hers. It was a gesture of joining, of partnership, that took her breath away. Then they ran back to the carriage.

This was her home—she was the mistress of her house, and had been since her mother's death. Why on earth did she feel so nervous?

Lucy felt her shoulders give an involuntary tremble as their carriage neared her house—or at least, she believed her family's Dartmoor estate was growing closer. In the dark, she could not recognize a thing. They had passed the village of Princeton, where the prison stood that had housed prisoners of war. The carriage had taken the road to the south.

She was nervous over so many things: defying her family and a possible confrontation with the servants of the house. But also, Lucy was quivering with anticipation. She wanted to have the boy safe—she was determined to rescue Sinjin's nephew. But it was going to take considerable wit to fool the members of her clan who must be watching over him.

And her brother might be at this house. Very soon, she might be facing Jack again. And she knew she had to confront him over his irresponsible behavior, and the horrible kidnapping her father had carried out.

From the road, the driver took a lane to the right. It consisted of two slightly worn tracks over grass and lumps of rock. The carriage wheels rattled along, slamming into outcroppings of granite. Sinjin sat at her side, her hand still clasped in his. Just having her fingers twined with his left her breathless.

They dipped down a hill. In the valley, long grass waved, and she knew the track meandered for only one reason—to follow the solid ground. The lane was a line of safety through the bog that stretched on either side. Originally, she had wanted to come here before the sun went down altogether. The lane would be almost impossible to see in the dark, the odds high they would wander off it and sink in the bog. Entire ponies could vanish in the bog. And there was a legend that someone plucked a hat off the soft ground, only to jump in surprise when he found a head beneath. The sinking man cheerfully asked to be helped out of the bog, and asked his rescuer to retrieve his horse, too, as he was seated on the animal.

But arriving before the sunset had been impossible. It was too dangerous for Sinjin.

Lucy gazed out the window at inky darkness. How the coachman stayed on the track, she didn't know.

She had only been to this house four times in her life—the last time had been five years ago. She had never come to one of her family's own houses feeling like an outsider. That's what she felt like now. She was coming as an *enemy* to the people in the house. Lucy did not know if the people who would be staying there, who would be watching over James, would be friends of her father and members of the Drago clan, or if they were servants of their family.

If they found out what she planned to do—give James back to Sinjin—they might fight her.

It was an unsettling thought. They would be far stronger than she was.

Sinjin's grip tightened, he squeezed her hand gently and reassuringly. The carriage stopped and he stood, still holding her head. "I asked the coachman to stop before turning into the drive of the house. Bring James out here in the carriage, and I will join you. I will keep watch over you—but you will not see me. I want to make certain you are safe."

Lucy nodded. "I *will* be safe." But she knew that wasn't true. Still she managed a small smile, and he finally unclasped her hand. He opened the door only enough to allow him to slip out, then he closed the door behind him.

* * *

Lucy surveyed the imposing house standing before her. The moors had always made her fancy it looked like a haunted castle. It was built of granite blocks, with two towers that stretched to the dark sky. High stone walls surrounded it. With nothing around it but hills, it looked imposing, dark, dangerous.

It was dangerous for her now.

She debated trying to slip in unnoticed. Lucy thought about windows and rear doors, and the secret way she knew to get in and out through a cellar window, because her brother, Jack, had told her about it.

In the end, she did the simplest thing. She sent a footman to the front door to announce her, and as she stepped down from the carriage, the large wooden front door was swinging open for her. A thin, tall, gray-haired woman stood on the threshold, flanked by two young footmen in her family's wine-red livery.

It was the housekeeper. Lucy remembered the woman's name—since Jack ignored all his responsibilities, she was the one who worked with their family secretary on matters pertaining to all the family's estates. The housekeeper here was Mrs. Billings, and she was much thinner, much more gaunt, than Lucy remembered.

Mrs. Billings stared in openmouthed shock for several moments as Lucy neared the door, then she seemed to gather her wits. She dropped into a curtsy. "My lady, I did not know you were to arrive. I apologize—I will have a suite of rooms prepared for you at once. I will rouse Cook to prepare a supper. For now, if you would go to the westerly drawing room?" Billings gazed at her anxiously, then looked back to the carriage behind her. The woman was nervous.

Apparently, the housekeeper believed there was something to hide. Which meant her father had intended for her to never know about this. Obviously, the words he had spoken on his deathbed had been brought out by the pain or confusion he must have been suffering as he died. Why—if Father had been doing this for James's good, had he wanted to keep it from her?

"Thank you." Lucy knew her clothes were crumpled, and saw the housekeeper's gaze begin to assess her with confusion. She had to act in charge here; she had to take command. "First," she said with autocratic firmness, "I wish at first to see a child who is staying here. A young boy, brought by my father a year ago." She said it without question, as though it was definite fact.

It worked. Billings pursed her lips, then answered, "The wee lad is sleeping, but if you wish, my lady, I will have him dressed and made ready and brought down to you."

"No, I shall go and check on him myself." Was it really to be this easy?

"Of course, my lady." And Mrs. Billings gave her the direction to young James's room.

Sinjin circled the house for the second time. Clouds had gathered, blotting out the moonlight, but it made no difference. He could see clearly. A stone wall, about twelve feet high, surrounded the house and grounds. It had been chiseled to a smooth surface, making it impossible for a mortal to climb. With his vampiric strength, he could easily jump over it.

But he had promised Lucy he would do as she had asked.

For the first time in his existence as a dragon slayer, he was going to do what a dragon had asked him to do.

The room was illuminated by a crackling fire in the grate, along with candles on the vanity. The bed was large, and the boy huddled under the covers was tiny. A thick counterpane showed only the smallest bump and when she approached, Lucy saw he was curled into a ball.

She crouched down beside him at the head of the bed. He

was turned away from her. Hair, the same golden color as Sinjin's, stuck up and brushed the pillow. "James?" she whispered. She kept her voice soft and barely audible. Mrs. Billings stood at the doorway, her ring of keys clasped in her hands. Lucy sensed the intensity of the woman's stare and suspected the housekeeper was straining to listen.

Lucy stroked the tiny shoulder beneath the sheets. "James, I've come to take you back to your uncle. To the Duke of Greystone, who will take care of you."

The boy didn't turn his head. Was he sleeping? She shook the boy gently and bent over. Clasping back fallen tendrils of hair, she whispered by his ear. "Wake up, James. You are going home." She could see a little bit of his cheek where the covers had slipped down. He was terribly pale.

Heart thudding, she rolled the boy onto his back and she jerked in shock. His dark eyes—a deep brown and fringed with thick lashes—were wide open. He stared upward, but he made no sign he had seen her.

He couldn't be blind, could he? Surely Sinjin would have told her. "Your uncle is outside," she said, as loudly as she dared. "We will get you out of bed and you can go to him."

It was as if he could not even hear her. But a soft creak came from the corner of the room, and he turned toward that sound. He faced the shadows in the corner, solemn, unblinking. The child looked lost in his own world, as though he had been so very afraid when he was taken from his uncle, he had receded inside himself.

Lucy's heart stuttered. What had her father done? She whirled and saw Mrs. Billings, her hands clasped in front of her brown skirts, watching. "What has happened to this boy?" she demanded. Even though her voice was sharp and loud, James did not react. Had he been so frightened by other people—by the members of her clan—that he now blocked out human voices?

The housekeeper took a step forward. "I do not know, my lady. The child has been like this since he arrived here."

Lucy sat on the side of the child's bed. She gathered him up—he was so thin and small, he seemed to weigh almost nothing. From the duke, she knew he was only five years of age. She drew him to her chest, a bundle swathed in white, soft sheets. The boy leaned against her only because she pulled him there, and he kept his little body as straight and stiff as a fireplace poker.

Stroking the boy's back gently, she glanced to the window, letting thoughts race, forming a plan. She did not understand exactly what was happening. There was no one in this house of note. There was no member of her clan, someone who would be in charge of the boy. There was just Mrs. Billings.

To return James to his uncle, she simply had to gather the boy up and carry him to the carriage. But that made no sense. Why would her father steal the boy, then leave him unguarded?

She stared blankly at the panes of glass, wondering if she dared to just take James out the front door to the carriage. Was she wrong—and there were members of her clan close by? Would her own servants try to stop her?

Something white and strong flashed outside the window, as though the sun had exploded. Lucy jumped slightly on the bed, though James did not show any reaction. The loud boom that rumbled after the bright light explained everything. The flash had been lightning. A storm was blowing in, washing swiftly over the open moors.

Clouds had blotted out the moonlight. Beyond the grounds of the house, faintly illuminated by the light from the house, the moors were impenetrable darkness. Rain came with a violent burst of energy, lashing the windows, and now she could see nothing at all.

They couldn't go anywhere tonight. The tracks would turn

into a quagmire, and without light, they could wander off into the bog.

But there wasn't any reason to. There was nothing to fear here in this house. She was in charge and she could command the servants to prepare rooms. Gently, Lucy laid the small boy back into his bed and drew up the covers. She swept to her feet. "This child's uncle is waiting outside. We will stay here tonight, and then this child will leave with us tomorrow." She spoke quietly to Mrs. Billings, but issued a clear demand.

The woman twisted her hands together. "Oh my lady, your father's instructions were clear. We were to keep the boy here."

"My father is not here."

"But His Lordship is to arrive soon, and he was to give us further instruction."

Lucy jerked. Her brother had sent word he was to come here? "When did you learn my brother is to arrive? When is he to come here?"

"I received a letter a few days ago. I do not know exactly when he will arrive. It is to be before the end of this week. But my lady, surely if the late earl—"

"This child is ill," she said sharply, "and is suffering from his captivity here, Billings. We will leave this house in the morning tomorrow."

She hating leaving James, even for a few minutes, to go down to the door and bring Sinjin inside. Ignoring the footman standing there, she pushed it open. Rain drove in at her, whipped in by the wind. To her surprise, Sinjin stood on the gravel drive, and he stared up at the lighted bedchamber window—the window where James was lying.

Guilt surged. Lucy was so furious with her family. It would devastate Sinjin to see the child this way. As he strode toward her, rain pelting on his coat and hat, she impulsively hurried forward. She slid her hand into his. "I must warn you . . ." Oh God, what had her father done? "Bringing James here has affected him, I fear. Badly. Or . . ." Heavens, how to ask this? "What sort of boy was he?"

Sinjin's face was pale, his silver-green eyes stark with pain. "What do you mean? He lost his parents, which had affected him. It had made him quiet and withdrawn. But I had worked hard, and was drawing him out. He was becoming a smiling, happy child."

Oh no. Her family had ruined that. Heart in her throat, Lucy knew she must face this—she must watch Sinjin's heart be completely broken as he saw what had happened to his young nephew.

Christ, James made such a small shape in the large bed. He looked so tiny, so fragile. Sinjin almost choked on his guilt. James was all he had left. He should have never let the boy out of his sight. He should have ensured the dragons hadn't got to the lad.

His sister would have hated him for what he'd done.

Lucy moved to the bed, and he hung back, immobilized by the swamping pain that rushed up to his heart. There was only one pain vampires and dragon slayers were supposed to feel— pain that stoked a hunger for vengeance. He felt it. Sinjin felt a rush of pure white-hot anger toward the men who had taken James.

He couldn't feel it for Lucy.

Her dark blue eyes were huge and stricken in her pale face. Tears glistened in the corners of her eyes. She approached James and gently stroked the boy's shoulder. James did not move. He did not even stir.

Approaching the bed, Sinjin saw the boy's eyes were wide open. Wide open, but eerily blank.

Lucy sat on the bed and leaned over James. "Here is your uncle for you, James. You are going to go home with him."

James did not face him, did not look toward him. It was as though the boy was deaf and had not heard her.

"What happened to him?" His voice was a rasp. "Drugs? Magic?"

"I—" Lucy looked at him with anguish. "I don't know. I think . . . it might be fear. He was afraid of coming here, of being taken away from you. It might have been that he thought he lost you."

A tear streaked down her cheek. It dripped from her lip. Then she kissed James on his small forehead. The boy stirred suddenly. He twitched as though he was shooing away a strange sensation. Then Sinjin heard the worst word, the one that was like a knife to his heart. Tentatively, hopefully, James whispered, "Mama?"

Sinjin heard Lucy catch her breath. "No," she finally answered, truthfully but softly. "But you are with your uncle, and I am your friend."

The candlelight illuminated her with gold as she lifted James into her arms and hugged him to her snug bodice. It was appropriate, wasn't it, since she gleamed like gilt? She had a golden heart. A gentle, good heart.

He watched her. In the soft glow, her neck was a creamy curve, and dark tendrils of her hair spilled along the smooth arc. "You should sleep now, James," she murmured. "You must be very tired. In the morning, you will go home . . . you will go home with your uncle. He has missed you and will be so happy to have you home." Her lips parted, full and lush, as she hummed a soothing lullaby to his nephew.

Damn her family—James was as lost as he had been when Emma had died. But watching Lucy sing to James, while tears glittered in her eyelashes . . .

It made his heart lurch . . . made it ache.

Lucy would make a good mother.

But Lucy's children would be dragons. What sort would

they be—the kind that attacked and killed the innocent, the kind that ripped defenseless humans apart, the way his family had been killed? Wolves, people had said. That had been the explanation for the cruel devastation wrought on his mother, his father, and his siblings. How else to explain bodies pulled apart, faces destroyed by claw marks?

His heart should have turned to ice again, as it always did when he thought of dragons.

But he was watching Lucy, and it didn't.

James shuddered beneath the covers and made a mewling sound, but Lucy's stroking hand soothed him. Sinjin approached, keeping his footfalls soft. The boy's breathing grew rhythmic; the counterpane rose and fell slightly as the wee lad drifted into a deeper sleep.

Sinjin sat beside Lucy on the edge of the large bed. He laid his big hand on James's tiny body. He was a sweet, innocent child. It was not the boy's fault he was a dragon, but because of it, the boy was threatened by Sinjin's clan of slayers, and had been stolen by the dragon clan for their protection. The boy had suffered because of him.

Hell, he wanted to leave it all behind. Take James and live a quiet, safe life. Somewhere the boy could live like a normal child, protected from damned slayers and even more damned dragons.

But it was impossible, wasn't it? The boy was a dragon—that truth couldn't be ignored. Sinjin had given his eternal oath to be a slayer. He'd be hunted down and destroyed if he broke his oath. James might be killed, too. At the very least, if he was hunted and killed, James would be left without protection.

There had to be a way out. For James's sake, he had to find one. Once he walked out of this house with James, the dragons of Lucy's clan would hunt him. He would be expected to slay Lucy's family. And Lucy.

Until then, he had a night. One whole night ahead of him.

James was sleeping and the boy looked sweetly relaxed in slumber. James had spoken to Lucy, which meant he was aware of her. It was a good sign. It was remarkable Lucy had broken through to the boy. James had been like this after his mother had died. Then, it had taken Sinjin weeks to get through to James and have him respond.

He knew the best thing was to leave James to sleep.

Heart thudding slowly, he went to Lucy. He crouched down and murmured by her ear, "Thank you for comforting him." It was no act to gain her trust or manipulate her emotions or seduce her. He felt things he had not known for a long time. Gratitude. Thankfulness.

She turned and put her finger to her lips. "He's sleeping now. And he spoke...." Her voice trailed away, and in a throaty whisper, she added, "Thank heavens."

"Thanks to you, love," he said again. "I'd like to stay with him tonight, but first..."

Out of the corner of his eye, he'd noted a wing chair pulled up to one side of the fire and a daybed on the other, near the drapes over the window. Quietly, he scooped Lucy into his arms. As she gave a squeak of surprise, he carried her to the daybed.

Wanting to thank her.

To please her.

She had asked him if he intended to kill her, and he'd lied to her. Even a really good fuck couldn't make up for that, could it?

But with his heart all mixed up, and duty strangling him, and desire for her rushing hot through his blood, it was the only thing Sinjin could think of. Make love to her. Make love to her and forget what the morning would bring.

Lucy could not quite believe Sinjin had thanked her. She'd thought he would hate her, along with the rest of her family, over the terrible state James was in. At least the boy had responded to her, and because he had, surely she could break through more. Surely she could bring him back.

Sinjin laid her gently on the soft, elegant daybed, draping her as though she were fragile and delicate. He had seen her as a dragon, yet he carried her and arranged her like a gentleman with a revered lady.

She gave a shaky sob. Tears came—tears for James. Sinjin made a soft growl in his throat, then kissed her cheeks to whisk them away. His lips were like velvet, a quick caress to her cheeks that made her tremble.

How she quivered. She hugged herself and closed her eyes, letting her sealed lashes hopefully stop the tears until she got control.

But he murmured, "Open your eyes."

She did. Wide. Sinjin's long dark lashes swept over his glinting green eyes. His mouth was parted, poised for another kiss. His broad shoulders were right in front of her, so strong and secure. She laid her hands on them. "I am so sorry about James."

"You made him speak. Together we can help him. I'm sure of it."

"I've never—" She stopped. She had never felt so close to anyone. So willing to open her heart. It made her see how she had never truly cared for the man who had been her fiancé. That had been nothing to this tumult of feeling she had no idea how to express. She didn't know if she should. Ladies were taught to be demure. She wanted to say *I love you*, but she knew a lady was not supposed to be so bold.

"Lucy, love, don't speak. Let me love you."

A soft smile touched his mouth, touched her heart. He gave her a swift kiss, a burst of magic against her lips, then he moved down her body. But he never dropped his gaze from hers. Her breasts lifted with fast breaths as he kissed his way along her stomach. Her hips squirmed against the silky cushions.

He threw up her skirts and gave her a long, luxurious kiss to her clit, which hardened at once. Her legs tensed as sensation streaked through her, but she was comfortable with him now and she lifted her hips, seeking pleasure. He was delighting her, tasting her, teasing with his tongue. It was like waltzing with him: she brought her hips up and played, gliding her quim against his lips and tongue. She saw the hint of his smile. She felt his hands cup her bottom and hold her tight. He pulled her against his mouth and licked, licked, licked her clit until she had to bite her lip hard to keep from screaming.

Her body heated and shook. It wanted to change. But she wasn't afraid. Not anymore. She didn't grow tense and terrified. She relaxed and controlled the shift. She did not want to become a dragon now. She wanted pleasure. This connection. This glorious, wonderful dance.

Then he suckled, lavishly, lovingly on her throbbing clit. Pleasure surged, a silken wave that coiled around her, and spun her wits, and made her sob with sheer ecstasy.

She clenched her fists, rode the wave of pleasure that made her quim pulse, her heart pound, that made her gasp and Sinjin grin as he twirled his tongue and drove her higher.

When she flopped down, he rose over her. He kissed her lips. Salty—his mouth tasted salty, tangy, and tart from her intimate juices. Sinjin's kiss was openmouthed and hungry. He broke the wild mashing of their mouths for a moment to whisper, "Thank you."

And his eyes . . . they held such fire, such softness. It stole her breath.

"Make love to me," she whispered.

He undid his trousers, and joined tightly with her. They moved together quietly, and he buried his face in her tangle of hair and murmured by her ear, "I'm going to come quickly, love. I can't last."

She giggled softly, wrapped her arms around his neck. "Come now. I want to watch you, feel you, enjoy it, too."

He plunged deeply, his hard thrusts teased her sensitive quim, and she gasped. She'd wanted just to watch him—

But heavens, pleasure flooded her. Her hands made fists and she flailed them against his shoulders. Goodness . . . goodness . . .

His hips surged forward and collided with hers. His back arched, his shoulders jerked, and he panted hard. Sweat rolled down his face as his groin bumped hers. She saw how ravaged he was, felt the rush of heat inside her.

He was coming.

Then he withdrew with a quick move of his hips and kissed the tip of her nose. Swiftly, he fastened his trousers, then he helped her undress. He stripped her down to her shift, and once she was clothed in nothing but the filmy muslin, he fetched a blanket from a box at the foot of the bed.

Adeptly, he arranged the blanket over her. The care Sinjin took to ensure her feet were covered made Lucy smile. Her skin was damp with perspiration for all her bouncing and her climax, but the soft weight of the cover warmed her.

He was stretched out beside her, balanced at the edge of the daybed. He cradled her in his arms, tucked her cheek to his chest. "Sleep, love. I don't sleep during the night. I'll keep watch over James. And over you, my treasure."

12

Just a Taste

Lucy woke to feel a firm ridge pressing against her bottom. Her shift had hiked up, leaving the cheeks of her derriere naked. She knew exactly was the jutting hardness was, knew it was the firm head of Sinjin's cock poking her with the long shaft squashed between her curves and his rock-hard abdomen.

"Mmm," she murmured, wriggling her bottom so it slapped his erection to and fro. Sinjin gave a rasp of a laugh. A soft bluish light glowed in the room, touching the curved details on the ivory daybed, and lightly illuminating the large bed that stood across from them.

Then Lucy remembered where they were and she lifted her head abruptly, straining to see in the whisper of daylight. She had slept without waking all night. Was James all right? Heavens, how could she have been so selfish? She should have gotten up and checked on him. . . .

It was daylight. And as a vampire, Sinjin had to seek darkness—

She bolted up, forcing Sinjin to groan as her hip pressed hard into his groan.

"What's wrong, love?"

"I hadn't meant to sleep so soundly. I'd intended to wake and check on James—"

"He is all right. I watched him through the night and he slept soundly," Sinjin said quietly. "He is still sleeping so I think we should let him rest as long as he wants. But daylight is creeping in and I have to sleep for a while. I need to find darkness."

"All right." She frowned, thinking. In the carriage they had kept the curtains drawn and the interior lights extinguished. At the inns, which they had reached at night, he had been awake while she had slept. Where in the house would be dark enough? "You can use any bedchamber . . . with the curtains closed, will it be dark enough? There is also the cellar—" She broke off. For years she had been mistress of her father's household, since her mother had died when she was twelve. She had been hostess at dinners and parties he had held for their clan. She felt terrible offering the basement to Sinjin.

But he smiled. "A bedchamber should work fine, love. But first, I want to bang my hard cock deeply up your ass. Though we have to go at it quietly."

She smothered a giggle, but quivered at his words. They were rough but erotic and exhilarating. With Sinjin she could be everything she should not be as a lady. Wanton. Lusty. Even a dragon who could play in the sky. He gave her freedom in a way no one ever had. Almost as though he'd commanded it, Lucy grew hot, wet, aching between her legs. "Yes," she whispered. "Please."

"Then roll over, love, and expose your pretty rump to me."

Obligingly she rolled onto her tummy, her legs slightly spread. The lacy edge of her shift lay halfway over her bottom, the roughish trim tickling her skin. A firm push got it out of the way. Naughtily, she lifted her bottom, both to tempt him and because she was wild with arousal. The touch of his hand on her rump made her moan. Anticipation had her wet, had her toes curling, had her heart racing.

He eased her cheeks apart with one hand, stroked his erection between them with the other. The velvety head bumped her tailbone, slid into the dewy valley where her cheeks were so plump they tried to grasp him. Then the full, taut head touched her opening.

Lucy held her breath.

Her hand strayed down, between her stomach and the cushions. Past the wrinkled hem of her shift. Through her nether curls. She tapped her finger teasingly on her clit, and he pushed his cock inside.

Slowly, wonderfully, he began to thrust. Her toes were clenched tight, her fingers curled so hard, her fingernails drove into her palms. But she began to relax. The tight puckered ring of her bottom slackened. She rose to him, wanting to take him deeper.

He obliged. Dear heaven, he lifted her legs off the ground, then thrust so far, she felt his groin smack her rump. He held her legs just below her knees, then he rose up on his knees, forcing her hips to rise with him. She braced on her arms, and his cock surged deep, impossibly deep, incredibly deep. His flat, muscled abdomen smacked her bottom with each stroke. Held this way, she was utterly at his mercy. Her breasts swayed wildly with each punishing but delicious thrust.

"Yes," she whispered hoarsely. "Go deep. Pound *hard.*"

Each time he'd thrust so powerfully, she'd loved it. This time she wanted more. She wanted to feel his balls slap her. Wanted to feel his cock filling her bottom, pushing her to the limits of pleasure, where it flirted with pain but didn't hurt. Where it was shocking and enthralling and good.

"Can you lock your legs around my hips?" he asked hoarsely. She tried it and it worked. Then his fingers pressed to her bottom, pushing in beside his cock. Oh, it made her feel so full. And he slid his other hand to her pussy, and thrust his fingers in, as his thumb slid over her slippery clit.

Oh God. She tried to hang on. Lucy could hear his fierce breathing. He was close and she wanted to share this.

His hips gave a fierce thrust then they bucked wildly. He pushed his groin hard against her bottom, helpless in his climax, joining them completely. Heat spurted inside her and the glorious sensation made her climax, too.

They were coming together. It was wonderful. Amazing. For this was what she felt with him—as though she could share everything. She could share pleasure with him and she could share hope with him, the hope they would set James to rights. She could share her fears and doubts . . . fears over being a dragon, doubts about her family, and both for her brother.

She could share her heart with him.

Sinjin collapsed on her, and as he always did, he kissed her. This time it was tickling brushes of his lips against her neck.

He rose, and she felt a soft cloth move over her rump. "I should fetch you some washing water," he said.

"No. I will tend to that. You must go and sleep now. The sun is rising."

"I'm sorry to leave you."

"I understand that you must." She pulled down the crumpled skirt of her shift. And watched as Sinjin stood, smoothed his clothing. He left her, then went to the bed. Her heart gave a pang as he smoothed back the boy's hair, kissed the lad's forehead.

Sinjin blew her a kiss. Then he let himself out of the room, closing the door softly behind him.

Lucy didn't know a great deal about young children, and she was worried she was about to do the wrong thing. Poor

James had been through so much and her heart begged her to let him stay in bed, to have a tray of food brought to him.

But even though her heart wanted to coddle him, her head insisted that perhaps James needed to be pushed back into normalcy. She found his clothes lain over the back of a chair—a shirt, and short trousers, and braces. His shoes and stockings were neatly stored beneath the seat.

A maid brought a pitcher of steaming water and a basin. After the young servant left, Lucy sat James up in the bed. She had to move him as if he were a doll. Holding him with her arm around his back, she dipped a cloth in the basin and wet it. Coils of steam rose from the water.

"Here we go, dear," she said softly. "I am going to wash you." She pressed the cloth to his cheek.

James did not flinch; he did not look at her. His eyes stared ahead. His mouth was closed in a straight line.

The poor angel. She bathed his face, wiping away sleep from his eyes, crumbs of food from his lips. It was obvious no one had bathed him for several days. Small pimples dotted his skin and it was salty with dried sweat. No one had tended James, and fury swept through Lucy. What had happened to allow this child to be treated so badly? She could not believe it of her father. Was it because Father had died and no one had known what to do with this boy? Why had Mrs. Billings not asked what she should do?

She would find out.

Briskly, Lucy rinsed the cloth, then rubbed soap upon it, releasing the scent of sandalwood into the air. James's small nose wrinkled and he tried to pull away when she began scrubbing. "No, my little lamb, you need a good wash."

Had Mrs. Billings written to her brother—to Jack—and asked him what to do? He was the earl now. He was expected to take on Father's duties, duties such as protecting young dragons.

Except Jack couldn't even protect himself! He didn't think of anything but his own pleasure. He would hardly trouble himself to write directions for caring for a child.

She loved her brother, but here, now, she had learned one undeniable thing. Jack's irresponsibility hurt so many people. She might love him, but she could no longer try to clean up his messes, repair his disasters. She had to get him to stop making messes in the first place.

Lucy stood, got to the bell pull in three hurried strides, and tugged sharply. A maid came in moments, and Lucy sent the girl to fetch Billings.

As soon as the housekeeper presented herself, Lucy met the woman at the door, so James would hear her words. "Why has this child been so badly neglected? He has not been washed in goodness how long! And he is skin and bone. Have you fed him?"

"Of course, my lady." The pale blue eyes widened in panic. "I have tried, but the child won't eat. I would push the spoon between his closed lips and hope that at least something would trickle in."

"Did you ask my father what was to be done with him? Did you write to my brother?"

"Yes. I received no reply."

It was just as she'd thought. "You should have at least bathed him."

The housekeeper wrung her hands. "I did try, my lady, but he would turn vicious. He would kick and punch me and bite me. Every time I tried it, he would fight me as if battling to the death. I could not get near him."

Lucy frowned. "Is this true? With me, he has barely moved a muscle."

"It is, my lady, I promise you. Most of the time, the boy just lay on the bed, staring upward without moving a muscle, but when I tried to touch him, he fought like a demon. And sometimes he would writhe on the bed as though he were possessed."

Mrs. Billings did not know her employers were dragons. She did not know that some of the beings who stayed in this house were not human. Only a few of their servants did. It would be impossible to stay the tongues of many, many servants, so the secret was only revealed to the very loyal ones, like Creadmore, who had been in the family for years.

Arching a brow, Lucy commanded, "I will need some tooth powder, a fine comb, and some scissors."

Mrs. Billings rushed off, and returned swiftly, bearing the items. Lucy dismissed the housemaid, and laid everything upon the vanity. *There*, she thought, *I will do this.*

But it proved rather difficult to tidy up James. He struggled and spit when she tried to clean his teeth. Her face and gown were quickly covered with white spots, made from the tooth powder she had mixed into a paste, which James then sputtered at her.

When she had the scissors poised above his knotted, unruly hair, he tried to bolt off the vanity stool. She had to throw down the shears and pursue him around the bedchamber. Finally, she caught him, and asked, "Wouldn't you feel better with your hair tidied? I will have to cut out the knots."

Frowning, he shook his head.

Hmm, perhaps it had not been the best idea to ask. "Well, I believe you will. You are going to have your hair cut."

Teeth sank into her wrist. Astonishingly sharp teeth. Lucy yelped and her hand fell back from James's arm.

The boy ran toward the window. Panicked, she followed, but despite his small size and frail body, he sped toward the curtains like an arrow.

Was he going to try to get out? Was the window locked? She had never checked and James had reached the curtains. Velvet billowed around him as he tried to scuttle between them, and he got tangled. It gave her the time to reach him, and to grab him up in her arms. She held him against her chest, and he squirmed like a wriggling piglet. She had seen men try to hold piglets, and it had looked nearly as impossible as keeping James secured.

He almost fell out of her grasp. She grabbed him more firmly, and suddenly realized her fingers were too tight.

Then she was stunned. His skin, where she held him, was heating up. It was growing scorching hot, as hers did before she transformed.

"No!" the boy shouted loudly, something he had not done since she'd been in his room. "No! No! It hurts!"

She had lightened her grip, and drawn him against her chest, and she could feel his flesh move as his muscles and bone changed beneath. She could feel the quivers and trembles.

He was sobbing with pain and fear.

What was happening? She had not changed shape for the first time until she had been much, much older. Until she had been almost a woman. Boys did not shift shape until they were almost fully grown also.

The boy screamed in anguish and thrashed in her arms.

Stunned with shock, Lucy managed to stroke his forehead. "It's all right," she whispered. "It will stop."

She felt his arms and legs stretch and become longer. She felt the poor child's back pulsate, getting ready to form wings.

James cried, "I hate it! Hate it! Make it stop."

Could she? "Try very hard to make yourself small, James." Would that keep his body from expanding and growing? How exactly did she stop it? She didn't know. She had just tried and tried and eventually she'd managed to gain control. "Your body wants to change and turn into a dragon. Try to think about staying as you are now."

Crying desperately, he was tense and shivering in her arms.

But she couldn't stop it, and he transformed and she held a

small dragon in her arms. His wings beat fervently and his tail thrashed. As a dragon, he could not cry, but he made a pitiful mewling sound.

She cradled him. She stroked over his smooth scales, so much softer than hers. The spikes along his back poked into her arms, but she did not care about that. The poor sweet needed comforting. "Shh," she murmured. "It will be all right."

What foolish words. It hurt her to change—how must it have felt to James? Why was he changing now, when he was so young? What did it mean?

He let out a high-pitched roar that was more of a squeak, and in moments she held a shaking little boy in her arms again. His hair was damp with sweat and stuck to his forehead. Smoothly, she brushed it back.

"Has anyone told you why you do that, James?" she asked gently. "Do you understand that you are very special? That you can change into a dragon?"

"Not special." He sniffled and shook his head. "Told me I am a beast."

"Who told you that?" she asked, too sharply, for his lip quivered. Much more softly, she said, "That is not *true*, James. I am just like you—I can turn into a dragon. A bigger one than you, of course, because I am bigger."

His head had tipped back and he watched her, eyes goggling and his mouth wide open. Lucy set him on his feet and held his hand firmly. She led him to the large wing chair and placed him on it. He curled his legs underneath him and stared at her.

"You sit there and watch me. Do not move, and I will show you what I can do."

He stuck out his lower lip. She took two steps back, then she willed her body to change. She tried to not grimace and cry out as her body stretched and grew and rearranged. When she was finished, she bowed her head to James and flicked her tongue across his forehead.

"A dragon. Like me."

She nodded. She kept her wings tight to her body and she flicked her tongue playfully. The smile on the child's face was her reward. She stayed close to the floor so she would look long, but not tall and frightening. She waited, watching how his eyes showed increasing curiosity. He cocked his head as he examined her face, then he slid off the seat and tentatively put his hand to her scales. She let him stroke her. He made a murmuring sound in his throat. With her muzzle, she nudged him back toward the chair. He clambered dutifully back on it, and she transformed back. Now she could speak to him.

"Yes, James, I am just like you. I know it does hurt to change. Now come and let me make you feel better."

She held out her hand. The small blond boy slid off the seat, came to her, and placed his tiny hand in hers. His hand was warm, damp. She could tell his fingers would eventually be long and graceful like his uncle's. The thought of Sinjin brought guilt roaring up.

James did need help to cope with being a dragon—but to be taken from his family, kept here and frightened, was not the answer.

She walked James back to the vanity and set to tidying him up. Carefully, she tried to coax information from him. She wanted to know why he could shift shape at such a young age. Of course, he couldn't explain enough for her to figure out why.

But she did learn from his descriptions that it must hurt him more to shift than it hurt her.

Was this why Father had brought him here? Was it not to help the boy, but to study him?

What could she do to help James?

And could she return him to Sinjin? She had no idea what it meant that James could already shift shape. Beyond the pain the boy felt, was it dangerous for him? Could it hurt him?

Make his life shorter? She did not have any answers. Was there anyone in her clan who would?

Even if there was, would Sinjin trust anyone in her clan—other than her—to help?

Sinjin awoke as soon as the sun dropped. His body sensed the darkness. He pushed the covers off him. It had interested him, yesterday, to discover the bedrooms of the house were all kept in readiness. But right now, there was only James here, along with the housekeeper Billings, maids, two footmen, a couple of men to do gardening, and a groom. Mrs. Billings had been evasive when he had asked whether the bedchambers had been used by people who had just left, or if they were ready in anticipation of people arriving.

Sinjin swung out of bed, yanked on his trousers, his shirt. He pulled on his boots. Damn. He should have thought of hunger. His body shook with the need for blood.

Rain pounded at the window. He was going to have to go out and hunt for blood. He did not want to feed in the house. In country houses, it was easy enough to lure a maid, making her believe she was to receive kisses, but he didn't do that sort of thing anymore. It would hurt Lucy. And the maid would tell her tale, which would lead to servants and local villagers pursuing him with torches and pitchforks. The way other vampires survived was to kill each person they drank from. Dead prey did not tell stories.

Hell, he couldn't do it. He could not drink from some innocent in the house, or even in the nearby village. But what in hell was he going to do?

There was Lucy . . .

Would she let him take some of her blood, sating his appetite for a while? He could do it without hurting her, and it would protect the people of her household from him.

Could he make such a request of her? Deep in his heart, he

knew she would allow him to do it—she would do it to protect others. Likely she would also be sickened by it.

Wasn't that a good thing? He should want her to hate him. It would make what he had to do so much easier.

The high-pitched squeak of James's giggles stopped Sinjin in his tracks. He paused at the top of the stairs to the upper floor. He had come in search of the nursery—Billings had told him Lucy had brought the boy up here because toys remained in the nursery from when Lucy had been a child.

A clattering sound came, obviously blocks tumbling across a wood plank floor. Lucy's voice came to him. "Goodness, you little scamp. You asked me to build a castle and you've knocked it down before I could finish."

James cackled gleefully in response.

Sinjin had to grip the banister. Since the death of his sister, he had never heard James laugh. Not once. Now the boy was shrieking with merriment and commanding Lucy, "Make it again! Do it again!"

"And you will knock it down again, won't you?" Lucy's tones were teasingly suspicious.

"Won't!" James declared. "Won't! Promise!"

He had never heard James so happy even when Emma was alive. When Emma had been brought back by the slayers, she always found time spent with James to be a strain. His exuberance as a toddler had given her headaches and made her cry. She had always waved at nurses to take the boy away. Sinjin knew the grief she carried had hurt her ability to mother the boy.

But Lucy had done miracles with James. Hell, it didn't seem possible that Lucy could be a dragon. She was too . . . too human, too good, too warmhearted and sweet.

His heart felt lodged in his throat as he ran up the last of the stairs, and he followed James's uncontrollable giggles to the nursery. His nephew sat in a small rocking chair, waving his arms like an imperious monarch. Lucy, on her knees with skirts tucked beneath them, built another castle to the demands of the little tyrant.

Sinjin grinned. It proved to be as sweet a sight as he'd imagined. Lucy stacked block upon block, and frowned as she lined them up to sit precisely upon each other. But despite her care, the tower of blocks swayed precariously. When it did, James squealed with laughter.

Crossing his arms over his chest, Sinjin leaned against the door frame. Lucy exaggerated her expressions—drawing her eyebrows harshly together as she slowly lowered the next block. She gasped and quivered as the tower threatened to topple. James giggled in delight.

She went to put on the next block, the tower now to the height of her shoulder. But her knee snagged in her skirts. Lucy waved her arms wildly, and lurched perilously close to the tower. James's green eyes were as big as dinner plates as her body wove back and forth. Her chest would almost knock the tower, then she swayed back, only to swing toward the tower again. James squealed with excitement.

Sinjin shook his head.

She was delightful. Amazing.

Lucy did things to his heart he had never felt before. . . .

Or at least not since he'd been a boy, not much older than James, not since he had lost his family.

Lucy stopped her rocking with her chin over the tower and her arms spread wide. James was thoroughly enthralled. Sinjin was, too. Then she twitched her nose, as though she was going to sneeze. Her arm flew up to her nose, and she hit the tower on the way. Blocks flew everywhere and James laughed and laughed. He flopped on his tummy and kicked his legs laughing.

Then Lucy, picking up blocks, saw Sinjin. "Oh! Sinjin."

James leapt off the chair. "Uncle!" he cried. And the boy barreled toward him.

Not since Emma's death had his nephew rushed at him, acting like a happy, normal boy. Normally he had to go to James. And when he put his arms around James, he had to coax the boy to speak to him, to smile.

Stopping in front of Sinjin's legs, James pointed at Lucy. "She is a dragon, just like *me*," he said, in a proud voice, one filled with self-importance. "But her wings are bigger and she has a big, long tail and she can use it to tickle me."

"Can she?" His throat was so tight, he could only manage to get out the two words. He—a slayer—was close to disgracing himself by crying. Then he blinked. "You have changed into dragon form, James? You grew wings and a tail? And scales?"

The boy nodded solemnly. His golden hair fell in tousled curls around his face, and these bounced as he firmly agreed.

Sinjin reeled back. He rocked back on his heels for a moment, then he fought to behave normally. He hadn't known anyone could shift shape so young, but apparently his nephew could. He had been taught that dragons only began to shift when their bodies matured into adult size. This was something unusual. Something strange.

Why was it happening to James?

Was that why the late Earl of Wrenshire had taken his nephew? Not to use the boy as a hostage and force a truce with the slayers, but to study a dragon who was unlike every other shape-shifting dragon that had been born?

Was this why his prince had agreed to let the boy live?

"Sinjin?"

Lucy's soft voice, filled with concern, made him jerk around. He had so many things to keep secret from her, so he tried to remove the worry that must be showing on his face. He gave her a grin and a wink. "So Lucy changed into a dragon for you. Did she breathe fire?"

"No." James shook his head fiercely. "She would have set fire to the curtains if she had done that. Maybe even the bed."

He scooped James up. "We cannot have that, can we?"

"No." James pressed his head to Sinjin's shoulder. The boy's slim arms wrapped around his neck. Ah, how could such a small boy make him feel so weak?

"I'm sleepy, Uncle Jin."

Sinjin saw Lucy's brows raise. James had never quite grasped his name, a variation of "Saint John." He had been named for a man his mother had considered a savior. A dragon slayer of legend named John, whom all the people of his village had called a saint.

"Then it is bedtime for you."

Lucy smiled her approval. Her wide mouth lifted in a gentle curve. For a moment, the scene felt eerily domestic. Once, a lifetime ago, his father would lift him to carry him to bed. And he remembered his mother humming songs, smiling at him.

Then the dragons had come. . . .

Lucy was a dragon . . . and it was the fact that she could turn into a dragon, too, that had been the very thing that had broken through to James.

He carried James to bed, with Lucy following, carrying a candle. Maids rushed forth when they reached the boy's bedroom, and they helped change him into a small nightshirt. He shooed the girls away, and tucked in his nephew himself.

How had Lucy managed to help the boy so much in just one day?

Sinjin sat on the side of the bed, stroking James's soft hair until the boy fell asleep. Behind him, he heard soft breaths. They belonged to Lucy.

Sinjin turned to her, intending to ask her how she had worked her miracle. But her hand strayed to her neck, and smoothed along the white column, massaging her delicate skin.

Hunger rose in him like a wave. It clutched at his heart. Swamped his head. Made sweat bead on his brow. His normally slow heartbeat became a roar in his ears. God . . .

"Lucy, love, I need to feed. If I promise I will not hurt you, will you let me take some of your blood? Just a taste, sweeting."

The words had come out on their own, raspy and desperate, and he couldn't take them back now.

She gasped and took a sharp step back, away from him.

Christ, what had he just done? He'd seen her throat and lost control of his tongue.

Now he was losing control of his fangs. His mouth tingled, then two sharp jabs of pain shot through his jaw as his fangs launched out and lengthened.

13

Revealed

"You are asking me if you can drink my blood?"

Sinjin winced at the cold, emotionless way Lucy asked the question. She hugged herself, even though a fire roared in James's room. Her face went pale.

"I'm sorry, my dear, and I should not have asked you. Certainly, not so bluntly." He tried to sound light, as though he had asked her to dance, not bite her throat and drink her blood. In London, he subsisted on animal blood drunk from a glass, and there were brothels that catered to vampires—sating their cravings for blood or for pleasure, or both. How many people had he fed from before he managed to learn to control his feeding? More than he wanted to count. Each victim had struggled and screamed. At the very beginning, he hadn't been able to stop taking blood, and he had seen the faces of his victims, contorted in terror and agony.

He saw the same horror etched in Lucy's lovely face. It hit him like a blade—or a stake—through his heart. "But I have to feed," he added. He kept his voice soft, but he heard the note of grim resignation. "And I didn't want to be driven to take blood from the servants. Instead, I will find the nearest village. In places like these—isolated places—people trade stories of vampires all the time."

"No."

Lucy spoke quietly, but with decision. He searched her beautiful dark blue eyes for fear, for horror, for hatred. But she gazed at him calmly, now. Before he had read her thoughts, but he could not do it now.

"Are you certain?" he asked.

"Yes. You cannot go out on the moors and attack people as though you are some sort of beast. Anyway, it would do no good to terrify local villagers. I don't want them to chase me with burning torches."

He was about to try for a teasing remark when she shivered and stated, "Nor do I want people chasing you, wanting to stake you or set you on fire."

Christ. She was worried about protecting him. Yet at the end of this, when he had James safe, he was supposed to kill her.

She traced the neckline of her bodice. His throat dried as he watched her fingertip follow the scoop against creamy flesh.

"All right," she said. "I will let you do this. But not here, not when James could awaken."

She squared her shoulders and faced him with her chin tipped up. He remembered the first night she had come to him and offered her body in place of her brother's debts. She had made the same motions—she had straightened her spine, lifted her chin. Then, he'd been amused by her stubbornness, her pride. Now he was touched by her bravery.

"Would you like a drink first? Brandy for a touch more courage?" Sinjin asked softly.

She shook her head, and as she did, he moved to her side. Scooping her into his arms, he carried her out. The winds howled tonight, buffeting the house, rattling windowpanes.

The two maids were in the hall, speaking in low voices. They stopped abruptly as they saw him approaching, carrying Lucy in his arms. He lifted his brows, and they scurried away.

He carried Lucy to her bedchamber. His fangs were out, brushing his lower lip.

Damn, he was hungry. He hadn't felt the craving this hard for a long time.

But he wouldn't be uncontrollably hungry. He couldn't be. Not like when he was first turned into a vampire.

There was no way on Earth he wanted to hurt Lucy.

Lucy had never felt quite so much like a damsel from a gothic novel. Lamplight gleamed on Sinjin's loose, long blond hair as he carried her into her bedroom. His shirt was open at his throat and his eyes were a seducer's—heavy-lidded and sensual. But his teeth had changed. He now possessed fangs, long, curved white fangs that overlapped his full lower lip.

A breathtakingly handsome man held her in his arms—but he possessed fangs that looked like they belonged on a beast. He was like her: both human and something different. Like her, he was a mystical being that wasn't supposed to exist at all.

Sinjin had let her shift shape, even though, as a dragon, she could tear a human apart if she wanted to. He had trusted her.

And she trusted him. She *could* trust him to do this and not hurt her. He lowered her onto the bed, and she rolled onto her hip and drew her hair back to expose her neck. Gathering courage, she whispered, "Come, please. I want you to do it."

Easy to say, but it proved much harder to wait and try to look calm as he approached. Would it hurt? What a daft thought—he was going to bite her deeply enough to draw her blood. Of course it would hurt.

But surely, as a dragon, she could bear it better than a mortal woman.

He kneeled on the bed. He looked so serious. Deathly so.

He cupped her shoulders and rolled her onto her back. He did it all in silence, never moving his silvery gaze from her face. Broad shoulders loomed over her. She fought not to flinch as he cupped her cheek. Just hours before, she had loved his touch, now she was searching his eyes, to see if he had . . . well, lost all his humanity. What did a vampire look like when he bit into his prey? She knew what a fighting dragon looked like, and she did *not* want to see Sinjin look so fierce and brutal.

Lucy couldn't bear to see him look anything like her fiancé had done on the night he had raped that girl. On the night he had attacked her.

She let her lashes sweep down, so she couldn't see him. But the moment his lips touched her throat, she instinctively jerked back.

"All right, Lucy. I shouldn't do this—"

"You must. I am quite fine."

A sad smile touched his mouth. "You aren't, love. I promise it won't hurt. You will see. The fangs of a vampire actually take the feeling away from the skin when they touch. There is something else you will feel. Intense pleasure."

"Really? Well then, let us do this. Now I want to know what it will be like."

She tipped her head to the side on the silky counterpane. Lightly, he ran his tongue along her neck. Closing her eyes, she let out a breathy giggle.

Then his lip stroked her and she felt a jolt of sexual arousal. The light scrape of teeth—she'd thought it would hurt, but it didn't. It sent sizzling sensations down through her body.

The tips of his fangs grazed her skin. With her eyes shut, waiting for the pain that would surely come when he bit her. "Before you do this . . . are you still angry with my family, with me, about James?"

"Angry with you?" He cradled her waist, and lifted her so she was lying across his lap. She had never seen such tenderness in a man's eyes. "Lucy, you made him laugh. I have taken care of him since he was three years of age, and I could never do that. I'm not angry with you—I am forever in your debt. For eternity, I am in your debt. You can ask anything of me. Do you want me to stop? Have you changed your mind?"

"No. Oh no! Now I am ready. Now that I know you aren't angry . . ." Then she added, "Thank you."

His brows drew into a frown. "Sweetheart, why are you thanking me?"

"For forgiving me. For . . . for trusting me. So you can do it now."

Again Sinjin moved to her neck and once more his fangs stroked along her throat. Where he touched, it tickled at first, then warmth washed over her skin and she could no longer feel his touch.

"Mmm," he murmured. "Your skin tastes delicious."

Lucy gazed down. She could see his long blond hair, his lashes shielding his eyes. From where she lay, she couldn't see his mouth as he prepared to bite.

Oh! A swift, sharp twinge hit her, then an intense tingle raced through her neck. It wasn't pain. It was a jolt of pleasure and it made her tip back her head and moan. Dear heaven, she could feel him drawing her blood, yet it didn't frighten her, it gave her rhythmic tugs of pleasure, like the way it felt when he thrust inside her.

He cupped her breasts, and her nipples stood up at once. She felt so extra-sensitive around her breasts. Just the stroke of his thumb over her bodice made her squirm on his lap. His erection grew beneath it—it must be straining against his trousers. Each pulse of her blood reaching his mouth brought a wave of delight through her.

She'd never dreamed it would feel like this. She arched and writhed, and lifted her neck so he could take more.

He began to pull back.

No—

She was going to come, and she couldn't let him stop. She needed just a bit more. She grasped Sinjin's hair, so he couldn't go away, winding her fingers in the silky length.

"Love, you have to let me go."

"No, please no." She wriggled her hips, aching and needing and wanting just a bit more.

"No, Lucy, I can't take more. I wouldn't stop." His hand crept down, her skirts went up, and his fingers slid between her nether lips. All it took was one stroke over her aroused, aching nub, and all the coiled tension exploded. It was like cracking a whip. Her body arched sharply, she let out a keening cry, and she let ecstasy take her.

The pulsing, the delight, the throbbing of her body, and the twitching inside . . . it went on forever. Until she was floppy and weak, draped over his lap like silk ribbon.

He had given orgasms before, but this had been the most intense. She was still panting, still breathing hard. So much pleasure, caused by his fangs in her neck and his fingers playing between her legs. Heavens, now she knew what he meant. His bite hadn't hurt. It had been erotic.

Dazed, Lucy opened her eyes, seeking his face. Stark lines ringed his mouth. Blood smeared his lower lip and he hastily ran the back of his hand across it, sweeping it away.

She smiled and squirmed once more, purring with contentment. But no smile touched his mouth.

"You didn't hurt me."

"I could have. Hell, Lucy, I was afraid I wasn't going to be able to stop."

"You did." She rolled off his lap, landing on her bed. At least she wore only her short stays, which gave her some ability to move. She clasped his hand. Why did he seem so filled with anguish, with remorse? "I am not afraid of you, Sinjin. How could I be? You are not afraid of me."

Abruptly he rose from the bed, jumping to his feet. "It's late, Lucy, I should let you sleep." He yanked his fingers through his hair, brushing it back from his face. His hair was matted and tangled—he had not combed it in days. She remembered how he had looked on the night she had gone to his house to barter for Jack's debts. His hair had been beautifully styled, his cravat knotted with pristine elegance.

Now he looked like a haggard wreck.

Feeding from her had bothered him. She touched her neck, the tips of her fingers found two small punctures. Surely these small holes wouldn't have meant her death. She remembered how her fiancé had slashed her with his claws. Big, brutal wounds in her belly, on her legs. It had taken months for them to heal completely, even with the magical healing properties that dragons possessed, and still those had not killed her.

Had Sinjin truly come close to taking too much of her blood? Wouldn't she feel much weaker if he had? All she felt was the velvety sensation that came after a climax.

But something was tormenting him. He would not meet her eyes.

"Come to bed with me," she said.

"I can't. I don't know if my resolve will break—if my hunger will take control and I will feed from you again."

"I wouldn't mind."

"You would if I took every drop, Lucy. You said you weren't afraid of me. Love, you should be."

Obviously he believed those words would make her retreat, for he turned away and headed for the door. She had been in danger from a man before. She had seen a man she trusted turn into a monster willing to kill her. Every instinct screamed at her to believe him—that she was a fool to get up from the bed, cross her arms over her chest, and state, "Well, I cannot fear you. I care too much about you to be afraid of you."

"Christ, what more do I have to do to make you understand—?"

"You could talk to me! You could tell me why I am now supposed to be afraid of you when you didn't hurt me, when you stopped, when you proved you have control."

"Damn," he muttered. He yanked his hand so viciously through his hair that he pulled some out and glinting strands of gold fluttered through the air.

She had to admit, seeing his anger made her knees shake.

What was she doing? She barely knew this man, but she was letting herself trust him. Since Mr. Ferrars she had not trusted any man. Even her brother had let her down, had stamped on her faith in him. In the last two days, she'd learned even her father had kept secrets from her.

Why did she trust this angry man?

Was it because he was showing his fury—directed currently at his poor hair? Was it because he wasn't hiding what he felt behind kisses, hugs, kind words?

Sinjin was the most honest man she had ever encountered.

"Hades, Lucy, I do not deserve your trust," he snapped. Then he was gone and the door slammed behind him.

Blasted moors. Nighttime had brought a plunge in the temperature, and the pelting rain had turned into stinging, bouncing hail. Small ice pellets danced on the rocky ground and encased the matted grass in an icy coating.

Sinjin paced through the rear garden, alongside the high granite wall. He'd planned to smoke a cheroot, but instead, he hunched his shoulders and let the hail punish him as he prowled back and forth.

There was no way he was going to kill her. There was no question in his mind now, and his duty could go to hell. But how did he protect Lucy and her family from his bloody prince? For he suspected Lucy would never let him spare her but murder her brother and sisters.

That gave him a moment's pause—not killing Lucy meant he also had to save her damned brother, and he wasn't sure Jack Drake, the Earl of Wrenshire, deserved to be saved. There was a hell of a lot Lucy did not know about her brother.

But he couldn't take her family and leave her alive. He would be consigning her to the same hell he had endured. It would be torture. It would be worse than killing her.

How many times, when he'd been young, had he wished he could have been taken along with his mother and father, his brother and sisters?

Sparing Lucy and her family meant putting James in mortal peril. How did he ensure his nephew was safe?

He could take James and run, but that would leave Lucy in London without his protection. If he fled somewhere like Africa, America, Tortola . . . would Lucy come with him? Would she do it willingly? He would also bring her sisters, as they were younger, innocent, female, and therefore unable to protect themselves. Her damned brother could fend for himself.

The prince would try to hunt him down. The demon commanded disciples all over the world. Alone, Sinjin could survive. But encumbered with a five-year-old child and three women would he have any hope of evading capture? By taking them to "safety," would he be condemning them all to death?

Kill Lucy and he guaranteed James's safety.

Another child's screams echoed in his head. Desperate wails of terror and pain. He knew what a dying child sounded like. He'd heard his younger brother die.

Could he do it? If he coaxed Lucy to convert to dragon form, he would just be killing a beast—

No. No, he couldn't do it. He'd cut out his own heart first. He'd walk outdoors at noon and let the sun burn him to dust.

In fact, he would do any of those things now if he did not have to protect James. His death would serve no purpose—if he destroyed himself rather than kill Lucy, the prince would send another slayer in his place.

The only way to keep Lucy alive was to make her run away with him. They would never have peace, they would never feel safe, but at least they would be alive—

Beneath the clatter of hail, the howl of the wind, Sinjin heard a new sound. The low rumble of human voices. Male voices, he guessed, from the husky, deep tones. He pressed his hand to the wall, and strained to hear beyond the angry sounds of the storm.

Footsteps, coming up on the path he had spotted before, one that wound down through the moors. Two men, both striding quickly through the pelting hail, and far enough away he could not make out the words, only the pauses when one would wait for the other to speak. He couldn't hear the men distinctly with the wall between them, so Sinjin jumped to the top of the wall, and crouched there, listening.

He could see easily in the dark, but the reflective hail disoriented him for a few minutes. He trained his eyes hard on the empty expanse of the moors, the hills blurred by a veil of ice pellets and darkness. Finally, Sinjin distinguished the ribbon of the path. Then he spotted two figures on it.

Two greatcoats swung as the men strode up the hill. Beaver hats covered their heads, hid their faces. "What are you going to do?" one of them asked. "Take her to him?"

Her? They had to be coming to the house—the path led to it and there was nothing else around. Who did the man mean? Lucy? They were not here for James, then.

Sinjin tried to look into their minds, but there was a shield against his probing mind. Which meant they were not mortal. Dragons, most likely.

Hail hit his face, stinging like needles. Crouched on the top of the wall, Sinjin almost laughed—he had fought dragons, had almost had his limbs torn out, and he was, in truth, dead—but the prickling pellets of ice irritated him.

"It's the only choice I have," the other man answered.

"He'll destroy her."

At those words, Sinjin's heart thudded faster.

"He won't. He promised me that he won't. He wants her. He'll keep her alive, keep her for himself. She won't be harmed. And it's either give her to him, where she'll be kept safe, or die." The second man's voice was softer. It was hoarse and pleading, weak and desperate.

It was also a voice Sinjin knew. It was the voice of Lucy's brother.

Who in Hades was the "he" that the earl was talking about? And was the "her" actually Lucy, or one of her sisters? Lucy had told him that her younger sister intended to marry a lecherous old rake to save the family fortunes. Was it that union that her brother was talking about?

His instincts told him it wasn't, that Wrenshire was talking about Lucy. It explained why her brother was coming to this house—he had been told Lucy was here. The men were silent now—Sinjin couldn't hear anything else. Perched on the wall, with his hand resting on it for balance, he thought over the conversation he'd heard.

Wrenshire's companion had warned Lucy could be destroyed. Her brother had assured the man she wouldn't. Hell, the brother had racked up a debt of thirty thousand pounds to him. Sinjin suspected the brother would sell any one of his sisters' souls for his own purposes. He believed Lucy's brother was lying. Gut instinct warned that Lucy was in danger. He had no idea from what or from whom, but instinct had kept him alive when he battled dragons, and his senses were screaming at him now.

That damned brother would betray her.

He wasn't going to lose her.

James was in the house, potentially an innocent victim. Fear made his fangs explode out of his mouth. Coat swirling around him, Sinjin jumped down from the wall and ran back to the house.

Lucy stood at the window of her bedroom, her nose pressed to the cool glass pane.

Despite the sated exhaustion that came after orgasms, she had not been able to sleep. She had tried, tossing and turning in her bed. She had tried every position possible in which to sleep, even on top of the covers, with her head at the bottom of the bed.

Nothing had worked.

Finally she had gotten up. She had changed into her nightdress, had plaited her hair. She fiddled with the end of the braid as she looked out of the window. An hour earlier, she had watched Sinjin stride past. At first, she'd felt fear: Was he planning to go to the village? Was he still hungry? Then she had run down the corridor to an unused bedroom. She had plastered herself to the glass of the big window. There was almost no light, but she had spotted the reflection of his eyes as he had looked back to the house. She had barely followed that gleam as it moved alongside the garden wall—dragons did have superior eyesight. It took a while to understand he was pacing, up and down along the high stone wall, in the freezing hail.

Why?

What was tormenting him so?

She had returned to her room. Her dress and shoes waited for her—it had been so tempting to get dressed, then go to hunt Sinjin down and force him to talk. But she suspected he would refuse to tell her anything. Likely he would walk away from her again.

So she had stayed at the window, unsure what to do—she who had been forced to take charge in her family after her mother's death. She hadn't been able to allow herself to be uncertain. But she was doing so now.

She had been watching for him to come in, and now she saw him. Long legs ate up the stretch of paths that ran through the garden. His hat was gone, and ice had frosted his hair. Sinjin looked up at her window, and she recoiled at the fierce look on his face. It was a look of agony. Of fear.

Lucy pulled on her robe and rushed out of her room. She was halfway down the steps to the foyer when Sinjin ran in from the servants' door. Ice coated his shoulders and arms, crackling as he moved. His hair glinted with it, as though diamonds were sprinkled on his head. He charged to the door, and checked the bolt, giving it an extra, incredibly strong shove to ensure it was drawn tight.

"What is it?"

Lucy hurried down one more step, but she was so focused on him, she felt her foot stumble on a lump. Her skirt snagged tight and she lost her balance. She'd stepped on her nightgown hem. She slipped, the lace snagged on her foot like a noose, and she gasped, falling forward—

Sinjin grasped her in his embrace. He had leapt up half a staircase, and landed on the step in front of her, snatching her up in his arms to save her. "Careful, love, I'm not losing you now."

Confusion left her head reeling. His hands wrapped around her upper arms, holding her tight. She frowned into his glittering silver-green eyes. "Two hours ago, you voluntarily stalked out, determined to stay away from me. Now you are telling me you don't want to let me go. What do you want, Sinjin?"

"Apparently the impossible," he muttered. Then he began to run. He did not bother to set her on her feet. Instead he whisked her so quickly up the stairs, she felt as if she'd flown up them. He kept her cradled against his chest, and for the first time, she heard his heartbeat—fast and hard and exactly like a human heartbeat. "Your heart—"

They were racing down the corridor, toward James's room.

"We are in danger, love. All of us: you, James, and I. We have to escape."

Faintly, Lucy heard the pounding at the door. Her heart stuttered. "Who is it?"

"Get some boots on, love, and get your cloak. We have to get out—there won't be time to take a carriage. We'll go out on the moors, and wait for our chance to come back and get horses. Or we'll get to the village—"

"Stop!" She struggled in his arms. She trusted him, but she would not be carried around the house by a terrified man with no explanation. "Put me down! Who is it? We cannot go out on the moors in the night, in a hailstorm."

The soft scurry of boots over the foyer tiles made Sinjin curse. "Damn servants. Of course they will open the door."

"They won't. I will stop—"

"Open up! Damnation, come and open this door. This is the Earl of Wrenshire." Jack's enraged shout came through the door—Lucy could hear it from so far away because of her dragon's blood.

Sinjin had stopped, but he had not let her go. "You can put me down," she said firmly. "It is my brother. There is nothing to worry about. I will not allow him to keep James. I know how to handle my brother."

"Not this time, you don't, Lucy. I overheard him talking outside, as he walked up to the house. He has come to fetch you, love, for someone who might destroy you."

That stunned her. It was hard to find her voice. So when it came, it exploded from her lips. "*Who?* What are you *talking* about?"

A grating sound echoed up from below. One of the footmen

had pulled back the bolt. Then the door creaked open, and footsteps thudded hard on tile.

"I've come to see my sister. Is she still here?" The fierce, commanding shout had come from Jack.

"Yes, my lord."

Sinjin was listening, distracted, and Lucy took advantage to slide out of his grip. But as she took a step toward the stairs, his arm snaked around her waist. Gripping her tight, he hauled her against his body. Her back slammed against his rock-hard, muscular chest. "Don't go to him. He is going to betray you."

She tried to push against his arm, but she would have had more luck toppling the granite wall that surrounded the house. His arm didn't move. "He has already betrayed me," she snapped in a whisper. "He built a mountain of debt, then ran off to live in a brothel. I'm accustomed to his betrayals. There is nothing he can do to surprise me."

"There is, love. Believe me. He told his friend that he had come to bring you to someone—someone who promised your brother not to destroy you. What would he be willing to do to escape debt or to get money to pay his way out of it? Would he be willing to give you up to a dragon slayer? Or to something worse?"

"I—" She wanted to shout that Jack wouldn't do such a thing. But he'd been willing to marry Helena to an old lecherous pig. He'd deserted them rather than face his debts and problems like a gentleman. There was the dragon-slayer coin.

"Come with me, Lucy. I have to take James away now since I don't know what your brother would do to him. If you are with me, I can protect you."

She had hesitated too long—her brother's footsteps were racing over the floor. He would be coming to the stairs. She slumped back against the hard wall of Sinjin's body. In her heart, she wanted to keep him with her—she needed him for his strength, needed him as she had not allowed herself to need anyone since her fiancé's attack. But she had to be strong: a five-year-old boy depended on them both. "Take James and get him safely away, Sinjin. I can stall my brother, so you and James can escape."

Sinjin knew what he should do—he should run now and get James. James depended on him, and he had the chance now to grab the boy and escape. But even as logic told him to protect the child, he couldn't make his feet move.

Hell.

James was a defenseless boy. Sinjin had promised Emma he would not let anything happen to the lad. He had a clear choice: help Lucy and risk getting James killed or lose the boy forever to the dragons, leaving Lucy to her fate.

He was a dragon slayer. The choice should be obvious, but he was not going to leave Lucy's side. The fact that he had been personally responsible for the deaths of more dragons than he wanted to count? It should tell him to go, to accept what he couldn't change. At this moment, holding Lucy by the wrists and pinning her lithe, delicate body against him, those memories weighed heavily on his conscience.

Still, he couldn't let her go. He knew he was going to protect her.

Though in a few moments Lucy was going to find out what he was.

"Lucy!" her brother bellowed. "Where in blazes are you? Upstairs? Come down here at once!"

Sinjin looked down at her. Held tight to his body, Lucy stiffened. "I cannot believe it," she muttered, and even Sinjin winced at the fire in her tones, fire directed at her wastrel dragon of a brother. "He vanished off the face of the earth and he is commanding me to show myself at once?"

Sinjin remembered how Lucy's eyes had flashed fire at him on the night she had come to offer her body for her brother's debts. She had been trying to play the demure maiden, but she couldn't. Pride and anger had betrayed her. She had faced him with her stubborn chin held high, and her fierce, angry eyes and strident voice had all but singed him.

She would be very, very angry when she learned he was a dragon slayer.

He could try taking her with him by force, but he realized he couldn't do it. "Shall we go down and meet your brother?" he asked.

She frowned. "No, he can get himself up here and find me."

"If he had any sense, he would run for his life now," Sinjin murmured.

"Indeed," she said.

Footsteps rushed across the tiled foyer and her brother shouted up the stairs, "Hell and the devil, Lucy! I've had to ride like the blazes across the godforsaken moors to get to you. I'm soaking wet, freezing cold, and exhausted. What were you thinking to come haring off here?"

Sinjin had relaxed his grip on Lucy's arms. Too late, Sinjin realized his mistake. She wrenched free and darted down the stairs, with one hand crushing her nightgown and robe to hold up the hems. She stopped three steps down, and her brother was at the foot of the steps. "You tell me why it was necessary for me to come, Jack," she cried. "Why is a boy being held in our house against his will? Where in heaven's name did you run *away?* Did you really think I would let Helena marry that overweight, overbearing, slobbering ancient roué to pay your debts?"

Lucy stomped down the steps until she was only two from the bottom. Sinjin could not see her face, but he could imagine the fire was raging in her indigo eyes. Certainly the sight of her anger had stunned her brother. The Earl of Wrenshire stopped at the bottom of the stairs, staring up at his sister with his mouth gaping.

Sinjin stood in the shadows at the top of the stairs. Wrenshire would do one of two things: either grab his sister at once and try to physically haul her with him, or pretend nothing was wrong, hoping to lure her outside, likely to a carriage, so he could whisk her away.

The young, dark-haired earl crossed his arms over his chest. "I am the head of the household, Lucy. Decisions made by the clan are my concern, not yours. You had no need to come here about this dragon-boy. He is fine where he is. And I did not run away. You are neither my mother nor my wife—I do not need to explain my every action to you. I spent a few days with friends—"

"You were living in a brothel. Accumulating even more debt, I believe, considering the scandalous things you were purchasing—"

"How in—Good heavens, Lucy, you went to that *brothel?* You had no business going to a such a place. If you were seen, it will be a scandal."

"Do. Not. Make. This. My. Fault." Lucy enunciated each word clearly, coldly, distinctly.

Yet her brother was proving to be a complete dolt. He planted his foot on the first step and scowled at her. "Lucy, you are to come home with me immediately. It is not safe for you here—"

"Are you planning to take me home, Jack? Or do you have something else in mind?"

"What are you talking about, Luce?"

"Have you found some man to give me to, just as you were going to let Helena marry the Odious Earl? Jack—"

Suddenly, her shoulders jerked. Her voice broke on her brother's name, and she took in a sobbing breath. "You saved me from Allan Ferrars! How could you hand Helena to a man who is just as bad? How could you, just to save your own skin?"

"Enough, Lucy. You are coming with me now."

"No."

Another set of footsteps came quietly—it had to be Wrenshire's companion, believing he was moving with stealth. Sinjin listened carefully. Then he heard a sound he knew very well—it was the soft resistant "cry" of a string being stretched.

Hades. He jumped out of the gloom and tore down the steps. But the other man leapt out, leveled a loaded crossbow along his sight line. Sinjin halted on the stairs, frozen. If the crossbow was pointing at him, he would have attacked.

The blackguard was pointing it at Lucy.

In the moment Sinjin hesitated, the earl jumped up a few steps and grasped Lucy's arm.

"No, Sinjin," Lucy gasped. "Please go."

"Sinjin," Wrenshire repeated. He tightened his grip on his sister's wrist. Sinjin took a step forward, but the bastard with the crossbow grinned and Lucy cried, "Please don't move, Sinjin."

"You know him, Lucy? What in hell is going on?"

"Of course I know him," she shouted at her brother. "He holds your debts. Your selfish behavior, your awful plans for Helena forced me to go to him. I was going to beg him to forgive your debts—"

Wrenshire let go of her wrist, but he grasped her by her shoulder and pulled her down the steps. He barked a command at the frightened-looking footmen who stood at the door. The earl roared at them to leave, to make themselves scarce. Lucy had no choice but to follow her brother down the steps, stumbling as he roughly hauled her with him. Sinjin couldn't attack—not with a crossbow aimed at her.

"What did you do, Lucy?" Wrenshire barked. "Hell, what did you do? Do you know what he is?" He shook her, and Sinjin tried to calculate odds. If he moved, would the bastard with the crossbow turn the weapon on him and away from Lucy? Or was the bloody wretch willing to shoot Lucy?

No, there was no way the man would shoot Lucy, and if he didn't act, she would be in danger. Sinjin was ready to spring when the earl snarled, "The Duke of Greystone is a dragon slayer, Lucy. He's planning to kill you."

"What are you saying? It cannot be true. He is—he is a vampire."

"Yes, and a dragon slayer," Wrenshire repeated. "He was given immortality so he could hunt our kind for eternity. Did you ask him how many of our kind he has butchered? It is hundreds. That is why our father took his nephew—if Father had not kept the lad here, the duke would have killed us all. It was the only way to protect us."

Lucy whispered, "I don't believe it."

"Believe what you like. I, however, plan to take care of it." Wrenshire jerked up his head and gave the cold command to his friend. "Shoot him."

14

Rescue

"No!"

Lucy's shout of fear and fury came too late. The earl's companion had pulled the trigger even before Wrenshire finished giving his command. Sinjin anticipated it and he dove forward and to the side, somersaulting in the air. Something whistled past him and a cold sensation lanced his left arm.

Sinjin landed hard on his feet, then lost his balance and dropped to one knee as the cold vanished and his arm screamed with white-hot pain.

The shooter had anticipated he would try to jump out of the way and guessed he would go to the right, hoping to go wide of the shot. The damned blackguard had been right and the arrow had almost found its mark. As he lurched back to his feet, Sinjin touched the slice that crested the muscle just below his shoulder. His coat was sliced and blood oozed onto his fingers.

He released his arm, knowing the cut would begin to heal. Pain stung but he was used to pain. He rushed for Wrenshire's henchman before the man could reload. Recognizing the weapon was now useless, the man slid a stake out of his sleeve, letting it drop into his hand.

Even facing a man holding a stake, Sinjin had to see what was happening to Lucy. Her face was white, her hand clamped to her mouth in horror. She grasped her brother's coat and shook him desperately. "Stop this, Jack!" she pleaded.

"Lucy, stay out of the way. You are going to get hurt." Her brother pushed her back, and she fell over her skirts, landing on her bottom on the tile floor. "Dear God, Lucy, you must go. Go to the carriage. Now!"

Sinjin lurched toward her, wanting to ensure she was not hurt, and in his peripheral vision, he saw the stake slash toward his chest. He jumped into the air, vaulting over backward, landing on his feet. He swung his leg out instantly, catching his attacker in the chest and sending the man sprawling back.

But his assailant leapt back to his feet quickly, springing up with his back arched.

Strong. Damned strong and agile. Obviously not a mortal.

The thunder of footsteps warned that servants were coming. Wrenshire shouted at the first footmen to arrive, "This man is an enemy of our family, but you will stay back and leave this battle to us. I want you all to go downstairs to the kitchens. Wait there until I command you to return."

From the floor, where she had landed on her hip, with her skirts spilling around her, Lucy cried, "No, what he is saying is not true—"

"The poor girl is delusional," Wrenshire yelled. "I am the master here. You will listen to me."

The servants hesitated, but then their master howled, "Go. I will protect my sister. He is the one who pushed her down. If you do not obey I will have your heads."

Quivering, the few servants retreated, including maids and a frightened-looking Mrs. Billings, who clutched a brown woolen dressing gown around her.

As soon as the servants left, Wrenshire grabbed Lucy by the

arm, and dragged her to her feet. "Finish him," he barked to his accomplice.

As Sinjin and his attacker circled each other, Sinjin flicked his gaze back and forth between Lucy and the stake. She slapped her brother in the chest, digging her heels against the smooth tiles, which didn't do anything to stop Wrenshire. "You must stop this, Jack. You cannot kill him! He has done nothing to hurt me. I don't believe he is a dragon slayer."

"Lucy, you have to listen to me. It's the truth. Don't make this any harder for me than it is. You will do as you are told. If you want to save this blasted family of ours, you will go out to the carriage now. You will get inside, and you will wait for me to finish this villain."

"I am not going anywhere."

"This is madness," Wrenshire snapped. "How can you be championing a dragon slayer?"

"If he is a dragon slayer, why did he not kill me? He's had ample chances to do it."

Wrenshire's eyes bulged and a vein throbbed in his temple. "For Christ's sake, why don't you believe me? Of course, he kept you alive—he needed you to bring him to his nephew."

"Once I did, why didn't he kill me then?"

The fiend with the stake took another swing, slashing toward his heart. Sinjin landed a punch on his jaw, one that would have snapped the neck of a mortal. The man's head lurched back, but then he regained his balance and stabbed again. He missed, then stooped to his dirty boots and hauled a dagger out of a sheath in the leather. "Bloody vampire."

Sinjin knew what he planned: to gut him with the knife, which would bring even a vampire to his knees, then drive in the stake while he was too weak to move.

"I don't know, Lucy, why he waited to kill you, but I guarantee it was what he planned to do—" Then her brother roared with anger. Still gripping her wrist, he cupped Lucy's chin, and forced her head to tip. Wrenshire touched her wound. "He bit you?"

She struggled to shove his hand away. "I *let* him do it. This way, he would not drink from anyone mortal. He stopped when he was drinking from me. He willingly *stopped*. If he is a dragon slayer, surely he would have killed me then."

Her brother pushed her toward the door. "What did he do to you, Lucy? Did he touch you? Force himself on you?"

"No, you made all that unnecessary." Her voice was a choked whisper, but Sinjin could hear everything, even the labored thud of her heart. "I learned you owed thirty thousand pounds to him. What do you think I had to do to save us?"

"God . . . Lucy . . . no." Wrenshire's face went chalk-white. "Not with him . . . how could you?"

"I was trying to save this family." She threw the words at her brother.

Hell, her brother's reaction had obviously devastated her. She was fighting, but it was the pain of hurt pride, of despair.

Wrentshire drew out a pistol and Lucy gasped. "You are coming with me. *Now.*"

The gun wasn't pointed at her, but Sinjin didn't know how far her brother was willing to go. He had to go after her. It was time to bring an end to this irritating battle. He moved at preternatural speed, slamming his fists into the gut of his attacker. Silver flashed in the corner of his vision, and he felt the knife drive into his shoulder. Over and over, the blade flailed into him, but he ignored the pain, picked up the man, and threw him. Wrenshire's lackey slammed into one of the marble columns that surrounded the foyer and collapsed unconscious on the floor.

Sinjin strode toward Lucy and her brother when a masculine cackle reached his ears. "Not so fast, Yer Grace."

Then he heard a muffled cry. He jerked around. Another thug held James, with his hand clamped over the boy's mouth and a knife held near the small neck. Lucy gave a muted cry. Sinjin let his fists drop to his sides. "Don't hurt him," he said to Wrenshire. "Stake me if you want, but don't hurt the child."

Tears dribbled onto James's cheeks. Rage snapped and roared inside Sinjin. He wanted to kill, but he couldn't take the risk of getting James hurt. He would cause pain to these men later.

"How could you hurt him, Jack?" Lucy yelled. "Stop this!"

"Go outside, Lucy."

Out of the corner of his eye, Sinjin saw the earl's gaze focus on him, then on James. Wrenshire was not looking at Lucy, but she was glaring at her brother with murderous fury in her eyes. Before Sinjin could even move, she lunged at her brother. She grabbed the muzzle of the pistol and wrenched it out of his hand.

Lucy held the pistol, both hands wrapped around the handle to support it. But her shoulders jerked with the effort of keeping the heavy weapon pointed straight, and she was shaking, with her index finger close to the trigger. First she pointed it at Sinjin, then she moved and held the pistol with the muzzle pointed at her brother.

"Put it down, Lucy," her brother barked. "For God's sake, what are you doing? You could shoot me by mistake. And if you shoot me, Perkins up there will likely kill the boy."

"I don't know who to trust anymore," she whispered. She swung the pistol and pointed it back at him.

Sinjin nodded. "Keep pointing it at me, love. That way they won't hurt James. In fact, you may have to shoot me."

"Don't, Lucy," Wrenshire growled. "A pistol ball won't kill him. It will not kill a vampire. Unless you want the boy to be hurt, you will give the pistol back to me."

"Why did you take it out, Jack? Did you plan to use it on me?"

"For Christ's sake, Lucy, of course not."

Her eyes were wide with pain and Sinjin flinched as they focused on him and he saw the raw agony on her face. Her lips were parted, her forehead lined with anguish. "Is it true, Sinjin? Are you a dragon slayer? Were you planning all along to hurt my family?"

"It is my duty to slay, love. But in the end, I knew I could never hurt you, and because I care about you, I was not going to hurt your family."

"Charming." Wrenshire sneered at him, his lip curled in the sort of snarl a man gave before he kicked a dying enemy. "That is a blasted lie, I suspect. He is playing a game with you, Lucy. He is telling you lies so you will turn against me, your own brother."

"Tell your thug upstairs to let James go," she said coldly. "The evidence I have with my own eyes is that the duke loves his family, loves them enough to take any risk for them. You, however, are willing to terrify a young boy."

"Perkins, let the child go. My sister is right. This is inhuman. We are better than this." Wrenshire glowered at Perkins, then glared at Sinjin. "He is a dragon slayer, Lucy. Dragons destroy slayers every time they have the chance. I cannot leave him alive."

"You will. We will let him go, and let him take James."

"No. No, that I cannot do. The boy is a dragon. Father explained that he is in danger from the slayers. The duke will tell you that, if he decides to be honest for once." The earl's lips cocked up in a smirk.

Damn, the bloody twit had him there.

"Is this true? Is James in danger from other slayers? From you?"

"God, not from me." His mind flicked over his options. He couldn't get James away from a man with a knife. What he needed to do was buy time. "Yes, what your brother says is true. James could be in danger from the slayer who commands me. But I intend to protect James—"

"And that is why we have him?" Wrenshire goaded. "Because you were taking such good care of him?"

"Stop, Jack. Stop!"

"Go with your brother, Lucy. Take James with you and keep him safe. I trust him with you. I know you can help ease his fears and comfort him. I will leave you alone."

"Oh yes, you will." Wrenshire's eyes narrowed.

Sinjin sensed motion—he had been focused on Lucy and James and had not heard the sound of another man's breathing until now.

Swinging around on his heel, he turned right into the crossbow bolt as it shot across the foyer. The other lackey of the earl's had reloaded his weapon.

Sinjin grasped at the shaft of the arrow—it had missed his heart, but the pain was excruciating. He knew the best thing to do. Buy time. He let out a groan and collapsed.

He heard a little boy's howl of fear and anguish.

Damn them for doing this in front of James. The poor boy had been through so much, and now he had been terrified by a thug and had seen his uncle—the last of his family—shot.

Hell, Sinjin thought, he cared for Lucy, but he was going to make her brother pay.

"Wrap your arms around my neck, James," Lucy whispered in the boy's ear. "Hold me tight. I'll carry you."

Trying to stay calm for James was the only thing keeping her from falling to pieces. She wanted to shake her brother. She wanted to hit him, then scream at him until her voice went hoarse.

She knew Jack was careless, knew he had all the worst traits of wealthy gentlemen: he could be arrogant, he was selfish, and he always fell in with the worst of men. But he had transformed into a monster. Into someone she was ashamed of.

At this moment, she hated him. How could he have allowed Sinjin to be shot? How could he have let such a thing happen in front of a child?

Poor James was sobbing, but quietly, as though he feared punishment if his tears were heard.

"It is all right to cry," Lucy murmured, cuddling him tighter. She was astonished he had not sunk back into his vacant, unresponsive state. She stroked his soft hair, growing damp where pellets of ice melted on his head. Her brother had not allowed her to dress James. The boy wore only his nightshirt, which was also wet, clinging to his slender frame. His feet were bare. She was wearing only her nightdress, her robe, and slippers. Cold seeped into her feet, and the wind-whipped hail pelted against her face. Her clothes were swiftly becoming wet. She kept James's head tucked against her neck to protect him.

Jack held her by her shoulder, propelling her to the carriage.

"I am sorry, Lucy," he said.

"No. I do not believe you are, anymore. I don't know what you have become." To think she had hated changing into dragon form because she hated to think she was not human. Her brother had become more of a beast than she could have dreamed.

"I cannot explain things in front of the boy, but when we are back in London, I will tell you everything. I will tell you what the Duke of Greystone has done to our people."

"He spared me. Perhaps he has changed—perhaps he changed for the better as much as you have changed for the worse."

At the pained look in her brother's indigo eyes, Lucy felt a twinge of guilt. But why should she? He had killed Sinjin. Why should she feel anything for Jack now? She could remember so much good—playing with Jack in the maze in their Hampshire home, chasing each other up and down between the thick, tall hedges. She remembered Jack teaching her to fish. He had taught her to swim in the cold lake; he had taught her to dive to the bottom and she used to pirouette in the silt-clouded water, with sunbeams streaking through the depths, making believe that she was a mermaid, not a dragon.

Jack had saved her life when Mr. Ferrars had attacked her. It was not a good memory, but she had remembered that night with deep gratitude for her brother.

But Jack had washed away all the joy in her sweet memories and the thankfulness she had felt for how he had protected her from Ferrars.

And what about James? Did he have many good memories to fight against the grim power of the bad ones? He had lost both his parents. Now he had seen his uncle killed in front of him. How did he recover from this? But she must make certain he eventually did.

She was going to protect James. He was her responsibility now.

Her brother pushed her toward the black carriage that sat in the drive. It would have been invisible in the hail-strewn dark if not for the lamps burning on it. Fingers of gold feebly traced the glossy black doors, the box, and the large wheels. The horses whinnied in anguish, for they must be cold and miserable in the rain. It looked like the devil's carriage. The men lurking around it, in black cloaks with the collars turned up, looked like demons.

"Come on, Lucy." Jack's voice had changed—she noticed the difference now. He used to speak like most bucks of the *ton,* with the exaggerated drawl and with a great deal of charm when he wished. Now his voice was hoarse and raw, as though he had been breathing in the fumes of Hell's brimstone.

"Lucy, get inside the carriage. There is no point standing out here in the hail."

She wanted to go back to Sinjin. He had not been dead when

he fell. He had probably died—a stake killed a vampire. But what if he was still alive, what if there was a faint hope he was? What if he was still alive and needed help?

The family's servants were there. The instant Sinjin had collapsed, Jack had hauled her outside, and his wretched lackey had brought James. Jack had not even bothered to speak to the stunned servants. He had just stalked out of the door.

Why? Why was he rushing her away?

One of Jack's men pulled open the carriage door. Her brother held the pistol—he had taken it back from her when she had been standing in shock, watching Sinjin fall. Would Jack shoot her if she turned now and ran back for the house?

He might. That was the horrible belief she had. That her brother might shoot at her and that he might miss and hit James. Risking her life was one thing. She could not risk James's life. She knew that was why Sinjin had been shot—because once her wretched brother had commanded his lackey to take James, Sinjin would not put his nephew in danger. He would have stood there and have taken a crossbow bolt directly in the heart, she was sure, before he would put James at risk.

Anger surged, but Lucy had no choice—she trudged to the lowered carriage steps. A stink rose from the man holding the door. The stench of sweat, smoke, spilled ale, and rotting teeth. He was not one of their servants; he was some thug her brother had employed.

As she put her foot on the step, she turned to Jack. It hurt to see his familiar face and know she could never look at him with love in her heart again. "What did you tell these men to do? Kill me if I try to escape? Are they instructed to shoot me?"

"Lucy—"

Good heavens, they were. Why else would he look so pained? And put on that irritating drawl, the way he did when he wanted to hide something?

She had to take one hand from James's back so she could retain her balance on the steps. As soon as the weight of her palm left him, he let out a plaintive bleat, like a tiny lost lamb.

Her heart twisted in her chest as she grasped the door handle. Jack's brute reached out to offer his hand, but she tipped up her chin. She would not even look at such a man who was willing to do such horrible things for money.

James was heavy in her arms, but she stumbled up the steps and managed to carry him into the carriage. She plopped down on one of the seats, cradling James on her lap so his tiny, cold feet were snuggled against her robe, and she hugged him tight to warm him. Immediately she thought of escape.

Could she leap out of the carriage on the road, holding James? There was too much risk she would hurt him. Even if she managed to get out without injuring the boy, they would likely be recaptured in minutes.

Or was there a chance they could get away? It was eerily black on the moors and if she ran off the road, into the grass, she could disappear.

Or she and James might literally disappear if she ran off into the bog.

Her brother had said they were headed for London. They could not travel all the way to town without stops at coaching inns to change the horses. James would need to be fed; he would need trips to relieve his bladder. At any one of those times, she could try to engineer an escape.

The carriage rocked as Jack hoisted his tall, muscular frame up the steps and into the doorway.

Revulsion washed over her. James shuddered in her arms, and she made a soothing, humming sound. She whispered very, very slowly beside his ear, "Sweetheart, I understand your instinctive reaction. You sense he is bad. He didn't used to be, but he is now. But I will take care of you. No harm will come to you."

James whimpered and pressed hard to her. The odious villain Perkins had stepped up to the threshold, obviously expecting to ride within. Jack cocked his eyebrow and the man blustered, "I thought you would be wanting me to watch 'em as we travel, guv."

Her brother frowned. His gaze met hers for a moment, then slid away. "Indeed. It would be a good plan."

Her mouth dropped open in outrage. Her brother had brought one of his toughs into the carriage, so he could simply give the order to hurt her or James, if they disobeyed.

There had to be an escape. . . .

Then what? Where would she go? She could not simply run away and leave her sisters in Jack's power. His mind had turned, he had gone mad, and if she deserted Helena and Beatrix, who knew what he would do to them.

Nausea clawed up Lucy's throat as her brother shouted over the howl of the wind to the coachman. In seconds, he whipped the horses, hooves began to paw at the ground, and the carriage lurched ahead on the gravel.

Somehow she had to escape with James. But she needed to return home before her brother could, so she could take Helena and Beatrix away with her.

Yes, and somehow do it without any money. She had no money to engineer an escape for her, James, and her sisters.

She knew of no place where they could safely hide.

The carriage rattled along the worn track. It was not much of a road, since it was barely used, but they were going faster, as though the coachman was lashing the horses, forcing them to gallop. That would be dangerous even on a good road. Lucy had no idea how the coachman could see. Even a dragon's senses would not be enough to steer a carriage on a rough, rock-strewn path in the pitch dark.

One of the wheels slid and the carriage lurched ominously to the side. Condemnation of Jack's idiocy danced on the tip of her tongue. She wanted to rail at him. Demand to know why he had dragged them away so quickly, and where they had to race to, at the risk of accident.

She wanted to ask, then the coachman shouted loudly and the carriage swayed violently.

"Damn." Her brother got to his feet. He changed position, so he could see ahead, and pushed down the window glass. "What is it?" he shouted.

They were going faster. The horses must be thundering at full speed, and the animals pulled at the traces in a lopsided way, which caused the wheels to hit rocks and bounce harshly.

Perkins grinned, revealing a lack of front teeth. He pulled a pistol from an inside pocket of his coat. "Could be that vampire weren't dead," he said cheerfully. "Get Coachman to stop us. I'll hunt the beast down and put a ball in its heart."

"That will do nothing," Jack snapped.

Lucy could hear the fear in her brother's voice. She launched up on her feet and slapped her hand against the ceiling. She surged forward to the seat that backed along the driver's box, got up on her knees despite the wild swings of the vehicle. Clutching glass, she pushed it back. "Stop!" she screamed.

The coachman half-turned. His beefy face was white, his colorless eyes large with terror. "I cannot. It's as if the beasts are bewitched."

Suddenly the door swung open—she saw it in the corner of her eye. It flew wide, then thrashed wildly against the side of the carriage. Again and again, it battered against the side, then the wind yanked it, and the hinges tore free. Wood splintered as the door was slammed against the rocky ground.

Lucy sat, grasped James, and pulled him tightly against her body. She slid into the corner away from the door, holding him tight.

She could change and fly free through the open door. There was risk—she would be too large for the carriage if she changed. Could she also ensure she could keep hold of James as she did?

Perkins pulled out a pistol and pointed it at her. "Stay put," he growled.

"Put that bloody thing away," Jack shouted. "You'll end up shooting me! Or her by accident." Jack reached for the pistol, then the carriage flew violently to the right.

Lucy pushed James into the corner, shielding him with her body.

The pistol went off with a roar. Smoke filled the carriage and the sound was deafening. Splinters of the floorboards flew up.

Stupid Perkins had fired, but had only hit the floor.

The carriage suddenly slid to the left. She slid along the seat. Perkins and her brother flew to the side and crashed into the wall. The impact sent the carriage tipping up onto the two left wheels. It lurched over and fell.

End over end it went. Lucy clutched James to her. Her head hit the wall, her bottom struck the floor, and her shoulder hit something hard. She was battered, turning in agonizing spirals.

Then it stopped and she slammed hard against the wall of the carriage.

There was silence inside the carriage. There was no sound of men in pain. Just the frantic whinnying of the horses, the clatter of hail, and the creaking of the carriage and the wheels.

Her arms were *empty*. Raw horror washed through her. She stared in shock at her hands. Where was James? She thought she had been holding him. It was pitch-black and she couldn't see. Panicked, she sat up. Her bottom was resting on the shattered window. "James?" she shouted. "James?"

Strong arms lifted her. She struggled. "Where is James? Let me go. Leave me. I have to *find* him."

"It's all right, Lucy, my beautiful angel. James is safe. I already found him. Now I have you. Despite what your brother told you, I intend to protect you."

Sinjin. She tried to break free of his embrace, but as always, it proved impossible.

Where was her brother? Where were his vicious, horrible lackeys? Dead? Safe? Were they going to jump out and attack at any second?

"Your brother is gone. He's disappeared. The other men are all dead."

"What happened?"

"I don't know. I ran after you, and managed to get ahead of the carriage. The coachman drove around me, but then the horses went mad and started racing. He couldn't control it."

Blinking she saw another carriage.

"Ours. The one we arrived in. I'm taking you and James back to London. I know the perfect place we can hide."

"You are a dragon slayer. I can't . . . trust you."

"It isn't a matter of trust, Lucy. You are mine now. I am not letting you go." Sinjin's lips touched her neck, warm and soft. Then something scraped. Weakly she clasped his cheeks. She tried to push him away. But she couldn't. She felt the rushing sensation inside as he took her blood. Weakening her. Making her languorous, dazed, sleepy.

Lucy struggled to stay conscious, to keep her eyes open. She fought to keep her lids as widely spread as she could. But enveloping blackness still rushed up and wrapped around her. Tumbling into the void, she cursed Sinjin. Dimly, she knew what he was doing. Making her faint so she would be completely under his control.

Blast. Fight it. Fight—with every scrap of strength you have.

But Sinjin tweaked her nipple and her body betrayed her, lurching into an orgasm that she couldn't control or stop—a pulsing of her body that was strong and physical and that she didn't want. It sapped every last bit of her strength. Then darkness claimed her.

15

Surprises

She was warm. She was dry. She possessed a pounding pain in her head.

Lucy's head hurt so much she couldn't bear to open her eyes. Slowly she lifted her arm and pressed her hand to her temple. A strange warm weight lay on her limbs and her chest.

She wasn't dead, though. Lucy was quite certain of that.

Dragons had tales of what happened when they died. She knew a little about human heaven—at least the differences between it and a dragon's heaven. She had grown up with stories of a sun-filled world, lush with greenery, warmed by soft breezes, filled with the perfume of beautiful flowers and the music of waterfalls and dancing brooks. Where berries, fruits, and wild boar were plentiful. Where one stayed in dragon form for eternity.

There was no glow sneaking in the seam of her closed lids, no babbling streams. Anyway, if she'd died, she wouldn't ache so much, would she? Not only did her head hurt, so did all her limbs. Her throat was parched and dry. Even before she opened her eyes and saw her skin, her limbs, her hair, Lucy knew she was definitely not in dragon form. But what had happened to her? Memories were flirting with her and she couldn't quite grasp them. . . .

Then it all came slamming back into her brain.

James.

Sinjin.

She bolted up in the bed. Crisp white sheets tumbled off her, and cooler air struck her skin. Her nipples hardened in the slight draft as she realized she had been put to bed naked.

She slid out of the enormous bed. An exquisitely woven rug protected her bare feet from the cold wood floor. The bedchamber was opulent—purple silk covered the walls and set off the ivory hangings of the bed—but she had never seen it before. Where was she? She saw bruises on her arms and below her breasts, near her ribs. She hadn't dreamed the accident, which meant she could not have just dreamed that Sinjin was alive. It had been real, hadn't it?

She must find him. She must find James.

But her nightdress was not in the room, nor were her slippers. Frowning, she walked around the room naked. A few days ago, she would have felt awkward. Now modesty seemed the least important thing. A large wardrobe stood in the corner, but it proved to be empty.

Had Sinjin taken her clothes so she could not escape?

Her stomach gave a painful lurch. Lucy let go of the wardrobe doors and they swung closed. She hurried to the bedroom door and rattled the knob. It didn't turn. It was locked. She raced to the window, threw back the drapes, not caring that she stood naked in front of it. Lacy sheer curtains adorned the window. As did wrought-iron bars, on the outside.

Sinjin had imprisoned her.

She could not *believe* it. Though, really, given the evidence, she had no choice.

Driven by fury, and by the fact that she really wanted to put something over her bare skin, Lucy ran to the door. She slapped her palms against it. Then her fists. She beat on the door and shouted. It didn't take long before she shouted herself hoarse and the only sound she could make was a furious growl. She kicked the door once.

Dear God, she must have broken her toes. Cupping them, she hopped around.

Damn Sinjin, what was he doing?

An awful but coolly logical voice in her head said: *He has captured you in preparation for slaying you, you daft trusting girl.*

Tears wanted to come: she wanted to let out a veritable waterfall of frustration. But she held them back. She had been an utter fool. One man had betrayed her in the worst way: he had attacked her and tried to kill her. One man had shown her what a selfish, vicious brute could do.

Yet she had given her body to another man—to Sinjin— when she knew nothing about him. She had believed every lie he had told her, and she had foolishly opened her heart to him.

She had even asked him directly if he were a dragon slayer, and of course he had openly lied to her face.

Really, had she thought he would tell her the truth?

Love. What an awful emotion it was. Did it ever survive? Was there any man alive who would not take a woman's love and crush it by doing terrible things? She had loved Allan Ferrars, and he had turned out to be a sadistic beast. She had loved Jack, and he had grown into a monster. She had loved her father, and he had stolen a child. Even if it had been for the best of intentions, it had been wrong. It had badly hurt the child, and there was no excuse for that.

And Sinjin . . . well, at least she had not fallen in love with him.

True, her heart had almost stopped beating when the arrow had torn through his chest. Fear had squeezed her heart, horror had frozen her, and when he'd fallen, she thought the pain of grief and loss and terror would crush her. When she'd gathered James in her arms, she'd feared she would start to cry and never stop. She had tried to run to Sinjin, and her brother had snatched the pistol from her hands. For one moment, she hadn't cared if he shot her in the back, she was so desperate to ensure Sinjin wasn't dead. Then she had realized she had to protect James, and she had let her brother drag her out of the house, not knowing if Sinjin was dead or not.

She had been sick with the fear that he was.

But it didn't mean . . . it couldn't mean . . . that she was in love with a dragon slayer. This couldn't be love. That emotion did not feel like this at all. She had admired Mr. Ferrars before she had fallen in love with him. Love had grown from admiration and she had never had any reason to doubt him *before* she had fallen in love with him, before she learned the truth. Her feelings for Allan Ferrars had not started with the kind of tumultuous mix of fear and desire and anger and longing that tormented her now. Love was the comfortable warmth Father made her feel. The affection she had for her sisters. It could not be this awful pain in her heart. . . .

Stop. She couldn't deny it, could she? How many debutantes in love had she heard speak of unbearable pain? She had done the most idiotic thing possible: she had fallen in love with Sinjin.

With a man duty-bound to destroy her.

The lock on her door clicked and before Lucy could run for the blankets to cover her naked body, the door opened. A sapphire blue robe appeared—the man had his back to her. But it was Sinjin—no one else had such golden hair that spilled long past his shoulders.

She would turn into a dragon. She would fight for her life.

Do it now, her instincts urged inside her head. *Don't wait. Waiting will give him the chance to attack. Waiting could mean he will kill you—*

She summoned the change, but Sinjin spun around. "No, Lucy. I don't mean you any harm." Swiftly his hand twitched the belt of his robe, opening it. Blue silk parted, revealing his muscular body, as naked as hers. "No weapons. I'm not here to hurt you."

Shaking, she struggled to stop her change. Knowing she was stupid, even as she did it. He could have weapons anywhere in this house, ready for his use. He *had* to kill her. Had to. Or else he would be destroyed. That was how the code of dragon slayers worked. A man could not walk away without killing his enemy.

Breathing harshly, she faced Sinjin, naked, human, and vulnerable. "I don't believe you. You took an oath to kill me. Did you become a vampire so you could slay dragons for eternity?"

Sinjin walked around her slowly, the robe whispering around his skin, teasingly revealing his body. "At the beginning, love, I had planned to do my duty," he said heavily.

Damn. She had been such a complete fool—

"But I cannot do it anymore."

"I don't believe you. I don't believe you would be willing to die to protect me."

"I can prove it, love." He stopped moving and opened his arms wide. "If you want, you can change into a dragon and rip me apart. However, before you do it, you have to promise you will look after James. Keep him safe from the slayers. Keep him safe from any of your kind who mean him harm."

From her brother's enormous debts, she knew Sinjin had great skill in gaming. Obviously he must be able to bluff. Lucy searched his eyes. Glittering, green, as beautiful as ever, they gazed back at her. His eyes were shadowed, his forehead lined, and the only emotion she could truly read in his gaze was self-mockery.

"You know I wouldn't kill you. I can't even bring myself to attack first." She sighed. "However, I would appreciate some clothing. It's one thing to keep me prisoner in this room. I refuse to be trapped in that bed, hiding under the sheets because I have nothing to wear."

"I'm sorry for the bars on the window, and for locking the door. This house is an informal sanctuary for vampires—one of a network that has grown up across England in the last year." He shrugged out of the robe, letting it slide off his shoulders, and he caught the mass of silk in his hand. "I brought this for you."

"Then you will be nude."

He eyed the bed. "I don't mind."

She laughed. What else could she do? She was so shocked, so astounded, that rippling laughter fell off her lips. "You really think I am going to go to *bed* with you?"

"I do recognize you've been through hell, love. Which means you should be resting. And I suspect the only way to keep you in bed is to hold you in there."

"You are a dragon slayer. I am a dragon. Of course I am not going to let you get into my bed. And I must go and find James. Is he all right?"

"He's sleeping. He's been asleep since we reached here."

She heard the worry there.

"The ladies told me I would not be doing any good sitting by his bedside. And it's daylight, time for me to rest. So I came to find you, love."

"Ladies? There are ladies here?"

A cheeky grin flashed his white teeth, but he quickly sobered, and his eyes softened so much it startled her. "This house is also a brothel. The women here are delighted to look after James."

Sinjin was thinking of his nephew, and it was the deep love he felt for James that was responsible for the deep look of tenderness. It had nothing to do with her. . . .

Then Lucy focused on what he'd said. "A brothel?" she squeaked. "This is the safe place for us to hide?"

"It worked for your brother."

Pain welled. "Don't. I don't want to think about my brother right now." She threw the words at him, angry with him, with Jack, with her father. "I do not want to stay in a brothel. I must go home—my sisters are there, and at Jack's mercy. I need clothing. I need a carriage. I have a family, just as you do, and I intend to protect mine just as fiercely." She stalked to him and groped at the robe.

His lashes lowered. "I thought you hated me now."

She pressed her naked body against his, and she grasped the silk robe from his hands. Staying up against him, she began sliding her hands all over the robe. There had to be pockets. To get in the door, he must have used a key. Where had he hidden it?

Nothing. There was no bulge, no hard shape—at least not in the two small pockets of the robe. His erection nudged and bumped her stomach as she searched.

"Your groping seems more industrious than seductive." His palms pressed against hers, guiding her hands away and he threaded his fingers between hers. "If you are looking for the key, it's not there. I left the door unlocked."

"Then let me go."

"You have slept through two entire days, Lucy. I watched over you for part of the time, when I was not watching James. You woke twice, and I don't think you were fully awake. You cried out, and thrashed around. When I drank your blood, I exhausted you, and the accident did not help. Nor did the shock you received regarding your brother."

Sinjin turned her, so her back was to the bed, nudged her backward, and continued to press her until the bed bumped the backs of her calves. "Sit, love. First, you need food. Then clothing."

"I have to go to my family."

"So you shall, when you are ready. Your sisters are here."

Surely he was joking. Her lips flapped for a moment then she managed to gasp, "In a brothel?"

"In one of the private apartments. They will have no contact with the male clientele."

Oh dear heaven, only a man could be so utterly obtuse. "But if they are seen—"

"They won't be. Trust me to protect you."

Exhaustion and despair overwhelmed her. She'd intended to stay strong, to fight with him. She slumped with her fingers still twined with his. "I simply can't. For my entire life, I've been taught to fear dragon slayers. Now that I've finally met one . . . you're nothing like what I expected. I don't know what to think."

"I've never hurt you. Think of that, love."

"But you told me you intended to." Heavens, her eyes could not be burning. There could not be tears lurking, ready to spill. Lucy took a shuddering breath, seeking strength. Pulling her hand free of his, she moved back from him. Tugging fiercely, she pulled one of the white sheets out from underneath his derriere and clamped it against her body. Never could she forget what he had told her: she could not forget he had admitted he had intended to kill her, because he was a slayer. She was far better to trust no one.

He reached for her cheek and she pushed his hand away. Pain tugged his lips downward. "I'm sorry. Lucy, it's impossible to look at you without wanting to touch you."

He would not make her feel wrong or bad. She wrapped the sheet tightly around her body. "You will have to learn."

On a groan, he stood and pulled on the blue robe, then tied the belt. "You need breakfast, love."

She buried her face in her hands as he rang the bell pull, and he went to the door and instructed someone on the other side to bring her breakfast. Suddenly, her thoughts went to her brother. She jerked her head up, forced words through her tight throat. "Jack . . . he is still alive, isn't he?"

"Yes. He shifted shape when he saw me and flew away."

"He deserted us?" She meant her and James. Why should it surprise her? She'd seen enough to now know Jack had become a coward.

She could not simply take this in stride and move ahead. For she had no idea where she was supposed to go. Her whole world had been turned upside down. She knew Jack was careless, but she'd never thought he could do deliberate evil. Now she was in a bedchamber with a man sworn to kill her, who was waiting by the door to receive a breakfast tray for her, and who was showing her more concern and kindness than anyone ever had.

She had always taken care of things since her mother's death. She had been the one to look after her family, because Father was busy with looking after the Drago clan. But her brother had betrayed her, she was in danger from both slayers and her own kind, and she couldn't see any solutions to those problems.

It had only been a few days ago that she had gone to Sinjin's house, thinking all she had to do to solve problems was give him her body. Lucy couldn't stop a desperate laugh at the insanity of it—one that sounded like a half sob when it came out.

"I don't know what happened to Jack." She should not be revealing such things, now she knew what Sinjin was. Heavens, she should keep her thoughts, her secrets, and facts about her family to herself. She could put her family at risk.

But she needed to talk to someone, or else she thought her heart would explode.

The madness of the thought made her draw a shuddering breath. How much worse could their lives be? Well, there were more horrifying prospects. She could be running with her sisters, scrambling across London, chased by dragon slayers. Or she and her sisters could be dead.

Instead, at this moment, they were all under the *protection* of a dragon slayer.

A discreet rap sounded at the door. Sinjin opened it and took a large silver tray—one stacked with covered dishes—from a servant's hands. He brought it to the bed, set it down on the elegant table that sat beside the headboard. "What do you mean, love?"

Lucy closed her eyes. That was why she did not see his hand come to her. His palm, warm and soft, settled against her skin. She felt the light scratch of his fingertips and swallowed back a moan. She was too tired to fight. Or perhaps she finally didn't know what to fight for. She had always fought, in her own way, for her family's safety. She had been willing to be ruined to protect her family. But now she had no idea how to beat back enemies, for she no longer knew who her enemies were.

With eyes closed, she whispered, "I mean Jack has changed. He was always careless, but I never would have dreamed he would willingly, deliberately hurt us."

"I don't know how willing he is, Lucy."

"What do you mean?"

"When I overheard him, he said he had no other choice. He might have captured you because he feared for his own life."

"Of course he would sacrifice mine in place of his," she said bitterly.

"I expect he was very afraid, love."

She opened his eyes. Sinjin's image was watery, as though a shimmering wall stood between them. It was the glossy barrier of tears. She blinked fiercely. "He is a coward. And you—you could have taken James and run away. It would have been better for James. Instead you stayed."

"You know why, love, don't you?"

How soft and coaxing his voice was. Her own kind had

turned against her, yet the dragon slayer had not hurt her. "I have no idea why."

Before he could answer, she added numbly, "I keep remembering all the things I used to do with Jack. Now that is all lost to me. It is as though he is dead—the brother I knew certainly is."

"Shh. I know what it is like to lose family." His arms encircled her, his embrace firm, warm, and strong. One stubborn tear dropped out of her eye and splattered on her cheek. Oh God, she should not do this. It was madness to cry against his chest.

But he pulled her there, with his arms around her. "It is all right to cry, Lucy. It will help."

Heaven help her, she trusted him.

He insisted she eat.

Lucy did not know how Sinjin was fighting his need to sleep. He had explained to her that it was not like human sleep: it was almost impossible for a vampire to deny; his body simply shut down during daylight. Yet somehow, Sinjin fought it to stay with her. Finally, when she had filled her stomach at his command, though she had no appetite, she became the one to make demands. She forced him to get into bed. His arm had locked around her waist at first, until she begged him to let her go to her sisters.

"All right," he said. "But don't try to escape, Lucy. Your brother would likely catch you. Or a slayer could. I suspect by this point, my prince—the vampire demon that commands me—has guessed that I'm not going to do my duty. He will send someone else. Someone who will be instructed to kill us all."

Her stomach threatened to toss up all the food at that thought, but she gained control. She nodded, then left him. Armed with Sinjin's directions to her sisters' rooms, she made her way down the hall. She wore the dress he had acquired for her. It was deep blue silk, and surprisingly demure, with a rounded neckline that came high on her bosom.

Lucy moved down the hallway as quietly as she could. Carpeting absorbed her footfalls. It seemed silly but she imagined there were women resting behind the various closed doors and she . . . didn't want to disturb them. Then she reached a gallery—an open curve of the hallway, framed with wrought-iron railing, and from it she could see down into the foyer.

She'd always thought brothels were active at night. Apparently, they were very busy during the afternoon. Two gentlemen stepped into the foyer, admitted by a footman in powdered wig and immaculate scarlet livery. Each doffed his hat at the same time, revealing identical curls of white-blond. Two women sashayed out to the gentleman, their full bosoms jiggling in low-cut dresses. Both men grinned, showing dimples in the exact same place on their right cheeks and flashing matching blue eyes. Twins. Remarkably handsome twins. The men were perhaps two-and-twenty, slender and broad-shouldered.

Lucy squinted, trying to look at the teeth as the men spoke and laughed. No fangs. They looked normal. Ordinary. Not vampires.

Then she blinked. One of the blond gentlemen had bent to his lady's breasts and was licking and suckling them, leaving damp marks on her pink silk dress. The other had pressed his woman to the wall and was sliding his hands up her skirts.

A plump woman waddled forward. Diamonds glinted on her large expanse of bosom, and she had a rounded stomach and generous hips, obvious beneath her filmy cream silk gown. Her gray hair was piled on her head. Withdrawing a fan, she sharply tapped the shoulder of the man suckling the woman's breasts. He straightened abruptly, blushed, and gave an apologetic bow. He called something to the other man, who removed his hand, let the girl's skirts fall. Both ladies grasped their gentlemen by the wrists and towed them down the hall.

What had she been doing? She'd intended to find her sisters, yet something had compelled her to watch the scene.

Suddenly she realized the girls had been smiling. They had looked delighted to receive the . . . gentlemen callers.

The door opened to admit more men—in the space of a few minutes, five came through the door, one at a time, and each man went off with a girl. It happened so swiftly, it seemed the women knew to expect the men. A great number of gentlemen, it appeared, liked to seek pleasure in the afternoon.

Lucy's cheeks were warm with a blush. She had to stop gawking and find her sisters. Turning abruptly, she rushed down the corridor. The private rooms were at the back, but she must have made a mistake—she followed four twisting, twining corridors, and she had no idea what would be the "back" of the house. The brothel must be made up of several houses joined together. Either that or it was an enormous mansion.

Finally she found a door at the end of a hallway, and there was nowhere left to turn. This had to be it. She turned the knob and eased the door open.

Goodness. She glimpsed a woman, nude, bent over at the waist. A man's erection was rhythmically disappearing in the woman's mouth as her lips bobbed up and down on it. And a man was thrusting into her from behind.

Two men. One woman. Lucy was stunned. For a moment, she couldn't move and she stared as the man's hard stomach collided with the woman's generous bottom. Then both men turned at once and saw her. Both *smiled*. One crooked his finger in invitation.

She retreated, pushed the door closed, and fled.

Now her face was flaming. Even after all the naughty things she'd done with Sinjin, she wasn't able to see other people do it and not run in panic.

She rushed back the way she came. At the end of the hallway, she turned to the right—certain she had come from the left. In seconds, she was hopelessly confused.

Doors had been left ajar here, and erotic scenes were taking place in each room. Lucy tried to walk without looking, but she couldn't seem to stop taking peeks.

A woman bound hand and foot, writhed on the carpet while a gentleman licked her pussy. In another, a man stroked his large erection while one woman slid an enormous ivory wand in and out of another woman's bottom. Then she saw a group of four all making love together, in a laughing tangle of arms and legs.

In this place, sex was supposed to be a commodity, bought and sold. Yet each activity she had seen involved delighted participants. She knew she should not look, but it fascinated her.

Was nothing as it seemed? She had thought brothels would be terrible places, the women hurt and unhappy. She had thought dragon slayers were dangerous. Thought brothers should care about their families. And she had thought she must try to be proper, like a normal English lady. She had thought she could be proper, if she simply tried hard enough.

But all of those things she had thought had been wrong.

Then she saw one scene through the door that made her stop in shock.

A woman was moaning, obviously in pleasure, and a man was drinking from her neck.

Like her and Sinjin. Her quim ached at the remembered ecstasy of this.

A throat cleared and she squeaked in shock. "Lady Lucinda?"

She whirled to find a servant standing behind her, an elderly man with a completely impassive expression. She was about to ask him to take her to her sisters when he announced, "Mrs. Simpson wishes to speak to you."

"Mrs. Simpson?" she echoed, mystified.

"The owner of this establishment."

The madam. Lucy felt her eyes widen. But then, she was a guest in the house. It made sense, didn't it, that the madam would wish to see her? She had spoken to a madam before, when she had been searching for Jack. She had spoken to the woman with Sinjin.

Perhaps, Lucy thought wryly, she was going to have to forget all the things she had learned from mortal society, all those ways she had tried to behave like a proper lady. For being a dragon trumped it all, didn't it?

"All right. But I was searching for my sisters. Would you take me there afterward?"

"Indeed, Lady Lucinda."

Lucy expected the madam would prove to be the woman with the gray coiffure, with the enormous spray of diamonds. What she had not expected was to be led to a very fashionable and tastefully appointed drawing room. Nor had she imagined she would discover a thin young girl painstakingly tapping the keys of a pianoforte.

The madam, Mrs. Simpson, rose and clapped her hands. "That is enough for today, Rosemary. You may return to your duties now."

The girl curtsied, then hurried out. Lucy saw the girl was older than she had thought—Rosemary was definitely a young woman. *Duties.* She stared after the young girl, watching her graceful steps, measuring her age against her sisters. If this young woman had "duties," it must mean she—

"My ward, who is like a daughter to me," the madam said, as if she could glimpse thoughts. "The work I refer to is the account books. Rosemary has a remarkable head for figures and I would trust my finances to no one but my family."

The words *trust* and *family* brought an odd sensation to Lucy's stomach.

"Do you not agree?"

Lucy studied the madam's face. She wore a mild, agreeable expression, but she possessed sharp, intelligent gray eyes. Her lashes had been darkened, and kohl encircled her eyes to make them appear very large.

"I agree that women should be well versed in finances," Lucy said, though to her own ears, her voice sounded rigid and tight. "It is fortunate you can trust her. But just because a person is a member of a family . . . it does not mean they are definitely loyal."

"I agree. That is quite true." The madam waved toward a small table. A silver tray sat there, adorned with a gilt-rimmed teapot and two cups and saucers. "Now, you must have a seat so we can talk. Greystone spoke of your troubles, my dear."

"Sin—the duke spoke to you?" She crossed her arms over her chest, fighting for pride, though she supposed she looked to be shielding herself. "About what troubles?"

The madam wore cream silk gloves. She tapped her index finger. "Your brother's debts." Then the next finger, to count the next trouble. "His nefarious plans for you." More fingers. "Your poverty. The loss of your father. The threats to your life. Your worry over the duke's poor nephew."

"He told you . . ." Lucy stared. "Everything?" It was an idiotic question. How could the woman know if she knew everything or not? But the madam merely sat, then poured tea, filling two cups close to the brim. After that, Mrs. Simpson withdrew a flask from her skirts and poured a generous tot in the cup. Balancing cup upon saucer, she held it up.

"You should take this, my dear. It will calm your nerves."

Lucy took the cup but she carefully set it down. "At this point, I do not believe anything could possibly do that."

"Keeping your hands busy will help. You will see." Mrs. Simpson took a healthy swallow, and the bite of brandy filled the air. Holding her cup, the madam patted Lucy's knee. "My dear, I wish to assure you that you can remain in this house as long as you wish."

Another thought struck. *Payment.* Heavens, she had not even thought about that. Even if Jack had not been draining their money, she had no access to anything other than her modest allowance. "Thank you. His Grace did not mention what the cost is—"

"Of course not, for he has taken it on himself."

"He cannot!" Lucy gasped.

"Of course he can. He brought you here when you were unconscious. I assume it was quite a surprise to you to wake up in one of my bedchambers, with no memory of how you got here. I expect he did not ask you, or even tell you about his plan. He just did it. Thus, he should bear the expense. Besides, that is what men are for."

But he should not. They did not have that kind of . . . arrangement, or relationship? Lucy could not think of an appropriate word. She did not know what was between them. She had agreed to be his lover for a fortnight, but that was for debts, and the agreement must be meaningless now.

The woman's friendliness was disarming—other than Sinjin, Lucy had no one to confide to anymore. She wouldn't tell truthful things to her sisters; her duty was to reassure them. She had never really been able to talk to Jack. He would claim to be bored, or he would simply not listen. Even if he did, her admonitions never seemed to sink into his head.

"You may ask me anything," the madam said. "For I suspect the duke did not tell you everything. In fact, it appears he told you little at all."

She frowned. "You cannot read my mind, can you?"

"No. But I can read your eyes, my dear. I can see questions flitting through them. I can see worry. Perhaps I can help you with some answers."

So tempting, but was she being lured into making a terrible

mistake? On the other hand, she could possibly learn things, things Sinjin wouldn't tell her. Did she think he would deliberately lie or keep information from her?

She didn't know . . . she didn't yet know. "The duke told me this is a sanctuary for vampires," Lucy said carefully. "What does that mean?"

"Yes, that is true." Mrs. Simpson smiled. "It is a sanctuary for you and your sisters."

"Do you think I am a vampire?"

"No, dear. I do know that you are a dragon. I had you brought to see me for another reason, Lady Lucinda. I suspect Greystone did not tell you very much about your brother this morning. He would not have wanted to trouble you. However, I know men never give women credit for the strength we obviously possess in spades. I felt it would be better for you to know the truth."

When women said something like that, like "it would be better for you to know the truth," Lucy was unnerved. Sometimes women were not always honest—a young lady had said that to her to try to drive her away from a particular gentlemen. Of course, the lady had not needed to waste her breath—Lucy had known she could not fall in love with a normal gentleman. "What did the duke tell you that he did not tell me?" It was an odd way to ask the question, but she knew Mrs. Simpson would understand.

"While you slept, Greystone spoke with other dragon slayers who were here. He questioned them about your brother. You see, Greystone is in service to a demon that commands the dragon slayers. This man is an immortal and is many hundreds of years old."

"He commands Sin—I mean, the duke."

"Yes. He turned Greystone into a vampire. The duke is in his service for eternity. If the duke disobeys his orders, he would be destroyed. That is the vow all of the vampire dragon slayers make—service for eternity."

Her stomach dropped. Sinjin had promised he would not hurt her but how could he not, if he was sworn to slay dragons forever? "Why...why would Sinjin want to do this?" she whispered.

"I see he has explained nothing about himself. Why does any man make such a drastic choice?"

Lucy shook her head. She had no idea.

"For revenge."

"Revenge?" she echoed, and she waited, barely able to draw breath. She waited for more, but the madam lifted her tea to her lips and sipped. Revenge. Why would a man become a dragon slayer for revenge? It had to mean that dragons had hurt him once. Or dragons had taken someone he loved...

"What was it?" she whispered. "What did my kind take from him?"

The clink of cup and saucer made Lucy flinch as though someone had fired a pistol.

"His family," the madam said coolly. "Each member of his family except his eldest sister. He lost his father and mother, his younger brother, his two littlest sisters."

"Oh. Oh God." Lucy's hands went to her mouth. Imagined scenes rushed through her mind. Father had paintings...paintings of battles between dragons and slayers. He had kept them hidden, but once she had found some. Pictures that showed dragons attacking villages, goring people with their claws and sharp wings, breathing fire. Father had told her such things were not real, that dragons were peaceful, that they had been painted for the slayers to justify the reason for having men to hunt dragons. But what if it were true...what if that had been what had happened to his family?

Mrs. Simpson gently patted Lucy's knee. "Now you understand what a struggle it has been for him to care so deeply for you. It is probably why he has not told you about your brother."

"What about my brother? Please tell me. Stop hinting at horrible things, and tell me."

"Your brother is being controlled by the prince."

That made no sense. "By Prinny?" What on earth would the Prince Regent have to do with this?

"No, by the demon who commands the dragon slayers. He is called 'the prince.' "

"My brother would not go to the prince of slayers—" Lucy began to protest, but the teacup was pushed back into her hands.

"Greystone fears your brother made a trade: his life in return for you. The duke fears your brother was going to give you to the prince, and in payment, your brother's life would be spared."

"Jack—" Horror numbed her lips. It made her choke on a small sip of tea. She sputtered. But it was possible, wasn't it? To save his own skin, what would Jack be willing to do?

"Just me. Or my sisters also?"

The madam shook her head. "We do not know. The duke will want to find out."

"What can he do? How can this . . . be stopped?" For there was no way of stopping this, was there? The dragon slayers killed dragons. They had vowed not to stop until all dragons were dead.

"I have lived a long time, my dear. Much longer than you might think. *Centuries*," the madam said, and she rose to her feet. "Come now, my dear, we will find a way. There is *always* a way. Now, let us take you to see your sisters."

16

Ultimatum

"Not four times in a row! That is not *fair!*"

The feminine voice came through an open door as Lucy stepped into a small but exquisitely decorated sitting parlor. Four doors led off from the sitting room, and she recognized her sister Beatrix's indignant cry. Mrs. Simpson smiled, and stayed back, letting her rush past. But Lucy stopped at the doorway to the bedroom.

It was so good to see her sisters, see they were both safe, and utterly oblivious to her. Lucy hugged herself in the doorway and sniffled. Taking a minute to compose herself—it would do her two sisters no good to see her teary—she watched Helena triumphantly slap down a playing card, obviously delighted to win the game. Helena was curled in a wing chair with a woolen shawl around her shoulders and golden-haired Beatrix was stretched on a chaise, with a blanket spread over her feet. Beatrix tossed her cards down on a small table in disgust. "I think you are cheating, Helena."

"I am not! I am just very good at cards. You never pay attention!"

They were behaving like normal girls, having a dramatic and

meaningless argument. And Lucy had Sinjin to thank for her safety, not her brother. The world felt as if it was tilting beneath her every time she tried to take a step. Mocking her for thinking she could be normal.

Sinjin, the dragon slayer, had promised to protect her from his "prince." He was the one she could trust to protect her sisters. Her brother wanted to drag her to the demon, not caring if she died. She had no idea what he would do to Helena and Beatrix, all she knew was that she could not trust him.

"Helena, Beatrix, I—I want you to both play fairly."

At the sound of her voice, Helena turned in the wing chair. Beatrix kicked off her blanket and leapt from the chaise. "Lucy!" Beatrix cried. Her blue eyes widened, her hands waved dramatically. "We thought you would never wake up. I was afraid you were going to *die*. Helena was so afraid, too—at first she told me not to be foolish, then she started to cry!"

Beatrix rushed forward and launched at Lucy. Lucy found herself wrapped in a hug, and she embraced her sister back, stroking her hair.

Helena flushed. "I shouldn't have done that. As the next oldest, I was supposed to take care of Beatrix—"

"Helena, you are not *supposed* to do anything but be . . . be normal," Lucy whispered. "If you need to cry, don't try to stoically stop the tears. You are not supposed to bear the weight of so much responsibility."

"You do," Helena pointed out. She slowly stood. "Because Jack will not."

"I—" She was about to say *I have to.* But that was what Helena had felt: that she must take charge of the family because there was no one else. Now she had to warn them about Jack. If she did not tell them the truth, to spare their feelings, to keep from hurting them more, they would still trust Jack, which meant he could approach them and capture them. She had not even asked the madam if Sinjin had told her sisters why they were here.

"What happened, Lucy?" Beatrix asked. "Why did you go to the house on the moors? The duke came for us and told us we must go with him, and he would bring us to you, and keep us safe."

"He told us we must not speak to Jack," Helena added. Deep lines creased her forehead. "The duke told us that Jack had hurt you, and that, to pay his debts, he was willing to do something dangerous to us all. I didn't know what to do. Creadmore tried to have the duke thrown out of the house. He did not want to even let me speak to the duke. When I refused to obey, he became furious. He tried to have the footmen drag Beatrix and me upstairs. I didn't understand—Creadmore has never acted in such a way before."

"I don't know. Perhaps he thought he was protecting you. Perhaps he thought the duke had hurt me, not Jack. I was hurt in a carriage accident, but it was one that was caused because of Jack."

Gently, carefully, she explained everything she knew. She told them about James, about the fact Father had taken the boy, and she told them about the duke, who had ruined Jack to get his nephew back. She told them how she had decided it was not right for her family to hold James, and how she had taken Sinjin to the house on the moors to retrieve the boy. And she told them about Jack—the conversation Sinjin had overheard, the fact Jack's lackey had shot Sinjin, and the fact her own brother was going to haul her off and give her to some mysterious, dangerous man.

"Jack did this?" Helena echoed. "And Father kidnapped a child?"

"Yes, this is how it appears to be. The young boy, James, is a dragon and he can already shift shape—"

"The Duke of Greystone is a dragon slayer!" gasped Beatrix. "Was he going to hurt his own nephew, though, Lucy?"

She shook her head. "He would never do such a thing—I am sure of it. He wants to protect his nephew. He was willing to risk his life to try to rescue James."

"He is a dragon slayer, Lucy," Helena said, softly. Deep concern showed in her eyes.

"I know. He has never hurt me, but it is true that he is a dragon slayer. We have to be careful—we must also protect ourselves around the duke."

"It is like Romeo and Juliet," Beatrix breathed. Ingenuously, she coiled a black curl around her finger and gave a romantic sigh.

"It most certainly is not," Lucy said sharply. "They both ended up dead." However, both her clan and Sinjin's prince were threatening his life. Sinjin's clan and her brother threatened hers. Sinjin was duty-bound to kill her and also her sisters. How could she keep her family safe? How could she hope to survive? Or would Sinjin be killed? She must push those thoughts away. She could not show fear in front of her sisters. For them, she must put on a brave front—

"You do care about him, don't you?" Helena asked. "Are you in love with him?"

"I—No, I am not in love with him. I would not do anything to risk our lives. But we are safe while we are in this house. Mrs. Simpson has promised me that."

"You believe her?" Helena looked startled. "You never trust anyone, Lucy."

It was true—why should she trust a madam? "I do trust her. She seemed to be speaking the truth. However, she did point out that she cannot protect us outside of this house. You two will have to stay here, and you are to stay to your rooms. This house is not the sort of place you can run around in—"

"I know," Beatrix said. "It's a brothel. Though I long to see what happens in such places. This morning, I saw two of the most handsome men ever, and they were identical in every way—"

"Exactly where did you see them?" Lucy broke in.

"Oh, I was looking out the window, and I saw them alight from a carriage," Beatrix answered, her eyes wide and innocent.

"Indeed." Lucy did not believe her sister's exaggerated guileless expression. "Make sure looking out of the window is all that you do. You cannot go anywhere in here, not even to satisfy your curiosity, or to gawk at men. This place is *dangerous.*"

Beatrix's lower lip wobbled. "Then what are we to do? We cannot go home—that is too dangerous! We cannot trust our own brother, because you have told us he is desperate and therefore, *dangerous.* This house is dangerous, and the man you are trusting, the Duke of Greystone, is a dragon slayer. Therefore, dangerous!"

The truth of it all struck Lucy. She had no safe sanctuary for her family. She had promised her dying mother to take care of them all—and she was failing miserably.

But Helena shot Lucy a look: a firm, no-nonsense look. She went to Beatrix and put her arm around the girl. "We are dragons, Beatrix. Unfortunately that means there are many dangers in our lives. We are together, all three of us, and because of that, I am not afraid."

"I'm not scared," Beatrix mumbled. "I'm frustrated and bored. Shouldn't it be exciting to be in so much danger?"

"It's not exciting," Lucy said firmly. "It is just exhausting."

But a rap on the door made them all start and turn around. A footman bowed. "I beg your pardon, Lady Lucinda, but you are needed at once in the bedchamber of Master James, the nephew of the duke."

The moment Lucy hurried into James's bedroom, Mrs. Simpson surged forward and clasped her by the arm. The woman's hair was falling out of its elaborate style and her face was distraught with worry. "Good heavens, my dear," Mrs. Simpson cried. "I have no idea what happened to the boy! I came to see him, and he suddenly began to writhe on the bed."

Lucy moved past the woman, quickly asking, "Did he change his form?"

"No. No, he did not. But he lifted off the covers and he hovered over the bed. At once, he stopped moving, and he stayed perfectly still, floating."

Heavens. Lucy had never heard of a dragon doing such a thing. "Did he say anything?"

"No. He did not speak at all."

As she reached the bed, Lucy looked to the window. The curtains were partly open and some sunshine fell into the room. Sinjin could not come yet. Looking after James, helping the boy, was something she must do.

Bother, she could not summon Sinjin, anyway. Now that she knew he was searching for revenge, shouldn't she accept that he wanted to kill her? That he had to?

Before, she had argued with him. Before she had known why he hunted dragons. Deep in her heart, she still wanted to believe in him. But then, she had been so very wrong about Alan—she had thought she could marry him because he was kind, charming, and good. In truth, he had been none of those things.

She knelt in front of James and clasped one of his hands in hers. Surprise and worry spiked: his hand was as cold as ice, yet he was bundled in a blanket and a good fire burned only a few feet from him. What was wrong?

Lucy lifted his hand and gave it a kiss. Then she turned over his palm and sucked it, which tickled madly, she knew. A smile flickered at the boy's small, cupid's bow lips.

"Aha," she said, with cheer that was false but hopefully convincing. "You are teasing me. You know I am here, and I will tickle you until you greet me."

She released his hand and snaked her fingers into his armpits. He squeaked, jumped on the chair, and clamped his arms against him. Almost against his will, a giggle escaped, then another.

She tickled and tickled him until he was slapping at her, and gasping, "Stop, stop, stop, Lucy! I don't want to be tickled!"

She did stop, drawing her hands out from his underarms. She gave him a long cuddle instead. "There. Now you are speaking to me again. I was so afraid you would not. Your uncle is safe, you know. He was not hurt and I don't want you to think of what you saw. You are safe now, and you are with your uncle Sinjin again."

He nodded solemnly. "I know Uncle is alive. He took me when the carriage crashed. It was very exciting. The carriage was all smashed to bits."

"Well, we were both all right, and that is the most important thing."

"The horses galloped very fast. Were they running away from my uncle? Where were we going?"

That she did not know—though the madam had told her Jack was working for Sinjin's prince, which meant they were probably being taken to him. "I don't know, but I did not want to go and I know you did not either. But you are not going to be taken away from your uncle again."

He nodded. "I love Uncle," he said, with a deep seriousness that fractured Lucy's heart.

The poor boy. It must have been the shock of seeing Sinjin shot that had made the boy so cold, so wild, and had sent him back into his own world. But . . . why had he lifted above the bed? She had never heard of a dragon doing such a thing, but since dragons could fly, wasn't it possible that they could levitate?

She let go of James, went to the door, and asked Mrs. Simpson to bring food for the boy. Once she was alone with James, Lucy sat with him. She sang him cheery songs, but her heart was not in them.

What was she going to do to protect Helena and Beatrix? She should take her sisters and they should run. But to where? Could they really escape both Sinjin and Jack?

Should she not at least try, rather than wait like a fool to be killed? Should they not run in the day?

Yes. They would have to.

He knew he was dreaming. Knew it wasn't real, what he could see and feel. He knew it in the way that dreamers did. He was standing at the precipice of a cliff and the sea pounded below. His sword was gripped in his two hands and he slashed it at the chest and stomach of an enormous dragon.

Flames flew out of the beast's mouth and licked at him. By dodging, jumping, somersaulting in the air, he managed to avoid being burned. Roaring, the dragon sent a burst of flame that ignited bushes around him. While they burned, the beast attacked again. Claws slashed. Its teeth gnashed toward him. It caught his shirt and tore it. He tried to jump back, but the beast had him against the cliff edge and he had nowhere to go. A slash of claws brought a row of wounds to his chest. Pain lanced him and blood poured. A fresh stream of flame came and caught his arm and the side of his face. The stench of burning skin filled the air. The pain was incredible, but he was a vampire, and he could survive what mortals could not.

The dragon was fighting for its life. So was he. And he was not going to lose.

He had chased the dragon here, filled with hatred, filled with the need to make one more beast pay.

Now he was going to kill it.

He launched forward and drove his sword into the beast's

chest. As soon as the blade drove in, the dragon collapsed. It was dying and it suddenly transformed back into human form. Into a man, years younger than he was when he'd been turned into a vampire.

Fear filled the man's blue eyes.

"I've never killed," the man whispered hoarsely. "Why . . . why attack?"

"You are a dragon. A dragon cannot be suffered to live."

The man whispered a name. A woman's name. Obviously the man's beloved. But she was a dragon, too, and she would have to die.

Sinjin watched the life drain out of the man's face. Any sense of victory and satisfaction was gone. He felt empty. The wind howled around him.

Suddenly, he was looking over the edge of the cliff. He could see faces, hundreds of faces. The human faces of dying dragons. All reaching out to him. Pleading for life. Pleading that they had never killed, that they should not die—

Sinjin jolted up. He was in a bed, not a coffin, so he didn't slam his head into a wooden lid. It had been a dream. Just a nightmare—he'd had these dreams every day since he had brought Lucy to the brothel.

It had been easy to kill dragons before, when he'd believed he was killing beasts to protect mortals.

Hell, how many dragons had he killed who were like Lucy? Who had good hearts? Who were good and loving and kind? How many lives had he taken for a vengeance that had nothing to do with those victims?

He hung his head. It felt like he had been buried alive, with earth pressing down on him.

Kicking the sheets back, he got up. Something compelled him to find Lucy, though he didn't know why, not when he felt so damned guilty for what he had done.

It was early evening, and at this time of day the brothel was

218 / Sharon Page

quiet. Almost quiet: his vampiric hearing picked out soft footfalls and muffled voices. Someone was creeping through the house.

Senses on alert, he moved with preternatural speed to follow the voices. He tracked them to the rear of the house on the main floor. Rounding a corner, he found three lithe forms in cloaks huddled at a door.

"Lucy," he barked. "Where in blazes do you think you are going?"

The two other Drake girls jumped into the air in surprise. Lucy whirled around and faced him. "I thought it was better to take our chances, rather than pray that we aren't killed by dragon slayers."

His heart clenched in his chest. "I vowed I would never hurt you, and I will never let anyone else hurt you. It's not safe for any of you out there. Please, Lucy—" His voice broke. He tried again. "Lucy, please don't go. Not yet. Mrs. Simpson told me what happened with James, and how you were the only one who could break through to him. Just as you did before."

He had managed to convince her to stay.

As Sinjin went with Lucy to see James, he knew exactly what he had to do to protect her. But first, he wanted to talk to her about his nephew.

He found the boy playing with blocks with a footman. The liveried servant was on his knees looking distinctly uncomfortable. Sinjin dismissed the man, and he grasped James under the shoulders and tossed the boy in the air. James squealed with delight. Sinjin caught him. They roughhoused on the bed, then he sat with Lucy as James had his dinner.

Since the activities of the brothel were going on downstairs, James was having his meal in his bedchamber.

Sinjin had requested sherry and had poured a glass for Lucy.

They stood by the mantel and he said the words that had been burning on his lips since Mrs. Simpson had told him what Lucy had done, again, for his nephew. "Thank you, love," he said through a tight throat. "Thank you again."

She was leaning on the mantel, studying the licking flames of the fire. He moved to her, and stroked her dark curls. But Lucy flinched and took a step away.

What had he expected? She was now coming to accept what he was. Hell, when he thought of what he had done to dragons, what he had seen in his nightmares, he didn't blame her for walking away from him. But he had promised her he would not hurt her, and he would ensure she and her family were safe. He now knew how to do it.

"I'm sorry." She faced him. "I don't understand," she said quietly, her beautiful, darkly lashed indigo eyes gazing at him. "James was not like that with me, when we were in the carriage. He was unhappy and he was crying because he was afraid and he thought he had lost you. But he did not retreat inside himself. I was amazed that he didn't. I feared he would, since he had been through such a horrible shock so quickly. When Mrs. Simpson brought me up here, and I found him in this blank state, I was stunned at first. I managed to break it by tickling him. I thought it must be because of the shock . . . but now I am not sure."

"I believe I know why he did not retreat into a vacant, lost state with you, Lucy."

"Why?"

"It was because he was with you. He felt safe with you—he didn't need to hide. You brought him out again. Despite what he endured, you made him laugh. You are the only person who can do that with him, Lucy."

She shook her head in a firm, matter-of-fact way. "I don't think it is that. I am not sure the shock did affect him. . . .

Would it take so long to do that? Perhaps it could. He did endure the carriage accident. Though, when he spoke about that, he described it as exciting."

"If not the shock, then what would put him back in that state?"

"I don't know. I wondered if you did. Perhaps it was just delayed."

"Or perhaps it was because he had you there with him before the accident, and then after it, he might have feared he had lost you, too," Sinjin said. "That it was the fear of losing you that did it."

She frowned. "But he knew you were safe then. No, it doesn't make sense. There is something else. Mrs. Simpson told me that she saw James levitate over the bed. It is possible he did that because he is a dragon, but I am not sure. I've never heard of dragons doing such a thing. But then, James is obviously a special and unique dragon." She narrowed her eyes, obviously considering deeply. "His father was a dragon, obviously. Was he a special dragon? What clan did he belong to?"

He shook his head. "I don't know, love. Emma ran away with him to marry him. Dragon slayers pursued them, killed him, and brought her back, with James. I don't know anything about the man she married. She would never talk about him."

"I am not surprised—if she loved him and he was taken from her so violently." Tears glittered in Lucy's eyes. "Poor James."

She was so very correct. Emma had suffered so much and that had to be why she had taken her own life. James had known so much loss and pain. It had been the prince who had sent slayers to hunt down Emma and her husband. And now the prince was threatening to take more innocents. "This has to end," Sinjin said.

"What do you mean? End?" Lucy paled.

He could guess what she was thinking. That he meant to end

things by doing his duty and slaying her and her family. "I am going to ensure you, your sisters, and James are safe."

He wished he could kiss her. One last kiss. But she would pull away from him, and hell, he didn't want that to be his last memory of her.

"Will you look after James for me? While I am gone?"

Her dark brows made a deep vee. "Where are you going?"

"I am going to the prince, love."

"Why?"

"To put a stop to this. To make sure he cannot have you. Or James. Or any other member of your family."

Lucy's eyes went saucer wide. She crossed her arms over her chest. "Well, I am not letting you go alone."

17

Horror

Fog coiled up the streets, slithering around their faces, muting the light from the burning street flares. Lucy pushed back her hood and gazed up at the elegant mansion inhabited by the dragon slayer that Sinjin called "the prince."

"He lives only three streets from my home," she whispered. Civilized society was surely madness: mortal enemies could live, separated by only a few streets, and never encounter each other. Anyway, what would have happened if they had met on the street, or in a park, or at a crowded ball? She doubted the prince would have attacked—he was pretending to be a Russian count, visiting England, and it would hardly be good *ton* to launch an attack out in public.

Sinjin snarled at the elegant house. Literally his lip curled like an angry, defensive dog and he let out a growl. "I should not have let you come."

"You didn't let me," she pointed out. "In the end, I had to follow you."

"Yes, and once I discovered you I should have spanked your pretty bottom and sent you home. This man wants to destroy you. Do not make his work easier by presenting yourself on a silver platter." He grasped her wrist and hauled her away from the faint glow of the streetlamp. "We are going to return to the brothel. You cannot go into that house with me. Come, let us go."

He began to walk and with his hand clamped around her right forearm, she had no choice but to match his long strides. She knew he was hurrying her back to the elegant brothel—which was situated only a few blocks away, on the fringe of Mayfair.

"What were you going to do? Did you hope to convince the prince to not hurt me? To leave my sisters and James alone?"

Still he didn't answer. He just stalked relentlessly toward the end of the street. The jingle of carriage traces, the clop of hooves, the rattle of wheels came out of the fog.

She took quick steps so she could walk at his side, instead of being dragged behind him. "Do you truly believe the prince would listen to you? Or were you going to fight him—?"

He stopped so quickly she walked into his chest. His hands settled on her upper arms. "Love, I was not planning to go to him and plead for your life. I was planning to kill him."

She cast a longing and frustrated glance back to the massive house. "Then let us go and do it."

He bowed his head, gently shaking it as though he was bemused and holding in a grin, or a harsh, jaded laugh. "It's not as easy as that."

"If you could do it, how could my presence make any difference?"

"You could become a hostage far too easily."

"I am a dragon—"

Her words were lost, for he pulled her to him, wrapped his arms tight around her back, and covered her mouth with his. It shocked her, lifting her onto her toes. His mouth was hot. Searing heat sizzled all the way to her toes.

People passed them on the sidewalk, and she heard sniggers

and gasps. Sinjin kissed her with fierce passion until all the strolling couples and servants had moved on. Then he let her go abruptly. He dragged his hand through his hair. "You are young, female, and have no experience with fighting."

She touched her lower lip, it was soft and plump from the pressure of his kiss. "Since this prince wants to kill me, I am going to have to fight for my life, aren't I?"

His expression hardened. "I will never allow you to be in that kind of danger."

"But won't that mean you will be killed?" At his frown, she added, "Mrs. Simpson gave me tea, and told me quite a bit about you."

"Did she?" He stared at her guardedly.

"She told me you could be killed, yet you walked over to this demon's house, with no one to help you. Do you even have weapons with you?"

To her astonishment, he shook his head.

Then she realized . . . his family was gone, and he had made a vow to serve the dragon slayers for eternity . . . or at least for as long as he "lived." Suddenly, a horrible thought occurred to her. "Were you willing to die? Is that it? Is that why you came unarmed and alone?"

His lip twisted. "You are a very astute woman. The prince would never believe I would try to kill him and be willing to destroy myself to do it."

Impulsively she grasped him, pressing her fingers into his hard biceps, through his coat. They were in the middle of a sidewalk in Mayfair, but her heart ached so much for him she had to speak. "You have never stopped grieving for your family, have you? It is not just about revenge. You aren't afraid to die, because . . . because you miss them, but you have James and he needs you."

"Killing the prince would give him better protection than I could. The slayers take all their guidance from him. Without him, there would be battles for power, internal struggles, and it would give you time to ensure your family was safe. It would even save your brother."

"But what of James? It would devastate him to lose you."

"I've lost all of them. They are all gone. Emma was the last—and now she is gone, too."

"All the more reason for you to ensure you stay alive. For James! You know what it is to suffer from losing your family. If it hurt you so deeply, what would it do to him?"

"You are telling me I am selfish for thinking of sacrificing myself to kill the prince?"

"Not selfish . . . but I will not allow it."

"God, Lucy." He clasped her waist, lifting her off her feet. In a heartbeat, he had taken them around a corner of the street and into a narrow mews. Here, there was a little bit of light spilling out of the stables, but it was almost completely swallowed by the damp fog. Sinjin stopped, his chest heaving, and he set her gently down. Her back brushed against the hard stone of a garden wall and he braced his arms above her head. "It's hell, you know. To want something so much and to know it is impossible to have."

"What do you want so much? Perhaps it isn't hopeless. Perhaps we can make it possible."

It was torture now to hold Lucy and kiss her. Sinjin looked into her eyes and remembered . . . not his family dying, but the deaths of dragons. The images that haunted him in his dreams during his day sleep now flashed through his thoughts.

How could she let him kiss her? Hell, hatred at what he had done was rushing through his veins.

Tenderly, her hand stroked his cheek. His pulse, which was normally the slow, lazy thump of a vampire's heart, was now pounding in his throat.

"I cannot imagine how horrible it must have been for you to

lose your family. To lose so many people you loved," she whispered. How soft and sweet her voice was. It almost made him believe he could capture her love. But how could he? At some point, she would realize what he had done and how many deaths he had on his conscience.

Caring for Lucy had forced him to put a human face on the dragons he had killed, and it was tearing him apart.

"It was." But his voice went harsh. "Did you lose family to the slayers?"

Her eyes widened. In their dark blue depths, he read so much—a lifetime of memories of pain and loss. "Not any of my closest family. Father took care to protect us."

Yes, and her father had taken James to keep Lucy and her family safe. Sinjin could no longer dredge up anger toward her father for that. Perhaps he could understand it. He had been driven by vengeance, and her father was driven by the immediate need to protect. All it revealed was that violence led to more violence and desperation made men commit hellish deeds.

"But I know other families who did. My father had friends who lost children."

He flinched. He had never personally attacked young dragons, but he knew there was a faction of vicious slayers willing to kill anyone. He had fought the prince over it, and he had lost every argument. But he should have taken a stronger stand. He should have stopped those slayers before they could kill innocents. It would have been the noble thing to do, but he had not been noble.

"I had friends who lost gentlemen whom they loved. But I know that some dragons would fight back and they would try to destroy as many dragon slayers as they could. I don't think it really helped them, but I understand why someone would do it, I think. I think I can understand the rage and the hurt that would drive someone to do it." She touched his forearm, and he felt the soft graze of her fingers. "You lost your family, Sinjin,

when you were young—it is horrible. Can you speak about it?
It must have been very long ago."

For years, he had been driven by revenge, but he had kept
the memories locked away as deeply as he could. He never
thought of his family. Never let himself try to imagine their
faces, their voices. Across his heart, he had pulled thick gates of
ice, and he was afraid to let them crack.

"Did you kill the dragons who took your family?" she
whispered.

"I will never know," he admitted. "I was nine years of age.
My memories of who those dragons were are vague. I just remember pieces of that afternoon." Christ, it hurt to remember,
but he wanted to tell Lucy. "My family had taken curricles out
to a picnicking place on our country estate. My brother Will
and I were flying kites. I remember Will being so happy because he could finally get his kite to take off. He ran as mad as
his little legs would carry him, clutching his string, with his kite
rising and dipping precariously. He was only six and he was so
small he could barely see over the tall grass of the meadow."

These were memories he had never spoken of. As though
Lucy knew how hard it was for him to dredge them up from
deep in his cold heart, she cradled his jaw, letting her fingers
stroke his lips. The gesture was comforting. He had no right to
take comfort from this woman—hadn't his nightmares reminded him of that? But he could not turn away from her
warm hand, from her calm, entrancing eyes.

"It was the smell," he said softly. "The smell was the first
thing I noticed that was wrong. I smelled fire. At first, I feared
the meadow had caught fire—it had been a dry summer, and
there had been several blazes that started at cottages and farms
and had spread wildly. I gathered up Will, and he was furious
because his kite fell. He'd dropped its lead as I ran with him,
and he'd lost it. When I reached my family, my father was trying to get us to safety. He got us all together—my mother, my

three sisters, and I still carried Will—and we ran as quickly to the carriage as we could. But the servants had vanished and the carriage was also gone. To this day, I don't know if they abandoned us, or whether our attackers killed them first, then removed the carriage so we couldn't escape."

Strangely, his body seemed to be trembling, just as it had on that afternoon. He remembered being confused and shaking as his father shouted at him. He had Will on his back and he was holding Will's ankles and his younger brother had whined at the tightness of his grip. Then his father had yelled at him to be more careful. He remembered how his shoulders had been jerking uncontrollably, how tears had burned at his eyes. Will's arms had been locked around his neck, making it hard to breathe.

"My father pointed to the woods. He told us to run to there and find places to hide. With Will on my back, I raced through the meadow. My father told me not to look back, but I did. The sun had dropped and the light burned into my eyes. They started to water, then tears came, and I stopped, which I wasn't supposed to do. But my vision was a blur and I wiped at my eyes. I stopped running so I could see what was happening to the rest of my family. There were men wearing black cloaks. My father fought with them with his sword, and the blade was a strand of gold in the light. He plunged the sword into one of the men. The howl of agony echoed through the meadows and when my father pulled out the weapon, it no longer shone. Red blood coated its sides. One of the men pointed at me, and two others ran toward me. My father whipped around. Pure anguish was on his face as he saw I had disobeyed him, that I had not kept running and taken Will to safety—"

He had to stop, afraid to go further. It was mad, but he also wanted to keep talking. He had never poured it out to anyone before. Not even after it had happened. His rescuers had asked him as they tended to him, but he had kept his mouth clamped shut. Had feared the men who had saved him would think he was mad, if he said he had seen dragons. Then, when he realized they knew about the beasts and hunted them, he still would not speak. He had tried to bury it all. He had suddenly become an earl and was supposed to be strong. Anyway, he'd been too twisted up inside to say a word.

Lucy slid her arms around his waist, her cheek pressed to his chest. Her embrace must be meant to soothe him, but it brought guilt rushing up to war with the pain of his memories.

"I tried to run again, and I got close to the woods. My legs were wobbling and I tripped. Will flew off, and the men were almost upon us. I ran back to grab him, but they were so close . . . I picked him up, but one of them lunged at us and he grabbed Will. I should have fought the blackguard . . . should have done something . . . but I ran for the woods. I managed to get in, crashing through it. It was dark in there—the trees were dense, the sky screened by a thick canopy of leaves. All the shadow made it a good place to hide.

"It also made it hard to see. I glimpsed a creature at the edge of the woods. It stood almost as high as the trees, and was a monstrous thing with enormous wings, a huge snapping mouth." At once realization dawned and Sinjin shut his mouth. Shutting his eyes, he dropped his head forward on a groan. He was almost unable to lift his lids and look at her. He mumbled, "I'm sorry, love. It was the way it seemed to me at the time."

Lucy's hand cupped his chin, forcing his head up. When he looked at her, he saw stark pain in her eyes, but she whispered, "I *understand*. I can imagine how horrible it looked to you."

She was amazing. She knew what he was, yet sympathized with him.

"I thought I was imagining things," he said, "until I saw fire licking out of their mouths. There was a thick bush right in front of me, so I dropped into the dirt and scurried under it on my stomach. But I kept thinking of Will. I had to save him. I was halfway out of the hiding place when I heard Will scream. I wanted to run out and go to him, but . . ." God, the memory crippled him. The surge of guilt made him want to be sick.

Lucy stroked his cheek, and her touch gave him the strength to face his memories. He saw the glimmer of tears in her eyes.

"God, it was the most awful noise," he whispered hoarsely. "It went so loud, then it stopped altogether. I knew I had to go, but I couldn't make my legs move. I lay there, under a bush, half-buried in rotted leaves, quivering. Then I imagined what had happened to my brother, and my stomach clamped tight and I vomited. I fell down beside the pile of my own sickness, and lay there sobbing, hating myself. It was only when I heard a roar and knew the woods were ablaze that I ran out. I did it then, to save my own arse. I didn't do it to save Will."

"I am so sorry." Tears streaked down her face. "You were only nine years of age. You were a boy, fighting against grown men."

He looked down. Her fists had clenched into fists. "God, love, please . . . don't cry. Not over me."

"I'm sorry. I can't help it. I keep thinking of your poor brother, only six years old. And your sisters. But your sister, James's mother, was spared?"

"I didn't know it until later. I found all their bodies in the grass. Emma was lying in . . . in a pool of blood. I thought she was dead. Later, I found out the blood was not hers. Before I could even touch any of them, I saw that the whole meadow behind me was burning, and it was coming for me like a wave."

"They had set the fire."

He nodded. His tongue felt strangely thick. "At first, I was going to stay there and let myself die, too. I didn't want to live; but I guess I wanted to survive—I stumbled out, lost and sobbing. Smoke and tears blinded me. Then I heard hoofbeats. I thought it was the dragons coming back. That I was dead for certain. They were men I had never seen before, and I fought like a wild man, kicking, punching, biting, and finally one of them grabbed me by the shoulder, pinched my neck, and everything went black. I'd passed out. It took them days to make me understand that they were dragon slayers."

"Had they rescued Emma, too?"

"Yes. They had worked quickly, with the fire almost upon her. They had saved her. I felt so damned guilty I had not checked all of them to see if any had lived. If they had not carried her away from the flames, she would have burned to death."

"Dear heaven, you should not have felt guilty!"

But he let her go and fell back against the wall at her side, letting the back of his head slam hard against unyielding, gritty stone. Again and again, he let his head fall back, letting the pain slide down his nerves.

How could he not feel guilty? Memories of his family—of his brother and sisters' deaths—bludgeoned him. There was no respite now. When he shut his eyes he could see them. When he opened his eyes wide, even though he could see in the dark, his sight could not penetrate fog and he could see their struggles against the silvery backdrop of the mist. In his head, he could still hear their screams. But he could also hear the roar-like screams of dying dragons—the ones he had killed.

Being a dragon slayer had just given him more guilt, more regrets, more nightmares. It hadn't given peace or any sense of satisfaction. It hadn't eased pain.

"Please, let me help you," Lucy said softly. "You must not feel guilty about this. You were right to blame the dragons. The ones who did this were horrible. They deserved to pay."

"I thought all dragons were bad, Lucy. I did inhuman, brutal things because I believed that. I was wrong. There is no way you can forgive me—I know that."

"I think . . . I think you must feel torn inside. That is how I feel. All mixed up. I do not know what to believe anymore. All

I can use is the evidence I have seen. Though you had every reason to hate my kind, you have not hurt me. You love your
nephew and are determined to protect him—but you did not
kill to do so."

Any man with sense would wrap his arms around Lucy's
slender back and let her believe in him. Strange, he had surrendered every shred of humanity when he let himself be changed
into a vampire so he could hunt dragons, but now he felt the
stirrings of a conscience. He grasped her arms gently and met
her eyes. "When you first offered yourself to me, Lucy, I intended to hurt you. My duty was to kill you, and I was willing
to accept that duty. At first I let you live because I needed you
to find James. So, do you hate me now? I am no better than that
fiancé who hurt you. What he did still haunts you. It hurt you.
I know you cannot forgive him. And I know I deserve the same
fate."

"I—"

"No woman can say she will forget that a man wanted to kill
her, love. Do not even try."

But Lucy tipped up her chin. "If I had known that you were
a dragon slayer, I would have been duty-bound to see you dead
also. I have to admit: your harsh words shocked me. Will you
tell me why you changed your mind?"

To his shock, she pressed her hands on his chest, even after
what he had said. She slid them up toward his neck. "Once you
had found James, you did not hurt me. You could have easily
done so." Softly, she added, "I don't think I hate you as much
as you hate yourself."

"Perhaps. But it doesn't change the fact you should hate me."

"Tell me why you changed your mind—about slaying me, I
mean."

She deserved some answer, but he couldn't form the words.
He admired her. He had grown to respect her. To care about
her. But his heart was hammering and he was shaking hard.

Damn, the feeling creeping into his heart was fear. Panic. He had a choice—he could try to claim Lucy, or push her away forever.

He should push her away. Let her go.

But he cupped her face delicately. Closing his eyes, he let her scent guide him—the sweet earthy unique smell of her, tinged with lavender. With his lashes down, Sinjin drank in her quick breaths. It was like tasting salvation. Like seeing dawn after more than a dozen years in the dark. Parting his lips, he kissed her.

18

Together

Lucy closed her eyes and kissed him. Fear, she realized, had been a powerful thing.

Her greatest fear had been to trust a man. She had been afraid to open her heart again to someone who was willing to hurt her. Sinjin had warned her to fear him. He had all but commanded her to hate him.

But she couldn't. She, who had never wanted to trust any man, could not hate the man who was duty-bound to kill her. Why?

Instead of retreating inside, as she had done every time she thought of Allan Ferrars, she pressed her body tight against Sinjin. She wrapped her arms around his strong neck, and responded to his melting kiss as passionately as she could.

He thought she should not forgive him for being willing to do his duty as a slayer. But she understood what had driven him to hunt dragons. He had been so deeply and badly hurt; he had felt so helpless, so guilty and angry. When Mr. Ferrars had attacked her, it had forever changed the way her heart worked. Sinjin was the only man who had touched her heart since.

Sinjin's warm palms cupped her breasts. His full lips pressed kisses down her throat, moving around the taut ribbons of her bonnet to touch sensitive skin. He reached the hollow at the very base and suckled. A throb of pleasure clutched at her quim and she tipped her head back, letting out a sob of need and desire.

Was she mad? She was in the arms of the man she should fear most—but she wasn't afraid of him at all. Now matter how deeply she tried to dredge up uncertainty and doubt, she couldn't. Not when she met his shimmering green eyes, and saw the vulnerability within them.

"Touch me," she urged. "I don't want to think anymore, or worry, or doubt, or try to fear. All I want is to hold you."

"Lucy, you have such a beautiful, forgiving heart. It is more than I deserve." But he tweaked her nipples with each forefinger and thumb, and swept away all her thought.

He pulled her against him, which forced his back to the stone wall, and he let out a groan as he buried his mouth in the crook of her neck again. She closed her eyes, savoring his touch. His hands cradled her breasts, fondled them through her bodice in the firm, hungry way she loved. Then his hands were on her back, massaging, while his tongue laved her neck and made her quiver.

Lower and lower, his hands went. His knee came forward, to press through her skirts against the fierce ache between her thighs.

"Yes," she whispered, arching her hips toward him. She shamelessly rubbed the juncture of her legs against his thigh. Pressing and pushing and flooding her mind with dizzying pleasure.

"What did I do to deserve your forgiveness?" He whispered the words in a raw rasp by her ear.

She didn't know. But she tried to find words to explain what she felt. "You showed love. To me. To your nephew. How could I not open my heart to a man who would do that?"

Words were such a dangerous thing. She had never known that. More dangerous than fangs and talons, for they totally exposed a woman's heart.

"You are so good," he murmured. "So noble. So perfect."

Words could also be beautiful and give strength. She had never known that either.

She wanted him. Even though they were outside and only yards away from the bustle of a Mayfair Street. All that existed was this moment. It was as if nothing bad existed: no battles between dragons and dragon slayers, no men with mad delusions of power, no threats to their safety, no fear. Lucy felt as if she had shattered through all the fear and prejudices that should keep a dragon and a dragon slayer apart.

Sinjin's hands curved around her bottom at the same moment she grasped his hips. Joining. It was what she yearned to do. For it would be more than just the collision of their bodies, the desperate search for an orgasm. It would show trust, and caring, and . . . and possibly love?

Deftly, he undid the ribbons of her dark bonnet and licked the length of her neck. Her eyes shut tight, the pressure causing little bursts of light against the dark. Wool was beneath her clutching hands, her fingers coiled and digging in. She was tugging on his trousers hard enough to tear.

He lifted his head, meeting her eyes. Green eyes sparkled, but his gaze looked drugged with desire, and his fingers traced tickling, lazy circles around her nipples. "So perfect," he whispered again. "You are what a damned man like me should never dream of."

He was a large, powerful man—a vampire who had been taught to slay. But it was as if the strength and the coldness had been stripped away, leaving the nine-year-old boy who had lost everything and did not know how to cope with so much pain and grief. She understood. She would have wanted to destroy everything she could.

But how could such a thing be coped with? Lucy slid her hands up under his coat, but it was easy to touch his body, and somehow she had to touch his heart. She had to help him to heal from all the pain. He had never let himself heal.

"Why shouldn't you?" she whispered. "You were damned by what happened to you."

"You leave me speechless, my love. I will have to show how much I adore you a different way."

Never had she dreamed Sinjin would drop to his knees in the dirt in front of her. Slowly he pushed her skirts up, and the mass of fabric tumbled over him again, so she clutched her hems and lifted. Possessively, his hands curved around her hips, pulling her quim toward his questing mouth. His tongue licked over her nether lips, twirling around them in the most intimate way. Then he parted them, stroking her clit. Shivers of pleasure rolled down her spine. He lifted, balancing her on his mouth, and her shoulders fell back against the wall. Vines trailed down the smooth stones, tickling her cheeks.

He began rocking her, so she rode lightly and gently on his face. The roofs of Mayfair mansions towered above her. The night was filled with the sounds of the streets: clopping horses, voices calling from the stables in the mews, chatter and laughter rising from gardens and balconies, the strains of music. It all whirled away from her.

This. This mattered. Being with Sinjin. Being adored.

Moans left her lips. His fingers pressed more deeply into her bottom, holding her to him. She loved this—the exquisitely intense twirl of his tongue around her clit. His hot tongue circled her, making her shiver and quake. Then he flicked it, swiftly . . . such wonderful speed, her mind melted.

With a glorious cry, she climaxed. Her hands clutched, her bottom thrashed in his firm grip, and she gasped and squeaked and wailed as she came. "Sinjin," she cried. "Oh, Sin!"

She whirled through the air, landing back on her feet. She

had barely opened her eyes, when his hands cupped her face, and his mouth, tasting of her, slanted over her lips, claiming them.

"I like that," he murmured. "Having you call me Sin."

"More," Lucy whispered, when he let her snatch a breath. "I want more."

She coiled around him, arms locked around his neck, her leg wrapped around his hips. Sweat tingled beneath her dress. He pushed up her skirts, bunching them at her waist. She giggled giddily at the slap of his erection between his thighs as his trousers dropped.

His eyes, normally silvery green, were alight with desire, burning to an almost white-gold hue. He saw her smile, his lips curving up in answer. The white glint of his fangs lapped his full lower lip.

She reached down, wrapped her hand around his shaft. She wore gloves, but could still feel the heat of him against her palm, the rush and pulse of his blood past her fingertips. It was glorious to hold his cock, to caress it. For each press of her fingers, each stroke, she saw the answer flicker in his gleaming eyes, the dip of his lids, the tightening of his mouth.

Her heart ached over what Sinjin had gone through. To lose his family . . . to have been chased by dragons, fearing for his life, and forced to hide, buried under leaves. To have wanted to go and save his family but be unable to . . . it was awful. Who of her clan could have done such a thing? To exist with mortals, dragons were taught to be peaceful. There were many, though, who used their special strength and power to shift shape for evil purposes.

But what those dragons had done . . .

She pulled a shuddering gasp through her lips. She couldn't think of it. Only him. She must think of Sinjin, of pleasuring him, of easing the pain he had never lost. Squeezing him tightly, she brought her fist up, along the length of his shaft, to the base of the head.

He gave a guttural moan.

Delighted, feeling powerful, Lucy stroked again, savoring his groan of pleasure. The way his shoulders shook. In this, she was strong—strong in a very positive way. Pumping him, she giggled as he cried out. He shouted in pleasure until horses whinnied and raucous male laughter came from down the misty mews, then a man's voice called, "Blast the fog. Can't see a thing. Must be a bloke 'aving a poke of a tart out there."

A tart. She blushed, but Sinjin leaned his head beside hers, his forehead pressed to the cool stone behind her, and murmured, "I'd better keep my mouth shut, love. We have to be quiet. But you steal all my control." Gently, he brushed his lips along her neck. "I always felt like there was ice inside me. But you warm me. You make the ice melt."

Another suckle to the base of her throat, a lush, delicious caress. "You make me melt, Lucy."

A whisk of fabric and his hands were under her skirts. She'd released his cock, to grasp his hips and steady herself. The rigid length slapped the juncture of her thighs lightly, making her gasp.

She still held her skirts and he drew her to him. "Put your leg over my hip, love."

Lucy did as he asked. He cupped her bare thigh, holding her. The position opened her quim to him, spreading her lips wide, letting him slide in to the hilt. He was so long, and he buried deeply inside her. Deeply enough she felt a twinge of agony, pleasurable agony, with each thrust.

"Stop, my love, or I won't last. I want to be inside you. I need to be joined with you."

It was exactly how she felt. She needed to be joined, connected with him. She had to bite her lip to quell moans as he thrust deeply into her. With her hips open to him, he bumped her sensitive clit. And she felt a wonderful, curious, exhilarating tug inside with each stroke of his shaft. He was touching something sensitive.

Something so sensitive . . .

She arched up to him, heard him gruffly say, "Yes. Yes, love, work against me. Pleasure yourself."

She was so sensitive that the orgasm washed over her gently . . . gently at first, then it grew strong, and intense, and her legs shook and she made fists and she let out a fierce moan.

"God, Lucy, love . . ." His head reared back. Through half-closed eyes, she could see his struggle: how he fought to stay quiet, as his body quaked in his orgasm, how he bit his lips, fangs drawing a bead of his own blood. Then his lips parted, and he let out a lusty yell of delight.

More male laughter came from down the mews, but she didn't blush. She was watching Sinjin buck with his pleasure, watching the whole journey he took, from his first grimace, to the sudden relaxing of his lips, the sag of his muscles, as his orgasm subsided.

Sweat cooled on her cheeks. He kissed her damp lips, then smiled as he gently tidied her hair, brushing it back from her face. "Now, Lucy, we have to go back to the brothel."

She hesitated. She had tried to show him love, but did sex actually do so? Suddenly Lucy realized it felt so intimate, but was it truly a joining of hearts as well as bodies? She had made love with him, but she didn't know what was really in his heart. And fear pricked hers.

"Are you going to come back here? If you are, you cannot do it alone." Had she done anything to change his mind—to make him want to live and not risk his life so dangerously?

"You are not to follow me again. The prince could be watching the house, waiting for you to come out. I do not want your sisters to go outside either. As for me . . . don't worry, love. I will take care not to be destroyed."

But she did not believe him.

The walk back to the brothel took only minutes. They left the larger, more elegant streets of Mayfair for the ones on the fringes, where rows of new white townhouses gleamed, even in the gloomy fog. Lucy had been unconscious when she had come to the brothel, but she had seen the house, of course, when she had rushed out to follow Sinjin.

He had told her to stay behind. But she hadn't been able to.

When they reached Mrs. Simpson's house, Sinjin rapped on the front door. A doorman pushed aside the wooden cover of the grill, peered at them, then opened the door. Bowing, he bade them to enter.

Jewels flashing at her wrists and throat, the madam hurried toward them. Lines crossed her forehead, and there was such fear in her eyes, Lucy's stomach plunged, as Sinjin rushed to the woman. He laid his hands on her upper arms, his face sheet-white. "Is it James?"

"He is now awake," the madam murmured. "But there is something wrong—"

Sinjin released Mrs. Simpson so fiercely she stumbled back. He ran for the stairs. Lifting her skirts, Lucy raced after him. Her disordered hair bounced in her eyes and her bonnet slid back. She grasped the banister and propelled herself up two steps at a time.

He left her behind, rushing down the hallway. She could never hope to catch up to him, so despite the urge to run as fast as she could after him anyway, she waited for Mrs. Simpson. The madam was panting hard as she hurried up the stairs and she stopped at the landing, her hand to her large bosom.

"What is wrong with James?" Lucy asked.

"He is not speaking once more. He has awoken but he will not move. He will not eat. And he is cold again, even though the fire is roaring in the grate. I do not know what is wrong. He must be ill. Do you think he is?" Mrs. Simpson bit at her fingernail, despite the fact she wore gloves.

But he had gotten better when she had been with him. What had happened? Was he ill? "I don't know," Lucy whispered.

She whirled, to go to Sinjin, but she saw he had stopped outside of the room. He hung his head, then slammed his fist against the wall. His body shuddered and she came up to him. She rested her hand on the small of his back.

"It is all right," she murmured. "We will face this together, but I think James must be scared. He needs our love, our help, and he will get better."

Sinjin swallowed hard. Lucy saw his hand shake as he clasped the doorknob. He pushed the door wide. He was frozen in place, and she darted around him.

The boy lay in the bed, motionless, just the way he had been earlier and the way he had been when she had first seen him at her Dartmoor home. Lucy knelt in front of James and she clasped both of his hands in hers.

She lifted his hand and gave it a kiss. Then she turned over his palm and licked it, which tickled madly, she knew. But he gave no response. His eyes were open, but glassy and blank. She wriggled her fingers into his underarms, but this time, tickling him did not provoke any response.

Panic rose like a torrent. What should she do? What was wrong? Should she shake him? Try to snap him out of this strange trance?

Instead she gathered him into her arms and embraced him tightly. Surely she could break through this. Cradling his small body against her, she rubbed his arms, trying to warm him. "James? James, it is Lucy."

There had to be some way—

What did her sisters used to do to make her laugh when she refused to? Memories came—of her trying to be responsible and keep order, and her sisters running about, defying her and wildly giggling.

She picked up his hand and blew into the palm. A loud, rude bellow resounded in the room. She caught Sinjin's eye—he was staring at her as though she were mad. But James . . . a smile flickered at his lips.

"Aha," she said, with cheer that was false but hopefully convincing. "You are teasing me. You know I am here."

She made more rude sounds—she strung them together to play a tune and finally James began to giggle.

"Lucy, you can work magic with him, thank God," Sinjin said gruffly.

She stroked James's head. "What happened, love?" she asked him softly. "Were you afraid?"

James frowned. "Afraid of what?"

Sinjin approached and knelt beside her. "What happened, James? Why did you not see us or speak to us?"

James stared at him, obviously mystified. "I was sleeping, I think."

But he had not been sleeping. Sinjin bent close to her ear and murmured, "Is this because he is a dragon? Is it something that happens?" He whispered it so quietly, James did not hear.

She shook her head and softly answered, "I don't think so."

But she wanted to ensure James was calm and happy. Lucy settled down, and began to tell James one of the stories her mother used to tell her. In these tales, there were dragons, but they were happy and gentle, and lived in a mythical world. She wrapped her arm around his little waist to keep him secured on her lap, and she told him about dragon heroes who could fly around the world.

Finally, James leapt off her lap and ran around his bedroom, his arms outstretched, pretending to fly.

Lucy laughed, but her heart felt heavy. "Come, little scamp. It is very late at night and you should be in bed." Even as she spoke cheerfully, and hustled James into his bed, where she pulled up the covers, she wished she could understand what kept happening to James.

Her heart gave a savage twist as Sinjin bent and kissed his nephew on the forehead, then whispered, "Sweet dreams, little one."

Now she had to ensure Sinjin did not go out alone, into danger.

Lucy was settled on his lap in a wing chair in his bed-chamber—this way he was pinned to the chair, and he could not get up, go out, and put his life at risk. His hand rested on her back, drawing her into a kiss.

She could not ask him if he could forgive dragons and put his awful past behind him. How could he? Even though she knew that dragons who had attacked slayers in vengeance had never felt any less loss or pain, she knew she had no right to ask Sinjin to forgive her kind for what those dragons had done. And even though he kissed her and gently stroked her back, she felt the distance in him. His lids were lowered, his eyes focused beyond her head. He was kissing her, but not looking at her. His thoughts were obviously elsewhere.

Was he thinking about the past and remembering how much he had lost? Or was he thinking about what he planned to do next—attack his prince to protect James and her?

Panic rose as he slid his hands under her bottom and began lifting her rump off his thighs. He was going to put her aside, and go. Lucy knew it.

She tightened the grip of her arms around his neck. "Don't go."

"I wish I could pretend I have a choice. I don't. This is the only way to ensure you and James are safe."

"But will it? Won't another slayer come in pursuit of us?"

His face was hard, as though chiseled from rock. "If I can destroy the prince, I promise you, no slayer would cross me again. And if I can destroy him, the other slayers will be too busy fighting each other for power to come for you or James."

She swallowed. She knew what his first statement meant. It must mean his prince was almost impossible to kill. Destroying such a man—a vampire, demon, whatever he was—would put fear in the hearts of all the others.

She couldn't let him go. She would probably never see him again.

That thought turned Lucy's blood to sluggish ice. She stroked her fingers up the corded lines of his throat. Her heart stuttered as she felt the slow thump of his heartbeat. How could she let him go? And lose him? She *couldn't* do it. Tears burned in her eyes. Trying to stop them before she dissolved into a blubbering mess, she laid her head against his shoulder. "I can't bear to let you go and die. I couldn't stand living without you."

There. That was the truth. She had known him for mere days, and on the very first night she had gone to his house she had been determined to dislike him, but now she could not imagine being without him.

She suddenly felt a spurt of anger. "You have been wounded your entire life by the pain of losing people you loved. Do you wish to make James suffer the same agony? If you are killed, he will have lost all of his family! Do you want to make me suffer? If I lose you, it will hurt me for as long as I live."

"You would get over me," he said gruffly. "It is not as if I am your family. You barely know me. Believe me, the more you grow to know me, the less you will like me."

"You want me to think that, but I can't."

How did she keep him with her? Was there a way she could keep him until dawn? Sinjin would not be able to leave then. . . .

Suddenly, she knew a way to stall for time.

"Would you make love to me once more?" Lucy whispered. "In case you do not come back." She must tempt him to stay with her at least a little longer, while she thought up a plan. With her family, she had always taken care of things. She must do so now—she must think up a plan, she must take charge—to save Sinjin. "I—I want to see what a brothel is like. I want to see what fascinates men so much about such places. But I don't want to go alone. Will you show me?"

Sinjin groaned and tipped his head back. "You want me to give you a guided tour of a brothel?"

Lucy smiled. "Exactly."

Lucy hadn't expected to hear music—to hear the lively tune of a country dance joyously played on a pianoforte. This was a brothel . . . surely gentlemen did not come here to dance? But as she reached the threshold of the ballroom, she saw this was like no dancing she had ever seen. There were many things that were exactly as they would be in a *ton* ballroom. Young women with bouncing curls executed the complex steps of a dance. They lightly passed from one elegantly dressed gentleman to another, taking each man's hand, smiling brightly. But they wore only corsets, stockings, and slippers. Their breasts were bare, bouncing above the shelf of their tightly laced corsets. They wore satin corsets—in blazing pinks, scarlet, emerald, and sapphire. Some wore daring black, which made their breasts, bare legs, nude bottoms look like porcelain. And their nipples—they had rouged them so dozens of red tips jiggled and swayed.

It was a mesmerizing sight.

"You look astounded, precious," Sinjin murmured. He had ducked his head to whisper by her ear.

"I thought . . . I was expecting . . . well, more like a . . ." Words failed her.

"An orgy perhaps? Unfettered sexual activity happening everywhere?"

His question gave her a pang of sexual awareness, low in her tummy. "Well . . . yes. I did not think they would be dancing."

"It's intended to entice. To build anticipation." Sinjin flashed a naughty grin. "And I think the women like to dance. Would you care to dance with me?"

She had once tried to be a model of propriety. So no one would suspect she was different from all the other young ladies. So no one would guess she was a shape-shifting dragon who could breathe fire. "Everyone would see me. I would be ruined. . . ." Had people in the brothel seen her already, when she had been brought in? Could she really hope to go back to being who she was—the very normal, staid Lady Lucy Drake?

"In this place, where vampires come for refuge, no one speaks of anything that happens here. That I promise you."

She took a deep breath. It would be a risk. Ever since she had gone to Sinjin's house to offer her body, she had taken one daring risk after another. . . .

She was no longer afraid. Risk did not frighten her anymore. And her toes were tapping within her slipper to the lively music. It had been a very long time since she had danced. When she had decided she would never marry, after Allan had attacked her—since she would not marry a mortal, and she was too afraid to consider marrying a dragon again—she had not danced much. Dancing was part of the game of attracting a husband. She had tended to stand back in the shadows and let other girls dance. Each time she had watched other girls whirl and execute steps up and down the row, she had yearned to be there. How she had missed it. "All right," she whispered.

Sinjin swept a deep bow. As he rose, he reached for her hand. "Then dance with me, Lucy."

* * *

Sinjin took Lucy's hand in his and led her into the set as the next dance began. She took her place in the set between two bare-breasted women, yet he could not stop looking at Lucy.

Before he had met her, he had gone from woman to woman to slake his cravings. Now he knew he would never want anyone but Lucy.

Her black hair looked like lush, soft sable in the glow the candlelight. A blush touched her cheeks with fetching pink. Her mouth was full and beautiful, her eyes flashing with excitement. In her ivory silk dress, she was the most demurely attired woman in the room. But she was enchanting, dazzling. He could not look away from her.

A glow seemed to come from within her. Despite being decently covered, she seemed more sensual, more tempting, than all the other women. As music wrapped around them, he bowed to her and she curtsied gracefully.

He could not believe she really could not bear to lose him. He was her enemy. Eventually, she would come to realize that. She would learn of the dragons he had killed. Some would be her friends, people she cared about.

That damned afternoon when his family had been taken from him . . . he should have died that afternoon. His destruction had just been delayed. It was inevitable that he was going to end up dead.

Now he knew he couldn't live without Lucy. But he couldn't ask her to live with him. How could they have a future together when he was a dragon slayer?

He moved forward and took Lucy's hand, passing by her. Her lips parted as if she wanted to speak, but she didn't. Which was good—his throat was too tight for words.

She had told him James needed him. Unabashedly, she had used his nephew to play on his guilt. He watched her dance as he moved mechanically through the steps. He saw other men watch her. Despite naked breasts and bottoms displayed for their delight, gentlemen stole glances at Lucy. She beamed with such delight as she danced. She displayed natural grace, natural beauty, and she looked so lovely yet ladylike it obviously enticed men.

Possessiveness surged through him.

He knew what was going to happen as the dancing ended. He intended to ensure Lucy did it with no one but him.

He was going to miss her. And James. It was going to hurt James if he didn't come back. But it would free the boy from danger. Wasn't that more important?

Sinjin knew he would never be able to kill the prince if he tried to do it and survive the fight. But if he went in willing to sacrifice himself . . .

His sire would never suspect he was willing to die. It might give him the advantage he needed. If he was going to be destroyed, he was going to damn well take the prince with him.

The music stopped. Suddenly, in the midst of the dance. Lucy came to a halt, staring in confusion around her. Everyone else knew what to do, of course.

Sinjin pushed through the other dancers to reach her. He got to her side just as a hopeful gentleman lifted her hand for a kiss.

Sinjin pulled her hand free of the bloke's grasp. "The lady is not available," he warned.

With a shrug, the man turned, and claimed a pretty redhead in a green corset. The brothel's client pulled the wench tight against him, squashing her large breasts, and kissed her.

Sinjin backed Lucy to the fringe of the crowd on the dance floor. He wrapped his arms around her and pulled her back against his body. He cupped her breasts, nuzzled her earlobe, and listened to the shocked squeaks Lucy made as she looked around her.

A couple beside them . . . the gentleman was nibbling the nipples of his partner. Not sucking, he was lightly scraping with his teeth, and the woman was writhing in pleasure in his embrace. Some gents had dropped to their knees to lick and devour the cunnies of their partners. Others had leaned against walls and columns and were already thrusting vigorously.

Lucy gasped. "It is an orgy after all!"

"It becomes one. It is the special event of the week. One you are not going to take part in."

"No, I wasn't—" But her voice died away.

Behind him, Sinjin heard one young girl's voice gasp, "Oh goodness!" Another girl giggled. Lucy pushed his arms away and whirled around.

"Helena! Beatrix! You must go upstairs at once!" Lucy's expression was of shock and outrage. She wagged her finger at her sisters.

Sinjin laughed. "Here, love. Let's shoo your sisters upstairs. This is not for them."

Her pretty sisters wore bright red flushes. Lucy strode to them, turned them with her hands on their shoulders, and marched them out of the ballroom.

He had to smile at her motherly behavior. She herded her sisters out through the doors, and he followed the three of them upstairs.

As she ensured the girls were in their bedrooms, he retreated. Ready to leave.

But a soft, aching voice stopped him. "Please don't go."

He turned to face Lucy. She held her hands out to him. "Please don't go yet," she whispered. "I want to make love to you . . . one more time."

He should go. It was late—past two o'clock in the morning. But he knew she had meant to say "one last time." Christ, tears sparkled in her eyes.

One last time. That was what it would have to be. And he couldn't say no.

19

Tied Up

"Champagne, my love?"

Lucy blinked. The bedchamber in which she stood was pitch-black. Warmth filled the room, but the fire was not lit now. Darkness was like a velvety blanket around her. Sinjin moved with ease through it, since he could see in the dark. The room did not belong to either of them. When Sinjin had agreed to make love with her, he had brought her here.

Something gave a soft *pop*, followed by a fizzy hiss. It must be the champagne. It made a sloshing sound as it hit the glass.

On instinct, she opened her eyes wide, but of course it made no difference. "I wish I could see in the dark as you can." She had her arms crossed over her chest, and she turned in a circle, too nervous to move so she didn't walk into something. Despite the cozy temperature of the room, she felt cold—cold with nerves, with apprehension, with the fear that if she did not act quickly she would lose Sinjin forever.

"Sorry, love. I should have been more thoughtful."

A sulphur smell touched her nose, then a small light flared. Illuminated by the tiny flame, Sinjin touched it to the wicks of several candles. Slowly, the room filled with soft light.

Lucy bit her lip. She had to do something that would keep him with her, but she didn't know what. She rubbed her arms as he returned to the bottle of champagne. He poured a tall flute of the ivory-gold liquid and brought it to her. She took it and lifted it to her lips. She took a sip, then giggled nervously. Holding the flute, she walked around the room. What could she do . . . ?

She passed a wall on which velvet ropes hung.

Now she knew. Exactly what to do to prevent him from leaving.

She was adorable. Sinjin swallowed hard as Lucy drained her champagne. She gave an endearing little hiccup. Coyly, she sashayed up to the wall. He loved the gentle sway of her hips, enhanced by the rippling movement of her ivory skirts. Curls of silky black hair bounced against her neck.

Lucy plucked a length of black velvet rope from the wall.

Teasingly, he asked, "Do you want me to tie you up?"

She faced him, a frank and open expression on her face. "What if I want to tie *you* up again?"

He blinked, instantly aroused. He could picture her doing it once more—straddling him on the bed, and tying him to the bedposts, leaving him vulnerable to whatever she decided to do to him. He hoped it involved naughty things with her fingers and her lips and her sweet pink tongue.

He brought the champagne bottle and refilled her glass. Her gaze captured his, and it was magic. He had been given eternal life, but this moment was the most magical thing he'd ever experienced. "I am yours to command." Strange, how hard it was to speak. "Do as you will, love."

He didn't touch the champagne, but he felt as though he was intoxicated, just by watching her lift the glass to her lips. She drained it in one drop.

"You, love, are going to be drunk."

Indeed, she wove a bit as she came right up to him, her body moving unsteadily. A silly smile played on her lips. With her right hand, she pulled pins from her hair. A river of black silk poured down, falling over her shoulders, tumbling down her back. He plucked the glass from her hand and put it aside.

Lifting her hands, she planted them on his chest. He let her push him to the bed. It was a different room, and the bed was a large circular concoction, with an enormous canopy and mounds of pillows.

This one last time was going to be beyond his wildest dreams.

The bed bumped the backs of his legs and she gave him a firm shove. He let her knock him over and fell on his back on the bed.

"Have to undress you," she said, her words slurring a little.

"I'll do that, love." He didn't want to waste time—so he could get to the fun as quickly as possible. He was breathing hard. Wanting her. He stripped off his boots and tossed them. Peeled off coat, waistcoat, shirt, then trousers. Damn, but an Englishman's proper dress was a pain in the arse.

Lucy had swayed back over to the ropes, giggling as she examined several more that hung on the wall. He watched as she tapped her lips and cocked her head, apparently making a decision over length, thickness, softness the way most ladies would assess their ribbons and lace. She draped several over her arm, nodding with satisfaction.

He was overwhelmed by emotion. By the sweetness of the way she studied the ropes. By the delightful surprise of discovering how wanton she could be. By the eroticism of the moment. By his hunger to spend the rest of his life with her. He, who had needed to provoke emotion, was swamped by it.

Sinjin swallowed hard as she returned to him and commanded, in husky tones, "Lift your arms over your head." As he did, stretching out his body, her gaze raked over him. She seemed to be savoring the view, and she slowly ran her tongue over her lush lips.

Lifting her skirts, she clambered onto the edge of the bed at his side. Her bosom strained at the lace-trimmed scoop of her bodice. Her skirts flowed demurely over her hips and legs. Candlelight caressed her face. She was a devastating mixture of angel and temptress.

Then she leaned over him, lowering her breasts close to his face, and she tied his wrists together. His cock bucked, his balls tightened, and he almost came as she looped the rope and made a snug knot.

It took every ounce of his control to stay his climax. He took deep, ragged breaths and she diligently threaded a second rope through a ring in the headboard and proceeded to secure that to the rope holding his bound wrists.

There was something alluring about being bound and at the mercy of a beautiful woman. Or was it simply that he enjoyed being at the mercy of Lucy, whom he trusted and adored?

"Love, I can't help you take your dress off now," he murmured.

"Oh dear, I suppose you cannot. What should I do? I shall have to summon a maid."

She would not do that. Not with him bound to the bed—

He was wrong. She slid off the bed, marched to the bell pull, and rang. When the young maid arrived at the bedchamber door, Lucy led the young woman into a dressing room off the bedchamber, but not before the young woman had seen him. Her eyes had been as large as saucers.

He was left on the bed for many, many minutes. But he could hear every aspect of Lucy undressing. The whisper of silk as her dress was removed. He heard the maid tell Lucy she was going to undo the laces of the corset. He heard the soft swish as petticoats fell. He heard Lucy announce she wanted to wear only her robe and nothing more.

Sinjin gazed down at his cock. It had bounced up and down at every word as if nodding its approval, as blood had surged into it and his groin had tightened. His ballocks were pulled up tight, his cock aching with each pulse of blood.

There was no way he was leaving now. He was in an agony of lust and hungering for satisfaction. He let his hands fall back on the bed. His hips were moving of their own accord, his buttocks flexing, wanting to pump against Lucy, wanting to shove his cock deep inside her.

Then she returned. Naked. Her loose hair flowed over her shoulders and shielded her bare breasts. Hard dark nipples peeped at him between the silky strands. Lucy looked beautiful, wanton, primal, standing there.

Then she brought her hands forward from behind her back and she revealed the lengths of rope. "Now I shall secure your ankles," she said saucily.

Lucy had to admit: Sinjin looked so sensual and tempting and delectable all tied up. She felt a bit guilty as this seemed very naughty, but Lucy also could not resist sitting back and admiring her handiwork when she had his legs spread and his ankles secured to the bedposts by the velvet ropes. His arms were stretched over his head. He obviously enjoyed it—he was rock-hard.

She was wet and creamy with anticipation. Her womb ached with wanting him, and she could feel how damp she was between her thighs.

As she had sat back and surveyed how Sinjin looked tied up, she had yearned to stroke between her legs, to touch her clit, because she knew one light touch would make her come.

But she wanted to share the orgasm. She climbed on top of

him, straddling his thighs. Slowly, she lifted his rigid shaft. It was incredibly thick and hard, almost like iron, and obviously a sign he was very, very aroused. With a soft, graceful stroke, she ran her hand down the shaft, then back up, where she cupped the head. His juices bubbled up, wetting her hand, making her hand slick so she could play with him.

But he begged her to stop. "I won't last, love."

She lifted, bracing one leg straight and she stroked the swollen head to her wet nether lips. Then she took him instead. Deep inside, all the way inside, in one stroke, until she collided with the firm planes of his groin. Oh God. She moaned fiercely.

Then, planting her hands on his chest, she rode him.

In three wild strokes, she came. In an explosion of cries, and moans, and bursting lights, and squeals, and gasps. Her head lolled back and forth. Pleasure crested in her, and she slumped forward on him.

He drove into her twice more, then his hips jerked up so hard they lifted her off the bed. He growled and roared and thrashed against the ropes that bound him as he came.

When his orgasm stopped and Sinjin fell back, Lucy let her body collapse over his, while she gathered strength for another bout. After that . . . and surely after several more orgasms he would not ever want to go.

His body sensed dawn approaching. Weakness worked at his arms and legs. Sinjin felt his muscles grow tired, his arms sagging against the ropes that held him. Dawn was coming and it was draining his strength.

Tossing back her tangled hair, Lucy sank back on her haunches. She splayed her hands on his abdomen and sucked in deep breaths. "Oh heavens," she whispered.

Smiling, Sinjin watched her try to regain her senses from her orgasm—her third since she had tied him up. He wanted more, he wanted to savor this, but he had to hope she finished soon and undid his bonds. An hour or two was all he had left.

Then she arched back, made a sound of pleasure, and ran her hands over her bare breasts, caressing herself.

God, he had to fight not to grow hard again. "All right, Lucy," he urged, huskily, "untie me."

She dipped her head, then lay on top of him, pressing her cheek to his chest. "No."

"No? Lucy, hell, do it right now."

"I won't. I won't let you go and be killed. We must think of a plan. We can do this together. It will be dawn soon and then you cannot go."

Sinjin let his head fall back on the bed, shutting his eyes. The poor sweet love. Her ropes would not hold him, no matter how tightly she believed she had bound him. Now she was sprawled on top of him, apparently hoping she could keep him pinned to the bed.

Did she really care about him so much? How could she?

But there was no point in arguing with the woman. He knew exactly what to do. He had to exhaust her with pleasure, until she fell asleep, and then he would deal with her.

There, she had done it.

He was tied to the bed—very well tied, Lucy thought. There was no way Sinjin could get free. She was lying on top of him, also trapping him. If he tried to escape, she would know. She had lied to him, but she had no other choice.

She refused to lose him. She had intended to stay awake all night, but after so much sex, so much pleasure, she was yawning. She would just shut her eyes for a moment. . . .

But the next thing she knew, she was opening her eyes to daylight.

And she was alone in the bed.

20

Pursuit

The first thing Lucy did was hasten to Sinjin's bedroom and ensure he had fallen into his day sleep. He had left her a note, a few brief lines.

You exhausted me, love, and I needed to seek darkness to rest. You were right. I cannot leave you.

From the doorway to his bedchamber, she saw him sleeping. He did it motionlessly. But he did not respond to her when she had whispered his name. And he could not go outside now, not now that it was daylight.

She had won. She'd managed to protect him.

Satisfied, Lucy closed the door and she went to James's bedroom. He was awake and he looked happy. He held out his arms to hug her when she went into his room.

Touched, she had hugged him back. Tears leaked from her eyes, but she quickly brushed them away. Then she helped him dress.

Coaxing him to eat breakfast proved difficult. One of the maids had delivered an assortment of gleaming covered dishes. Tempting scents drifted into the air but James did not want to eat at first. She lured him with ham and eggs, and finally he began to devour the food eagerly.

He burped, giggling after he did, then looked longingly at the window. Sunshine streamed in, and it was promised spring warmth. "Could I go outside, Lucy?"

Hope shone in his large green eyes. But to go outdoors would not be safe. She shook her head. "I'm sorry, James, but we should stay inside."

His lower lip protruded, and she tried to reassure him. "We will make lots of fun inside today. I promise."

To keep her word, she spent the morning playing with him in the upper rooms of the brothel, the rooms reserved for them. Surprisingly, there had been a room in the attic with toys stored in a large trunk. She did not know what was happening down below in the house, but it was quiet. Last night she had extracted a promise from Helena and Beatrix that they would never go exploring in the brothel again. The madam, Mrs. Simpson, seemed to be working to keep James and Lucy's sisters separated from the scandalous business of the brothel.

Sunlight spilled in through the window of the attic room. Skirts tucked beneath her, Lucy sat on the carpet and watched James play.

He looked very much like Sinjin when he worked with great seriousness. He patiently stacked his many blocks. He built a castle with soaring towers. A bridge, and a house, and a pile of scattered blocks that he claimed was a battlefield of war. Finally, though, on his third castle, he swept all the blocks down with an angry swipe.

He crossed his arms over his chest and cried, "Want to go outside!"

On her hands and knees, Lucy began to gather the scattered blocks. She had to jockey her skirts out of the way. As she pushed the blocks toward James, she thought of how to explain this. "I am sure you do, sweetheart. But you cannot today." Sinjin had warned her that the prince would be watching the house. "There are bad men outside and your uncle does not want you to leave here, where you might be . . . vulnerable." Bother, this was a wretched way to go about it.

As though she could save him from anything.

The boy's faith in her touched her heart. It also was a great responsibility. But she could not take him outside—she could not protect him from a powerful vampire, or from Jack and his lackeys. "Very soon, you will be able to go outside," she said soothingly. It was not quite a lie, but it was not true. If she did not let Sinjin hunt down his prince, would it ever be safe to let James outside? To let him live like a normal young boy?

Perhaps it would never be safe. But even then, she couldn't let Sinjin risk his life. She couldn't let him die, even to give James and her and her sisters safety.

Lucy moved around the room, gathering up fallen toys and setting them up on various chairs in James's bedroom. She was lost in a maelstrom of thought. James was like her—he could never live like a normal boy, could he? She had tried so desperately to be normal, but that was a path that led to loneliness. If James tried to act like a normal boy, he would spend his whole life hiding what he was, as she had tried to do.

He had to, didn't he? There was no other way for a dragon to live. No dragon could be open about what they were. . . .

But she had been frightened of what she was. Ashamed of it. She did not want James to grow up feeling ashamed of being a dragon. Or hating what he was.

What if Sinjin took James away from England? Was there another place in the world where it would be easier for a dragon to survive . . . ?

Bother, some of the blocks had rolled under the armoire. On her hands and knees, Lucy got down as low as she could, and reached. She gathered up two, and stretched her arms, trying to reach two more—

She frowned. In the background, James had been humming. Blocks had clacked together as he'd thrown them around on the floor.

It was now utterly silent.

She scrambled back, and jerked around. A pile of blocks sat in the middle of the carpet. But there was no James sitting beside it. Almost tripping over her heavy skirts, Lucy struggled to her feet. "James?" she called, even as she guessed she would receive no answer. Her heart plunged into her stomach.

"James?" she shouted, sharply. "If you are hiding, I want you to come out at once."

Nothing. The door gave a soft creak, but it was only a breeze giving it a push. "James?" she called again, and her voice was growing shrill. "If you are hiding as a joke, I want you to stop. You are making me frightened."

She rushed around the room. She dropped to her knees to check beneath the bed, praying she would see the blue-eyed scamp grinning at her. But there was nothing underneath.

Swiftly, Lucy searched behind the curtains, and the door, and under the covers of the bed. Her heart pounded in her throat—he wasn't in the room. He must have gone outside. She ran out to the stairs, and almost tumbled down them. Clutching the banister, she steadied herself and started running down the steps again.

Heavens, James had wanted to go outside. Had he decided he wouldn't get permission to go, he would just run out and do it?

She had to stop him.

She raced all the way down to the first floor of the house, clutching her skirts clear of her feet. Where would James go? Surely not out the front door—one of the footmen would have likely caught him. He would go out the back, probably, into the garden.

She reached the kitchens and almost barreled into a young maid. The cook, in the process of chopping up a chicken with a heavy knife, looked up. "Are ye after that lad?" the burly woman demanded. " 'e ran through 'ere just now. Almost knocked over me pies."

Lucy managed a stumbling sentence somewhere between "thank you" and "I'm sorry," and she rushed past the woman, wended her way clumsily around large worktables, past an oven, and between hanging pots. She shoved open a low, narrow door, and flew out into the yard.

Sunlight dazzled her eyes after the darkness of the kitchens. The yard was narrow and long, stretching back to a stone wall that threw a line of shadow over neat gardens. Her heart flip-flopped in her chest. James stood in the shadows, near a wooden gate set in the wall. A brown-haired man stood with him.

"James, come here!" she cried, forgetting it was probably not the wisest thing to do. She ran down a small gravel path toward them.

The man's hand snaked out and grabbed James's wrist, capturing the boy. Then the stranger looked up and glared at her. Shock hit her so hard Lucy stopped on the path.

Blue eyes. Coffee-brown hair. A rugged line of jaw; a straight, perfect nose; long eyelashes; and the look of gentlemanly disdain.

Scowling at her, sneering at her, this man looked like Allan Ferrars. Like her former fiancé.

This was guaranteed to destroy him.

Even with his beaver hat pulled low, his collar high, gloves on his hands, and his greatcoat covering him, Sinjin could feel the warmth and power of the sun sapping away his strength.

Each step felt like he was lifting a ton of stones and slamming them to the sidewalk.

He'd come in daylight because his sire would never expect an attack while the sun was up. He wasn't strong, but the prince would also be weak, and that might give him the chance to win.

Lucy would not expect him to leave the house during the day. He knew she had come to his room to ensure he was sleeping. Once she saw him, she had left the room, and he had then forced himself up, and had left the house. This was the best way to sneak out without her catching him.

A grin tried to tug at his mouth, but even the muscles of his face were too exhausted to work. He was behaving like a disobedient gentleman trying to sneak out on his wife.

Wife. When he thought of marrying Lucy, of spending the rest of his life with her . . . hell, it was a sweet dream, but an impossible one.

When he had first left the house, he had gone to Charing Cross Road, to a bookstore owned by the vampire historian Guidon. There he had learned several interesting things. He had learned about Lucy—and why the prince was determined to have her.

Swinging a walking stick, Sinjin forced his heavy legs to move to the house as though he was a gentleman paying an afternoon call.

His prince's house was only a block away, but suddenly, in the depths of his heart, he felt a stabbing pain. Fear raced through him—the same ice-cold, terrifying horror he'd known when he'd lost his brother. It rooted him to the sidewalk.

He could hear her roars—they were a dragon's sounds of fury and hatred, but they were also Lucy's. How he could hear them from so far away, he didn't know. How he knew they were her roars he didn't know. But it was like a voice in his head, telling him to get to her. To help Lucy. Save her. Fighting for strength, he spun in the street and forced his numb, shaking legs to run.

It *couldn't* be Allan Ferrars. He had died. Lucy was certain of it. She had seen her brother attack him and she'd heard her fiancé's howls of pain as Jack had lashed into him with his claws. She had seen Allan's large dragon body collapse to the ground. He had lain there, unmoving, and his eyes had been open and blank.

She had been shaking with shock and horror, and sobbing with tears blurring her eyes, but she knew what she had seen. Jack had tried to pull her away, but she had gone to Mr. Ferrars and she had seen him change back into human form. Her brother's arms had wrapped around her waist, stopping her before she could touch the man who had betrayed her, and Jack had hauled her swiftly away for her safety. But she had been *sure* Allan Ferrars was dead.

Father had told her he was. Father had told her Mr. Ferrars would never bother her again.

"Wh-who are you?" she cried at the man, cursing the tremble of her voice. "Let the child go."

"But he is not a child, is he?" the man responded, his lips curving into a mocking smile. Heavens, it looked so much like Allan Ferrars's smile, Lucy felt as though she had been hit in the stomach.

"The boy is a dragon." The man waved his hand and murmured something to James. The boy gazed up at this eerie man, as though held under a spell.

James's body began to jerk and stretch and change. Fear turned the boy's face pale and he whispered in terror, "No. It hurts—no!"

She ran forward. "Stop this! It is too hard on his body and it is hurting him. You must stop it."

James let a shriek of terror, a yell of pure pain. "Uncle," he sobbed. "Help me. Lucy . . . Lucy, make it stop. Please."

She reached the man who held James. She stared into his gloating face, not caring if it was Allan—if he actually wasn't dead, or he had become a demon or a ghost that had returned. She didn't care. Shoving his arm, she tried to break his grip on James. But he laughed. A low, amused, tired laugh. Then he swung at her, and his open palm slammed into her cheek so hard it drove her to her knees.

Pressing her hand to her stinging cheek, Lucy got up on her haunches. Wings sprouted from James's back, large blank and green wings, unusually wide for such a small body. His clothes had been torn by his change, and pieces of white cloth fluttered over the lawn. Scales were appearing over his body as it changed to dragon shape—as a tail grew and his arms became smaller, his face took on the shape of a muzzle.

He was screaming.

Lucy pulled up to her feet, and ran at the man again.

This time he threw her, and she tumbled like a rolling log across the grass and into a garden. Her body bashed against gravel and stones, and prickly twigs snagged at her skin. She dug her fingers into the earth to stop her, and got up painfully.

She had to stop him.

She hadn't been able to fight Allan Ferrars, who looked exactly like this man.

It didn't matter—she had to try. She understood Sinjin, understood why he was willing to face his prince alone, even though he knew it would be hopeless: to protect James, she had to be willing to die trying.

Lucy bit down on her lip and summoned her transformation into dragon form. The moments it took to do it were excruciating, and it felt as if it were taking forever. Her clothes seemed to explode off her body as her shape changed. As she grew and grew.

Then it was done.

The blackguard who looked like Allan had transformed, too. He was an enormous black dragon, as dark as coal, as shiny as smooth jet. He clamped his teeth into James's neck and gave a powerful flap of his wings, lifting from the ground.

No. She leapt off the ground and took flight. Lucy threw all her strength into the beat of her wings. She managed to fly over his head, then blew a stream of fire across his back. She had to take care not to hit James. Since the horrible night she had fought for her life against Allan, she had never battled in dragon form.

James beat his wings wildly and struggled, but he could not break free of the grip of the other dragon's jaws.

Lucy breathed another blast of flame, singing the scales on the other dragon's back. Smoke curled up. Suddenly, the dragon whirled and his mouth sent a shot of flame at her.

Thank heaven she had flown that night in the moors. She was able to move agilely, to spin swiftly aside and let the fiery blast go by her. But the heat singed her, and she cried out in pain as it scorched her scales. Flapping her wings, she somersaulted in the air, drawing away from the dragon. She spun back quickly, and she breathed fire again—she put all her strength into the attack. She shot flames at him, then whirled around and slammed her tail into his back.

The male dragon whipped his tail around, and the end of it struck her stomach with so much force, the sharp scales dug into her skin. She let out a roar at the pain. Blood welled.

James was making desperate sounds—a dragon's equivalent to cries of fear. She tried to make sounds to reassure him, the quiet, musical sounds she had heard her mother make. But they were unfamiliar to James and he was shrieking.

She pressed her clawed hand to her wound. Damn—the other dragon would go and she was too wounded to catch him—

No, he was turned back to her. With James caught in his mouth, with his claws extended, he rushed toward her. He wheeled his feet up so the long, razor-sharp claws on his toes were sticking forward. He could rip her apart.

But if she retreated, he could escape with James. She had to engage in a fight. Breathing flame as quickly as she could, Lucy turned to protect her belly and she charged at him. She stopped the fire when she got too close and she tried to aim her claws to take James without hurting him.

The other dragon swooped at her. His claws dug into her back. Pure pain. God, it was unbelievable. She was screaming, roaring . . . falling. . . .

As she spun toward the ground, she saw the black dragon prepare to come at her. To finish her. Desperately, she fought for control, but she still fell heavily into the garden, sinking into the rich earth.

Her body hurt too much for her to take flight again, and she heard the low, hissing sound of victory coming from the black dragon—

"Lucy!"

Sinjin's voice. The sharp tones of it stunned her. She arched her neck to see him racing across the garden. A long sword in his hand glinted in the sunlight. Gripping it with two hands, he leapt into the air and swung the blade so quickly, it became a blur of light.

Light. *Daylight*. What was he doing? He could not be out in the daytime.

The blade caught the black dragon's leg. The dragon shrieked in fury and blood sprayed.

"Give me the boy," Sinjin shouted. "I will let you live if you give me the child."

The dragon hissed, then took James from his muzzle, and clutched the boy in his claws. He shot fire at Sinjin. A blast of flame larger than any she had ever seen. Cursing, Sinjin leapt to the side, rolling out of the way.

Lucy clutched her stomach. Blood leaked between her scaly fingers. Then she saw Sinjin's face as he got to his feet. He was swaying. His face was turning black—it was burning with the rays of the sun. Smoke rose from his cheeks. His skin was angry slashes of glowing red and burnt black.

The sunlight was going to kill him.

The black dragon swooped down to him, wearing a grin on his long mouth. Sinjin lay on the ground, struggling to grasp his sword. Lucy tried to fly, but the pain in her stomach was too great.

Howling with victory, the black dragon dropped James— she managed to pull her body across the ground so she could catch him. The dragon flew at Sinjin. It dove in. Then Sinjin leapt to his feet and swung his sword. It should have taken off the beast's head, but the dragon slid to the right and the sword took off its foot.

It spun, losing blood, then rushed at her. She tried to hold on to James's small dragon form, but the bigger dragon hit her with his tail, driving her down, then grabbed James. It flew upward.

"Lucy! Lucy, are you all right?"

Arms came around her. She tried to struggle up. She couldn't speak, only make a low moaning sound. Sinjin's face—it was so horribly burned . . . but he lifted his wrist to his mouth. She waved her clawed paw at him, trying to send him inside. They had to get James, but Sinjin was going to die.

His fangs came out, and he drove them into his wrist. Blood leaked out. He pushed his wrist against her mouth. She tasted the coppery fluid. Panicked, sick from the thought of drinking blood, she tried to struggle away, but she was cold now and her body was numb.

"Drink, Lucy. Please. Drink and survive."

She did. With her tongue, she lapped up his blood. Then he moved his wrist away. Warmth flooded through her. The pain eased in her stomach, and a tingling sensation spread through. Through her dragon eyes she gazed down. The wound was knitting itself together, slowly disappearing.

She was healed.

She knew what she must do.

Beating her wings hard, she rose off the ground.

"Lucy, no! Lucy, don't—"

She ignored Sinjin's shout and she flew out of the garden, into the brilliant sky. Far ahead of her, she saw a dark spot in the air. It must be the black dragon and James. She didn't care how strong this dragon was, she was going to rescue the boy. Sinjin was probably dying, he had been so badly hurt, but if she let herself think about that, she would panic or burst into tears.

James needed her to keep her head.

The other dragon—the one who looked like Allan Ferrars— had bigger wings, but she flapped hers wildly. Her dragon body ached with the pain of trying to beat her wings as hard and quickly as she could. Her lungs burned with the exertion. Even in dragon form, she was showing what happened to ladies— with their restrained living, their bodies fell apart. She had tried for so long to act like a proper normal lady, she had lost all her strength.

The black dragon turned in the sky, heading toward the lush green of Hyde Park. Lucy followed, amazed to see she was closing the distance. At least, she thought she was. She rose above the park. They soared so high, they looked perhaps like birds to the people below. Below the Serpentine snaked through the park, the rippling water glittering in the sunlight.

Suddenly a searing pain shot through her wing. Twisting to the side, she saw a thin dark shape hurtling through the air as she felt the delicate membranes tear apart. Her wing pulled inward as she reacted to the pain. She lost her balance in the air. Spinning.

An arrow had been shot through her wing. Crippled, she couldn't control her fall. But then a force grabbed her—something unseen that slowed her plunge and brought her down slowly toward the trees that dotted the park. She landed with a thump on soft grass between two trees. The shock made her lose control of her shifted body. Pain rushed over her as her body twisted and writhed and she transformed back into human form.

She was naked. In Hyde Park. In the distance, she heard shouting voices. People had seen her fall. They might come to investigate, and she had no clothes on. Nor could she change back into dragon form. Her wing would not have healed. So she was going to lose James as well.

Tears of fury pricked. She got to her feet, too sore and pained to move quickly. Footsteps made her turn in panic. A gentleman was running toward her—an elegantly dressed one. Remarkably, his beaver hat stayed on his head as his long legs swallowed up the ground. She tried to cover her breasts and privates, then turned and ran for a tree. Why did there have to be one man who could run so fast?

The footsteps behind her sped up.

She was running like wild, naked. Where could she go? She couldn't run out of the park.

Out of the corner of her eye, she could see he almost was upon her. Suddenly he reached out and grabbed a hank of her hair. He yanked her back, winding its thickness around his wrist. "Now I have you, my dear. Finally."

Lucy twisted, staring into bright silver eyes. They were almost blinding.

"Who are you?"

A white-blond brow arched up. "I suspect you know, my

dear. Do not worry, Lady Lucy Drake, your dragon slayer will come for you." His hand cupped her neck, then slid down, nearing her breast. "I know he will. I have known Sinjin for a long time."

"No!" She shoved his hand away. She tried to pull away, but he had her clamped by her hair. She knew who he was—Sinjin's prince, the leader of the dragon slayers.

He was going to kill her.

"Not yet," he said, as though he had seen her thoughts. "I have no intention of killing you now. Not when I know Sinjin will come to save you. But he will fail—he won't free you and he won't survive. It will please me first to take something he wants so very badly."

"What?"

"You."

21

Poisoned

In the prince's grasp, Lucy tried to change shape. She closed her eyes and willed her body to shift into a dragon form. Even with a broken wing, she could fight better as a dragon, with far more weapons: claws, fire, and a powerful tail—

"No, you don't, my dear."

The prince's right hand suddenly clamped around her neck. She felt pressure, as if he was choking her and as she struggled for breath, something cold and hard gripped her neck. It made a soft click, and then he moved his hand away. He kept her hair twined around his other wrist, using it like a leash to bind her to him. She sucked in a deep breath and looked down. But all she could see were her naked breasts and her stomach. She could not see the thing around her neck, but she could feel it digging into her flesh. Grasping it, she tried to pull it off. It suddenly grew as hot as fire and sizzled against her hands, burning her fingertips, and she had to release it, hissing in pain. She had felt something that was flat and shaped like a large, wide ring.

"A collar," the prince informed her, in cold, hard tones. "It will prevent you from shifting shape and escaping me. This will make you more obedient."

With his hand in her hair, he wrenched her head to the side. Her neck muscles pulled in protest and the hot necklace at her neck gouged into her skin. She tried again to shift shape but she couldn't. With no other way to fight, she kicked at him. Wildly, she slammed her feet against him. But he wore a gentleman's boots, and all she got were sore, bruised toes.

"Feisty," he murmured, jerking her head even more to the side, until she feared he would break her neck. "A fiery dragon. I can see why Sinjin was willing to give up so much for you."

He touched his mouth to her neck.

"Oh no, you will not!" Lucy cried. She struggled, willing to lose her hair to his hands if she could get free. But her stupid hair would not give. She kicked. She screamed. What did it matter if all the *ton* came running across Hyde Park and saw her naked? She would be saved—

"Shut up," the prince barked. Then he lunged forward and bit her neck. The pricks of his teeth were like two fierce burns. God, it was nothing like when Sinjin bit her. This hurt. And she could feel her blood rushing to his mouth.

Dear God.

Dimly, she wondered how he could be out in the sunlight. How was this vampire not burned, as Sinjin had been? *Sinjin.* Was he alive or had he died of the wounds to his face?

Her blood was rushing out of her. Suddenly, her legs gave out and she sagged into the blackguard's arms. He was going to kill her. He was going to take all her blood and she was going to die here, with grass whispering around her and the sun beating down on her—

"Enough," he growled. "That will be enough to keep your feisty nature subdued."

The prince, the hateful, evil monster, swept her into his

arms. Then suddenly he changed shape. He grew wings and his body turned black, like a large bat. A whirling light whipped around them. A sparkling white light.

"No one will see us. But do not fret. Sinjin will know where you are. He will sense you, he will track you, he will come to you."

Would he? Her heart felt ready to explode in despair. Or was he already dead?

He strode into Guidon's bookstore. He had not even bothered to let Guidon open the door, he had shoved it so hard, he almost tore it off its hinges.

"I need to find her," he barked. "I need to find Lucy. Guidon," he shouted, "where in blazes would the prince have taken her?"

The troll-like librarian came out from between two stacks of books. His thin yellowish-gray hair stuck straight up from his head, as though he had run his fingers through it. The vampire librarian was tiny, with a curved spine, but knew everything there was to know about vampires, dragons, and other shifters in London.

"He has taken Lucy," Sinjin roared. He slammed his fist into the end of a wooden shelf. "Where would he take her?"

"If she is not at his official London residence, then he might have taken her to a house he rents on Curzon Street. That is the only other home I know of that he would use."

"Curzon Street. Thank you." He turned.

"Wait one moment, my lord," Guidon called. "I have discovered there is another being who also wants her. Another dragon. His name is Lionel Ferrars."

Ferrars? That was the surname of her fiancé.

"Tell me about him," Sinjin said coolly. "Make it swift. I have to get to her."

*   *   *

Of course she was still naked when she woke. Nude, chained to a bed, and covered only by a scrap of pink satin sheet. Once she would have died of embarrassment and shame. Now, she was just determined to escape.

Lucy strained her arms as hard as she could, but she only pulled her muscles, made the chains rattle, and gained absolutely nothing toward freedom. The collar was hot and itchy at her neck. If only she could get rid of it, she could shift shape and break the chains in seconds. She shook her head, then her shoulders, but that didn't dislodge the controlling band around her neck. She tried rubbing and banging it against the bed, hoping to break open its clasp.

Again, it didn't work.

From the bed, she could see both the window and the door. She was in a bedchamber, one with ivory walls. The window was shut, but the black curtains were open. A golden-red hue glowed against the pane. The sun was setting. Was Sinjin still alive? Was he aware the sun was going down and it would soon be night, when it was safe for him to come out? Or was he gone—lost to her forever?

What of James? Was he hurt? Had that monster of a dragon hurt him? Who was the dragon-shifter who had taken him— the man who had looked like Allan but who couldn't possibly be Allan?

Bound to the bed, Lucy knew she should plan a way to escape, but her mind continually fell back into the same pattern. Her stomach roiled in agony as she worried if Sinjin was dead. She worried about James. She kept trying to figure out who the black dragon was. Could it be someone *related* to Allan Ferrars? A brother? A cousin?

As time ticked by, she kept forcing her memory to dredge up the face of the man who looked so much like Allan. Were his eyes really exactly the same? The same color? Was the shape of his face an exact match? Or was his jaw heavier, his skin rougher, his nose crooked?

Then she thought of the horrible wounds on Sinjin's face, and her heart thudded and thundered. She couldn't even remember how he had been wounded, only that his face had been a striated mess of black burnt areas and red, oozing welts. It made her sick to think of it. It must have been so painful.

The door rattled. She watched the knob turn, the door swing open. She saw the white-blond hair of the prince, then his elegantly dressed body as he came into the room.

Hatred. Fear. Revulsion. Fury at being powerless. Emotions exploded in her, lending her strength, stoking desperation. She tugged as hard as she could on the chains, praying she could pull them free. That she could win.

He crossed his arms over his chest, watching, and an amused smile played on his cold, ruthlessly perfect face. "Stop," he said, and his voice seemed to echo inside her head. "I have come to unlock you. There is no need to thrash as though you are having a fit. You are to be taken downstairs, where you will wait for your hero to arrive." His lips split in a leering grin.

"I need clothing." Really, given what he intended to do to Sinjin, if Sinjin had survived, it hardly mattered.

But he threw something upon the bed. A slither of dark purple silk. "A robe for you. Now I will unlock you, but I warn you not to try to overpower me. Or try to escape."

Of course she nodded, to show she would behave. As soon as he unlocked both her wrists, she struck at him. She tried to throw all her strength behind the blow. But he caught her fist before it connected with his face.

"Naughty girl. You will be punished later, dragon. After you have done your job and brought Sinjin's heart to me."

But Sinjin might not even be alive. Yet she did not say anything to the prince.

Minutes later, bundled in the silk robe, she was being propelled downstairs. Even after just a few hours of being chained,
her feet were tingling and half-numb and her legs did not want
to move. The prince gripped her arm, forcing her down one
step after another. He directed her down a large corridor, one
with niches filled with statues, and an ornate ceiling. The
painted frescoes showed men battling dragons, and the statues
were all of dragon slayers wielding swords.

"Why do you want to kill all of us?"

The demon stopped, apparently astounded by her question.
In fact, she had never intended to ask it out loud. It had been a
desperate thought in her head and had just slipped out.

He jerked her around to face him. A sneering smile played
on his lips. His expression—it looked like the one Jack had
worn when he confronted Sinjin in Dartmoor.

The prince lifted his hand. She flinched, expecting a slap.
What he did proved far worse. He caressed her cheek, traced
her lips with his fingers. Cold fingers—cold, lifeless, unfeeling.
His touch made her shudder, made her stomach lurch in revulsion. His eerie eyes glittered like black marble.

But her reaction only widened his smile. "Dragons kill mortals, my dear. It is imperative for humans that they are the strong-
est creatures on earth. So they chose to prey on the more
powerful animals to destroy them: the great cats, bears, wolves
. . . and dragons. Humans kill what they fear. They want to
eradicate the things that can kill them. They are a lazy species,
and for them it is easier to decimate an entire type of animal
than it is to be constantly vigilant."

His index finger stroked her lip, tugging at it. She tried to remain impassive, for she guessed he wanted a reaction. The way
Jack used to when he would tease her. "You are not human,"
she said coldly. "You are a demon."

"I am no different from Sinjin. Do you consider him a soulless monster as well?"

He was goading her, she was sure. "That is not true—you are very different from Sinjin. You are heartless."

"Indeed? As a young man, I was indentured to serve for eternity as a dragon slayer. I did it because dragons killed my family. Just as your kind destroyed Sinjin's family."

He wanted to hurt her—he was using those words like a knife, jabbing them into her heart and twisting them.

"But I do not know which dragons did those terrible things," she said. "I certainly did not do it. I think it is awful. Why should I die because of the actions of some other, brutal dragons?"

"Dragons kill slayers. They do not stop to question the morality of their prey. They just kill."

"Most dragons don't kill that way!" she cried. "Of course dragons attack dragon slayers. They do it to save their lives. Just as you would kill a dragon to save your life. Do you not see? It is the fear of an attack that drives each side to kill the other. It should just stop! Surely there could be peace."

"Not when both sides are living to mete out revenge." The prince pushed her and continued on down the corridor, his hand at her lower back. "You should be thankful, Lady Lucy. This is what will bring Sinjin to you. His fear that you will die."

But he might be dead. . . .

He shoved her and she stumbled against one of a pair of smooth, glossy black-painted doors. "In this room," the prince said, in a rumbling, accented baritone, "my dragon slayers work off the thrill and heated blood that comes after they have killed a dragon. It is exciting to face such an enormous, dangerous beast, and be the victor. It arouses men incredibly. This is what tempted Sinjin to slay dragons. He got the revenge he craved, and he also received incredible sexual arousal."

Lucy shuddered, but said defiantly, "I do not believe you. I do not believe he ever felt pleasure over what he did."

Suddenly the wall pressed into her back. The prince had propelled her against it. His face hovered in front of her, his lips separated from hers by mere inches. She was trying not to breathe, so she did not smell him—even though he smelled like Sinjin. He smelled of cool crispness. On Sinjin, the scent was alluring. The prince smelled like ice—cold, hard, inhuman.

"Did he tell you what dragons did to his family?" the prince asked.

"Yes," she began, but he spoke over her, hissing, "Each one was destroyed. He lost his mother, his father, his younger brother, two of his sisters. Only he survived. Along with one sister, who was the mother of his beloved James. She was driven to such madness she took her own life."

Tears welled as she thought of how much it must have hurt Sinjin to lose her, and in such a way. It must have made him feel so helpless. No wonder James had been so wounded by grief. He had lost his father, and his mother had not been willing to live for him.

"You can guess at the torment he must feel—caring for you and hating you," the prince went on, like a serpent hissing and spitting venom. "Each time he is with you, he must remember how it felt to be pursued by a dragon. He told me everything. How monstrous and terrifying the dragons looked. How he saw his younger brother be caught and killed."

His words fell on her like blows. What was truly in Sinjin's heart every time he was with her? Was it pain? Did he think of all he had lost when he saw her? He had kissed her and made love to her, he had told her he adored her, but was it the truth? Was he being honest about what he truly felt? The prince's words were what she feared—that she would constantly re-mind Sinjin of all he had lost.

"His mother begged for the lives of her children. She sobbed and pleaded, but she was killed anyway. His father tried to fight to protect Sinjin and his brother and sisters, but a dragon slashed his heart out with one swipe of claw. That is what you will remind him of. Always."

The prince shouted out a curt word. She did not understand it—it was not English—but it was obviously a command as the door flew open at once.

After the brothel, she thought she could not be shocked. She was wrong. This was not like the lighthearted, playful dancing that had led to the orgy in the brothel's ballroom. Darkness permeated the room, despite all the burning lamps. The room was hot, steamy, and smelled of sweat. The glow was golden but it was not a warm, welcoming, mellow gleam—it was the type of garish coloring that should be cast by the fires of hell.

The room was dark, paneled with black wood, filled with settees and chaises covered in black silk. Women were everywhere in the room. Naked women. But all the ones Lucy could see were bound. Their hands tied at the wrists, their legs tied at the ankles. Some were balanced on their forearms and knees with their bottoms in the air. Others were tied to chaises. Some were standing upright, but their bonds were hooked to eyelets that hung from the ceiling. There were men, of course. Fully dressed or half-naked, the men smacked the women's bottoms with whips, or they held flat, round paddles and used those to spank the fleshy, jiggling rumps.

Squeals, throaty moans, and sobbing, agonized groans filled the room.

Then she glimpsed the faces of some of the men. Recoiling, she tried to step back, but the prince's hand was at her back, forcing her to stay put.

They looked . . . driven by something wild and awful. They barely looked human. Their eyes were bright and filled with lust. Their faces were distorted, their mouths open, demonic grins twisting their lips. They were panting as they delivered blow after blow to the women.

They looked like monsters. Like she imagined vampires would be—treating humans like insignificant prey. Something to consume, destroy, throw away.

Sinjin was not like this.

He could *never* have been like this. Could he?

"Yes, Sinjin has been here." The prince wore a leering grin. "He is notorious for his skill with a whip. Shall I ask some of the women to describe the things he has done?"

"N-no." Then Lucy cringed at the quake in her tone. He would know how devastated she was.

But Sinjin would not do this *now*. Perhaps he was like one of these slayers before, but he had changed now. She was certain of it.

Yet her heart still felt heavy. It felt as though it was turning to ice. How could he ever have done this? How could he believe that hurting others would make up for losing his family?

"Would you care to join them?" the prince asked, his tone insolent and goading.

She drew herself up, and coldly informed him, "If you are planning to whip me, I would suggest you do not try. If you do, I will hurt you."

His laugh boomed out. "There is nothing, sweet nymph, you can do. I think it is time to show you what dragon slayers are truly like."

The prince whistled and footmen sprang forward. Two grasped her by her arms and dragged her across the floor. They wound through the various scenes of domination, and as they passed, the male dragon slayers stopped their work and stared at her.

Several left their bound partners and followed.

Heavens, no. She twisted in the confining grip of the two young, strong footmen. The prince was behind her, smiling and . . . and humming a melancholy tune that sounded like a dirge, though he looked incredibly pleased. Six men trotted behind him. Two were dressed in gentlemanly attire, two were wearing the rough-looking clothes of tradesmen, and two wore nothing but their trousers and boots.

All looked large, strong, intimidating. Four carried whips. The two bare-chested ones had riding crops.

God, no.

If only she could get this thing off her neck. For she could guess what was going to happen. She was going to be tied up and whipped and struck. Perhaps raped also. The prince obviously wanted to torture, abuse, debase her so much she would pray for death. The odds were that she would not survive the night.

If only she could get the collar off. But the prince had bound her hands together at her wrists. He had done a thorough job of tying them up. She'd wriggled and struggled, but couldn't loosen the rope.

The footmen pushed her into a second room, a smaller one. A fire burned in here, along with lamps, but it was empty. A smooth black wall, one covered in a stone that shone like obsidian, ran the length of the room. She was pushed to it. Then the footmen took gold chains from the wall and secured them to her collar. It was so close to her, she could not see how the chains attached.

The servants left her. Footsteps approached. A male chuckle fell over her—was it the prince? She didn't know, but hands grasped the belt of her robe and tore it in two. It fell away, her robe fell open, then it was whisked off her. Even though her hands were bound, the robe came off. With a loud rending sound, it tore at the seams, then fell to a warm puddle at her feet.

Behind her, men drank in sharp, appreciative breaths. One let out a low whistle. Again, footsteps approached her. Something tapped her bottom lightly, something hard. It made her fleshy cheeks jiggle.

"Voluptuous, and lovely. Unwilling, I take it?" The voice was hoarse, gravelly, and one she did not recognize.

"This one is a dragon. A strong and very beautiful dragon."

Murmurs fell over the men behind her. Her cheeks burned with humiliation, her heart thudded with fear. There had to be a way to get at the collar, but her hands were tied behind her back.

"Step aside, Roberts. I will be the one to begin. I want the first strike."

A boot landed heavily on the floor, something whistled through the air, then snapped against her high back, above her hands. Stinging pain lanced her. She screamed. God, dear God, she had never known anything like this.

"Too hard," another man shouted. "We want her to last."

"Just a few to soften her up. To get her blood running."

The lash of the whip had been unbelievably strong. . . . It wouldn't take long before it would cleave her flesh open. It was strong enough to—was it strong enough to break through metal? Even a magical type of metal?

She heard the whistle and she dropped at the last instant, tugging the gold chains to their limits. The lash smacked against the collar around her neck. It slammed the metal against her flesh then she heard a slight crack. The collar sprang open and dropped free.

"What the bloody hell—?" shouted the prince, his voice an enraged bark.

The instant she felt the collar give, Lucy summoned the change. Her body wriggled, stretched, heated to burning, and transformed, all in a heartbeat of time. Larger and larger she grew, her dragon's body filling the small room. Her arms broke the bonds and were free as they changed. The dragon slayers were armed with only whips and crops, and they lashed her with harsh, wild strokes, but the devices made no impact on her shimmering scales. They were trying to beat her, trying to wound her.

She craned her head and blew a breath of fire at them. Two of the men were in the path of the flames and they stumbled back. Fire licked at the furnishings, and a chair seat caught. The men ignored it—two ran for the door, shouting for weapons.

She swung her tail, hoping to knock them down. She caught one, but the other escaped. Then she lashed her tail to and fro as the remaining men whipped her mercilessly.

She charged for the window. If she could break through it, she could fly to freedom. Behind her, something released with a twang. She lunged forward, but not fast enough. An arrow drove into the back of her dragon leg.

Another arrow shot, and she snapped her wings to avoid it. The wound slowed her and the pain hammered in her brain. Lucy fought toward the window, but more arrows came—a volley of them. Some bounced off her scales. One ripped through her wings again. Another hit her arm.

She was slowing. There was something about these arrows. Some kind of magic or potion or poison. Her muscles were seizing.

The window was only yards away. She flung herself forward, but a huge black shape appeared in the window. It was the black dragon, with James held in his claws. His huge wings beat as he hovered in front of the window. Then he rushed forward, and broke the window with one of his wings, smashing all the glass out, so it fell like raindrops. Through the opening, he flew with James, landing in the room. In an instant, he transformed back into the shape of a man.

A silvery-green dragon followed and she recognized him even before he changed.

It was Jack.

*   *   *

In dragon form, her brother advanced on her, snapping at her with his jowls. He forced her to retreat against the wall. The black dragon, still in human form, stood there, holding James. The man was naked, but still exuded arrogance and control.

The dragon slayers rushed forward, swords raised.

Jack roared in the language of dragons: *Change, Lucy. Change back. It's your only hope to survive.*

She wanted to roar at him. Shout *no* at him. But the poison was flooding through her. Against her will, her body began to shift back into human form. Her muscles jerked and trembled. The floor tipped and wobbled beneath her feet. She lost her balance and the floor flew up to meet her.

A thunderous crash exploded behind her and a male voice roared, "Touch her and you will bloody well die."

She knew that fury-tinged bellow. Knew the deep, beautiful baritone that had barked those words, and did it with such mad fury, he had frozen everyone in place.

She tried to move, but her limbs were numb and cold. All she could do was flop over.

"Who did this?" The man shouting this was the prince. He loomed over her, his eyes burning with such anger they were red. "Who poisoned her?"

Her eyes were blurry, but she could see him whip around, screaming the question at his slayers. No one answered. Then suddenly, the prince was jerked off his feet and thrown across the room. Sinjin dropped to his knees beside her. Half a dozen swords immediately pointed at him. The dragon slayers closed in on him, standing only inches away. So close that if Sinjin moved, the lethal points would stab him.

He bent over her, apparently not caring about the fact that six men were prepared to kill him. "Drink this, Lucy," he murmured near her ear. Suddenly he pressed his wrist to her lips. She tasted his metallic, slippery blood. She tried to pull back, but then the blood flooded her mouth and some impulse drew her to suckle. To drink.

"Let me save her." She heard Sinjin speak the words, saw he was imploring the prince, her brother, and the other dragon to leave him while he gave her blood.

"Stay back—let Sinjin rescue his damsel," the prince barked. "Do not touch the other two dragons. Not yet."

The other dragon slayers obeyed their prince, moving immediately away.

Why had Jack come here? Why was he with the man who looked like Allan? Why had they brought James to the dragon slayers?

It was some kind of betrayal. With a heavy heart and a dizzy, drugged head, Lucy knew it must be.

Sinjin cupped her face, stroking her cheek. The more of his blood she drank, the more she wanted. Warmth spread through her. The numbness of the poison subsided.

His blood was saving her.

Clutching his arm, she tugged and he understood, coming closer to her so she could whisper in his ear. "They . . . want to . . . kill us. Get away."

His face. Suddenly she realized—his face had healed. The skin of his cheeks and forehead was still wrinkled and slightly scarred, but mostly he was as perfect as he'd been before the sun had burned him.

"I have to ensure you are safe."

"How did you—?" It was hard to force out words. She wanted to ask how he had known she was here. If he knew what her brother wanted. Why Jack was here. Why the slayers were not attacking.

"Your brother told me," he said softly. "He needed my help to get close to this house. I took care of the prince's guards, allowing him to get in. I didn't know his friend would bring James."

"The black dragon . . . he looks like Allan Ferrars. Like my fiancé."

"I believe he is the brother of that bastard, Lucy. But I am not going to let him have you. You are going to live. You are going to feel very strong very soon. Then we will get James and get to safety."

Brother . . . she didn't know he had one. . . . "But why—why would he want me?" she whispered. She could not even hear her thoughts over the loud drum of her heart. "The prince wanted me to lure you. Why would Allan's . . . brother want me?"

22

LOSS

Sinjin rested his hand on Lucy's heart. She was naked, and he wanted to rip apart the other men in the room, since every male except her brother was looking at her. Exploring her with appraising, lust-filled gazes. Sinjin moved his hand, pulled off his greatcoat, and draped it around her. Then he wrapped his arms around her, held her close, and slid his fingers under the lapel of his coat to check her heartbeat once more.

It proved strong and steady now. His blood had destroyed the poison inside her and had healed her wounds. The problem: she was now a vampire.

He didn't know if a dragon could be turned into a vampire and survive. To save her from the poison used by slayers, had he sentenced her to certain death?

She would have died if he had not acted. But he had not told her what he intended to do—he had not told her that she could die if she drank his blood.

Hell.

He had been so afraid to lose her, he'd reacted without thought. Out of the corner of his eyes, Sinjin watched the vampire slayers, the prince, her brother, Jack, and the black dragon, the brother of her former fiancé. They were all shifting restlessly, waiting . . . ready to attack if the bargain they were about to strike did not work.

He knew what they wanted. His prince wanted James, because James was growing up to be the most powerful dragon they had ever encountered. No dragon had been able to shift at so young an age. The prince would want to study James. He would want medical experiments carried out on James, the way some vampire slayers performed experiments on captured vampires. Sinjin suspected the damned prince wanted to see if he could acquire James's ability to shift into dragon form. He knew the prince wanted to try to be both a vampire and a dragon at the same time—to find out if the combination would make him stronger.

Sinjin knew the prince had tried to combine vampiric powers with those of a shifter dragon before. He had tried it on other people that he referred to as "subjects." It had never worked—every subject he had tried it on had died. The prince believed it was possible, believed it like a fanatic.

Sinjin didn't know if it was possible, and it meant he had turned Lucy into a vampire without knowing the consequences. He did know from the prince's experiments, that if a vampire tried to acquire dragon powers, the vampire died.

Damn. He had to pray it didn't work the same way if a dragon became a vampire.

From the gleam in the eye of the black dragon, it was obvious he was determined to have Lucy—even if he had to kill everyone in the room to get her.

"Enough," the prince growled. "Release her, or I'll send so many crossbows into you, you'll be fractured into pieces and her blood will spurt out of you like a fountain."

Sinjin drew Lucy closer to him. He glanced around—half

the weapons in the room shifted to point at him, and the rest remained trained on Jack and her former fiancé's brother, Lionel Ferrars.

First he had to take care of the prince—and he knew Jack and Ferrars would not stop him from doing that. They would want him to take down their opponents, then they would get rid of him.

The prince moved over and stood, towering over Lucy. "Fascinating," he growled. "She is still alive. She appears healthy, and she has the powers of both a vampire and a dragon inside her."

His sire's eyes glowed like silver discs, bright with a fanatical gleam.

Sinjin knew if he destroyed his sire, he would die. But he had to keep Lucy from becoming the pawn of his prince or of the black dragon. He had to protect her. Guidon had not been able to tell him how long he could survive after killing the prince. Would it be long enough to fight the black dragon and save Lucy? Or would his death be instantaneous?

In the heartbeat it took him to think it through, the prince reached for Lucy and tried to pull her from him. A crossbow string gave a sharp twang, and a bolt streaked for his head.

He kicked the prince and pulled Lucy away from the shot. The arrow slammed into the wall where he had just been standing.

He shook his arm lightly, letting the stake drop into his hand. He pushed Lucy back, hating having to treat her so roughly. The prince followed her with his gaze, ready to pounce, and Sinjin jumped forward. He heard the whistle of arrows past his head, and he slammed into the prince.

His prince looked down, saw the stake, and screamed, "You fool, you can't kill me! You'll destroy yourself."

But he drove the sharpened piece of wood upward and punctured his maker's heart.

The prince jerked back. His hands clawed at the stake, but it was in so deep, it stuck out through his back. He slumped to the ground. His body began to instantly decay—it was something Sinjin had never seen before. Right in front of their eyes, the prince's body began to shrivel, then the skin turned gray, then collapsed into dust.

Sinjin stepped back. Was this going to happen to him?

The other slayers gaped in amazement and weapons suddenly lowered. He knew why. The king of their clan was dead, and now there was doubt as to whether he would be the new king. They were staring at him because he was still standing. He wasn't dead. But he didn't know whether that was temporary or not.

He whirled around and ran to Lucy. He had to fight the black dragon while he still had time, but he had one thing to do first.

He pressed Lucy against the wall and clamped his lips on hers for one precious instant. "I love you," he said, then he turned to face the black dragon.

But it was her brother who stood in front of him, a stake in his hand.

Lucy screamed at her brother, "Jack, stop! No!"

He turned wild, desperate eyes to her. "I have no choice, Lucy. If I don't do this, I'll be killed. I have to do this to protect you."

"Protect me? If you want to do that, help Sinjin! Put down that stake!"

But her brother hesitated, then tightened his grip on it and took another step toward Sinjin. He met her frightened, horrified gaze. She saw the agony in his expression. Was he going to die because he had killed his sire?

No—he couldn't be dying. He looked too strong. Surely he would have died the instant he had driven the stake into the prince's heart. He was going to survive—only if he attacked her brother. He snatched up one of the fallen swords.

She knew he had to kill Jack, but she couldn't stand it. Jack had turned against them, but he had been forced to.

There must be a way for her to stop this.

Sinjin lifted his sword, poised to drive it through Jack's heart. She winced, shutting her eyes for an instant, but she couldn't stop her lids from lifting.

Sinjin turned his sword in his hand, so he held the hilt with the blade pointing down, the tip pressing into the floor.

He wasn't going to attack Jack. He was going to spare her brother. Thankfulness welled in her, choking her, making her throat dry and tight.

But the next sound made her knees shake and her heart fall. It was a howl of pure fury. She jerked around to face her fallen brother.

Opening his muzzle wide, Jack let out another roar. He hauled his wounded dragon body up, and flew at Sinjin, his jaws wide, and pouring out flame, his claws extended. Heavens, Jack was going to take advantage and kill Sinjin.

"No! Jack, he spared you! Do not do this!" she shouted.

She expected to see Sinjin lift the sword again, but he didn't. He stood his ground, holding the sword pointing to the floor, and watched Jack rush toward him. She was staring at Jack—then she saw a flash of movement in the corner of her eye.

Sinjin must have seen it, too. He jerked around. Just as Allan's brother slammed a wooden stake into his heart.

Shock seemed to grip her like a force of magic. She couldn't move. She stood helplessly, staring as Sinjin tried to clutch the stake, then fell over, sprawling on the ground.

It had gone several inches into the left side of his chest. It could not possibly have missed his heart.

Finally, the horror snapped—she forced her feet to propel her forward. But as she fell to her knees at Sinjin's side, his eyes went blank. Before she could help him, save him, even tell him how much she loved him, he died.

23

Magic

As soon as the stake had driven into his heart, a red haze had formed in front of Sinjin's eyes. Now the red glow was gone and he couldn't see anything. The room was pitch-black around him. He had been able to see in the night for so long, he'd forgotten what it was like to feel blind.

Was he alive or dead? Hell, he would have thought it would be easy to tell.

Heat surrounded him. He heard the roar of flames. Something stank, like sulfur, like foul gas. Sinjin tried to shake his head, but he didn't feel any movement. His body felt weightless, like he was floating in a hot, steamy, stinking void.

He remembered wrapping his fist around the stake in his heart, then trying to pull it free. Remembered that, like the one he had plunged into his sire's heart, this one would not budge.

He had to be dead—and his soul, which was in some kind of dormant state when he was a vampire, was on a swift descent to hell, by the smells surrounding him.

He had lost James. He had lost his precious Lucy.

At least he had told her he loved her.

Hell. *At least.* What a pile of horse dung: It wasn't enough. He wanted more. He wanted a lifetime to show Lucy he loved her.

He had thought it would be worth dying to see the prince die. He thought it would be worth it to know he had made James and Lucy safe. But they weren't safe.

Was there a way he could cheat death? He wasn't finished. He still had to ensure they were all right. . . .

Something was dragging him down into the void. A force he couldn't resist. He was going to hell, he was sure of it. He'd surrendered his soul so long ago, he had killed so many creatures, where else would he be going?

Sinjin fought to hang on. He strained to hear Lucy's voice. To smell the subtle fragrance of her skin. To see her and hang on to her and stay with her.

He fought, but he was losing—

He had saved her life by giving her his blood.

Tears streaked down Lucy's cheeks. Scalding tears that blurred her vision and made it hard to breathe. She brushed at them fiercely, ridding her face of the signs of anguish. Dry-eyed, she looked up. Jack had taken James by the hand, and was holding the boy at his side. James strained at her brother's grip but Jack yanked the boy back, snapping at him to behave.

She wanted to kill her brother.

Sinjin was dead because of her, because he had wanted to save her from the pain of losing a brother.

The man who looked like Allan Ferrars stalked forward, his bare feet coming to rest in her field of vision. She stared up, craning her neck, and flinched as he held his hand down for her.

"Don't touch me," she snarled. "Leave me. Go away. I will not go with you."

"Yes, you will, you stupid woman. Push him off your lap

and stand up." He snarled at her, baring his teeth. Even though he was in human form, his teeth were long, curved, and sharp. "We are leaving."

She wrapped her arms around Sinjin's fallen body. Wishing that by hugging him, she could breathe life into him again. Fury made her body shake. In a low voice, fighting for control, she growled, "Who are you? You look like the man I despise most in the world and I want to know who you are!"

He gazed down, sneering with disdain. "My name is Lionel Ferrars. Your fiancé—murdered by your family—was my younger brother."

"Younger brother? But he never even told me he had a brother." Allan had lied even about his family to her. Why had he ever asked her to marry him? She didn't understand. He hadn't loved her. Or wanted her. Or even respected her enough to be honest about anything.

"Get up, you little whore. You belong to me now."

His words struck like a slap. Then he did hit her—striking her across the face with the back of his hand.

She roared at him. The sound burst out of her instinctually. It came out with a dragon's power and she felt a strange pain shoot through her upper jaw. She clapped her right hand to her mouth, but her teeth grew. They shot forward and stabbed her palm.

Fangs. She had fangs.

Sinjin's blood . . .

It was how people were transformed into vampires. They were taken to the point of death and then fed the blood of a vampire and they became one.

She was a vampire, which meant her blood had the power to transform a dying mortal. Dear heaven, what if she gave her blood to Sinjin? Would it save him? Would it turn a dying vampire back into a vampire? Was she too late?

Ferrars, the brute, hit her again. "Leave him," he shouted. "Get off your arse, you stupid tart, and come with me."

"I will never go with you."

"I have only let you live so long because I need your power, you piece of whoring filth. Obey me. Or I'll break your neck now."

What was this madman speaking of? She kept her arms around Sinjin, and she willed one of her fingers to transform, so her fingernail grew and became a claw. Amazing. She hadn't even known she could do such a thing. Out of the corner of her eye, she saw James, still held by her brother. The boy was white with fear and was shaking.

She felt different. Stronger. She felt utterly in control. Yet how could she? She was in the clutches of a vicious maniac of a dragon and she had lost the man she loved. . . .

She hadn't lost. Not yet.

She would save Sinjin, then she would protect James.

Slicing her wrist, Lucy shifted her arm, so the wound in her flesh touched Sinjin's mouth. The cut stung and blood flowed out. Sinjin was dead so of course he couldn't drink. She feared she was too late. And she couldn't let her wrist bleed out. She must survive to try to protect James.

Ferrars roared, "Stop it! Goddamn you, whore, stop feeding him your blood. Stop or I'll kill you—"

He reached for her with both hands and she stiffened, expecting him to grab her head and try to snap her neck. She couldn't move, for that would take her blood away from Sinjin.

Suddenly Ferrars howled in anguish. The curved blade of a dragon slayer's sword was protruding from his chest, just below his heart.

His eyes, the same blue as Allan's had been, bulged with sheer fury. Awkwardly, he stumbled around, blood pouring down his chest and back. It was covering his skin like an eerie, grotesque red veil. Her brother let go of the hilt of the sword, stepping back, and he grasped James by the shoulder and pushed the lad behind him. He was shielding James with his body.

Ferrars, amazingly, was still standing, despite being gored through his body. But the blade had missed his heart and a dragon had to be stabbed through the heart to be killed. The blackguard bent, letting out a roar of pain, and snatched up another sword. He slowly, menacingly approached her brother.

She looked around desperately for a sword. For something she could throw. She couldn't move her wrist—

Her arm was pushed away from Sinjin's mouth. Astonished, she gaped down at him. His eyes were blinking. They sparkled with . . . with life. He grinned. "Enough, my love. I don't need more."

She tried to slide out from under him, as Ferrars glanced back at them. He wore a gloating smile. "The bloody dragon earl first. Then you, Greystone. It will be a pleasure to kill you."

"Not as much pleasure as killing you," Sinjin murmured. Then he jumped to his feet. He rushed at Ferrars, who jolted around and stabbed with the blade. But Sinjin vaulted over his head, turning over in the air. Her brother pushed James out of the way, to the corner of the room where it would be safe.

Lucy saw the glint of silver in Sinjin's hand as he landed. She barely understood it for what it was—a dagger—before Sinjin plunged it into Ferrar's chest, just above the penetrating sword.

Ferrars lurched. He swung wildly with the blade he held, but missed all of them. Then he fell to his knees and blood poured out of his mouth.

James screamed. He had been standing behind her brother, his face expressionless. Now he shrieked in terror. Sinjin gathered the child into his arms, and cupped the boy's head, pressing James to his shoulder. It was as if he had been under a spell, one that was now broken. He looked down at the blood that had soaked into his uncle's shirt and he whimpered.

Lucy got to her feet. Her legs were wobbly, but she wanted to go to James, and help Sinjin comfort the boy. Their foes were dead, were gone . . . all except Jack. What would he do?

Sinjin picked up the sword dropped by Ferrars. He took a step toward her brother. Fear spiked in Lucy's heart. He wouldn't spare Jack now. Not after Jack had tried to kill him. She was going to see her brother die—

The sword clattered across the room. Sinjin had tossed it aside. "You saved her life. Thank you," he said simply.

Jack gaped at him in amazement. "I—I staked you. And you are thanking me?"

Sinjin kissed James on the head, then faced her brother. "I assume he tempted you with the promise with power or forced you to help him with threats."

"Both." Jack hung his head, looking guilty. "He promised power first, then threatened to kill me if I didn't help him." Jack turned to her, but he did not look her in the eye. "I never would have given you to him, Lucy. I was trying to play for time, to find a way out of the mess."

"A way that would spare your life—" Then she put her hands to her face. "Jack, you betrayed us. I don't know if I can forgive that."

"I know." Grimly, her brother looked to Sinjin. "If you spare my life, I will disappear to the Continent. You will look after Lucy, won't you? Will you look after all of them? I can see how much you love her and she loves you. I've never known love—"

"Yes, you have!" Lucy jerked up her head. "You are a stupid fool, Jack. I love you. Helena and Beatrix love you! For some reason, you've always seemed to want us to despise you, not love you." Then she stopped and she hurried forward to James. She took James from Sinjin and gathered him into her arms. At once, the boy seemed to relax against her and she stroked his head.

"I am not going to kill you, Wrenshire," Sinjin said. "I would not put Lucy through so much pain. I owe you for saving her life and for protecting my nephew. In the end, you proved you had a heart."

She was kissing James on his head, soothing him, when Sinjin came to her. He wrapped his arms around her. "Your brother should be free now. Ferrars was a powerful dragon—one that had demon blood in him, which gave him abilities beyond those possessed by normal shape-shifting dragons. He had the power to control James's mind. He wanted to use James and study him, because James is an unusual dragon. The only one who has ever shown the ability to shift shape so young."

She knew she was gaping at him in astonishment. "How do you know this?"

"An intriguing man told me. He is a vampire who is also a historian." Sinjin told her about a strange, wizened little man who owned a bookshop in Charing Cross and recorded all the secrets of vampires and demons and shape-shifters.

"He told me about you," Sinjin said softly.

"About me? What could he tell you about me? You already know I am a dragon and who my parents are."

Sinjin lifted her chin. His eyes glittered at her. "How do you feel, Lucy? Strong? You don't feel weak or sick, do you?"

"I feel fine . . . well, considering what we have just been through."

"I have a confession to make, love. When I gave you my blood, I took a huge risk. I didn't know if it would save you . . . or kill you." He looked so guilty. So ashamed. "I did it because I was desperate to save you. You will hate me for taking that kind of risk—"

"It didn't kill me," she interrupted firmly. "And if you hadn't done it, I would have died."

He lifted her hand and bestowed a gentle kiss to her palm. "I made you a vampire, love, without your consent."

"I—I will learn to live with that."

"Guidon, the chronicler, told me who your mother was. It is something you must know, Lucy."

"But I know about my mother—" She stopped. His face wore such a serious expression and her heart gave a flip-flop in her chest. Whatever he believed he knew, he expected it would shock her. She squared her shoulders and steeled her heart for what she would hear. But then she thought of James, and of where they were—in the prince's house.

"Don't tell me now. Let us take James to somewhere safe."

Sinjin bowed. "You are correct, as always, love. But first, I have something I have to do." His mouth set in a hard line for an instant, and determination burned in his silver-green eyes. "I defeated the prince and survived. That means, in theory, I now have control of the dragon slayers. It is time we stopped fighting and killing each other."

She gaped at him.

"I want to put an end to the slayers. There will be no more killing. I want both of us to learn how to live peacefully. Lucy, love, will you help me with this?"

"Yes, of course I will. But you—are you certain you wish me to help you? You see, the prince told me—" She couldn't continue. Her tongue felt thick and clumsy, her throat was tight with tears she was struggling to keep inside.

"What did he say to you?" he asked gently.

"That when you look at me—every time you do—you will remember how your siblings died. You will remember your mother pleading for your life to be spared. You will remember how your father fought to try to protect you and your siblings."

He frowned, looking grim. Her heart made a slow, painful twist in her chest.

He was thinking of those things now, and there were deep lines framing his mouth. "He couldn't have known that."

That stunned her. "What do you mean? He told me what your parents endured—"

"He could not have known it because I didn't know what they went through. My father told me to run, with my brother, and I did. I didn't see my parents die. I never heard what they said. He could not have heard those details from me."

"Your sister perhaps?"

"Possibly. Or there is another possibility. One I was too blind to see before. For him to know so many details . . . it is like he was there."

Her stomach lurched. "But you saw dragons—"

"I saw what I thought were dragons. I was only nine and I'd never seen dragons before. The prince had a great deal of strength, and the power to manipulate a mortal mind."

"He lied . . . you think he lied. That he killed your family and made you think dragons did it. But why would he do that? To make you into a dragon slayer?"

"I don't know, Lucy. But I intend to get to the truth. For now, we should go home."

Home. It had been so long . . . would home even feel the same anymore? She nodded. "Yes, I should go home. I must get my sisters from the brothel and take them home." She stared at Jack. "What are you going to do?"

He flushed, and flinched, obviously embarrassed. "I don't know. I guess I can't go home. Not after what I did. Maybe I'll go to the Continent—"

"Jack, you can come home." She reached out and gently touched his arm. "Sinjin is correct. You did save my life, Jack. And you protected James. Come home, Jack. I don't want to lose you."

* * *

Sinjin watched Lucy's brother walk uncertainly into her embrace. She truly was a queen amongst women. But when he had said the word *home*, he had meant his home. And he wanted her there with him. He wanted his house to become her home.

But he couldn't ask her that now. She needed to recover from all the horrors of this day. She needed to be with her family.

He had lost his family and he knew how much he longed to be with them. He knew how much it would mean to her to be with her family.

And he had James to take care of.

He watched her and her brother walk away, and wondered . . . would she marry him? Or should he let her go? She had said how she feared she would remind him of pain. Would he do that to her? If he asked her to be with him, would she be forever reminded of the horror of this day?

Did she deserve to be with one of her own kind?

What if he opened his heart and she refused him? What if he asked her to marry him, and he ended up losing her for good?

Hell.

He didn't want to lose anyone ever again.

The door opened slowly, as if by magic, and the scent of dust and old books made Lucy sneeze. A tiny gnome-like man hurried forward, almost dancing from foot to foot. "A dragon!" he cackled, and he rubbed his hands together. "What an honor! I have never met a dragon before." He stopped in front of her, and swept a deep bow. "Do you take tea, my dear? What of biscuits? Honey? Jam? I am so afraid I have nothing more to offer you."

Taken aback by his breathless questions, Lucy tried to focus on him as he leapt from side to side, then turned swiftly away. "Are you Guidon?" she called after him.

"Indeed. Indeed."

She followed, winding through stacks crammed with books. She smelled leather bindings and titles flashed by her eyes as she hurried behind the tiny, stooped man.

She caught him as he reached a small kitchen, set off the bookshop, and was putting a kettle upon his stove.

"I was told that you know about my mother. That you know something special about her. I—I wish to find out what it is. Whatever the price, I am happy to pay you—"

"I require no payment." He whirled around, his tufts of yellowish-gray hair flying up to stick out from his face. "I would wish to tell you, my dear. Truly I would. But I think it would be best if the Duke of Greystone explains the tale to you. He wished to do so. You are very important to him." He cocked his head. "The only other union of a dragon and a vampire was the one between the duke's sister and the dragon Nadezda, who came from the old country. But you are now a vampire and a dragon. It shall be interesting . . . I will be delighted to follow the births and lives of your children."

"Children! I am not married to the Duke of Greystone. There are no children. I am sure he—"

"He has not yet asked you to marry him? Even though he survived the death of his sire? Even though he took command of the slayers? I was certain, when he left my shop that day that he intended to propose marriage."

"He—he said that?"

"Eh?" Guidon had set two dainty white cups on a tray. He held a tin of biscuits from Fortnum and Mason's. "Of course he did not say it. No gentleman ever would. It was obvious from his agitation that he was preparing himself to take that frightening step."

"Frightening step?"

"A proposal is a very terrifying endeavor for a gentleman to make, my dear Lady Lucinda." Guidon's eyes held a twinkle.

"You will not tell me about my mother?"

"Not now. Not when it might be the only thing to force the two of you together again."

The kettle whistled and he swiftly put in his tea leaves, then set the pot on the tray. "But you will, of course, stay for tea."

"I—"

"There are many things I would like to tell you about dragons! I am the chronicler of all the preternatural beings that inhabit England: the vampires, the werewolves, all the shape-shifters. There is so much I want to ask you as well. Please, Lady Lucinda, would you indulge me with a little of your time?"

He was such a strange little man. She glanced around. "These books—they are not about vampires and werewolves are they?"

He chuckled merrily. "Some are, but only accountings of legends and tales. The books that chronicle the truth, I keep well protected. I had lost all my books before, and fortunately I had memorized every word of them. I have spent much time writing them all again."

"Heavens," Lucy breathed. "How many books?"

"Hundreds. But let us have our tea."

She stared suddenly at the tray he held and the pot that wobbled slightly on it. Remembering what she now was. "I—I am now . . . I mean, I cannot—"

"Oh, you can drink this tea, my dear. It is specially created for we vampires. Do not worry. And I am so delighted to be able to have tea with the future Duchess of Greystone!"

The footman brought her to Sinjin's study and from the doorway, she saw Sinjin raise a tumbler to his lips, just as he had done on the very first night she had come to him. That night she had come to offer her body. Tonight she wanted to surrender her heart.

He had sent instructions to her house—pages of written

guidelines on what it meant to be a vampire. He had sent her bottles of his special blood, for her to drink, and he had sent her notes of apology. Even though she had told him she understood he had given her a chance to live and survive, he did not seem to think she could forgive him for making her a vampire.

Was that why he had not seen her for so long? Why he had not come to her house? Or was it because of what he had learned about his family's deaths? Had he learned that dragons were to blame after all?

Guidon, who had proved to be both charming and gentlemanly, had insisted the duke intended to marry her. But she . . . she did not know. But where she would once have been afraid to hope, now she was willing to do so. Her heart was filled with hope, so much it felt it would burst.

She stepped forward into the room, and he jerked his head up. She had asked that the servant not announce her. What would be Sinjin's reaction when he saw her?

"Lucy," he said. And a large smile lifted his lips. He set down his drink and came to her, arms outstretched.

She could not have dreamed for a better greeting.

As he gathered her into his embrace, she whispered, "It has been a whole week. And I was afraid to come to you. I was afraid you had learned that . . . that you do have a good reason to be angry with dragons—"

"I'm sorry, love. I had to track down some of the vampires who had supposedly rescued my sister and me that day. It has taken me all this time to find them, but eventually, from them, I got the truth." He lifted her hand and bestowed one of his melting kisses to her palm. "They were the men who destroyed my family. It was not the dragons. They had killed my family for blood, then when the prince discovered my sister and I had survived, he decided to turn us into vampires. He also engineered my sister's marriage to a dragon, to produce a child. He wanted to see what powers such a child would have."

"Oh my goodness."

"My sister deeply loved her husband. The prince was responsible for my brother-in-law's death. The prince wanted him out of the way so he could eventually take control of James. I learned that my sister's despair and melancholy was caused by the prince. He used his powers to affect her emotions. Again, she had served his purpose—she had borne a half-dragon child, and the prince then wanted to get her out of the way."

Lucy cupped his face with her fingers. Deep lines gouged into his forehead and framed his mouth. "And because of you, the prince can no longer hurt James. He can no longer hurt anyone." She took a deep breath. "Did you destroy those other slayers—the ones who killed your family?"

"It may surprise you, but I didn't. I had decided there would be no more death. I also decided I am not going to run the dragon slayers, and I put another slayer in charge. A man who also believes there should be peace between our clans. He had those vampires arrested under the laws of our clan. Their punishment was destruction."

"Then it was done because it was the law. Not vengeance, but because they broke the laws of your clan."

"Yes." He took a deep breath and his sparkling, glittering eyes held hers. "Lucy, you gave me the most amazing gifts in the world. You gave me the truth. You forgave me for what I did, because I was misguided and wrong. You helped me to crack the ice that had formed around my heart. You gave me my life back, a future, a nephew who can grow up to be strong, healthy, happy. You've given me peace, Lucy. I don't know what to give you in return."

"There is only one thing I want," she whispered and her heart ached.

"If you want my heart, it is yours. On a silver platter."

"I want to spend forever with you."

Sinjin smiled, then he batted his lashes, making her giggle. "Are you proposing marriage to me, Lady Lucy Drake?"

"Were you ever going to propose it to me?" she countered, but she knew she was blushing. The heat of it scalded her cheeks.

"In matters of the heart, I don't have as much courage as you do. I had to be certain I wouldn't offend you if I asked."

She sighed and rolled her eyes. "You won't."

"Then . . . Lady Lucy, will you do be the honor of becoming my bride?"

"Are you certain? You will be marrying a dragon, you know."

"You will be marrying a vampire. I love you, Lucy, and I still think it is too much to ask of you to take me on. I want you to be happy. You wanted normalcy, Lucy. Marrying a vampire won't give you that. By making you a vampire, I took away any chance you have to try to live a normal life."

"I'll never be normal and I would never want you to try to be 'normal,' either. I love you, Sinjin. And if you will let me give you my answer, I will."

"First, love, I have to tell you what I learned about your mother."

"I spoke to Guidon," she told him. "I went to him to find out what he had told you."

"So he told you?"

"No! He said he would not, as he wanted you to be the one to do it. He hoped it would force us to be together. He gave me tea, then made me promise I would come to you. So tell me— what is this secret truth about my mother?" She heard the catch in her voice. Memories flooded of her mother, of Celia, Lady Wrenshire, who had been beautiful. Lucy had only seen her mother as a dragon twice in her entire life. But her mother had possessed silvery scales and large dark blue eyes. Her mother had always smiled. She had been wonderful.

"What is the truth?"

"Your mother is a direct descendant of the first female dragon. She was a queen of dragons, though she was never officially called Queen. She was of such a pure line, she had all the best qualities of dragons. She was beautiful, strong, but always possessed a noble heart. It appears that at the very beginning dragons were very peaceful creatures and they had to become aggressive when people began to hunt them. You have all her strengths—including her good heart. But also, according to Guidon, you possess certain magical skills."

"Magic? I've never done anything magical!"

His gentle, loving smile made her heart wobble. "You helped James, Lucy. Thanks to you, he is now a happy little boy and seems to be putting his sad and frightening memories behind him. You saved me. You've done many magical things."

"I mean I cannot wave a wand and make things fly into the air."

"Guidon promised to explain more about your magical skills, once you knew about your mother. He insists you are filled with magic, and I have to admit that I agree, though for different reasons." His sparkling eyes softened.

It was so wonderful to be looked at in such a way. With so much love. It stole her breath.

Sinjin swallowed hard, and Lucy suspected he was finally willing to hear her answer. Though, really, should he not already know what it was to be?

"Yes," she whispered. "Yes, I will become your bride. Your wife. Your fire-breathing, but besotted, devoted, and thoroughly happy partner."

Laughing, he lifted her in his arms, and carried her to her bed. On the way, she tugged desperately at his clothes. She freed him of his cravat, and suckled the firm muscles that defined his neck. She unfastened his shirt at the collar and licked him with abandon. Massaged his chest muscles, stroked his nipples through his coat. Slid her hand down and stroked his rigid cock through his trousers.

That made him jerk. "Careful, I don't want to drop you."

But then he tossed her onto the bed, so she bounced on the mattress.

"Our fortnight ends today," he whispered.

"Fortnight?"

"Do you remember the first night you came to me, when you promised to be my lover for two weeks? I have one night left."

"One night? I just promised to be your lover for eternity."

"Eternity starts tomorrow, my love. Tonight, I want to end our fortnight of illicit carnal pleasure with a big bang."

A big bang? Lucy had no idea what he meant. Until he pushed up her skirts, then arranged her so her legs hooked around his neck. Her pussy was creamy and wet, ready to be filled with his thick, hard cock.

She moaned as he slid inside. Then she wrapped her arms around his neck, too, to keep them joined. Joined forever. Joined with his groin kissing her swollen, eager clit with each thrust. Joined so he could reach between them and tease her bottom. She helped him, sliding her finger beside his up her ass.

It ignited her. Sent an orgasm streaking through her. She moaned, screamed, wailed. "Goodness," she whispered. "I can't wait to begin on eternity."

He tried to laugh, but she could see he was close to the brink himself, straining to keep his orgasm leashed, and unable to do more than grunt.

With her finger still up her bottom with his, she slid her hand down and found his rump. As he slid back, preparing to thrust again, she shoved her index finger greedily up his arse.

It was like pulling a trigger. On a loud, animal-like howl, he exploded inside her.

Sinjin collapsed, grinning, then he kissed her mouth hungrily. "I," he whispered, "am the luckiest man in the world."

"Indeed," she said.

He laughed, heartily, warmly, like a man who was truly happy. Her heart soared.

They were attending their first ball as the Duke and Duchess of Greystone. After traveling along the receiving line and thanking people for their congratulations on the marriage, Lucy began to move toward the wall of the ballroom. It was where she had always stood when she was unmarried, and it was where the married ladies congregated.

"Where do you think you are going?"

"Over to the wall to stand with the other matrons."

Sinjin's golden brow lifted. "I don't think so. You are coming with me."

Lucy let her gaze slide to the whirling dancers. Hope blossomed in her chest. "Do you mean . . . you wish to dance?"

He winked. "Later. I have something to show you first."

Lucy felt many gazes follow them as Sinjin clasped her hand and led her across the dance floor. Matrons had snapped up their lorgnettes to peer at him. Young ladies, making their debuts, goggled at him. Other gentlemen stared with curiosity. Of course, she had forgotten—he never came into Society. She had hidden in the shadows; but he had been mysterious and intriguing to the *ton* for he had behaved as a complete recluse.

It was strange to be here. She had always felt out of place, terrified something might happen that would reveal her secret to the *ton*. She had always hidden.

Now that she shared her secret with Sinjin, it felt like a special thing. Something wicked and illicit, kept just between them. It felt rather naughty to be walking amongst the cream of Society, knowing that she was a shape-shifting dragon and a vampire, that her husband was a vampire.

Sinjin led her out onto the terrace. Fairy lights dotted the gardens and when the warm spring breeze blew, the tiny diamonds of light danced in the trees.

"You brought me out to appreciate the view? Did you wish to walk in the gardens?" Dancing would have been delightful, but this was rather romantic. Many couples were already taking advantage of the warm weather and inviting gardens. She could hear laughter rising behind lilac bushes and manicured hedges.

"I planned to, but I don't believe I can wait that long. The thing with dying and getting a second chance—it makes you realize you can't hang around and wait for things."

Taking her hand, he guided her to the stone balustrade that ran around the terrace. They were at the end, beyond the lights that spilled out from the paned terrace doors. It was not exactly dark, but more shadowed.

"Lean against the railing, love," he whispered hoarsely and his breath was a hot tickle against her ear.

Trembling, anticipating, she did. With a soft whisper, her skirts flew up, cascading around her waist in a silken wave.

"Won't someone see us? We could cause a scandal."

"Someone might catch us. But you are my countess now. My bride. I love you, and I promised you an eternity of pleasure."

"An eternity of scandalous, naughty, dangerous pleasure?" she asked.

"What else would be enough for my fiery dragon?"

Lucy wriggled, batting her bared bottom against the front of his trousers. "I want you to set me aflame." Then she giggled, suddenly shy. "I trust you more than I've ever trusted anyone. I love you completely. But to daringly make love on a terrace in the middle of a crowded ball? I am not sure if I am ready to be that daring."

"Trust me," he answered, and she felt the brush of his hand as he undid his trousers. "You are."

She did trust him. With Sinjin, she had visited Guidon and had begun to explore her magic. When she had jokingly told Sinjin she could not wave a wand and move things, she had been wrong. She could actually move objects with her magical powers by waving her hands.

Here, now, she wanted to let him show her just how daring she could be, how thoroughly aroused she was when he thrust deeply inside her. She knew she had become very daring for she was certain the entire crowd heard her cries of pleasure when she and Sinjin reached their climaxes together.

Laughing, she slumped against the railing, cradled in Sinjin's embrace.

All her life she had been afraid of being a dragon. Now Lucy knew how lucky she was. For she loved the fiery, wanton side that came with being a dragon.

From behind, Sinjin nibbled her neck and spoke the most magical words of all. "I love you, Lucy. For ever and ever."

Turn the page for a sizzling preview of Logan Belle's

NAKED ANGEL

An Aphrodisia trade paperback on sale now!

There is simply not a single ugly move in ballet. Not one ugly move. I like to hold burlesque to the very same standards.

—Dita Von Teese

1

"Are you nervous?" Mallory Dale's boyfriend, Alec, asked her.

"No. Should I be?" She surveyed the room, finally seeing the tangible results of nearly a year of work.

"It's a big night," Alec said.

"The first of many to come, I hope," she said, putting her arms around him. "And I'm ready."

In one hour, the club they had created would be unveiled to New York. Standing alone in the room, holding Alec's hand, she felt confident in the world they had brought to life. The Painted Lady was unlike any burlesque club in the city: After careful research and their investors' generous open checkbooks, they had managed to create a glorious throwback to the roaring twenties.

Mallory had always loved flapper style. It was fashion liberation. In that sense, flappers did for women of the 1920s what burlesque did for her: It shocked her, then irrevocably changed the way she saw herself. And now she'd helped create a space that would have made Zelda Fitzgerald proud: The Painted Lady burlesque club was a decadent tableau of unrestrained art deco. The red walls were decorated with portraits of Josephine Baker and iconic flapper Louise Brooks, a collection of Grundworth and Yva Richard fetish photographs, and illustrated *pochoir* prints by Erté. The brass and bronze chandeliers had been designed for the 1925 Paris Exposition. And the topnotch sound system was already playing Irving Berlin's "Puttin' on the Ritz."

"You definitely look ready. You are by far the sexiest flapper ever to grace a stage. Were women allowed to be this hot in the 1920s?" Alec asked. He pulled her over so she could see her reflection in one of the mirrored picture frames.

She'd never been more excited about a costume. Her former boss—and onetime owner of the famous burlesque club the Blue Angel—had created the pink satin flapper dress and beaded headpiece for her. Then, after scouring the best vintage shops in the city, she and Alec had found the perfect accessories: ropes of pink and black beads to wear around her neck, and black patent leather heels with ankle straps. Even her face was transformed to Old World glamour: Her best friend, notorious burlesquer, model, and actress Bette Noir, had spent an hour at her apartment earlier applying her makeup to look flapper chic.

Alec kissed the back of her neck, running his hands up from her waist to her breasts. She sighed, a swell of desire rising in her chest. But she forced herself to push his hands gently away. "We don't have time. Save it for later, okay?" she said. Still, she felt a twinge between her legs. Alec could always get her going, even when she had less than one hour before the beginning of the biggest night of her New York life.

"Now that you mention it, I *am* saving something for later," he said, the tone of his voice especially devilish.

She turned to look at him. "Oh, yeah? What's going on?"

"I have a surprise for you."

"You know I don't like surprises," Mallory said.

"Hmm. The last time you told me that, things turned out okay, didn't they?"

She knew he was referring to the night he took her to her first burlesque show on her twenty-fifth birthday at the Blue Angel. Now, just two years later, it was the opening night of her own club. Well, The Painted Lady wasn't technically *her* club. But she was the creative force behind it, along with Alec. It was their baby, and after designing the look and feel of the club, hiring the staff of dancers, choreographing the début show, and writing the script for the opening night's MC, it was finally the moment of truth.

Bette Noir strutted over to them. With her signature black bob, she already looked like a modern-day Louise Brooks.

She carried a large flower arrangement wrapped in plastic. "Someone has a secret admirer," she said, handing the package to Mallory.

"Is that my surprise?" Mallory asked Alec.

"No. It's not from me." He raised an eyebrow, as if looking at her with suspicion.

"Busted—my secret lover," she teased. A year ago, it might have been true. But all of that was behind them now.

Mallory tore the plastic wrapper away to reveal a remarkable bouquet of pink flowers that happened to match the exact shade of her costume.

"Will you look at this!" she said, almost afraid to move the arrangement, it looked so delicate and perfect—more like a sculpture than a flower arrangement. A dozen or so Phalaenopsis orchids brimmed over the top of a long, rectangular vase. Underneath the flowers, circles of grass were arranged inside the glass walls, as if an artist had painted green loops with a delicate brush.

Mallory detached the card. "For Mallory: Thanks for all your hard work. Tonight, we see it bloom. Our love, Justin and Martha."

"You gotta love those guys," Bette said.

Justin Baxter and Martha Pike were the money behind The Painted Lady, and they were among Manhattan's most visible—and unusual—couples. Martha had made her millions in the vaginal rejuvenation field: She'd invented a device called the Pike Kegel Ball, and many a bold-faced name over the age of thirty, when pressed, would admit it had helped take years off her vag. Justin was a drop-dead gorgeous former playboy who'd settled down with the less-than-attractive Martha when he was in his early thirties, and the two seemed extremely happy together. They both had an appetite for beautiful young women and kinky sex, and they happily indulged their desires together. They also threw the most decadent, incredible parties on both coasts and were major patrons of the arts. When their favorite burlesque club, the Blue Angel, was bought out by a woman they knew would run it into the ground, they decided to open a club of their own. That's when Mallory and Alec had gotten their dream jobs: The club was theirs to create and run. Martha would write the checks.

"Now I'm tempted to give you my surprise," Alec said, putting his arms around Mallory. She tilted up her face so he could kiss her.

"So give it to me, baby," she said.

"Ah, my favorite thing to hear," he said, pulling her close. "But you're just going to have to get through the show."

"You're such a sadist," she said.

"And you wouldn't have it any other way."

Violet Offender paced the dressing area of the club formerly known as the Blue Angel. She ran a hand through her short-cropped, white-blond hair, her cheeks flushed with irritation.

"What do you mean it's by invitation only?" she snapped at the petite redhead busily getting into costume. For once, the sight of the woman's luscious breasts bound in a corset wasn't enough to calm Violet's nerves.

"I did what you told me to do: I went to get a ticket for the show tonight, and the woman at the door told me the opening night was by invitation. Press and friends only."

"Jesus! Why do I have to do everything myself around here? Give me a phone."

The girl scrambled to hand over her iPhone. Violet punched in the number of her reluctant business partner and bankroller, the magazine publisher Billy Barton. "Billy, I need you to get off your ass and do something for this club for once: We need press passes to the opening of The Painted Lady. Apparently, I am the only one around here who seems aware of the fact that a major competitor is opening up shop tonight. I didn't buy this fucking dump to get steamrolled by Mallory Dale six months later. Call me back ASAP."

"Baby, there's nothing to worry about," said the redhead, half-dressed in her costume, a sexy equestrian ensemble complete with riding boots and crop. "We've already been open for months and months."

"Don't be an idiot," Violet snapped. "This isn't the Internet: Getting there first doesn't mean shit. It just means you're old news. Change back into regular clothes. I'm getting you into that show tonight one way or another. And I want you to report back everything: the music, the girls, the costumes. Take photos."

"They probably won't allow photos," said the redhead.

"I'm not asking you to get permission, I'm *telling* you to get photos. God, I'm tense," Violet said. She knew there was only one way to relieve her stress. Now that she was running the club, she barely had time for her former day job and favorite pastime, her work as a professional dominatrix. Fortunately, her latest fuck toy, a five foot two inch former investment banker with enormous breasts and the burlesque name Cookies 'n' Cream, was always willing to bend over backwards—sometimes literally—to accommodate her needs.

Violet locked the dressing room door. "Take off your clothes," Violet said. "But leave on the boots."

Cookies wordlessly complied, unfastening her corset and stepping out of her lace panties. Her legs were covered in black English riding boots with zippers up the sides. The rest of her costume, including a black riding helmet and riding crop, was by her feet.

Cookies' delicate porcelain skin was red from the pressure of the corset, and it gave Violet the irresistible urge to see matching welts on her ass.

"Turn around," Violet said, picking up the crop. Cookies obeyed, letting Violet push her down so she was leaning on a vanity table, her ass in the air. "Don't move," Violet ordered. She paused for a minute to look at Cookies' pale, creamy ass, a hint of russet pubic hair visible between her legs. She resisted the urge to get on her knees and lick the girl's pussy. She knew in order to get true satisfaction she had to do things in the proper order. Violet understood the need for control, something most of her lovers did not. At least, not until she taught them.

She raised the riding crop and brought it down hard on Cookies' left ass cheek. The girl cried out, but did not move a muscle. A satisfying red mark emerged almost immediately on her flesh. Violet repeated the lashing on the other side. She dropped the crop and kneeled behind Cookies. She pressed one finger into Cookies' pussy and was satisfied to find it very wet. Violet was surprised to feel the building pressure in her own cunt. There was something about Cookies that always got her excited. She wasn't sure what it was, but it was a relief to not be bored yet.

She worked her finger in and out, reaching up to graze

Cookies' clit before resuming the sharp strokes inside of her. She slipped one hand inside her own underwear, mirroring the motions inside herself as she worked Cookies into a frenzy. She felt Cookies' pussy contract on her fingers, and the girl cried out as she came.

Violet quickly pulled off her jeans. She tugged on Cookies' hair to turn her around. Violet sat on a chair, spread her legs. Cookies knelt in front of her, hands on Violet's thighs, her tongue lapping at her wetness.

"Fuck me," Violet growled. Cookies darted her tongue in and out of Violet's pussy. Violet pulled on her head, trying to get her deeper. She felt a rush of impatience. "Use your hand."

Cookies moved her mouth to Violet's clit, her fingers pressing inside with the sharp, fast strokes she knew Violet liked. Sure enough, Violet shuddered to a silent climax. Cookies sat back on her heels, wincing when she accidentally put pressure on the freshly bruised skin on her ass.

Violet noticed her discomfort and said, "If you think your ass hurts now, you don't even want to know what it will feel like if you come back here tonight without photos of The Painted Lady show."

2

Mallory stood behind the red curtain. On the other side of it, center stage, Alec warmed up the crowd, reminding them that the more skin the performers revealed, the louder he expected the audience to get. "Foot stomping is appreciated, but not mandatory," he said to a few laughs.

"I see some familiar faces out there," he said. This was met with shouts and clapping. "As you know, this is a huge night for New York burlesque—and I don't just mean because Supersize Suzy is visiting us tonight." This brought another round of applause: Supersize Suzy was a six foot two inch, double D–breasted British transvestite who had recently been made infamous by her unbridled performance in a burlesque documentary called *Fan Dancers.* "And if that isn't enough, we are starstruck to have with us tonight—fresh off her latest movie set—the mysterious, magnificent, Mistress of Delight: Bette Noir." More applause, whistles, and a few random shout-outs of her name.

From her perch behind the curtain, Mallory smiled. She remembered how, at the first show she'd gone to, the audience had gone wild when Bette's name was announced. And that was before she became world famous for dating the pop star Zebra, appearing in a national Dolce & Gabbana campaign, and getting rave reviews in an indie film directed by Jake Gyllen-haal. "But first, I have the great pleasure of introducing to you our opening performer: the sexy, sassy, incomparable Moxie!"

At the sound of her stage name, Mallory reflexively straight-ened her back. She tugged on her elbow-length white gloves to make sure they were easily removable, and straightened her headpiece. These were nervous, unnecessary tics. She was, as al-ways, perfectly prepared for her performance. Maybe more so tonight than ever before.

The song "Puttin' on the Ritz"—the synth-pop 1983 cover version—filled the room. The curtain receded to one side, and Mallory felt the heat of the stage lights bathing her in a red glow. From the darkness in front of her, the full house roared. She knew she was a sight in her costume, but this wasn't a fash-ion show. Being a sight wasn't enough. Burlesque was all about the reveal—revealing parts of her body, yes. But in doing so, she would elicit a reaction from the audience that revealed something about them.

Mallory shimmied to the front of the stage, twirling the fluffy pink boa draped over her shoulders. She sensed the audi-ence's collective anticipation. Although she'd practiced on the stage many times, it felt dramatically different to be in front of people. In the months since the Blue Angel had changed ownership and she'd stopped performing, she'd almost forgot-ten what it felt like to play off a crowd.

As the song kicked up-tempo, she swiveled her heels in op-posite directions, launching into an improvised Charleston. At the same time, she tugged off one glove, throwing it into the au-dience to an appreciative roar. She loved the way the pink beaded fringe on her dress moved with her hips, and she exag-gerated her kicks in the front and back to maximize the dra-matic flair of silk.

When the song came to the lyrics "walk with sticks or um-ber-ellas," she retrieved a black walking stick from the floor and used the tip to tease off the spaghetti straps of her dress. With another shimmy, her breasts were exposed, her nipples covered in pink sequined pasties with pink tassels. The audience shouted her name, and she let the dress fall to the floor so she was clad in only the boa, pasties, a pink thong, thigh-high white fishnet stockings with garters, and her black patent heels. She used the boa to tease the crowd, covering her breasts and then revealing them in flashes. She turned her back to the audience, holding the boa in either hand, stretching it across her nearly bare ass and rubbing it back and forth. Then she bent forward and moved the boa so she was rubbing it between her thighs from the front to the back. This whipped the crowd into a frenzy, and when she turned to face them again, she dropped the boa and shimmied her shoulders so the tassels on her pasties twirled dramatically.

The red curtain closed.

"That performance would almost make Prohibition tolerable," said Bette.

Mallory was breathless and could only smile her thanks. She heard Alec retake the stage to introduce the next act.

"Another round of applause for Moxie, the sexiest flapper to grace the stage since Louise Brooks," said Alec. The audience clapped. "Moxie, come on back out here."

"What is he doing?" Mallory asked Bette. "He's interrupting the whole flow of the show."

"Better go humor him," Bette said. She handed Mallory a black silk robe.

Mallory quickly covered herself and returned to the stage. A few people stood to applaud her. This was embarrassing. What was Alec thinking?

"I don't know how many of you are aware of this, but in addition to being The Painted Lady's opening performer, Moxie is also the creative director of the club and producer of the show you are seeing tonight. And I'm hoping she might take on one more role—that of my wife!"

Alec got down on one knee. Mallory looked at him in shock.

"Oh, my God! What are you doing?"

He pulled out a small black box and opened it to reveal a beautiful art deco, antique diamond ring.

"Marry me, Mallory," he said, his voice low and husky with emotion.

Mallory wasn't sure if the low roar she heard was the sound of blood rushing to her head, or if it was the sound of the crowd, or if this was simply what it felt like to be truly shocked for the first time in her life.

"Oh, my God," she repeated.

"What do you say, Mal?" he asked with that wonderful teasing glint in his eyes.

Was this really happening? After all the years, the mind-blowing sex, the jealousy, fights, uncertainty, missteps, soul-searching, and compromise, could it really culminate in this one perfect moment?

"Yes," she managed to breathe. "I'll marry you." He stood up and hugged her. Through a blur of tears, she watched him slip the ring on her finger.

He held her tight, and all she could think was that she didn't ever want this happiness to end. She had no idea how to leave the stage. She didn't want to. She didn't trust the magic of the moment to follow her into "real life."

But on the stage, anything was possible.